I0585275

Albion W. Tourgée

A Son of Old Harry

A Novel

Albion W. Tourgée

A Son of Old Harry
A Novel

ISBN/EAN: 9783337041885

Printed in Europe, USA, Canada, Australia, Japan

Cover: Foto ©Andreas Hilbeck / pixelio.de

More available books at **www.hansebooks.com**

A SON OF OLD HARRY.

HE STRAPPED A SHEEPSKIN ON THE BACK OF THE COLT.—*See Page 12.*

A SON OF OLD HARRY

A Novel.

BY

ALBION W. TOURGÉE,

Author of "A Fool's Errand," etc.

WITH ILLUSTRATIONS BY WARREN B. DAVIS.

NEW YORK:
ROBERT BONNER'S SONS,
1891.

A Son of Old Harry.*

Albion W. Tourgée.

PROLOGUE.

IT did not need the verdict of Science to assure me that I am doomed. Yet, I have just heard it announced. Calmly, quietly, without a quaver in his voice, one of the most eminent of his profession, has declared : "There is little, I may say no hope of recovery, nor any immediate prospect of death. You may live weeks, perhaps months, possibly years ; but you will never be—other than what you are."

Other than what I am ! I expected this decision—knew in reason it must be so—yet the words fell upon my consciousness with a strange, numbing sense of horror.

"Other than what you are !" I repeated to myself, as I heard the firm, elastic steps echoing along the corridor of the great hotel outside my room when the physician went away. What am I ? It did not need knowledge such as his to determine. Half dead and half alive !

This body which has served me so well at need, and
which, whatever else I may have done, I have never
abused, has been cut in twain.   One-half has already
passed beyond the realm of consciousness.   The inert
limbs chain me to the couch.   The nerves which traverse
the yet unshrunken tissues, bring only dim, vague mes-
sages of need—dull, prickling appeals for aid.   I live,
but it is only a half-life.   The brain is alert ; the soul
alive ; the body slipping helplessly and hopelessly into
the tomb.

It is a strange ending of a strange life—a life strange
enough without such tragedy—a life already curiously
dismembered by Fate.   Has it been one life—or two—
or three ?   Am I the lad who set out on life's journey
half a century ago unmindful of the destiny that awaited
him ?   Did I grow to be what I was, or did some strange
alembic transform my nature ?   It is hard to tell.   Perhaps in the earlier life was hid the fruitage of the later
years—and the one was but an evolution from the
others.

What shall I do with this interval between life and
death ?   Review the past ?   I cannot change it.   Nay, I
would not if I could.   Not that I have always done the
best or chosen always the wisest course.   Perhaps I
sometimes did the very worst.   But the one act which
colored all my after life, I committed purposely, with
full knowledge of its import, and I have no desire to
repent or to be forgiven.   Whether it was right or
wrong, I do not know ; worse yet, I hardly care.   Nay,
looking backward at it from this vantage-ground of
truth, my dying bed, I do not hesitate to say that I am
glad I did the thing which made my name a synonym of shame, so bitter that Cain himself, even with
the ineffaceable mark upon his brow, might well pity
the man condemned to wear it.

It cut my life in twain even as my body is now cleft. What I had been, I was never to be again. The child my mother bore has already been dead more years than he lived. I have had two lives—two lives with a black, bottomless gulf between them. Yet the past has no terrors for me. As to the future, I do not know what it may have in store. If I am to live hereafter, and I hope I may, I trust my destiny with Him who shaped the past which He will judge. I do not fear His judgment. I have no need to prepare for death. I am ready for it —at least as ready as I ever shall be—as ready as I ever can be.

No living mortal save myself knows who I really am, or even guesses what I was. Why should he? I died a score of years ago—died and was inurned in infamy. A continent thrilled with horror at the obloquy of my act. My name is remembered only to be detested. Even I can hardly realize that it was once mine. My life seems bounded by the red horizon of my shame. He who lived beyond it, and bore that other name, was not I, but another. I never think of him but in the third person. Men blotted this name off the tablets of friendship; women denied with angry vehemence all knowledge of him who bore it. It was erased from the roll of honor on which I had written it with the sword— from the records of the church; from the scroll of fame —for I had made it famous in a way, by honorable endeavor. Even the brethren of the " Mystic Tie " disowned me. In all the world there was not one to offer me the hand of sympathy or speak my name with pity.

Why should I not write the story of this strangely disjointed life. The future is denied me—why should I not recall the past ? I do not know that any one will care to read the tale. Indeed, I do not think I desire so much that it should be read as that it should be fairly stated. I wish to tell the truth, and am not sure I would always do so, if I thought what I write would be read by many.

I have often wondered that men should care to write about themselves, or that others should care to read what people think, or, rather, desire others to believe they think about themselves—their dreams, acts purposes and achievements. A man's testimony for or against himself is not apt to be reliable. I have always thought there was no greater liar that St. Augustine in his "Confessions." I read them when I was young. If I had believed them, they would have done me harm. In his desire to glorify his Redeemer, I think he slandered his Creator. His idea of evil was delusive, too. The sinful thought is not the full equivalent of wrongful purpose ripening into harmful act.

Yet St. Augustine was probably as nearly truthful as any one can be who writes of himself in order that the world may read.

I have read many so-called "Lives" of men who desired to extol their own purity, demonstrate or defend or explain the acts they feared the future might not estimate as they desired. I have no such motive. What I did cannot be extenuated. Why I did it is a matter of no consequence. I expect nothing of to-morrow and have no defence to make of yesterday. I could at the best only admit that of which I am accused, and affirm the very motive which was assigned. I do not regret it, and can derive no benefit from its confession. The world would demand either a show of repentance or a display of boastful depravity. I can offer neither. I would be glad if one who knew *her* might read the plain, unvarnished tale of my life that *she* might be judged aright. That is all I desire. So far as *I* am concerned, it is a matter of no moment. There is but one whose good opinion I would greatly care to retain ; and hers, of all persons in the world, I think would be least likely to survive a knowledge of the truth. It is strange that I should care for the judgment of one who wears a nurse's cap and apron, more than for all the world beside ; but it is true. So I will write and she shall read ; and whether she excuse or condemn, it shall be of none the less advantage to her.

PART FIRST—JACK.

CHAPTER I.

A TIMELY PHENOMENON.

It was forty years ago. A man of middle age, whose frame was wasted by disease, lay upon a bed opposite a bright wood-fire, by which sat a woman weeping bitterly and wiping away her tears with the blue-checked cambric apron which she wore. A sturdy boy of twelve years stood near the foot of the bed, digging his chubby fists into his eyes and sobbing dolorously. A man younger than the invalid, but so closely resembling him as to leave no doubt that he was a brother, stood with flushed face at the head of the bed and looked angrily down at the offending youngster. The countenance of the sick man evinced great anxiety. The stubby beard gave his emaciated face a somber look. Jet black hair hung in a dark, almost forbidding mass across his sallow forehead. Blue eyes shone with a tremulous, humid glow beneath the knotted, beetling brows. A full under-lip showed through the dark beard moving nervously. A red flannel shirt was visible beneath the coarse white cotton one with its unlaundried bosom.

The hand that rested on the coverlet, though pale and shrunken, still bore the tan of accustomed toil, and the great joints and broad, stiff nails told that the sick man

"I CANNOT COUNTENANCE BETTING," ANSWERED SETH.—See Page 39.

had been of powerful physique. Tufts of black hair showed upon the shrunken phalanges, revealing a ghastly story of the ravages of disease. His face was kindly but severe, and his voice trembled more from excitement than feebleness, as he said, sternly :

" What is this I hear, my son ?"

Seth Goodwin was a very sick man. His friends, relatives, and even the attending physician, said that he had not long to live. They told him so, too, with that reckless disregard for consequences which characterized a life in which preparation to die was considered a much more important fact than death itself. Lest he should perchance forget the fate impending over him, a preternatural gloom pervaded the room in which he lay, which was kept at a stifling temperature, with every breath of air excluded, lest Nature should refuse to submit to the general verdict. Apprehension was written on the countenance of every one who approached the bedside. Many asked, in solemn tones, after his spiritual welfare. Several insisted upon praying with him. The wife wept and tried to hide her tears. The brother, recently arrived, had put a stop to some of these things. He had insisted on cheerful faces, few callers and no prayers. The wife thought him cruel ; the neighbors called him wicked ; the doctor said he was sensible. He himself said that Seth had made his will, was ready to die, and probably would die ; but he shouldn't be worried to death nor lose any chance of life through fretting over what couldn't be helped.

The sick man was only a common farmer, one of those sturdy men who, when the middle West was but half subdued, undertook to win competence by completing the conquest the pioneers had begun. It was before the days of railroads and telegraphs. The highways of traffic lay along the great lakes, a hundred miles to the

northward, or up and down the great river, a hundred
miles to the southward. Wagons and boats were the
sole means of transport. The stage-coach was the only
carrier-pigeon. Roads had been hewn through the
forest on the lines blazed by the government surveyors,
until every State west of the Alleghanies must have
looked to an aerial beholder like a great checker-board
cut in the arboreal verdure. Here and there the dull-
yellow roadways were flanked by green meadows and
thrifty homesteads. Villages and towns, the ganglia of
traffic and precursors of a new civilization, were clustered here and there. The forest, which represented the
stored-up wealth of unnumbered centuries, was still
accounted the enemy of the thrifty settler, who warred
against it with fire and steel. The mighty walnuts,
whitewoods, maples, beeches, oaks and elms which
hedged in the clearings with a continuous living wall
a hundred feet in height, even though of the finest
grain and clearest fiber, were counted worthless to the
owner. Men were still hired to destroy these monarchs
of the forest. Only from their ashes, leached and boiled
into crude forms of caustic soda—"potash," it was
called—could a merchantable product be obtained by
which the owner might get pay for the labor of "clearing." The value of the land depended upon the cost
of cutting away the forest. The denser the growth and
the richer the wood, the heavier the cost of removal.

The land teemed with the promise of unexampled
productiveness. Horses and cattle, sheep and swine
were abundant ; but only the first were highly prized,
according to more recent standards of comparison. It
was a tedious and costly matter to drive the cattle and
swine a thousand miles to market. The fleece was
more easily transported, and despite the disadvantages
of production, wool became one of the first articles of

commerce of this region. Grain and cheese were exported also, but the cost of carriage made the prices very low.

With the irrepressible energy which marked the epoch in which he lived, Seth Goodwin and his young wife had set out a dozen years before to overcome these obstacles —to build a home and acquire a competence. They had succeeded well ; but before their plans had reached entire fruition, one of those great financial revulsions that sweep over the world had touched the products of toil and they had shrunk almost to nothing. His desire to increase his possessions had induced him to mortgage what he had already acquired to secure money to buy more. When the shrinkage in values came, he fought bravely, working with redoubled energy ; and for a time his hope for ultimate success was not without reasonable basis. Whatever courage, integrity and good credit could do to avert disaster, that Seth Goodwin could be relied upon to accomplish ; but after a time disease came, and with it, very soon, despair. The sick man faced his doom with composure, but the thought that he would leave his wife and child unprovided for, filled both his waking moments and his dreams with agony.

The boy had been a source of constant anxiety, especially to his mother, ever since he had been able to find his way into danger. He had now been summoned to his father's bedside to be reproved for an offence which derived the greater part of its enormity from the condition of his parent's health. Among the duties which this illness had imposed upon the lad was the care of a colt which from a suckling had been the pride of the boy's heart. It had been " broken," as the process of training the horse to work is barbarously called, the summer before. The boy had ridden him to plow corn,

and to and from the field, and since he had had him in
his care, had ridden him, perhaps, oftener than was necessary, to the brook, which babbled along under the
hill-side half a furlong from the barn, for water. This
fact, not having come to the parents' knowledge, had
never been forbdiden. He was a resolute lad and had
shown a capacity to "look after things," as the mother
had expressed it, which was a great comfort to the
afflicted woman, and being reported to the father had
won his warm approval.

A fortnight before, the brother of the sick man had
come to assist the wife in taking care of him. He was a
somewhat gay young fellow whose pride centered in a
mare noted throughout all the region as a "quarter-
horse," of great speed. Since he had owned her she
had done some notable work, but was not regarded as
quite strong enough for the long distance races then in
vogue. This mare the uncle had brought with him and
she had occupied a stall next to the boy's colt, Pompey.

Racing was at that time a popular amusement in that
region. The tracks were often "straightaway," and the
equipments of the sport very crude, but good time was
often made, and the associations of the turf were far
more reputable than they are to-day. Almost in front
of Seth Goodwin's house stood a beech-tree, which was
the beginning of what was known through all that
region as "the measured mile," a level stretch along the
State Road, which was a favorite place for trials of
speed between the fancy nags of the neighborhood. In
these trials, the boy had always manifested a lively
interest, and was well aware of the reputation the brown
mare belonging to his uncle Horace had earned in many
a hard-won race as the "Queen" of that particular bit
of turf. Her fame did not, however, in the least eclipse,
in his opinion, the glory of his own pretty bay, in whose

capacity to distance the " Queen " herself, the boy was
a firm believer.   This belief he did not hesitate to avow,
and when some of his playmates made light of this
theory, he promptly offered to put it to the test by a
race between them along the accustomed track.

It was not the season of races.   A heavy snow had
fallen, but the weather was mild, and it had been beaten
down into two smooth parallel tracks, bordered on either
side by a white flocculent cushion.   There happened to
be among the boys one who boasted of some experience
as a jockey, who volunteered to ride the Queen, and
young Goodwin declared his readiness to back his own
favorite in a literal sense.   It is not in boy nature to
" take a dare," and words quickly grew into deeds.   The
horses were bridled.   Cooper, the challenger, who was
some years older than the colt's champion, insisted on
having the only saddle in the barn.   The boy made no
objection.   He had rarely ridden with a saddle.   He
merely strapped a sheep-skin on the back of the low,
rangy bay colt, which stood beside the bony, flat-limbed
mare on the great barn-floor during the controversy,
and declared himself ready for the trial.

The jockeys mounted and rode out, the colt leading
the way.   The other boys followed on foot.   They went
down the lane toward the brook, and took the cart-track
up the hollow out of sight of the house, to the road,
instead of going through the yard.   Nobody gave any
specific reason for taking this course, but the boys all
knew it was to prevent their being interrupted and the
race spoiled by any interference of the elders.   The
house was quite a distance from the road, and they
trusted on escaping observation until too late to put an
end to their sport.   When they reached the road, they
trotted up to the big beech ; a mark was made in the
snow on each side of the track ; one of the boys was

named as starter ; the horses were turned back and brought carefully up, neck and neck, to the starting-place.

" Go !" shouted Billy Wayland, the starter, throwing his cap in the air.

" Go !" shouted the other boys at the top of their voices.

Mrs. Seth Goodwin looked out of the kitchen window just in time to see two horses, with boyish figures on their backs, flash across her field of vision. A swift intuition told her who they were, and she sank into a chair with a low, shuddering moan. She was a weak, nervous woman, whose reliance had been in her husband's magnificent strength. Now that this support was likely to be removed, she was already looking forward to a widowhood in which the son, so wonderfully like his father in self-reliance, should be her chief dependence. If there was one thing that she feared more than another, it was a horse. From the first, the boy's fondness for the colt had filled her with apprehension. A thousand times she had in fancy seen him bitten, kicked, torn, mangled by the spirited beast he would persist in fondling. Now she beheld him borne headlong to his doom on the back of this same winged terror.

There was a shriek from the group of boys by the roadside—an unmistakable cry of alarm. She saw them gazing in terror along the level vista of the " measured mile." There were more shouts. Some ran in one direction and some in another. She heard louder, more terrified cries. She was sure one voice said : " He's down ! He's killed !" She did not stop to ask who was slain. Her heart told her. She was not only to be a widow but childless ! The snow grew red—bloody red —then yellow and green to her dazed vision. The room whirled round and round as she sank to the floor in a dead faint. Here her brother-in-law found her when, startled by the noise of her fall, he came from the sick-room to inquire its cause. Taking her in his arms, he laid her on the bed in an adjoining room. By that time more than one of the frightened boys were clamoring at the door.

It did not take many inquiries to learn the facts. Even his heart stood still with fear at the thought of two unpracticed boys starting out to ride a race with a a hard-bitted flyer and a half-broken colt. He was in the road in an instant, snatching off his coat as he went, clenching his hands, throwing out his chest and shutting his lips close as a man must who is going to take a long run. Away up the road he could see two moving spots —or was there only one? He did not stop to question. A quarter of a mile away there was a black heap by the roadside. It was alive and audible ; there was no doubt about that. Two of the boys reached it about the time he struck the roadway. They raised it into a sitting posture. The clamor grew louder.

" I never thought the whelp would make such a fuss as that," said the runner to himself, disgustedly, as he drew near. " Ah, it's not Jack ! What's the matter ?" he asked, pausing and shaking the boy by the collar as he spoke. " Stop your yelling, Sam Cooper, and tell me what's the matter !"

" Oh, I'm killed ! I shall die ! I know I shall !" howled the frightened boy.

The questioner soon found that however frightened the lad might be, the deep snow had saved him from serious injury. All he could learn about his nephew was that he was " sure to be killed ;" a result he thought not unlikely, but man-like consoled himself with the contemptuous remark :

"If he is he won't make such an infernal fuss about it."

Having thus expressed himself, Uncle Horace resumed, with the pertinacity peculiar to the Goodwins, the apparently hopeless pursuit of the runaway.

It was an hour later when he returned. He was riding the Queen, whose head drooped down as she swung it back and forth in a long fox-walk, while the steam rose from her heaving flanks, and clouds of vapor poured from her distended nostrils. He held the colt's rein, while a worn switch, which he carried in his right hand, seemed a sufficient explanation of the lachrymose condition of the lad on the colt's back. Both horses were evidently tired, as was natural after a two-mile heat in the snow, for they had passed the limit and only been stopped when nearly a mile beyond.

The colt's condition did not escape the horseman's eye as he put the animals in the stable and blanketed them carefully lest they should take cold. He was drenched with sweat by his unaccustomed effort, but not in the least blown, and his steaming flanks throbbed evenly and steadily, as if he had merely had a fling in the pasture, instead of trying conclusions with the best horse in that region. When the uncle had attended to the horses he hooked his fingers in the boy's collar and led him to the house. Seeing her child safe, the mother had already informed the father of the main facts in the case. After a short consultation with his brother, the lad was called in. His mother followed, taking her station on the hearth and weeping as if her heart would break—whether from joy or sorrow, it would be hard to tell.

" What is this you have been doing, Hubert ?" repeated the invalid, tremulously.

The boy's name was John Hubert. His mother gen-

erally spoke of him as John ; his father always addressed
him as Hubert ; his uncle and playmates called him
Jack.

"I didn't—mean—no harm," sobbed the boy as he
industriously rolled his fists in and out against his eyes,
as if seriously contemplating the removal of the offending members.

"You knew it was wrong ?"

" I—I—s'pose so."

" Then, why did you do it ?"

" Well, you see, sir—Sam Cooper—he—he—we was
all in the barn and talking about—about Pomp and—
and the Queen, sir—that is, the boys was talking about
old Queen, and—and I told 'em Pomp was a better
horse'n she'd ever been ; and he is, too."

" Pompey is a good colt, but he has never run a race ;
so you should not have said that. It is not nice to
brag."

" It wasn't any bragging, father ; I was sure of it,"
said the lad, stoutly.

" But you had never seen him run."

" Oh yes, I had," answered the boy, quite cheerfully ;
" and rode him, too."

" When and where ?" demanded the father, sternly.

" Oh, lots of times ; last fall, after the races." '

" My son, answer me : Have you ever ridden him on
the measured mile before ?"

" Yes, sir," answered the lad, bowing his head and
beginning to sob again.

" How was it that you were never seen before ?"

" It—it was at night."

" At night ! Didn't you know you were not old
enough to do such things ?".

" But I went after the doctor at night when you were
first taken sick," sobbed the boy.

"So you did," said the father, softening.

"And you said that was right, though I didn't let you know about it."

" That's a fact, my son—"

"And Doctor Kelsey said if he had waited to walk, it would have been too late," interrupted the mother, who could not help interceding for the child.

" But you know I do not approve of horse-racing," continued the father, changing his ground. " It is not a creditable business for any one to engage in."

" Uncle Horace races," protested the boy.

"You see, now," said the sick man, reproachfully, turning to his brother, " what your example is doing. The boy might have been killed."

" Well, he wasn't ; and I don't think he's likely to be, judging from what I saw of his riding." ·

" Oh, it's no trouble to ride Pomp," exclaimed the boy, eagerly.

" But Sam Cooper was badly hurt, I hear, and he is considerably older than you, Hubert."

"He would have been all right, too, if he had just stuck on—but he got scared—that's what was the matter with him.   You see, the old mare had the best of the send-off—'cause she was used to it, I guess.   But when Pomp see she was trying to get away from him, he laid down to it and shut the light out between 'em almost as if she was standing still.   Of course, she didn't like that, and just let out the best she had.   She went so fast, I guess it scared Sam, for he kind of slid off into the snow, and began to holler ; but the old mare kept right on.   'Twasn't any use, though," continued the excited lad ; " Pomp was on her quarter when we got to the bars of No. 7, and 'fore we'd got to the three-quarter maple, he was a neck ahead.   Queen was a-doin' her best, too, and I didn't touch the switch to Pompey, but by the time we got to the mile post, he was—well—quite a few lengths ahead—three or four—anyhow," said the boy, doggedly, looking up at his uncle.

" My son !" said the father stornly.

" It's so, father. Do you think I'd tell a lie ?" asked the boy, choking back the tears.

'" Why didn't you stop there ?" asked the uncle.

" I did try to, and I could have stopped Pomp easy enough, but every time I'd pull him up, old Queen would try to rush by."

" Just like her," muttered Horace to himself, appreciatively. " I'd risk the old girl to run a race all by herself, and win it, too, if it was in the cards for her to do so."

" My son, you cannot expect any one to believe you when you claim to have outrun the swiftest horse in the country with a snip of a colt."

" There's a good bit of a horse in that colt's hide, Seth," interposed the uncle.

"I did, father ; 1 did, truly !" exclaimed the boy, with passionate intensity. " And he can do it again any day —the best she ever see. I tell you, father, you don't know what a colt he is. Just let me try it. Uncle Horace may ride Queen, too, and if Pomp don t beat her, he can whip me all the way back just as he did to-day," said the boy, resentfully.

" Your uncle did exactly right."

" I wasn't to blame for the colt being smarter than his old mare," protested the boy, sullenly.

This was too much. The uncle laughed outright ; the mother chuckled under the apron she still held to her eyes, and even the father smiled.

"Hubert," said the latter, after a moment. " Can you think of nothing but horses ?"

" I—I don't know," answered the boy, rolling up the

skirts of his butternut " warmus " with uneasy hands.
" I s'pose so."

" Come here," said the father, tenderly. The boy
slipped forward and laid his hand in the great, gaunt
palm that opened to receive it. " You know your father
may not live very long, and then your mother will have
no one but you to care for her. It will be a hard thing
for a boy, and you must grow to be a man very soon.
Now, I want you to promise to take good care of your
mother."

" Oh, I'll do it ! I'll do it !" exclaimed the lad weep-
iny passionately. " Don't be troubled a bit ; I'll take
care of her, and you, too, if you'll just live and let me
have Pomp to do it with. I tell you, father, I could
make a thousand dollars out of him next summer, just
as easy as not. How much has Uncle Horace made on
Queen, and she ain't nowhere beside the colt ?"

There was no attempt to suppress the laughter now.
The incorrigible boy had disarmed reproof. The uncle
laughed as loud as he dared in the sick-room, the
mother whirled her chair quickly round, and catching
the boy to her breast, sobbed and laughed on his
shoulder. The father laughed feebly, too, until the
sweat started on his forehead and he motioned toward
the stand on the other side of the bed, on which stood
a blue bowl containing a cooling draught. The boy
caught the gesture first, and bringing the bowl, held it
carefully to his father's lips. When the invalid had
drank and the bowl had been replaced, he called the lad
to him, and putting his hand on his shoulder, said :

" You are a good boy, Hubert, and I hope you will
think of something beside horses, when the time comes.
I think I can trust you, and I want you to know that I
do trust you never to do anything unmanly, that will give
sorrow to your mother or bring discredit on your name.

But I want you to promise me that if I should die, you will not worry your mother by running horses or getting into needless danger. Will you do it?"

"Oh, you know I will, father—I will do—anything—if you only won't die!"

"Life and death are of God, my son," said the father solemnly. "When he calls I must answer. Will you make it easy for me by promising not to run a race or ride an unbroken horse until you are eighteen years old?"

"But, father—" pleaded the lad, desperately.

"I want to be sure that your mother will not be left alone in the world, my child."

The promise was given ; the weeping lad kissed the parched lips, and the mother led him sobbing from the room. The invalid sank down wearily, and the brother carefully arranged the pillows and clothing of the bed.

"Johnnie says he wants to ask you just one question," said the mother, re-entering the room after a few minutes, with the boy by her side. "He seemed so anxious I could not refuse him."

"Well, what is it?" asked the sick man, in a feeble voice.

"If—if—you shouldn't die, you can take care of mother, can't you?"

"I trust I may be able to do so," answered the father, with difficulty repressing a smile.

"Then—what I promised," sobbed the lad, "ain't no promise, if—if you don't die, I s'pose?"

There was a choking sound at the head of the bed as Uncle Horace caught a corner of the pillow against which the sick man leaned and stuffed it in his mouth.

"O dear!" sighed the father, petulantly. "Yes, yes —if I get well you may ride all the time. Seems as if you could think of nothing but horses and races."

"It ain't that, father," exclaimed the boy, as he ran forward and buried his face in the bed-clothes ; "but I should hate to think you hadn't as much confidence in me as other folks have in their boys. I wouldn't mind not riding—not so very much, that is—but I'd hate to own that you wouldn't let me ride at all."

The father's face lightened, and his hand stole out and rested on the bowed head.

"You are a good boy, Hubert, and it gives me great comfort to know that you think of others instead of yourself. Perhaps I was over-anxious."

" I would rather never see a horse again than have you so troubled about me !" exclaimed the boy.

"I've been talking with him, Seth," said the wife, hesitantly, " about—about the colt, and I would like to tell you what his idea is. I know you're tired, but I'm sure 'twould do you good just to know how far ahead the boy's been looking, and how much he's been thinking about the very things that are troubling you. If the worst comes, I'm sure you'd feel better to know about it."

The good woman was not afraid of her husband in the sense of having any apprehension as to his kindliness of heart. Seth Goodwin was a model husband, as he was a model man in all things that go to make up a good neighbor and a good citizen ; but he was masterful and strong, and felt himself quite competent to do the thinking for all those in whom he was interested. This characteristic had been emphasized by his illness, and his wife hesitated to offer a suggestion which might conflict with his imperious will and so prove deleterious to the welfare of the invalid. It was only as a result of the lad's persistence, who was as self-willed as his father, that she had ventured to prefer so extraordinary a request.

"I think you ought to hear it, Seth; I really do," the mother repeated.

"He's pretty tired," said the brother, after telegraphing in vain from his place at the head of the bed for her to refrain from troubling the invalid further.

"I'll hear it," said the elder, irritably, resenting the implication of weakness.

"Well, you see," continued the mother, smoothing out her apron and looking deprecatingly at her husband, "Johnny thinks he is—well—something remarkable—the colt, I mean."

"Boys always think their own things better than anybody else ever had."

"But he's hunted up the colt's pedigree, Seth," insisted the wife, desperately; "and you know you said yourself that the dam, old Fanny, was the most remarkable horse you ever owned."

"I didn't mean as a racer."

"But there wasn't anything in these parts that could get away from her in her prime, all the same," interposed the brother, emphatically.

"I s'pose you know," was the peevish rejoinder.

"I do that," was the unabashed reply. "I won more dollars on her when we first came here, than I made by day's work."

"That is no credit to you, Horace," said the sick man, reprovingly.

"I s'pose not," answered the brother, jocosely; "but it *is* to her foal; and you must remember there's not many people hereabouts that wouldn't take Hod Goodwin's opinion about a horse sooner than they would his brother's. He ain't half as good, but he knows a horse, don't you see."

"Well, what's all this got to do with the boy? I hope you don't want him to be a horse-jockey, Susan?"

" He says the colt is very fast, and has what he calls
'bottom,' " said the mother.

" Well, suppose he has ?"

" Why, don't you see, father," protested the boy, lifting his head quickly and speaking hurriedly, as if fearful that he might not be allowed to finish his remarks,
"if he's handled right he'll pay off every cent of the
mortgage, and you needn't trouble another bit about it,
but just lie still and get well."

" That's sense, anyhow," rejoined Horace, emphatically.

" I would rather my debts should never be paid than
be discharged by betting on a horse-race or any other
sort of gambling," said the father, sternly.

" Knew he'd say that !" muttered Horace, shaking
his head. " I'd have helped him out long ago ; could
have done it just as easy as not, but he wouldn't have
my money."

" You didn't have any," said the sick man, impatiently.

" But I could have gotten it, and you knew I could."

" By risking what you had ?"

" Of course. You know I don't bet except to get a
little spending money, and now and then to buy a new
horse, but I'd have strained my luck for you any time,
and will now, if you'll let me."

" You are very kind, Horace, but—"

" But John says it isn't necessary to do any betting
at all—of course he knows you wouldn't allow that. He
says if you'll let him and Uncle Horace handle the
colt, he'll sell for more'n the mortgage amounts to,
long before Kincaid can turn us out," interrupted the
wife.

" Now, that's an idea worth having," said the brother-
in-law, heartily. " Kincaid can't get you off the place

before October, anyhow ; you told me that yourself ;
and if Jack's right about the colt outsteppin' the Queen,
there's big money in him if he's handled, and I'm the
one to do it. Seth, if you don't take back all the scold-
ing you've given the boy over this matter, and thank
God for giving you such a son, you ain't the man I take
you to be—that's all. He may not be as careful about
his pronouns and adverbs as you'd like to have him, but
you just let him alone and he'll steer things. Hanged
if I wouldn't marry myself if I could have a boy like
him. You can go to sleep, now. Providence has taken
care of your affairs in spite of your thinking it couldn't
be done without your help. All you've got to do is to
get well and enjoy your good luck. Kiss the boy now
and let him clear out. You must go to sleep."

"I'd like some broth first," said the invalid, with a
look of relief on his face that had not been there for
weeks.

"Good for you !" exclaimed the brother. "How long
since he's asked for anything to eat before, Susan?
Hurry it up before he changes his mind. And Jack,
you can ride the colt as much as you're a mind to;
didn't I hear you say so, Seth?"

" If he'll only be careful," answered the father, humor-
ing his brother's conceit.

"Oh, I'll be careful, father—I won't ever get on a
horse without thinking of you—I won't, truly."

The boy leaned over and kissed his father tenderly.

" And see here, sir," said the uncle, taking the lad by
the coat-collar, "I'm going to lick you every day until
your father gets well !"

"You may, you may, Uncle Horace ; I won't mind—
if I may ride the colt," was the gleeful response.

" All right ; now go and rub down those horses and

give them a feed. I'll come and take ancther look at the colt after awhile."

A strange sense of peace and hope settled down upon the Goodwin household that night. The black giant Despair fled away, and sweet sleep rested upon the long-troubled home.

Seth Goodwin's illness "took a turn" that day, so the neighbors said, and from that time he began to mend.

CHAPTER II.

CONFIDENCE BORN OF KNOWLEDGE.

Why Seth Goodwin began to improve in health just when he did was almost as great a puzzle to his physician as why he had not done so before. The simple fact was that he had begun to hope. He had waked out of the fever which his stalwart frame had so long resisted, with the one thought still dominant in his mind which had been uppermost when he lost consciousness, that on the first day of January he must pay one thousand dollars, or his bond would be forfeited and his creditor might sell as soon as he could get judgment. The property covered by the mortgage was really worth several times the amount of his debt ; but in the existing condition of affairs it was doubtful if the whole farm would bring the necessary sum, though it was only a moiety of the price he had agreed to pay for half of it. Values had shrunk terribly, and he had already sold everything that could be spared, to meet a payment due six months before. His son's words had shown a possible way of escape, which, slender as it seemed to the brother, was sufficient to lighten his despair.

As is usual with persons affected with morbid fancies, he went at once to the other extreme. As hitherto he had no hope, he had now no doubt. He accepted without hesitation the boy's notion that the colt would pull him out of all his difficulties. As it was deemed important to keep up his spirits, no one questioned or contradicted what he said about the matter. The result was that when he was at length able to leave his bed, he was possessed with a hopefulness as unreasonable as his former depression. He was very weak, however, and it was decided that Horace should remain to assist, or, more properly, carry on the spring's work, to facilitate which the Queen and the colt were to constitute a supplemental team. After that was over, the brother was to take such steps as might seem desirable in order to realize upon the colt from the sale of which so much was expected. How this was to be accomplished, Seth Goodwin seemed to have no more idea than he had doubt as to the result. Forbidden by the physcian's orders from taking any part in the labors of the farm, he surrendered everything into his brother's hand with a calm confidence in the outcome, which, though at curious variance with his previous character, was the result of the same deep religious fervor which had reconciled him to the thought of death, even when he could foresee only want and difficulty for those he loved. His hope was of God, as well as his submission. As he had trusted Him in his darkest hours, so he praised Him now in his brighter moments.

To his family, this change in the father's character was very puzzling. He had always been a kind husband and loving parent, but anxious, severe and irritable. Every day he had discounted to-morrow's trouble, and

sought to anticipate to-morrow's burdens. Striving
always for the best, he had feared always the worst.
Now, however, he was light-hearted, confident, careless.
The boy, whose love for his father had before been
tinged with fear, found him now the pleasantest of companions; and his wife, who had regarded him with
something of awe, both from his riper years and somewhat stern and serious character, began to give way to
her natural light-heartedness as she saw how her gayety
harmonized with his inclination.

To his neighbors the change was so startling that one
and all attributed it to preternatural causes. His deep
religious character and the composure he had manifested
in the face of death, gave some color to this hypothesis,
and it was soon noised abroad that Seth Goodwin had
experienced "sanctification," and was "delivered forever from the power of sin." It is doubtful if this idea
had occurred to him until after it was suggested; but
it was eagerly accepted, and belief in its verity served
very greatly to confirm the mental composure on which
it was based. If he did not quite believe that sin was
impossible with him, he for the first time accepted the
idea that his purposes and inclinations were right, and
that what he desired to do could not in itself be wrong.

All this, his brother, careless and worldly-minded, was
unable to comprehend, and it was with unfeigned astonishment that he found him entering heartily into his own
plans for the colt, on whose qualities the hope of the
future seemed to depend. The invalid made frequent
allusions to the subject, and sometimes rebuked his
brother for seeming apathy in regard to it; but Horace
skilfully avoided any extended consideration of the matter until the spring's work upon the farm was well
advanced and his brother's health so far restored that
he was able to sit up the greater portion of the day.

His recovery was very slow, if recovery it was, and the
once busy, anxious man watched the springtime pass
away with a strange absence of apprehension for the
future, and without manifesting any special desire either
to assist or direct the work which was going on about
him.

"What are your plans about the colt, Seth?" he finally
asked one afternoon when the planting was over and a
warm April shower had just come in time to start the
waiting seeds. It had cleared away and the first rain-
bow of the season was painted on the retreating storm-
cloud in the eastern sky by the level rays of the setting
sun. Seth Goodwin sat in a great splint-bottom rocker
watching the pictured clouds, from the window of the
room which he had occupied during his illness. His
face had lighted up as if the effulgence of the bow of
promise were reflected in it. Horace sat near him, in
his shirt-sleeves, just as he had come scurrying in from
the field to avoid the rain. He had watched his brother
narrowly during the storm and seemed depressed rather
than cheered by the quiet contentedness of his manner.

"Oh, you just put him in shape, Horace, and take
him East and sell him. There isn't anybody else can do
as well with him as you. He's gained every day he's
been at work, and is looking splendidly now."

Seth Goodwin did not know the care that had been
taken not to over-work or even weary the animal on
whose value so much depended. Horace had allowed
no one else to touch the reins; and in addition to giving this team the lightest work, had taken the precaution to shift the pivot of the doubletree well over
toward the end to which the mare was attached, thus
lightening the colt's load. The colt had never been
allowed to get tired or discouraged, but had had plenty

of good, toughening exercise. When it was over, he was rather low in flesh, but his tendons were like steel and his coat as soft and shining as if he had been under the trainer's hand.

In the meantime, Horace had studied him very carefully. To the careless reader such prolonged scrutiny may, no doubt, seem to have been unnecessary. There is a general impression that certain men are gifted with an instinctive power to determine at a glance the qualities and capacity of a horse ; but every true lover of the animal knows that one might just as well attempt to select a lyric poet by inspection, as a successful race-horse. So many qualities are essential to a well-founded hope, so many mental as well as physical attributes to be considered, that the experienced horseman fully understands that only he who has "summered and wintered with a horse," studying his every movement, watching the play of his muscles, the action of his limbs, the beat of his pulse, the swell of his nostrils, his digestion, endurance, and especially his temper, is able to give a reliable opinion, not only as to what he is able to do, but what he is likely to be willing to do under given conditions. It was not without good reasons, therefore, that Horace Goodwin followed the colt day after day in the furrow. He knew very well that there is no place where one learns so thoroughly the real qualities of a horse as by constant observation of him while engaged in some regular work. In that manner alone can one become entirely familiar with his physical qualities, learn what reliance is to be placed on his power of endurance, and especially whether he be endowed with that courage which, while submitting to needed restraint, is of that fine quality which bids defiance to fatigue, and when he has done his seeming best, responds with willingness to the demand for more.

Horace Goodwin had determined to attempt a bold stroke, if his observations confirmed his nephew's judgment of the colt's qualities. While he did not rely upon the boy's opinion, he did not neglect the fact that the lad, though without extensive knowledge of horses, had a natural aptitude for horsemanship, and, by a careful study of his favorite, had arrived at an estimate of his capabilities, which was by no means to be lightly discarded. His own reputation as a horseman demanded, however, that this opinion should be confirmed by his own carefully matured judgment.

This young man was by nature a gambler. He delighted in great risks. He loved to do unexpected and surprising things. While not averse to labor, the drudgery of slow accumulation was intensely distasteful to him. Fond as he was of the horse, he had an ineradicable aversion for farm-life. He could endure any sort of privation in order to accomplish some startling result, but the almost inappreciable gain resulting from daily application was irksome beyond expression to him. He was willing to stake everything he had upon a single stroke, but he would not do it without full comprehension of the chances for and against success. Though a gambler by nature, he was something more than a mere dice-thrower. He delighted to base his hope upon knowledge, and had in him much of the material of which the successful speculator is made.

In the present case he had many incentives to caution. He had fully determined to effect his brother's release from the incubus of debt in one way or another. He had become satisfied that the mare, Queen, was possessed of trotting qualities of rare excellence, and as this sport had lately sprung into special favor at the East, he had intended to train her carefully and enter her as an unknown in some of the races where the odds would be tremendously in her favor. He counted upon borrowing enough to take advantage of these conditions, and hoped that what he might win in stakes and wagers, supplemented, if need be, by the sale of the mare, would enable him to pay off his brother's bond before he could be dispossessed by legal process. It was not a very large sum, but a horse worth a thousand dollars was then very rare.

The hope of discovering a winner was not so wild as it seemed. The trotting horse had not then become a scientific fact. Prodigies were still numerous upon the trotting turf. Each year developed some new wonder, and it was hardly an unusual thing to find the last year's favorite superseded by one which twelve months before had been hitched to plow or cart. Horace Goodwin had watched the principal events of the previous season, and felt that he could safely rely upon the Queen to give a good account of herself with such competitors. She was in her prime, sound as a dollar, toughened by exertion, familiar with the track, and only needed, as he thought, to have the trotting-gait she had always preferred developed and confirmed to show not only speed but the ability to win races.

The suggestion in regard to the colt had changed his plan by adding to it another possible chance for success, as well as another possible opportunity to enhance his renown as a horseman. Next to the relief of his brother's necessity, he counted the pleasure of a triumph on the turf. To have two strings to his bow and be the possessor of two " surprises " at the same time was a rapture he had never dreamed of before. The fact that he found himself dreaming of it now rendered him distrustful and uneasy rather than confident. He began to think that his imagination had run away with his judgment.

His study of the colt had been unusually careful,
therefore, and his disinclination to pronounce an opinion
upon his merits had proceeded not only from consideration for his brother's interests, but also from a keen
desire to avoid a decision that would reflect discredit
upon himself. He felt that his reputation as a horseman was at stake, and he would almost rather have
abandoned the hope of relieving his brother than have
suffered that to be tarnished. He understood how easy
it is to be mistaken in regard to an untried horse, and
determined not to err from any lack of study of the
subject. Twice, after a day or two of rest, he had tested
the colt's speed at night along the " measured mile."
Once the boy had ridden him and the uncle had ridden
the mare ; the other time he had gone out alone, lightly
clad, with spurred heels and a rawhide at his wrist, and
ridden the colt at speed along the " measured mile."
It was a race against time. He had no watch to tell
the seconds, but he could make a good guess at com-
parative speed. Besides that, he wanted to feel how
the colt would run under a heavy weight, so as to be
able to judge of his prowess, and to test for himself his
courage, to decide whether he would endure pressure,
and in the climax of his effort respond to an appeal for
more. When he had reached the end of the course he
dismounted, quickly applied his ear to the colt's chest,
counted the heart-beats, held the nostrils a moment,
and then listened at the swelling flank ; stood off and
watched him, as, with outstretched neck and observing
eye, he recovered from his effort with deep, even sus-
pirations. Then he felt of each leg, one after the other ;
stood in front of the animal and looked him over sharply,
while the colt's bright eyes watched curiously his own
movements. Having finished his observations, he
threw the bridle over his arm and walked briskly home,

nodding his head, now and then snapping his fingers at his thoughts. He did not trust himself to put them into words by whispering them even to himself, and the colt probably wondered why Mr. Horace Goodwin was so considerate as to walk back to the stable, instead of riding.

"Oh, I can put him in condition easy enough," said Horace, replying to his brother's suggestion ; "but he must—you see—well, I suppose you know his value depends on what he can do—how fast he can go."

"Of course," answered the other, simply. Horace looked into his brother's peaceful face in unaffected surprise.

"And you understand that what he can do can only be determined—in one way ?"

"By a race, you mean ?"

"Certainly."

"You might arrange one with the Queen."

The younger brother shook his head in emphatic amazement at his brother's innocence.

"No use," he said, shortly. "Everybody would say it was a put-up job, and it would hurt both of them. To make a reputation, the colt's got to run against something that *has* a reputation and is run to beat ; and he must either win or come so near winning that any one can see he ought to have won. You see, it isn't so much the question what he *can* do as what he *will* do on the track against another that makes a horse worth dollars instead of dimes."

"So I suppose."

"You don't object to my making a match for him, then ?"

"I cannot countenance betting," answered the other, firmly.

"But you have no objection to his running, if you are not required to back him ?"

"I can hardly say I have no objection, Horace," said the other, gravely ; "but if the Lord is kind enough to lift me out of trouble by sending me an exceptionally valuable beast, I do not think I have any right to scorn His bounty by refusing to allow an opportunity to show his value."

"Exactly. Well, that's sensible, anyhow," replied Horace, with an intonation of relief.

"I wouldn't want to keep on running him, but, just to find out what's in him, I think I've a right—"

"Of course you have," interrupted Horace. He was afraid the other would see the weakness of his own casuistry and revoke the leave he had granted. He need not have had any such apprehension. Seth Goodwin had decided that it was not sinful for him to take this course. This decision had made him happy, and he had come to test questions of right and wrong more by the "inner light" than by any established ethical rule. It may have been delusive, but it was a very comfortable way of looking at a troublesome question.

"What do you think of the colt, anyhow, Horace?" asked the owner, with some show of uneasiness.

"He's a good deal of a horse," answered the brother, cautiously, "and it's all the better it wasn't found out until he was well grown."

"I should have broken him before, but I had no use for him, and I thought it was just as well he should be in the pasture, so I only used him enough to keep him bridle-wise," commented the invalid, complacently.

"I suspect somebody else used him more than you did," the brother added with a meaning smile.

"What do you mean ?"

" I've a notion that Hubert has ridden him about the pasture more than you imagine."

" But Number 2, the pasture where he has always been kept, is a mile away, and only half cleared," said the father in surprise.

" Well, Jack is a dozen years old. Jumping over logs and stumps was good exercise for the colt and splendid training for the boy," answered the brother. " Don't be troubled, Seth," he continued ; "it won't hurt the lad for anything else to be a good horseman, and that he certainly is—the best for his years and inches I ever saw."

" And you think he's right about what the colt can do ?"

" Beat the Queen, you mean ?"

" Yes."

" I think so—haven't any doubt of it ; though no one ever knows just what the old girl will do to-day by what she did yesterday."

" His dam was a good one. Nothing ever discouraged her. You remember when we moved out here, Horace, we had to lay over for the other horses to rest three or four times ; but old Fan was always ready to start—too ready, in fact," commented the elder, musingly.

" And the colt was sired by Abdallah ?" rejoined the brother.

" I don't know," was the reply. " You remember I sold the mare, and the purchaser let her run down until she was thin as a shadow. That was always the way with the old girl—let a fool drive her and she'd run herself into the grave, no matter how well she was fed. She was getting on in years and the man thought she was going to die on his hands, and sold her back to me for a song. I turned her out to grass ; the fall feed was good ; she stood the winter well and the foal was as pretty a fellow as I ever saw. The next year she took a hard cold and went off in a month as if she had quick consumption."

" I suppose she had."

" Very likely. I don't see why horses shouldn't have it as well as people, and I never saw a place where there was so much of it as right about here. I've heard the sire was Abdallah, but never quite believed the story."

" There's no doubt of it."

" I'm almost sorry," said the brother, in a dissatisfied tone. " They're boasting a good deal about his stock now, especially for trotting nags, but I haven't much opinion of him or of trotters, either. It is a strained, unnatural gait—fast trotting, I mean ; and the horse that trots instead of galloping is a sort of monstrosity. I'm sorry its coming into favor again. As for Abdallah, I saw him once ; a mean, rat-tailed, ill-proportioned scrub, with the worst temper ever put inside a horse's skin."

" The colt's got his share of that ; but you must remember that descent from Abdallah means Messenger blood."

" Well, I, for one, don't think as much of Messenger blood as many do. I think it owes as much to what it has met with as to the qualities it brings "

The younger brother smiled. In that day, it was still permissible to doubt the excellence of the matchless gray whose blood has since become the most valuable that ever coursed in equine veins, and there were many very capable horsemen who still regarded the trotting gait as a serious mistake.

" At all events," said Horace, " Messenger blood means ' go ' to the very death."

" I suppose that's so. Belmont used to say it was a strain of that which made it so hard to keep old Fan ın fair condition ; but she got most of her good qualities from the other side."

" Did you buy her of a man named Belmont ?" asked the brother in surprise.

" Bought her at the administrator's sale. She was old Loren Belmont's favorite nag. She was past her prime then, and, as usual when she had her own way, in low order, and went very cheap. She used to be called the ' Belmont Mare,' and was a notable beast in her day."

" I should think so !" exclaimed the other, emphatically.

" I wanted her because she was the best walker I ever saw—the colt is just like her in that—and I knew such a horse would be worth her price in a team on a long journey, if she did nothing afterward. Even a dull horse will wake up if he has a quick-stepper for a mate."

" So ?" said the brother, with a long, low whistle. " That accounts for some things. The Queen is one of her colts, too."

" Foaled the second year after we got here. I was a fool to sell her, but I needed money badly."

" Lucky there was a scapegrace in the family to buy her back," rejoined the brother, jocosely. " I tell you, Seth, there's more money in Messenger blood than in any other stock that ever walked on four legs. You see they're always willing to do their level best. They may be coarse-built and high-strung and bad-tempered, but they're tough and determined. One of the best things that ever happened to this country was the landing of that scraggy gray who couldn't even be made sea-sick, but was all two men could manage the very minute he came down the gang-plank. His stock are mostly trotters, but I suppose the colt gets his gait from the other side. The Belmont Mare was a Bashaw, I believe."

" Her dam was by an Arab."

"From a daughter of Messenger ; that's what I've heard."

"And she was sired by Justin Morgan."

"You see the colt is very well bred—almost thorough-bred, except the Morgan strain."

"Well, I believe Justin Morgan was better bred than he gets credit for."

"It may be."

"Must have been to give out so even and strongly-marked a stock. You see, it's the average quality of a family of horses that shows the breeding, not the exceptions."

"I suppose so," assented the brother, absently.

"Of course it is," said the invalid, irritably, noticing the other's inattention.

Horace looked anxiously at his brother, took his pipe from his pocket, filled and lighted it, took a whiff or two, cleared his throat and said :

"If I tell you just what I think about the colt, Seth, it won't upset you, nor—anything, I s'pose ?"

The other paled a little, but answered brusquely :

"Of course not."

"Well, then, I don't think there's above a dozen horses in the country can show him their heels ; and if you can hold on to him until that's generally known, you needn't fuss about not being able to work."

The sick man, who had shown a strange weakness since his recovery, put his hand to his breast and looked steadily out of the window. His mouth twitched with pain, and there were tears in his eyes.

"The Lord has rebuked my want of faith," he said, solemnly.

"The colt will need to be given a fair chance, of course," interposed the brother, quickly.

"You will do what you think best with him, Horace,

I don't want to know anything about it. It may not be right, but I'll stand by you and take the blame. Right or wrong, it means comfort for *them ;*" he nodded towards the other room where his wife and his child were. "When I was at the worst and thought I was going to leave them unprovided-for, I promised the Lord that if He'd show me a way to do that, I wouldn't ask anything for myself. It seems as if He'd took me at my word, and I'm not going to back down, whatever the consequences. If there's any sin in what we're doing, Horace, I'll take it all on myself. If I knew it meant eternal punishment, I'd do it—*for their sakes.*"

His face grew pale and he leaned back in the rocking-chair, with a glance at the open door between the rooms. Horace rose and shut it softly, and returning, placed his hand on his brother's forehead. It was wet with heavy drops of sweat.

"Don't be troubled, Seth," he said, soothingly. "It can't be wicked to raise and sell a colt—and that's all you're going to do. If I choose to arrange a race and win or lose a few dollars on the result, that's my affair. It won't be the first time I've done it, either, and probably will not be the last. You just leave the matter to me and don't worry. I wouldn't have your name mixed up with such a thing—though I don't think there's any harm in it—any sooner than you ; but you know *I* can't be hurt, nohow."

The sick man smiled.

"You are very good, Horace."

" No ; I'm just paying off some old debts."

" I'm afraid I was too harsh with you sometimes, Horace—when we were both younger."

" That's just where you're mistaken. If I ever do take a turn for the better, it'll be because of your example," said the younger brother, with some show of feeling.

The elder raised his right hand feebly, the younger clasped it and turned away his head. After a little time he withdrew his hand and went out of the room wiping his eyes.

———•———

CHAPTER III.

"THE KING OF THE CORNERS."

Ortonville was the name assumed by the little group of houses on the State road a mile from the dwelling of Seth Goodwin. Why it was called Ortonville, or why a ville of any sort should have been located at that point, nobody knew. It was not even a cross-roads, since the township roads which crossed the great highway, did so, one to the northward and the other to the southward of the little village. Indeed, Ortonville had no legal status, boundaries or existence. It was located in Greenfield township; and sometimes arrogated to itself the name of West Greenfield; but the assumption was not regarded with approval by the inhabitants of other sections of the green parallelogram to which the name legally pertained. A score or so of houses, a store, two rival blacksmith's shops, a tavern, a grist-mill, a wagon-shop, a carding-mill, two churches and a select school may be said to have constituted about all there was of the pretentiously named little village. Small as it was, it was made more insignificant by being divided into two parts by a sharp gorge down which flowed a little stream, whose pent-up water lazily and reluctantly turned the mill wheels. The inn and one of the stores stood on one side of the gorge; the two churches, the school-house and several of the most pretentious residences on the other.

The magnate of the village from the first was Marshall Kincaid, who owned the store, the hotel, the livery stable upon the south side, and was the richest man in all that region. The store and the inn were under one roof and had a common sign—

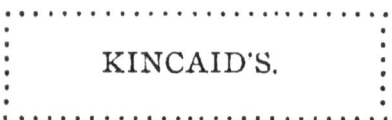

For a time the village was called " Kincaid's" also ; but the people, especially upon the north bank of the stream, rebelled at this assumption, and procured the post-office to be named Ortonville. This institution was also, after a bitter contest, located in a rival store on the north side, which the owner of Kincaid's chose to consider as arrogating some aristocratic quality, because of the possession of the post-office, churches and the select school.

Hard-headed, heavy-fisted and sharp-tongued was this magnate of Ortonville. The "best people" spoke slightingly of him. He retorted by calling the village, north of the ravine, Skunk Hollow. Coarse and democratic in manner, he was strictly honest according to his own standard. What he promised, that he did. He was not scrupulous or merciful. He did what the law allowed him to do ; what it forbade, he did not attempt. In spite of all opposition, the tough-skinned owner of Kincaid's remained the autocrat of the ganglion which had grown up by the great artery of trade and travel, along which the stage and the drover found their way towards the northern and southern outlets of the great East. What made this man a sportsman, it would be hard to say, unless it was that his strong nature craved the excitement of the gambler's life, while his prudence held him back from the gaming table. Certain it is that he prided himself especially upon his horses, and would rather have held a mortgage on Horace Goodwin's mare Queen than on his brother's farm.

It was early in May that Horace rode up to Kincaid's, watered his mare at the great trough which stood brimming over at the foot of the sign-post, hitched her in one of the long sheds across the way and sauntered toward the store, in the door of which stood the merchant, arms akimbo, clad in coarse white tow-cloth trousers, and shirt, then the usual summer wear, the sleeves of the latter rolled above his elbows, and having upon his head what was known as a " chip " hat, made of the braided filament of the buckeye-tree.

" Hello, Hod !" he exclaimed. " Come in here ; I want to see you a minute. Where on earth have you been keepin' yourself all the spring ? Workin' for Seth ? Didn't know he could afford to hire. What you been doin' ? Sugarin' and plantin', eh ? I've heard about your sugar—mighty nice lot they tell me. Got any for sale ? Sold it ? How much ? Eight hundred pounds ! Why didn't you bring it to me ?"

" Well," answered Horace, indifferently, " we found that we could get a cent a pound more at the harbor than you was offerin', and as I wanted to go East to see 'bout some matters, we thought 'twas best to take it there. Might just as well, you see ; don't cost any more to drive a loaded team than an empty wagon."

" Why didn't you go East, then ?" retorted the merchant, sharply.

" Found what I was after in Sandusky."
"Oh, you did? Must have been important."
" That's what it was—to me."
" Oh, 'twas your business, was it? Everybody knows that when Hod Goodwin has business on hand, it must be 'tended to right off or it'll spile."

He turned sideways in the door to give several loungers in the store the benefit of his rude wit. There was an approving laugh, and one or two of them sidled past him and stood upon the porch the better to hear the wordy encounter. Horace Goodwin, in the phrase of the region, was regarded as " able to hold his hand with most any body that chose to tackle him." He leaned quietly against one of the posts of the porch, holding a beech switch in his hand, with which he carelessly tapped his red morocco boot-top, as he joined in the laugh against himself. Horace Goodwin was inclined to be what the good people of the region termed " foppish in his dress." On the present occasion, though he wore the ordinary homespun of the country, it fitted his supple figure with a careless elegance, and the blue tie, which confined the flowing Byronic collar at the throat, the high, calf-skin boots, carefully blacked, and having red morocco tops, together with a pair of brass spurs so well polished that they shone like gold, gave him a suspiciously picturesque appearance. In truth, his reputation as a sport and reckless ne'er-do-well, was based quite as much on his good clothes and good looks as on anything reprehensible in his conduct. He had come to the village for a special purpose, and had studied his attire with especial reference to that object, giving it just that careless elegance which he knew was most irritating to the coarse nature of the landlord.

" Well, Squire," he answered with a provoking drawl, " I don't know 'bout that; but even if it was sp'ilt, I don't think my business would smell as bad as yourn does in good condition."

The hit was too apparent to be overlooked, and the laugh was on the magnate.

"Never you mind my business," he retorted, angrily. "I'll take care of that. Brought back a load from Van Wyck, didn't you?"

"B'lieve we did."

"Trust him?"

"Wasn't asked to."

"Owed him, I s'pose?"

"He paid cash at the dock—always does, I hear. That's how he get's his hauling done cheap."

"Oh, 'tis! Wal, he'll need to. I'll show him what it means to come and open a store right here under my nose. In less'n a year, the sheriff'll be auctionin' off his goods if I have to sell mine at less'n cost."

"Ortonville 'll be a cheap place to buy goods, for a while, then!"

"Kincaid's 'll be the cheap place, and that's where the goods 'll be brought, too."

"They say Day & Miller is backin' Van Wyck."

"Don't care who's a-backin' him. I'll break him down or bu'st up myself. I've made up my mind to that."

"That's what Wyck says he likes to see you doing. He says he keeps run of your prices, and sends all of his best customers here for big bargains. He furnishes them the cash to buy with, you see, and takes their truck at a fair price. He says it's cheaper to have you bring on his goods than haul them himself."

A roar went up at this sally, and the merchant, willing to conceal his vexation, joined in it.

"You're too sharp for me this mornin', Hod. I give up. Got any more of that fine sugar? They say you

Vermont folks beat the world at b'ilin' sap. What do you suppose makes the difference?"

" I don't know, unless it's because we use more water."

" More water? What has that to do with it? What's the use of mixin' water with the sap, when you have to bile out what's in it?" asked one of the loungers.

"Oh, I didn't mean waterin' the sap," answered Horace, dryly. " I meant washin' the kettles and the troughs and things of that sort."

" Hello, Hank!" said Kincaid, giving the one who had spoken a whack upon the back. " Who's hit, now? They say you're so 'fraid of wastin' water that you don't wash your hands above once a month."

" I'd wash 'em oftener if I had 'em in as many dirty things as you handle," retorted the farmer, desperately.

" Wal, never mind," said the merchant, relieved by the way the laugh had turned on another. " What I want to know, Hod, is whether you've got any more of that sugar. I s'pose I'll have to have a little, if I pay twice what it's worth. My wife's been at me 'bout gettin' some for a month. She don't like muscovado. Now I do. 'Tain't quite so white, but it's sweeter an' richer."

" Flavored with bits of nigger now and then, too. That's what makes it suit your taste, I s'pose," said Hank, willing to repay his tormentor for the thrust he had received.

" I don't know about that. I don't reckon there is anything in that story. I 'low niggers cost too much to be used to flavor molasses with. But whatever 'tis, I like muscovado. I think a green-apple pie, sweetened with muscovado, with white clover honey on top of it, is just about as good eatin' as a man ever gets. But my wife spleens against it, and is especially fond of Goodwin's sugar, 'cause she says she knows it's clean. I hope you saved some for us, Hod?"

"I don't know whether Seth's folks would think they could spare any more or not. We made about twelve hundred pounds."

"So I heard," remarked the merchant. "Mighty good bush, that."

"'Bout the best in the country, and well-equipped, too. Seven hundred buckets and troughs; two forty-barrel store-troughs, and a sugar-house thirty feet by seventy, as light and dry as a parlor, and a sixty-foot arch for boiling. It's hard to beat."

"Jest so," said the magnate, with a shrewd twinkle in his eyes.

"But you see, Marsh, the last run was after the buds had started, and wasn't quite as white as what was 'done off' before; a little sticky, too, as if it wasn't quite dry."

"Always will be that way after the buds start," remarked the farmer called Hank.

"Yes," continued Horace, "and I don't s'pose Seth's folks would like to sell that."

"Hurt his reputation, eh?"

"Seth's mighty particular 'bout such things, you know. Besides, it takes a good deal of sweetening for the family, 'specially when I'm there; then they're expecting a sight of company this year, and Seth being sick—"

"How is he now?"

"So's to be about the house, but don't seem to have no strength—no more'n a baby, hardly. Just gives out if he lifts his hands, let alone doing any work."

"I hear he's mighty happy, though?"

It was Hank who asked the question, and his face had assumed a sudden seriousness.

"Perfectly."

"So the Elder told me. I tell you, gentlemen, religion pays at such times," said the grimy-handed farmer, turning toward the others with an unconscious assumption of superiority.

" So I s'pose. When I git that way, I'll think about it," said Kincaid, lightly.

" You'd better begin pretty soon, Marsh. You'll need all the time you're likely to have, if half they tell about you is true," retorted Hank, shrugging his shoulders and winking at the others.

" How much was there of that last run ?" asked Kincaid, ignoring the rough exhortation.

" About eighty or a hundred pounds."

" What you goin' to do with the rest ?"

" Seth thought we'd better keep it. They might need it, you know."

" Need four hundred pounds of sugar! More'n I use in the tavern !"

" Perhaps the house'd be more popular if you used more," retorted Hank.

" No doubt it takes a good deal of that to sweeten Seth's religion," sneered the merchant. " Well, he can afford it—he's mor'gaged. By the way, when's he goin' to pay that thousand dollars I've been waitin' for since January ?"

" I don't know—not just now, I s'pose," answered Horace ; " but you needn't be at all afraid, Marshall ; he'll get it some time, and he might as well be paying you interest as any one. We've got in a good crop, and I'm going to help him this year. He's had bad luck, you know, but we're going into a little matter that promises mighty well, we think."

" Horses ?" asked Kincaid, sharply.

" Well, a little. I went on East last fall looking up this trotting business, that's come up so hot all at once. I've had a sulky built and am going to train the Queen for some of the fall races."

" 'Tain't no good," said the other, positively; "they'll beat ye out of yer eye-teeth. You ain't no match fer them fellers down East, Hod Goodwin."

" I don't know," answered, Horace, complacently. " I hain't ever got let in very bad on a horse yet, and I thought while we were at it, Seth and I might as well pick up a drove and take them on at the same time. So if one speculation flashed in the pan the other might amount to something."

" That ain't a bad idee. It'll take money, though, to buy horses cheap, an' they don' either on ye seem to have any too great a supply of that," sneered the merchant. " I don't see how y're going to do business, unless you've got either money or credit."

" Well, you see, Seth's wife's brother, back East, he's a little forehanded, and he's got a mighty good idea of Seth's judgment and my luck ; so he's going to furnish a little money for a starter. 'Twas him I went to Sandusky to meet."

" Jest so ; wal, 'tain't half a bad idea," repeated Kincaid. " Ef you'd been as stiddy as Seth, you'd been a rich man long ago with your luck—judgment, I'd call it —but Seth'll spile it ; see if he don't. He's too pious to make a good hoss-trader."

" I s'pose I'll have to do the buying," said Horace.

" You'll have to do the sellin', too, if there's any money made," answered Kincaid.

" S'pose I shall," was the reply.

" Then what in thunder's Seth going to do ?"

." Look after me and keep me straight, I guess."

" So you're goin' to turn pious, too," sneered the magnate of the double-headed village.

" Well, I thought I'd see if I couldn't turn my experience to some account, and help Seth along at the same time."

"GUESS I WILL HAVE TO TAKE YOU UP ON THAT, SQUIRE." See Page 55.

" Hod Goodwin," said the merchant, "you're jest as big a fool as ever. Ef you'd done that ten years ago, or even five, you'd made a fortune, both on ye ; but it's too late now. He's got no credit, and I'm goin' to harvest that crop you have been plantin' for him, unless—" here he looked around and winked at the loiterers—"unless he takes that brother-in-law's money and pays off my mortgage. That would be a good plan, now."

" Seth would starve, first," exclaimed the brother, angrily.

"B'lieve he would," rejoined Kincaid ; "but it's his only way out of the box he's in. I'm goin' to put the note in suit right away ; the place'll be sold in July— jest the tightest time in all the year for money—and he'll have to get off before the crop's ripe. I'm goin' to have the money or the place, and, if the corn does well, I'd a leetle rather have the place than the money."

" There ain't no doubt of that," answered Horace ; " but I'll bet something you don't get it."

" How's he goin' to help it ?"

" I can't say just now."

" You can't make nothin' on yer hoss spec afore fall nohow ?"

" I s'pose not."

" Wal, then, what's to hinder ?"

" I don't know exactly ; I just feel, though, as if something or other'd turn up to save Seth's place ; been feelin' so all the time."

" Bet ye fifty dollars that I git the place," retorted the merchant, slapping his brawny palm on the door-casing.

" Guess I'll have to take you up on that, Squire."

" All right," said Kincaid, going behind the counter

and opening his money-drawer, with a flourish; "put up yer available."

"It's about all I've got," answered Horace, taking out his pocket-book; "and it's a good while to wait for returns; but one has to back his kin, you know. What time did you say?"

"Wal—first of October."

"All right."

Horace counted out the money, and the two went across the street to put the stakes in the hands of a third party. They chose a lawyer, and when the deposit had been made, the terms being carefully written out and signed by the parties, the merchant said:

"Now, Kendall, you jest push that suit ag'in' Seth Goodwin, and the money in that paper is yer fee. I'm much obleeged to you, Hod, for helpin' me pay a lawyer to eject yer brother."

This incident put the money-lender in good humor, and on their return to the store he began to banter the other to make a race between his mare Queen and a noted gray horse which the merchant had bought the summer before. He was known as Gray Eagle, and was said to have a long record of victories on the turf. It was rumored that Kincaid had bought him especially to dispossess the Queen from her supremacy, his previous attempts in that direction having been rather costly failures. This was exactly what Horace Goodwin had come to the village to effect, but he was a keen judge of men and knew that the surest way to effect his purpose was to display entire indifference. So he answered nonchalantly enough to the eager banter:

"Can't do it, Squire. I'm going to train her to trot; made up my mind to that. Besides, it wouldn't be any

credit to her to beat that lop-eared old nag of yours.
You got awfully taken in when you paid twenty-five
hundred dollars for such a horse. He's seen his best
days, and never was worth anything like that money."

" Who told you I paid that ?" asked Kincaid, sharply.

" Why, I went down to Kentucky just to find out about
him ; and I found out all I wanted to know, too."

" We did call it twenty-five hundred," admitted the
other, " but part of it was trade. Anyhow, he can run a
mile quicker'n any horse in Ohio. Come, now, I dare
you to make a race with him and your mare, and bet
one horse against the other."

" Oh, I won't run the mare ; that's settled. I wouldn't
run her against him, anyhow ; it would spoil her reputation. But I'll tell you what I will do. I ain't the man
to spoil sport or take a banter. I'll pick up a horse
right out of the pasture that never run a race in his life,
and just give me a few days to show him how to pick
up two feet at a time, and if he don't beat your old Gray
Eagle the best two out of three, mile-heats, you may
take the Queen ; and, if he does, you shall give me as
much for him as you agreed to pay for the Eagle."

The loiterers highly applauded this challenge, all the
more, because they had no idea that it would ever pass
beyond the realm of braggadocio. Fond as the people
were of horse-racing at that time, large bets were
exceedingly rare. The merchant, knowing how attached
Horace Goodwin was to his pet mare, thought this
merely a bluff, and met it with one as bold.

" Done !" said he emphatically. " A word's enough
—between gentlemen—" he added, scornfully. " Come
right over to Squire Kendall's again and have the writin's draw'd up at once. There ain't no mortgage on the
mare, I s'pose ?"

" Nothing on her heavier'n a saddle," answered Goodwin.

"I s'pose my note 'll be security enough for the money."

" The money 'll do well enough for me, Squire, or anything that'll bring money, but not any note of yours, if you please."

" Do you think I'd go back on my word?"

" 'Fast bind, fast find,' Mr. Kincaid. That's your motto, I believe. If I put up a bill of sale of the mare, you've got to put up the money or the money's worth."

Again the sentiment of the crowd was unmistakably in Goodwin's favor. After some haggling, it was agreed that the race should be run on Tuesday, the third day of July, if the weather was fair and the track dry—if not, on the next day—it being admitted by both that it would not do to make a match over a hard clay track when it was wet with a recent shower. The landlord was to deposit two thousand dollars—good and lawful money—to abide the issue, ten days before the race, and in case of failure to do so, to forfeit the five hundred now deposited, and in that case the bill of sale of the Queen was to be returned to her owner. Proof satisfactory to the stakeholder, that the unknown horse had been reared in that or an adjoining county, and had never run for any stake, was to be made at the time set for the race, which was to be three heats along the "measured mile," Goodwin having the choice as to which end of the course the track should begin.

An hour afterward, when Horace Goodwin dashed past the window at which his brother sat, and up the lane to the low, rambling barn in the rear, the mare was unusually blown and he had chewed the beech switch until only a fragment of it remained. He felt that he had made a desperate venture, on which not only his own favorite but his brother's good name were staked, with the chances by no means certain in his favor. Yet when he came to the house a few minutes after, his countenance was as composed as if he had never dreamed that failure was a possibility.

" There is no betting about it, Horace ?" Seth Goodwin asked, when he was told that the colt was to run with the Gray Eagle.

" If he beats Kincaid's horse," answered Horace, evasively, "you can have twenty-five hundred for the colt ; that is all."

" And if he does not ?"

" You will still have the colt."

Horace did not inform him that his own highly-prized mare would be the forfeit for the colt's insufficiency. The answer satisfied the elder brother. He was a shrewd and thoughtful man, but he knew little about racing, and did not trouble himself to guess that there must be another side of the wager. Horace had made it one of the conditions of the match that its terms should be kept secret, so that no whisper of them came to the elder brother's ears.

" Very well," he responded after a moment's silence ; " if there is no betting about it, I have no objection. I think the colt will give a good account of himself. Who is going to ride him ?"

The brother glanced at Hubert, who stood by, eagerly drinking in every word of the conversation.

" Do you think it safe ?" asked the father, in an anxious tone.

" The colt will do more for him than for any one else, and you remember what the English turfmen say : ' Ounces at the start mean guineas at the finish.' "

" Well, I suppose that is true," Seth Goodwin replied.

A few days afterward, Horace Goodwin and his

nephew, with the Queen and the colt Pompey, suddenly disappeared from the neighborhood. It was generally reported that they had gone to find a horse to match the Gray Eagle. As the days went by and they did not return, there was a good deal of curiosity expressed as to their whereabouts.

CHAPTER IV.

SOLITUDE THE NURSE OF POWER.

It was a curious training-stable that Horace Goodwin chose for the colt on whose performance he had staked so much. The Queen represented the sum total of his accumulations, and he had no intention of losing her by neglect of any precaution. At a time when most young men of enterprise and respectability were land-owners at twenty-five, Horace Goodwin was approaching thirty without having become master of an acre. Patrimony he had none. His father, from whom he inherited only a happy-go-lucky temperament, had not only squandered the little inheritance he received, but had shown such utter lack of capacity, that the thrifty neighbors counted his death a blessing to his wife, who, aided by a remnant of her dowry, bravely undertook the support and education of her two sons. Seth, the elder by several years, she had consecrated with many prayers, to the work of the ministry, which was the destiny most desired by every pious mother of that day for her favorite child. Before his preparation for this exalted station was fairly begun, however, the duty of maintaining the family devolved on him ; and the younger had hardly reached the years of self-support when their mother passed away, leaving him to the guardianship of his elder brother.

The western fever had long possessed Seth Goodwin. The family once prominent and prosperous had " kind of run out," the neighbors said, as so many New England families do, if they stick too close to the ancestral acres. People pityingly compared their present with their past estate, and Seth Goodwin was not the man to endure pity. If he inherited nothing but pride from the past, he had enough of that and to spare—the real blue-blooded, Plymouth-Rock-and-Faneuil-Hall pride in the essential superiority of all things Eastern, which was not so comical in its absurdity then as it has since become. Upon their mother's death, therefore, he lost no time in transferring his household gods to the West. He did not expect to find an Eldorado, but he was ready to battle with whatever came in his way to competence, and was especially anxious to get away from all familiar knowledge of the Goodwin history and attributes. He shrank from exposing his wife and their baby boy to the privations of pioneer life, and so, with the usual short-sightedness of the over-cautious, pitched his tent in the middle West, where there was less of comfort and no more of opportunity than in the region from which they came.

He provided for his brother's sustenance and education, so far as the restless character of the young man would permit, and when he came of age, offered him the choice of a moiety of the little store which constituted their inheritance, undiminished by any charge for nurture, or an equal share in the land he had bought, if the younger brother would " settle down " and work with him until it was paid for. This offer was a very liberal one, so other people thought, but Horace unhesitatingly chose the bit of money rather than the half-cleared acres, and received it with some unsolicited advice, which as usual in such cases, he proceeded promptly to disregard. This conduct grieved the elder brother, but in no way disturbed the pleasant relations that existed between them. " The Goodwins aren't much alike, but they stick to each other," was the general verdict upon the brothers.

Horace's money very soon burned a hole in his pocket, through which his earnings as well as his inheritance dribbled away. A gun and a violin were presently the sum total of his possessions. Afterward he had purchased the mare, which was the extent of his acquisitions. His brother's house was still his home, where he never lacked a welcome for himself or a stall for his favorite. He did not want ability or industry, though the latter was of a fitful character and the former not always directed to the most creditable ends. While few excelled him in the harvest-field, he was admittedly unrivaled as a violinist, an accomplishment then deemed almost as discreditable as the skill for which he was also noted in manipulating those painted bits of pasteboard whose mysterious charm was then regarded as a device of the arch-enemy of mankind for the taking of unwary souls. Versatile, kindly, jovial, he was stable only in the pursuit of the pleasures he affected, and devotion to the mare, with which no temptation could induce him to part. This was a peculiarly unfortunate combination of good and bad qualities for a time when life was especially earnest and real to those who were waging a hard conflict with nature, with none of the excitement of the pioneer and few of the comforts of civilization.

He had led a roving, though it could hardly be called an idle life, which was not without advantage in an added knowledge of the world and its ways. He had been East in the employ of drovers, once or twice, an experience of no little value in those days when it took two or three months to get the stock of the West to New York "on the hoof." Afterward, because of his skill as a purchaser and excellent judgment as to the value of stock, he had been employed to buy horses and cattle for a firm doing business at one of the lake ports. He was generally in receipt of good wages, but none of his earnings stuck to his fingers, except the Queen. He had repeatedly offered to let his brother have a part of his wages to assist him in paying off his indebtedness; but Seth Goodwin was the very incarnation of that pride which would rather endure hardship than be indebted to another's favor, more especially one whom he had so often lectured for extravagance.

Horace Goodwin was, therefore, one of the best-dressed, poorest, most contented, best-liked and least esteemed men in that region of the country. It was said that he knew most of the men and women and every one of the horses in the five counties adjoining that in which he lived. Because of this, the owner of Gray Eagle, despite his confidence in the prowess of his steed, was somewhat uneasy about the wager he had made. Twenty-five hundred dollars was a big price to pay for a horse, even though by some scratch of luck he might be able to defeat the nag of which he had boasted so confidentially. The truth was that Marshall Kincaid felt that he had been overmatched in the purchase of Gray Eagle, and would have been glad to get him off his hands at a greatly reduced figure. He had been a very good horse, but the winter had revealed certain infirmities which caused his new owner to regard him with a feeling not very far removed from nausea. He had bought him without warranty, however, and the only chance he had to make himself whole was by wagers on his performance. It was possible that another horse of similar character might win by dint of superior management. The chagrin of such a possibility troubled the magnate of the Corners even more than the prospect of loss.

The fact that the Queen was excluded by the terms of the race gave him no little comfort. He knew it was not an easy thing to find a raw horse which had never run a race able to defeat even a second-rate veteran of the turf under good management. The latter he made sure of by sending to Kentucky for the colored jockey who had ridden the Gray Eagle in his best races. As the jockey was a slave, he was obliged to give security to the master for the negro's safe return to bondage.

Despite all these precautions, however, he did not feel exactly safe. Horace Goodwin was too good a horseman and too fond of his mare to stake her upon a mere chance of success. Could it be that he had discovered some phenomenally good horse whose merits no one else recognized? Do what he might, Marshall Kincaid could not divest himself of a fear that this might be the case. He accordingly sent trusty messengers through each of the adjoining counties to make inquiries in regard to horses of the description indicated, which Horace Goodwin might perhaps secure for the purposes of the race, and, if possible, to discover also where Horace was hidden. The result of these inquiries was a conviction that young Goodwin would try to palm off, on the day of the race, a horse which did not comply with the conditions. As this would result in a forfeiture of the stakes, if the deception were exposed in time, he determined to be prepared for it by securing the attendance of a large number of men well acquainted with the people and horses of the adjacent counties.

He did not give a thought to the colt which had grown up on the farm so quietly as never to have attracted the attention even of the owner's " horsey " brother.

In the meantime, by a roundabout way, Horace and his nephew reached the training-stable which had been decided upon in case a match was made, long before. It was not a very luxurious affair ; but for secrecy, and adaptation to the purpose intended, a better one could hardly be imagined. It was Seth Goodwin's sugar-house, the camp at which the sap from his sugar-bush was boiled into syrup. It was a log-cabin, seventy feet long, with a store-trough hollowed from a giant cucumber-tree stretching along one side, and a great stone arch, in which were set a half-dozen large iron cauldrons on the other. Ordinarily the cabin was used during the summer to store the vessels in which the sap was caught, but this year these had been piled up outside of it, and a snug partition had been put across it, giving the opportunity for two roomy but secluded stalls beyond. The camp was admirably located, both for its original purpose and the one to which it was now dedicated.

It stood beside a running stream in a narrow valley, closely shut in by a dense growth of beech and maple. Hardly twenty steps away, a cold spring burst out of the sheltering bank, while just below was a sandy-bottomed pool, which constituted an ideal attachment of the training-stable. The store-trough served as a manger, and the front end of the log-cabin was occupied by the trainer and the jockey, who thus literally slept with the horse they were preparing for the crucial test of equine merit. Their preparations had been carefully made, and everything that might be needed for the horses and their attendants had been brought there at night and with every possible precaution to secure secrecy.

For a training-ground they had the springy wood
roads, cut for hauling sap to the camp, which were perfection itself for the ordinary jogging exercise, while a
few days' work with a pair of steers had made a splendid
turf-course around "Number Two," a twenty-acre
pasture which lay just outside the verdant wall that
marked the edge of the primeval forest, and was
securely hidden from the road, a mile away, by a fringe
of second-growths along its lower side. The sugar-
bush was part of an unbroken forest which stretched
between the parallel section-roads two miles apart, only
cut by narrow cross-roads at equal intervals. Surrounded by this dense mass of giant *decidua*, there was
no danger of discovery, unless by some chance wan-
derer, and as it was not the season for hunting, this was
very unlikely. For two months, this sequestered sugar-
camp was to be the training-stable of the bay colt and
of the mare, which was at the same time to be fitted
for the trotting-course, on which it was hoped she might
win profitable distinction.

To the boy these were months of almost unalloyed
happiness. Not only did its secrecy give special relish
to a life intrinsically attractive, but it was the first time
he had ever been a day beyond the touch of parental
restraint, and the solitude of the forest is magical in its
power to develop self-reliance and individuality Manhood is a flower which unfolds its petals most readily
where only God and Nature can scrutinize their form and
color. There is no place where the boy ripens into a
man so swiftly as in the shadows of the forest or the glare
of the desert. Besides this, the knowledge that his father
was constantly improving in health because of the hope
resulting from his estimate of the colt's merits, and the
importance of the work in which they were engaged,
made the days of steady application to a single purpose

pass radidly away, while the flashing fire, the uncle's violin and the thousand voices which filled the verdant wood, made the summer nights a genuine fairy-land to his fervid fancy.

Absorbed in his surroundings, he hardly noted the daily improvement of the colt, until he suddenly awoke to the fact that the animal he rode was quite a different beast from the one he had been accustomed to bestride. That nameless transformation which comes to a well-bred horse when he is " in condition," had given a new fire and life to his favorite. Speeded daily on the springy turf of Number Two, with the mare whom he was usually allowed to out-strip without too much effort, the instinct of the racer was stimulated, until the colt would have given up his life rather than be outdone. Then he was taught to yield to his rider's judgment, hanging on the mare's quarter and trailing steadily after her around the course, to steal in with a rush just at the finish, she being held back to make his victory more apparent. At the same time the colt's master received a training not less thorough at the hands of the experienced horseman with whom he was associated. From toe-tip to fore-top he learned the anatomy of the horse, while having the benefit of practice in his management and care. It was an education none the less important, because rare even among those who profess a special liking for the noble animal. The teacher had found somewhere the cannon-bone of a horse, still attached by the curiously intricate combination of bone and ligaments of the fetlock and pastern, to that amazing system of self-renewing springs, the hoof. This he analyzed, dissected and discoursed upon for the benefit of his young pupil, in the intervals of their labor, illustrating his theories by examples drawn from his own experience, or which he had gathered from the conversation

of others. As a consequence, the boy developed almost
as rapidly as the colt, and when the period of seclusion
was over, had not only become a well-informed horseman, but desired nothing so much as the life of a jockey.
Happening to mention this ambition one night, after a
pleasant day's work, when his uncle was quietly smoking, as he reclined on the pile of hay which served them
as a couch, that worthy took his pipe from his mouth
and said, sharply :

" Now, look here, my boy, none 'o that. Remember
you're Seth Goodwin's son. He's set his heart and hope
on you. It is well enough for a man to come up
through a stable, but he cannot go down into one unless
it is ·for a special purpose—such as this—if he expects
to be anything in the world. I hope to see you
ride this race and possibly one more—if you win,
that is. Then you must give up all thoughts of such
things. It is well enough to know all about horses, but
it's a bad notion to think too much of them, especially
for a Goodwin with a red spur on his heel. It happens
to be the only way you can help your father just now ;
and it's a real providence that you can do this. I can't
help thinking about it, though I don't believe your
father half realizes how marvelous it is. He thinks the
Lord will look out for him and his, as a matter of course.
I'm just sure his prayers are going to be answered, but
it will be in a way he never thought of looking for help
to come. Everything is turned around, you see.
Always before it has been the pious, strait-laced Goodwins, who have helped the reckless ones ; but it's just
the other way now. If we hadn't the mark of the beast
on us there wouldn't be much help for Seth now, so far
as I can see, at least. I ain't blaming your father, lad,
nor I don't mean to speak lightly of serious things. I'm
afraid he won't be able to do much for himself—for a

good while, anyway—and it'll be a great relief to him
to have the place clear of debt. If we win, that'll be
off his mind ; if we lose, he won't be any worse for the
way it's done.

" But he wouldn't have had any chance at all if his
brother hadn't been a son of Old Harry, or his son hadn't
taken to horses as naturally as a duck to water. Now I
just believe that's the reason the Lord made us what we
are—so't we could help one that's been as good a servant
as He's likely to find in these days. I'm glad the Lord
has found a way to make me useful, too. I've been
afraid sometimes that I wouldn't ever be fit for anything
decent. I can make money enough, but I don't seem
able to keep it. It slips away while I'm trying to find out
how to hold on to it ; and nobody can be respectable unless he has more money than he has any use for.
Remember that, my son. It don't matter how good or
wise a man may be ; if he ain't rich, he's mighty little
thought of.

" That's always the way. There's sure to be one Goodwin in every generation that ain't of much account—
kind of sleazy, you know. It didn't make so much difference as long as there were two of them. One was
sure to keep up the name and make it respectable. But
you're all alone—the very last Goodwin there is—and
you've got to be steady like your father, and not wild
like me. Of course, you can't help being fond of horses,
and I think you ought to know all about them, so that
you won't be led away by any false notions. Horses
are like cards ; it's the man who knows the least about
them that gets taken in the worst by them. But you've
got something better to do than give your time to horses.
You've got to please your father—do what he wants you
to do—and show the world Seth Goodwin's got a boy
fit to bear his name."

"What does he want I should do, Uncle Horace?" asked the boy, not very cheerfully.

"Well, the first thing, you know, he wants you to go to school."

"Oh, that's easy enough," said the lad, brightening.

"Of course, it's easy," continued the uncle, approvingly. "I never cared much about book-learning myself; but your father would have made a great scholar if he'd had a chance. That's why he's so anxious to have you get a good education. Do you know he wants to send you to college?"

The boy shook his head, wonderingly.

"Yes, he does; I don't fancy the notion, but he wants you to be what he hadn't a chance to become. I don't know, being a baby when pa died, but I expect 'the gray mare was the better horse' in that team. Ma was a remarkable woman, and she made up her mind that Seth should be a minister—not one of those stub-toed, lickity-clip fellows that know about as much about preaching as I do about shoe-making, but a real, thorough-bred, college-educated minister. And I expect, if she'd lived, she'd have brought it about in one way or another.

"He'd have made a goer, too," continued the brother, with enthusiasm, "if he'd been rightly handled. But you see he had me on his hands, and that held him back. I've always thought it was a pity. There ain't many that can outfoot him in an exhortation now, when he gets waked up. Bless your soul, I've seen him at camp-meeting sometimes, when it would just make one's hair stand up to see his eyes flashing, his face pale, his lips quivering, and the words just tumbling over each other trying to get out of the way of those behind. And when it comes to praying, I've never seen the minister of them all that could hold a candle to him."

A flush of pride rose to the boy's face as he listened to these words of praise. He had more than once seen his father transfigured by strong emotion, and felt himself carried away by the rush of his rude eloquence, the effect of which had been to make him regard the stern, severe parent with an admiration akin to awe.

"And he don't preach what he don't practice, nor spoil a story for relation's sake, either," continued the uncle, "if he did whip Dạn Marvin for lying about me. I remember once, over in New Dorset camp-ground, I and three other fellows had crept into a thicket, on the outskirts of the meeting-place, for a quiet game of cards. We could hear 'em a-shouting and praying, but couldn't make out any of the words, and so didn't trouble ourselves about them. I had been a-hauling in the others' dimes and quarters pretty lively, for they were just about as green as grass, while I wasn't exactly a chicken, though the youngest of the crowd. They played, you see, because they thought it was wicked ; I played for the fun of the thing, and just took their money as a fair price for what they learned—or had a chance to learn, at least."

His eyes twinkled, and the corners of his mouth drew down, as he gave this ludicrous excuse. The boy laughed appreciatively.

"I guess I had got about all they had, when all at once we heard Seth's voice. He was praying, and I tell you the very birds kept still to listen to him. Every word came just as plain as if he had been only a hundred feet instead of half a hundred rods away. It was one of those hot summer days when the very leaves are still ; and his voice swelled and echoed under the maples, as if he had been alone with God. It had been growing dark under the trees for some time, but there had not been a growl of thunder nor a breath of wind. The clouds had settled down and seemed to rest like a blanket on the tops of the trees. I've heard that at such times sound travels farther than at others—it is kind of shut in, you know, between earth and sky.

"But I didn't think anything about it, then. We just stopped to listen—had to, you see. After awhile, I gathered up the cards and put them in my pocket. Just about that time, your father began to tell the Lord about me—not in any roundabout way, but naming me right out. It seemed as if he knew just where I was and what I was doing. He said I was on the outskirts of the camp engaged in a sinful play; not content with periling my own soul, but leading others down to destruction, also. The fellows looked at me; one of them laughed, though his cheeks grew pale, and Jim Force, who had got up the game, but had been losing pretty steady, said I made it pretty profitable being a devil's decoy. But the other fellow spoke up, and though his lips were white and his eyes had a scared look in them, he said that wasn't fair; Jim had got up the game himself and had coaxed the rest of them into it. 'Which I couldn't have done,' sneered Jim, 'if I hadn't known that Hod had a pack of cards in his pocket. It's a mighty smart game, I tell you, getting Seth to pray like a hurricane just as the luck's turning against him so as to scare the white-livered part of the crowd and break up the game. I suppose Seth gets part of the winnings for his share in the play.'

"With that I took out my wallet and gave back to each just what they'd lost, taking out of Jim's share what he'd won from the others. Of course, this left him short; for they had won something from him as the game went on—how much I didn't know nor care. But he insisted that I'd cheated, and one word brought on another—and—well, that was the cause of my fight with

Jim Force. I don't doubt but you've heard about it. He was bigger than I, and stouter ; but he lacked action. He wasn't in good condition, either. I'd been on the Lake ever since the season opened until harvest began, and swung a cradle every day after that. He'd been hanging around Kincaid's for two or three years, kind of tending bar—he was a relative of Marsh, you know—and taking the bigger part of his pay in what he could swallow, I guess. Anyhow, I got the better of him. As soon as we clinched, one of the fellows ran for the camp constable, and the others tried to stop us. Your father was the constable, and I knew I'd got to make quick work of it, or he'd be on before Jim got his lick- ing. So I caught a hip-lock on him, and when I threw· him over on his head and shoulders, he kind of moaned, trembled and turned white as if he was dead. Just then I felt Seth's hand on my shoulder and knew I was under arrest. I knew he'd do his duty without flinching if I swung for it.

"I thought Jim was dead, and I tell you I felt pretty streaked ; but it turned out he only had his collar-bone broken and had fainted away. They fined us ten dol- lars apiece for fighting on the ground and ten more for gambling. It was awful hard on your pa. All his trouble with the church came out of that fight. He wouldn't stand Dan Marvin's jaw, and when they wanted him to say he was sorry for knocking him down, he said he couldn't tell a lie ; he'd done nothing but stand up for his kith and kin, and was only sorry he had to do it. Then they took away his license as an exhorter, think- ing that would bring him around. But they didn't know my brother Seth. He told 'em he didn't need the church to help him on the road to heaven, and just drew out, entirely. You can bet I felt bad, then. I promised fair and square never to turn a card again for money ;

and I meant to keep my promise, too ; I did, in fact.
But, bless you, boy, I ain't like your father. If he promises a thing, it's as good as done, no matter how hard it
may be. I ain't built that way. I can't stand temptation, and it wasn't more than a month—just as soon as
I felt blue water under me, in fact—that I was at it
again.

"Your pa's been the best brother in the world to me ;
but it wasn't any use. I wasn't one of the 'elect,' you
see. That spur on my heel has been my undoing ;
always itching and burning whenever I tried to be
good, until I can't rest no more than a turkey on a hot
slice. I haven't done anything so very bad, but I can't
be good and pious and steady like Seth, and there ain't
no use in trying. But I'm going to pay him back now
for all he's done for me. I'll have to do it in my own
way, though, because I can't do it in his. He's set his
heart on your being a minister. I told him I didn't
believe there was any sense in it, for, according to my
judgment, you wasn't cut out for one. Of course, I
don't know the points of a minister as well as I do those
of a horse, but I'd a notion you'd do better as a steam-
boat captain, or something of that sort, than you would
as a salvation pilot. But he wouldn't listen to me, and
I don't blame him. He says that no man can tell
whether or not you'll get a 'call ;' but if you do, he
wants you ready to answer prompt, like a soldier armed
and equipped for duty ; and he made me promise that
if he was taken away I'd see to it that you went to college and came through all right.

"I couldn't deny him anything, if I wanted to, and
I'm going to do it. I owe it to him, you see. So you
may just as well make up your mind that you are not
going to be a jockey, nor have anything to do with
horses, more than a little buying and selling at least,

after we get through with this matter. Of course, there's no harm in buying and selling if you don't swap nor lie ; and I never could see why a circuit-rider shouldn't buy a colt every year, break him, put him in condition and double his value before he goes to conference the next year. But he must know all about a horse to do it, and that's why I've been giving you lessons. I should hate to see you taken in on a horse even if you were a minister.

"I don't quite know how I'm to manage it, though. It would be easy enough if I could have my own way. That colt yonder is something altogether out of the common. If I could just take and enter him in a few good races at the East, we could make enough on him to settle the whole matter. But Seth won't allow that ; and I suppose it would hardly be the thing to raise money to educate a minister by betting on a horse.

"I expect it will take a lot of money—I don't know how much, but they tell me them big colleges are very expensive. Then, too, you'll have to get ready. I fancy there'll be as much as ten or twelve years' steady schooling to pay for. You'll have to do the studying, and I'll contrive some way to get the money, or to hang on to it after it is made, rather, for that's the hardest part. Your mother'll have to be taken care of, too. She ain't such a manager as Ma was ; probably because Seth has always taken the brunt of everything on his shoulders."

"Is my father going to die ?" asked the boy, with a wondering sob.

"I hope not ; but I'm afraid he can't last long—a year or two, perhaps ; and the easier we can make things for him, the longer he is likely to stay with us. We'll clear off the mortgage ; I've no doubt of that, though there's nothing exactly certain about a race until after it's run. That colt can beat the Gray Eagle, and a good deal better horse than the Gray Eagle, too. It's amazing how easy he gets over the ground ; but he's got an uncertain temper, and is just the kind of beast to up and bolt or do some kind of devilment at the wrong time. He minds you, because you've kind of grown up together, I s'pose ; and I think you can get the best out of him every time you ask for it. My notion is, after we've won this race, to enter him for some big event, win that, and then sell him. Seth couldn't object to that ; but in order to win, you might have to ride him, and that, I'm afraid, your father wouldn't consent to. You see, the rascal don't show his temper until he's crossed, and he seems to think that what you want done is just the thing he wants to do, no matter what it is ; but every time I get astride of him and try to make him do according to my notion, there's a row. Yet there ain't many men have a lighter touch on a horse than Hod Goodwin. If your father wouldn't insist on making you a son of Theophilus, we could make a pile on that colt this year and next ; and I allow you wouldn't be none the worse for it, either. I don't believe in making ministers of people who have got the mark of Old Harry on their heel, anyhow, and you've got it ; I saw it when you were a little thing, not more than so long."

Uncle Horace extended his hands as he spoke to show the infantile proportions.

"It ain't so big nor so red as mine ; and I hope won't ever give you the trouble mine has given me ; but after all, a boy having it is sure to get mixed up with horses sooner or later. I don't know why he shouldn't, either. What's the use of a man digging and delving and toiling for money when he can get it without ? I tried to show your father that he made a mistake coming to Ortonville. There never was any chance for anything here. Why didn't he buy up on the Lake Shore or somewhere, where there was some likelihood of lightning striking, and not come here to the very poorest spot in the State, where it is a dead certainty things will never be any better than they are now. I don't say he's too honest ; but a man ought to take advantage of his opportunity and get in the way of any good thing that is going, and not hunt a hole in the backwoods and crawl into it and draw the hole in after him. I've told him, over and over again, that if he had some of my riskiness, and I some of his steadiness, we'd both be a deal better off. But if he will be a child of Theophilus, I suppose I shall have to go on being a son of Old Harry—just to keep up the average, you know."

"What makes you call him a child of Theophilus, if you're the son of Old Harry ? Wasn't his father yours, too ?"

"Why, of course—but—didn't you ever hear that story about the Goodwins ?"

The boy shook his head.

---•---

CHAPTER V.

''THROWN BACK.''

"You don't know about Sir Harry and Theophilus?" repeated Uncle Horace, in surprise.

"Never heard of either of them before to-night," said the lad, positively.

"Well, well, that's queer. I didn't s'pose a Goodwin

ever grew to your age without hearing that story. Perhaps your father didn't want you to know it, though I don't see why you shouldn't, especially as you have the mark ; but I don't know as I ought to tell you without his consent."

" Please—please, Uncle Horace," urged the boy in an anxious tone.

The young man rose from the pile of hay on which he was reclining, stirred the fire, took out an open-faced silver watch, looked at the hands by the firelight, glanced up at the sky where it showed through a rift in the green mass of foliage about them, went to look at the horses lying down in their stalls, and returning, said, as he sat down on the end of a log near the fire and refilled his pipe :

" I never saw two horses get along together as well as that mare and the colt. She seems to feel that the responsibility is on her, and lets the young one know its business we're here for, not pleasure ; and he takes to it just as kindly as if he had been used to it all his life. Have you noticed how much they lie down? That's the way with a good horse. One that don't lie down in training, won't do to bet on. He either gets so fine that he can't stand the pace, or so nervous that he can't be controlled. One would think, now, that the higher the condition a horse was in, the less he'd sleep, but it's right the other way ; the better the condition and the more work, if it's the right kind, the more a good horse will sleep. It's about as bad for a horse to fall off in his sleep as in his feed, unless it's one of the nervous sort that stay awake all night and stand nodding and staggering in the stall all day. It don't make any difference with those, because about the best thing that can be done with one of that sort is to hitch him to a

plow and let him work at a walk until he gets sense
enough to go to sleep when it comes night.

"Now that colt of yours goes at it systematically, as if
he knew what it all meant. He's up in the morning
bright and early, asking for his breakfast ; takes his sup
of water, eats his oats, and comes out stretching one leg
after the other out behind him, making the ribs show,
as he bends his back and draws in his wind with a yawn,
for all the world like a hound which is just spoiling for
a run. He's rested, you see. His muscles are live
springs that fairly ache to be pulled and stretched.
When you notice that, and find the white of the eyes
clear and bright, and see the ears all in a quiver, or, if
he's a little hot-tempered, lying flat on the head, and
his mouth opening to show his teeth on the slightest
provocation, and especially if he puts out a fore-leg, as
if he couldn't stand still or was anxious to take boxing
lessons, just touching the ground with the toe as he
draws it back, first one foot and then the other, then, if
his coat is shining and his hide soft, you may know a
horse is in 'condition' or getting pretty near it.

"That's the way with that colt, now. You'll observe
that, after he's had an hour's work, with a sharp little
dash at the end, just to spread his lungs and clear his
nostrils, and we bring him in and blanket him, give
him another little sup, and let him munch his hay
while we eat breakfast, he comes out to be rubbed
down with a step as springy as a lady's on a danc-
ing-floor, and is just as full of pranks as a kitten.
And when every part of him has been rubbed and
kneaded and washed and scraped, and he's stood in
the pool a while to cool his legs, soften his hoofs and
keep the fever out, drinking just as much as he's a
mind to, and you bring him in, dry off his legs, and
take him to his stall, you'll see him lie down, stretch

out, and, perhaps, roll over once or twice; then he'll
curl himself up, and before you know it he's off to
sleep and nodding like a judge. He isn't tired; he's
just taking comfort.

"When it comes dinner-time, he's ready for his feed,
and in an hour afterward, is pawing and fretting for a
chance to go. When a horse gets in 'condition,' he's
just *got* to go. He'll race with himself, try to outrun
his shadow, or match himself against time along a
worm-fence, if there's no other way. I've a notion he
makes himself believe that the fence corners are trying
to run by him. When you get a horse up to that point,
he'll not only do his best, but he'll do it just as often as
he has a chance to sleep up and get the spring back
into his muscles and tendons. But he's got to have
sleep. There isn't any feed or physic that'll take the
place of that. So I always want a horse I'm training
to be where there isn't much going on. One or two
other horses, just for company, you know; but no
crowd and no lights. When a horse lies down after
supper, he wants it dark—dark and still; and then, if
he's in condition and the right kind of a horse to put
money on, you'll find him lying as still as a mouse until
the birds sing and he begins to whinny for his oats
in the morning. They've both laid down now, but
they won't be ready to go to sleep for half an hour yet.
They are just taking comfort lying there, listening to
our talk."

The boy laughed at the idea.

"You don't think they care about that, eh? That's
because you don't understand horse-nature. I don't
mean to say that they comprehend exactly what we say,
though they make out a good deal from the tones. For
instance, they know whether we are angry or good-
natured. If I should begin to scold you now, they'd be

on their feet in two minutes. I saw a fight in a stable once where there was a string of thoroughbreds. It didn't last more than five minutes—just a lively fist-and-skull affair. The horses were in box-stalls with square holes in the front so they could look out on the big barn-floor where the fight occurred, but couldn't be hit nor hurt. I hardly ever saw a set of men take more interest in a row than those horses did. They listened to the quarrel, and, when the fighting began, there was almost as much excitement in the stalls as on the floor. The horses puffed and blowed ; some of 'em kicked, and when it was over, half of those colts were in a tremble of excitement, much as if they had been children who weren't accustomed to family rows.

"Now you think those horses don't enjoy hearing us talk, perhaps. Just let me light my pipe, and we'll walk around the foot of the hill out of sight, and keep still awhile and see what they'll say."

He took up a hickory splinter, the end of which was a glowing coal, and pressed it on his pipe.

"Come on, now," he said, as he rose and led the way. They walked on until the base of the hill shut the cabin from view ; a moment later their voices died away, and all was still at the training stable. An owl lighted upon a limb of an old chestnut just across the brook from the silent sugar-house, and hooted out his challenge to the fire-lit camp. Presently the colt whinnied a low, inquiring call.

"Keep still," said Uncle Horace. " He thinks we'll answer him ; but he's got to call louder than that before we do. There he goes again. What do you think of that, now ?"

It was a loud, impatient call this time, and was seconded by one somewhat less imperious from the Queen.

" You see the old mare is getting anxious, too. There, the colt has got up to see if he can't wind us. She's up, too, and they're calling to us in the imperative mood, now. You answer the colt, and I'll whistle to Queenie next time, and then we must hurry back, for it won't do to let them get too excited at this hour ; they wouldn't sleep a wink all night if they did."

They hastened back, to find the horses standing up, pawing and looking eagerly around, their bright eyes flashing in the firelight, as if making inquiry about the absence of their guardians.

" There," said Uncle Horace, laying down his pipe upon the jamb of the stone arch, "I'll leave the pipe there. I think horses generally like the smell of tobacco smoke if it isn't too strong ; but it certainly makes them dull to have too much of it, especially in their stalls. I wouldn't allow a man to smoke in a stable, but I've seen a horse follow a stranger all about a paddock for a whiff of his cigar. A horse is very sensitive about smells, as well as sights and sounds. Let's go in now so they can see we're all right, and while they're quieting down, I'll finish my pipe and tell you about Sir Harry. It's time you knew something about the Goodwin pedigree, anyhow.

" Now," continued the uncle, resuming his pipe and seating himself on a huge stump that served also as a corner-post of the cabin, "what was it you wanted to know about? O, yes, I remember. You asked why I called your father a child of Theophilus and myself a son of Old Harry. Yes, we had the same father and mother ; but, you see, that's a sort of superstition, or rather, a tradition of the family. The Goodwins are never alike. There's always some black sheep among the white ones. The white sheep we call the children of Theophilus, and the black ones the sons of Old

Harry. They're always sons—never daughters, at least I never heard of any—and there is always one in each generation who has Old Harry's mark on him. The children of Theophilus are just about the whitest lambs that were ever born into the world. Your father is one of that kind. I think a speck on his fleece, even if it was so small that nobody else could see it, would mighty near kill him. I'm not anyway sure that it wasn't the trouble with the church over the licking of Dan Marvin that brought on his sickness. The children of Theophilus are all that way. They may be hard-headed and strong-limbed, but they are thin-skinned—always thin-skinned and tender-bitted. They don't always get along well in the world, though they are the most industrious and deserving people that ever lived. Do all they can, they don't ever seem to get forehanded, though they're always pinching themselves and doing without what they want and sometimes what they need in order to get ahead.

"The sons of Old Harry aren't that kind of folks; they aren't near so good. They grade all the way from just kind of soiled and smutched to dead solid black— from mere sinners to great rascals. They're never forehanded, either, but they always have enough, and its generally about the best that's going, too. They don't own lands and houses, but they are sure to be good horsemen and generally have a good time while alive, without much thought of what may come afterward. They're almost always good-natured, and nearly everybody likes them, though but few speak well of them. The fact is, there's always a mistake somewhere in making up the family record. If the children of Theophilus weren't quite so good and the sons of Old Harry were just a little better, it would be a great advantage to the stock and no harm to the

world—so far as I can see, at least." Horace looked
into the fire and sighed deeply.

" But what makes you call my father a child of Theophilus ?" asked the boy, impatiently, looking up from the
block of wood which served him as a stool.

" O, yes, I 'most forget what I set out to tell you,"
said the uncle, starting from his reverie. " Well, you
see, the Goodwins are an old family—about as old as
any in the country, I guess. I don't know as any of
'em came over in the *Mayflower*—you've heard of the
Mayflower ?"

> " ' The breaking waves dashed high
>   On a stern and rock-bound coast ;
> The trees against a stormy sky
>   Their giant branches tossed !' "

quoted the boy, in shrill, quavering tones, that told how
often he had declaimed the lines.

" Exactly," said the uncle, nodding approval. " Well,
I don't know whether the Goodwins were amongst that
first company or not, but they weren't far behind. And
before they came to this country they were very respectable people in England—that is, I take it they were
respectable—for the first we knew about them—or the
first I ever heard of them—was of Sir Harry Goodwin,
or Godwin rather, for that was the way he spelled the
name, who was the Master of Horse for King Charles—
that's a sort of military officer who had command of the
cavalry. The story is that he was a pretty tough cus-
tomer, as was natural in those times, a hard-hitter and
about the best horseman in the whole army of gay
Cavaliers.

" They say at one of the battles with the Roundheads
—I forget which—he advised the king, when things were
getting bad for them, to charge with his whole army—

rignt, left and centre—and end the business then and
there. You see he knew the Cavaliers, as they called
King Charles's men, were better on the charge than on
the defense ; and he thought if he drove in the enemy's
flankers, they would get all tangled up in a certain lane
somewhere about the center of their line, so that all the
king's men would have to do would be to kill them off
until there wasn't enough left to carry on the war, and
then the king could just go back to London town and
carry on as he'd always been doing—riding rough-shod
over people and Parliament. They say King Charles
agreed to this, and Sir Harry rode back to his horse-
soldiers and charged with them as he promised to do,
but the king stood still and waited to see what would
come of it, instead of pitching in to help them. The
consequence was that Sir Harry's men got all cut up
and the king ran away. Charles blamed it all on Prince
Rupert, they say, claiming that he didn't obey orders ;
but everybody believes it was the fickle king's own
fault, who never knew his own mind and was always
willing to sacrifice a friend to save himself.

" The Master of the Horse was reported killed, but
he wasn't—only badly wounded—and, as it happened,
one of Cromwell's pious troopers took charge of him ;
he had been wounded himself, and so didn't have to
march with the rest of the army. When the Cavalier
got well, it was Hobson's choice, I s'pose, whether he'd
own up who he was and have his neck stretched, or join
the psalm-singers and fight against Charles. Of
course, he didn't feel very kindly toward the king, who
had left him in the lurch, and he'd been so near death
that he probably thought it might be well enough to
forsake his bad ways and take on a little religion for the
rest of the voyage ; for, although Charles himself was
well enough and even inclined to religion of some sort

at times, he seems to have had a pretty tough crowd around him, and Sir Harry, it is said, was the worst roysterer of them all. Besides, he had been one of Staffords's men and probably thought he stood to be abandoned by the king sooner or later, as the great earl had been. It seems he'd been plundered while he lay on the field, and so had nothing about him to show his rank, or even that he was a Cavalier, except his long hair. This all came out with the fever that followed his wound, and left his head as bare as a bird's eye, except a little scruff as white as snow around the neck from ear to ear. When his beard and mustache had been cut off and he began to crawl around in plain clothes, nobody recognized him as the dashing leader of the king's horse, but everybody took him for one of Cromwell's private soldiers.

" Well, the upshot of it was that he was converted and made a confident of the sergeant who had charge of him, and between the two it was fixed up that he should 'make a profession' and join Cromwell's own company of horse, called the Ironsides. It was the custom in those days, it seems, especially among the very religious crowd that followed Cromwell and the Parliament, to take all sorts of outlandish names on making a profession of belief and being baptized. As they considered it a new birth, they thought it was no harm to take new names. So men called themselves, ' Smite-them-to-the-quick Jones,' Praise-God Barebones;' and our Sir Harry, to keep up the fashion and hide himself at the same time no doubt, dropped his name and title and called himself Theophilus Goodwin, which wasn't so very bad, being a modest enough name, which means God-lover. I s'pose he put the other 'o' in ' Godwin' as the easiest way of disguising the name without getting far enough away from it to keep him from harking back if he ever wanted to.

" Indeed, I've heard it said that one of his reasons for the change might have been—I don't say it was—to save a nice little estate, which would go to his son if he was accounted dead, in case the king should prevail, and which he could claim if the Parliament came out ahead.

" I don't suppose either of these motives were entirely responsible for his changing his coat and his religion at the same time. Probably men acted then as they do now, from a variety of motives, of which very often the one that seems the weakest is really the strongest. At any rate, there seems to be no doubt that Theophilus Goodwin served the people and Parliament just as faithfully as Sir Harry Godwin had served the king. Cromwell knew a good soldier, and didn't leave the new convert very long in the ranks. Perhaps he knew the old swordsman in spite of his bare face and bald head, or perhaps Sergeant Comfort-ye-my-people Jacobson did not keep the secret as well as he might. Cromwell had a strange way of finding out things, they say. At any rate, he was soon promoted to a company, then to a troop, and presently given a regiment of his own ; so that Colonel Theophilus Goodwin became about as big a man with the Roundheads as Sir Harry Godwin had been with the Cavaliers.

" But, after a while, they had a worse fight than they had ever had before, at a place called Naseby. Old Sir Harry had a son, a hot-tempered lad, hardly sixteen, who joined the king's horse as soon as he heard his father was killed, and had been made a cornet, partly for the sake of his father, and partly because he showed himself as brave as Julius Cæsar. When the Roundheads under Colonel Theophilus charged the king's men in this last fight, they found young Harry Godwin in the lead, just crazy with the notion of avenging his father's death. He couldn't help seeing who the leader of the psalm-singers was, for the old fighter was always in the front, I take it, and he went for him just as straight as an arrow. His father knew him, of course, as soon as he set eyes on him, and tried to get away, but it was no use. The boy was on him hacking and hewing with his sword, before he could turn around. Of course, Colonel Goodwin wouldn't strike back, but just tried to parry the blows, until, finally, the same sergeant who had nursed him when he was wounded, came up and gave the boy a death-blow before the father could call out to stop him, thinking, no doubt, that he was doing his officer a great favor.

" That was the last of Colonel Theophilus. That battle ended the war. He quit the army; went off and hid himself somewhere for a time, and finally came to this country. He was a hard, stern man, always praying to be forgiven for the death of the boy he loved. Yet, he married again, and had two sons afterward. One of them, they say, was as sober as anybody could wish ; but the other, who was born with a red spur on his heel, took to wild ways, went to sea and came to a bad end along with a gang of pirates, somewhere in the West Indies. After this the old man concluded he had committed the ' unpardonable sin,' in having caused his oldest son's death, and that on account of this a curse rested on his children and their descendants forever ; one son always being predestined to go to the devil.

"In this he wasn't far wrong—at least, he hadn't been up to this time. Ever since there has been one in every generation of the Goodwins who has been a black sheep ; not always very bad ; but shiftless and reckless, instead of being steady and respectable. Queer enough, too, this has always been the one born with the mark of the red spur on his left heel. So we call them the sons of Old Harry, because they are likely to turn out something like the old Master of the Horse; and the others we call the children of Theophilus, because they are always glum and sober—the 'select infants,' pre-destined to salvation. They are like the old fighter was after he turned Puritan and sang psalms."

"Am I a son of Old Harry, uncle ?" asked the boy, who had listened with almost breathless interest to his uncle's narrative, in an anxious tone.

"It's hard to tell," answered the uncle, seriously. "You've got the mark, and nobody who's had that on his heel has ever yet been able to get along without showing some signs of it in his ways."

The boy turned his left foot to the firelight and care-fully scrutinized the heel. A narrow line of red ran along on each side almost to the hollow of the foot, branching downward in front of the heel and upward toward the instep.

"'Tain't nothing compared with mine," said the man, gravely, "and I've been told mine wasn't any-thing to compare with what they used to have. I've heard that one of the worst of 'em had a heel as red as if it had been parboiled. Mine don't trouble me much except during the racing season—it gets pretty hot, then."

He drew off his boot and held the foot toward the light as he spoke. The mark was heavier and redder than on the boy's, and had an unmistakable likeness to a spur.

"Does one have to be bad who has that mark ?" asked the lad.

"Pshaw, no. I don't s'pose it makes any difference. It's probably the unsteadiness that makes the mark talked about; though there's something in the idea that if you give a dog a bad name he'll deserve it. I suppose every Goodwin with that beauty spot on his heel has been told this very story until he has come to think himself elected to-go to the devil anyhow, and so don't try to do anything better."

" Do *you* think so, Uncle Horace ?"

" Well, as I said, I don't believe it was my heel that affected me. I guess I was naturally unsettled and trifling. I've sometimes thought that if your father had known just how to manage me I might have been a credit to the family ; but he didn't, and he ain't to blame for it. Religion and hard work are just about all he thinks a man is fit for. I didn't take to either ; but if he'd encouraged me to trade, I tell you what it is, I believe I'd have made my Jack long ago—I do, for a fact. But here I am, nigh thirty, and not been able to settle down yet. It really does begin to look as if I was likely to be one of Old Harry's genuine red-heeled, no-account Goodwins that thinks more of a horse than he does of a home, and more of his liberty than he does of his soul. I s'pose that's the reason I've never married. Very few of that sort of Goodwins do ; and I guess it would be as well if none of 'em did. Them that have married didn't make any too good husbands."

There was a moment's silence. The owl hooted from the chestnut-stub opposite, and a fox barked up the valley.

" Uncle Horace," said the boy, firmly, " I'm not going to be a son of Old Harry."

" Think you have struck back to Theophilus, eh?"

" No ; I don't want to be a minister, either ; but I'm not going to be a son of Old Harry."

" I hope you won't, but you've got the mark," said

the uncle, as he rose, put up his pipe and drew the ashes
over the fire with a wooden scraper. "Of course," he
continued, "it will wear out some time—the mark, I
mean, and it is mighty faint with you. Besides, you've
got lots of the Howel blood in you—that was ma's
family, you know—steady, forehanded folks, not very
pious, but always well to-do. Seth and I have often
spoken about it. You look like 'em, especially like Uncle
Hubert, that's why he gave you the name, and the older
you grow the more you act like 'em, too. He was rich ;
everything he touched turned into money without any
effort ; didn't seem to make any difference what it was.
I think you're lucky, too, and I hope you'll succeed in
whatever you undertake ; but you mustn't ever forget
you're Seth Goodwin's son. It's time to turn in now,
and give Old Harry a rest ; the colt'll be calling you
before you're ready to turn out, if you don't get to snor-
ing soon."

Long after they had retired to their beds of straw and
drawn the heavy blankets over them, the boy lay awake
thinking of what he had heard, and praying that he
might be spared the mysterious fate which the mark of
the old Master of the Horse stamped on one of every
generation of his descendants. Prayer was almost as
natural an act to him as respiration. From his earliest
memory he had heard the voice of supplication morning and evening. The story he had just heard shed
light upon many a passionate invocation to which he
had listened. He knew now why his father so often
prayed with such earnest tenderness for his uncle
Horace and himself. He understood, or thought he did,
the oft-recurring petition that the "mark of the beast"
might be washed out by the "blood of the Lamb." He
prayed now with childish simplicity that his father's
petition might be heard, and the fatal mark lose its

power with him, and had no doubt that his prayer would
be answered. He did not wish to be a child of Theophilus, but he promised, sobbingly, to be a very good
man, if he might only be spared from becoming a son
of Old Harry ; and with this petition on his lips he fell
asleep.

CHAPTER VI.

KARMA OR ATAVIA.

The student of heredity in the human family is ever
and anon confounded with seeming miracles.   The
weakest lives sometimes produce the strongest ; and the
converse is so often true that science has finally been
compelled to abandon one of its favorite hypotheses
and admit that, so far as man is concerned at least, the
rule of upward gradation may be forever broken by a
single instance of unusual brilliancy.   So it has come to
be an accepted corollary of the hereditability of human
attributes that the over-taxed brain cannot give forth
a healthful life.   But there are worse puzzles than this
which the scientific observer must meet.   In spite of
the principle that like produces like, we meet every day
with instances of unlikeness so startling as to confound
the observer, and, for a time at least, destroy all faith in
scientific theories of life.   From the most unpromising
stocks we see springing up the most consummate flowers
of human perfection.   Whence come they ?   Is the
mystery of life wholly insoluble, or is the oriental
dogma of pre-existence true ?   On what theory shall

we account for Delia, the sweet, gentle daughter of Marshall Kincaid and his wife Olivia?

"King Marsh," as he was nicknamed by a punning abbreviation of both Christian name and surname, was a man of striking appearance and pronounced characteristics. He was of powerful build; so broad as to create the impression that he was of less than average height, though in truth considerably above it; somewhat inclined to flesh, but of remarkable activity. His thick, round neck, which rose from a pair of mighty shoulders, bore a head as evenly balanced as if its centre of gravity were never shifted, which was covered with a heavy shock of reddish hair, among which the white was beginning to show. His round, full face was smooth-shaven, and except in the coldest of weather, he was usually found with his sleeves rolled above his elbows, and not unfrequently barefooted, his hairy breast showing beneath the white, unlaundried shirt. His small grey eyes, thin lips and upward-pointing nose gave character to a face by no means repellent, but which, studied in detail, gave a clew to his success.

Marshall Kincaid had set out early in life to become a rich man. He had far enough to go, for his family was of the poorest; but he had strength, cunning, unscrupulousness and will. He had a fair education for those days. He had mastered the three R's, and that was enough. Knowledge was to him a thing for use, not ornament. It was no wonder he had prospered. He had no thought for anything but gain, and to that gave night and day, never sparing himself. After a hard day's work at the store, he would, perhaps, lie down upon the counter and catch a few hours' sleep; rise, harness, his horse and by daylight be twenty-five miles away, still sleeping in the buggy, in which he sat bolt upright.

His wife was a fit mate for so marked a character. Thin-visaged, tall, sharp-tongued, and with keen, beady eyes set close beside the narrow promontory that ran down from the low, angular forehead and threateningly overhung the thin line of the mouth below, around either corner of which the wrinkles gathered in radiating groups. Her hair was black almost to blueness, but fine and thin. Her nature was one that could not tolerate profusion in anything. She was as unscrupulous as her husband and twice as keen and hard ; so people said. What he made, that she kept. What he did not think of, that she suggested. What he was unable to do, she never left undone. If he was absent from the store, she attended to it. If he was occupied with the store, she looked after the tavern.

The one thing in which they differed was his fancy for a good horse. It was his sole extravagance—his one fault, his wife said. Though he had sold more liquor than any man for miles around, he boasted he had never tasted a drop. Many a famous game had been played in his house, he watching the players' hands and sharing their excitement ; but he never turned a card.

The fair-haired Delia—the parents called her Deely —was the one ray of sunshine in their lives. The mother had heard that there was some magic potency in a hundred brush-strokes a day bestowed upon the golden coils, and the hard hands were never too weary to give them, nor the lips too cold to intersperse them with fierce, hot kisses.

As for the father, he dreamed of her, in hard, self-glorying phrases sang her praise, and saw his toils and sacrifices rewarded in the triumphs and attainments he meant she should possess through his endeavor. Both parents were agreed that she should be the most accomplished, as she would be the richest, and was already the fairest girl in all the country round. The mother exulted and planned social triumphs, as well as material supremacy. For her sake they attended "meeting" regularly. For her sake the father tolerated the aristocracy of the East village, though he still used the name of "Skunk Holler" to designate it. For her sake he subscribed liberally to the select school ; for her sake Seth Goodwin had been "accommodated," when in need of funds, and Mrs. Kincaid had "put herself out" to be on good terms with timid Mrs. Goodwin. An intimacy had grown up between the boy and the girl, therefore, which was strengthened by their attendance at the same school and the boy's fancy for the horses which thronged the inn-keeper's stable. Thus Delia became the ambassadress sent forth by Kincaid's to secure for the magnate and his wife the social rank which they had been too busy with material accumulation to acquire before.

"I'm goin' to send her to school over there just as long as they can teach her anything," Marsh Kincaid would say to his group of coarse-grained followers, as Delia passed by the door with her books, on her way to the select school ; "which, at the gait she's showin', won't be long, I take it. Then she's goin' to the best schools that can be scared up at the East, and if that don't satisfy her, by George, if there's anything better across the frog-pond that she wants she shall have that, too ! I'll just let people know that King Marsh has best of everything that's going. I reckon they'll open their eyes when I get through polishin' her off. She hain't bad to look at now. Just see how she picks her way among them big-footed, slab-sided, soft-headed Skunk Holler young uns, who have been raised on piety until they're so tender you can't look at 'em without their wiltin' like cabbage-plants in a June sun. She's got sense and pluck, too, if she isn't anything but a feather-weight. Why, she ain't 'leven year old yet, but she rides like a jockey. Took to it naturally, you see. She wasn't a month old 'fore I took her in my arms for a canter, and by the time she could toddle she'd laugh and crow if I offered her a chance to ride. Ever since she's been big enough to clamber up my leg, she's been on a horse most every day, and hasn't no more fear of one than if she'd been raised in a stable. I bought her a pony a year ago—she's the only gal in town that's got one—and she rides all over the country, till there ain't a man, woman or child, for ten miles around, that don't know King Marsh's gal and black pony just as well as they do the dog in their own door-yard.

"I'm goin' to get a pianner for her the day she's twelve years old, if I have to send to New York and hire a feller by the day to teach her to play it. Ain't no need of that? Well, perhaps not. I hain't made up my mind yet; but I ain't a-goin' to have no common key-thumper teachin' her. Everything's got to be A Number 1 that she has, and when she's finished off, we'll see who does the braggin'.

"She's first chop in school now. There ain't one of her age that's up with her, except that boy of Goodwin's, and he's most a year older. He's a smart chap, though —smart as a whip, and knows a horse, too. Takes after his uncle Hod there; and Hod's a deal smarter than Seth, if he'd only stick to something, or go in with somebody that would furnish the stick for him. Them two children's just as thick as if they was twins; always together when they're not in school, until Seth tuk sick and the boy had to stay out. Deely's mourned about it all the time, and been up to see him 'most every Satur-day all winter. Don't know what I'll do if I have to sell

Seth out. 'Spect it'll most break her heart; but business is business, and I guess she'll get over it."

Whence came into those hard lives the spark of loveliness which lightened and sweetened the air of Kincaid's? Had some forgotten stream of noble blood flowed for ages in coarse, ignoble veins, to show at last in the artless sprite who charmed by her grace and won by a gentle prescience beyond her years and apparently at war with her origin? It was merely one of the mysteries no man may solve; one of kindly Nature's riddles, who delights to hang jewels in swines' noses.

It was a few days before the time set for the race, when, one morning, Horace Goodwin and his nephew beheld a most unexpected apparition. The morning's work with the horses was over; they had eaten their breakfast, and the uncle was enjoying his pipe, when around the corner of the bluff came dashing a black pony, bearing a slender, bright-eyed girl, whose shining hair fell in a cataract of curls about her shoulders.

Horace Goodwin dropped his pipe, and, with a muttered imprecation, sprang up, rushed into the sugar-house, and shut the door which led to the stalls. At first they had been very careful to keep this closed, in order to preclude the possibility of observation, but they had been so undisturbed that they had grown careless. Startled by his uncle's movement, the boy looked around, and despite his surprise and the apprehension he felt for the consequences, he could not keep his face from lightening as he saw the short-limbed, shaggy pony cantering easily toward him, and recognized the light figure swaying to and fro upon his back, while the bright face above beamed with exultation.

" Well, I've found you at last," she exclaimed, with quiet satisfaction, as she reined in her pony beside the nonplused lad, who had risen from the log on which he had been sitting, and now stood looking up at her as if the power of speech had been suddenly taken from him. How absolute is the rule of imperious and precocious girlhood over awkward and bewildered boyhood ! Delia Kincaid knew that she dazzled Jack Goodwin's eyes as the sun-god does his worshipers, and enjoyed his confusion to the fullest extent.

" You thought you could hide from me, did you ?" she asked, mischievously shaking her whip at him. " You are a bad boy and ought to be punished. Won't you whip him for me, Mr. Goodwin ?"

She addressed her inquiry with artless simplicity to Uncle Horace, who at that moment re-appeared from within the sugar-house, his brow clothed with a frown as black as midnight.

" I'd like to thrash—somebody," he growled, savagely.

" Me, perhaps," laughed the saucy sprite, conscious of the annoyance her presence had given. " Now, Uncle Horace, I think you are real mean ! Just think how long it has been since you saw me ?"

" I could have stood it a few days longer," he answered, grimly, though the cloud on his brow was evidently lightening. Jack stood twisting a button of his jacket, as he looked from one to the other. Horace Goodwin had been " Uncle Horace " to the girl as well as to Jack almost ever since she could remember. His pleasant ways had won her heart, and his feats of horsemanship, together with the vague notion that his wanderings had covered the greater part of the earth's surface, had made her a breathless listener to the stories he told, and led her to regard him with hardly less of hero-worship than his nephew himself.

" Why, Uncle Horace !" exclaimed the girl, reproachfully, while the tears gathered in her eyes.

" There, there, Deely," said the man, subdued at once
by her grief : " I didn't mean anything. You mustn't
take on that way. Won't you get down ?"

" No, I won't !" sobbed the girl, angrily ; " I've been
sitting here ever so long, and you haven't asked me
before—neither of you. I thought you would be lonesome and glad to see me ; but you aren't—nor Jack,
either," she answered spitefully. " I'm going home,
and when you see me again—I—I—guess you'll be glad !
Come Dick !"

She lifted the reins and gave a vicious pull across the
pony's neck, to indicate that he was to turn instantly
and leave at the same accelerated, pace at which he had
arrived. But the pony had ideas of his own. While
she had been talking, he had been sniffing at the hand
with which Jack had been unconsciously caressing the
black muzzle. Dick found himself among friends, and
had no notion of leaving until he had partaken of their
hospitality. So, instead of heeding his mistress's
demand, he put his nose down, turned his sharp-pointed
ears back upon his neck, and shook his head until they
were almost hidden in the flowing mane, while his
black eyes shone like ebon sparks set in ivory rings.
At the same time he gave a threatening hitch with his
hind feet, as if to indicate what would be the next step
in his remonstrance.

" Whoa !" exclaimed Jack, instinctively reaching his
hand for the bridle.

Uncle Horace laughed ; he had no fear for the little
lady's safety. He had given her too many lessons, and
knew the tricks of the pony too well for that.

" You, Dick !" exclaimed the miniature horsewoman,
angrily. "Let him alone, Jack ! I'll teach him."

The slender rawhide which she carried came down
with the full force of her arm on the pony's flank as

she spoke, and his threat of an uprising in the rear was instantly fulfilled. Then the reins were tightened, and the curb forced his head up and his mouth apart. The lips curled away from the white teeth and the red nostrils showed like coals of fire in his black muzzle. Still the blows fell upon the quivering flank. Then he reared and pawed the air until the black hoofs and shining shoes were lifted above the head of the boy, who instinctively stepped backward to avoid them, still keeping his eyes anxiously riveted upon the girlish form in the saddle. The blows rained faster still upon the exposed flank, and when the fore-feet touched the earth again, the pony wheeled and bolted along the path by which he had come, glad to escape from the tingling strokes.

The boy darted after them, but his uncle called him back.

" Never mind," he said. " She's all right ; the pony 'll forget what he got mad about before he's gone forty rods. It's the way with them Canucks ; they're hot and peppery, and cute and tricky too, sometimes, but they know when they've got a boss, and Deely knows she's boss of that one. We've got something else to think about, now," he added seriously.

" What's that ?" asked the boy, noting his uncle's grave tone and the look of concern on his face.

" What ?" exclaimed the other in surprise. " Why, we've got to think where we'll go and what we'll do."

" Where we'll go ?"

" Yes ; where we'll go," repeated the uncle, pettishly, sitting down upon the big stump, picking up his pipe and filling it absently, his eyes roaming over the ground as if in search of something he could not find. " You don't s'pose we can stay here after Marsh Kincaid's daughter's had a glimpse of us, do you ? She's no fool ; and before an hour is past he'll know just where we are,

THERE WAS A CLATTER OF HOOFS ROUND THE CORNER. —*See Page* 101.

and then there's nine chances to one that our cake 'll be
all dough. I know Marsh Kincaid. If he thinks the
colt's likely to beat Gray Eagle—and he'll know there
ain't a chance for anything else the minute he sees him
at work—why, there won't be any colt to run when the
day comes."

" How can he help it ?"

" Help it ! Wouldn't a rifle-ball out of the bushes
help it any morning or afternoon ? I guess there
wouldn't be anything to fear from the colt after that,"
said the man bitterly. "Lucky I've got friends who
won't go back on me. The trouble is to get to them
without leaving any trace."

There was a clatter of hoofs around the corner of
the bluff, and Horace Goodwin rose uneasily, stepped
inside the cabin and took down the rifle that hung upon
a couple of wooden hooks above the doorway. Half
unconsciously he flung the bullet-pouch and powder-
horn over his shoulder at the same time. The region
was not wild or lawless, but its sparsely settled character gave opportunity for acts of violence not known in
more thickly inhabited countries. And everywhere the
utmost care must be exercised to protect the race-horse
in preparation from his enemies. The man who bets
upon a race is as unscrupulous as any other gambler,
and steed and rider are subject to many perils. The
deadly poison, the enervating drug, the weakening irri-
tant may come to him in food or drink ; may be sifted
down upon him from the loft above or ejected on him
as he passes by at work. The smith is bribed to prick
him in shoeing ; the groom to knuckle him or even to
drop leaden pellets in his ears to make him frantic with
pain ; the rider to vex his temper or cause him to injure
himself by a misstep. On every side the racer is encom-
passed with danger. Eternal vigilance is the only

safety for the man who backs a favorite. The risk is
half over when a horse comes safely to the start and
gets the word, without untoward accident.

It is told of a horse which became famous about the
time of our story, that for weeks before a great event
the owner always locked his groom and a bull-dog in the
stall with him, slept himself in the stable, and passed all
that the horse ate or drank into the stall with his own
hand, after making a personal test of its qualities. It is
not to be wondered at, therefore, that Horace Goodwin,
mindful of these things, was somewhat nervous over the
incident that had just occurred. If he had any impression that their privacy was at once to be invaded by
others, however, it was quickly dispelled.

Around the corner of the bluff came again the black
pony, still at his utmost speed. The rider drew him to
his haunches in front of the boy, and stretching out her
arms to him jumped to the ground. Snatching up her
habit she ran impulsively to the man and said :

" Don't be cross at me, Uncle Horace."

She looked up at him so pleadingly that he forgot his
chagrin, stooped and kissed her.

" Nobody could be cross at such a witch as you,
Deely," he said.

" I am glad of that," she rejoined, turning her head
archly on one side. " I didn't know but you were going
to shoot me."

She glanced meaningly at the rifle. Uncle Horace
flushed a trifle, but answered carelessly enough :

" Oh, I was just going out to get some squirrels for a
pot-pie. I heard a gobbler up the hollow this morning,
too."

" Then I'll stay with Jack until you come back," said
the girl, turning with a pleased look at her playmate.

"I may be gone a good while," answered Uncle Horace, uneasily.

"Well, I haven't seen him in a long time, and have got lots of things to tell him. I've been to his house ever so many times, but Aunt Susan wouldn't tell me anything about him, only that he had gone away. As if I didn't know that as well as she. That's the way I came to find you."

"How's that?"

"Why, you see, I was wondering where you both were and what you were doing, and I heard pa and a good many others wondering, too, only they didn't seem to care anything about Jack, and I did. They all thought you'd gone off somewhere to get a horse to run against Gray Eagle ; just as quick as I heard them say it was to be a horse that had never run a race I knew it was Pomp, and that was the reason Jack had gone as well as you. I couldn't imagine where you were, though, until I thought of 'Number Two,' and then of the sugar-bush right here beside it. I knew Jack used to ride the colt around the pasture and thought this would be just the nicest place in the world to train him. So I thought I'd come and see. Isn't it lovely here?" she said, taking a general survey of her surroundings. Jack was petting the pony and gazing at her with unmistakable delight.

"Where do you keep him? In there?" pointing to the stable. "Can't I see him? Oh, I'm sure he'll win. I've got ever so many bets on him."

"You have?"

"Well—on the horse you are going to run. Of course I know it's Pomp, just as well as I know anything. Please let me see him."

"How did you come here?" asked Uncle Horace, disregarding her appeal.

"As if you didn't know. Uncle Horace, aren't you getting a little loony? Didn't you see I rode Dick?"

"I mean by what road?"

"Oh, I didn't come by any road at all," she answered, gayly. "I knew you didn't want anybody to suspect you were here, so I just rode up Matthews's lane until I came to the woods, and then picked my way along through them."

"You must have found it pretty rough."

"Not so very," she answered ruefully, looking down at her habit, which was plentifully decorated with green burs. The others laughed at her brave denial of difficulty, in the face of such evidence. "There were one or two fences Dick had a hard time getting over," she continued. "But I'm so glad I came. Have you had a good time here in the woods, Jack?"

"Pretty good," answered the boy, with some embarrassment.

"Oh, it must be nice!" the little lady exclaimed. "I wish I was a boy—but where is Pomp? I wanted to see him most as bad as I did you?"

The lad's face flushed with pleasure.

"There isn't any 'Pomp' now, Deely!" he answered, jauntily.

"Isn't any Pomp? What do you mean?"

"We've given him a new name."

"What for?"

"Uncle Horace thought 'Pomp' wasn't fine enough for a horse that was going to run a real sure-enough race."

"What do you call him now?"

"I wanted to call him Curtius, but Uncle Horace didn't like it, so we named him Belmont's Abdallah."

"'Abdallah?'" repeated the girl, sounding the word carefully. "'Abdallah!' That's a pretty name; but

why do you call him Belmont's Abdallah ? Have you
sold him ? Who is Belmont ?"

" You'll have to ask Uncle Horace."

" Who is he, Uncle Horace ?"

" I'm sure I couldn't tell you," answered the young
man, who was leaning against the cabin-wall, still holding his gun.

" Then why did you call him that ?"

" Because—well, because it's a respectable name for a
horse to have," smiling.

" So there wouldn't anybody know him ?" she asked
shrewdly.

" Well, that was one reason," Uncle Horace confessed.

" I thought so," gayly. " I hope he'll win."

" You do ?"

" Of course," with a gay laugh at his surprise. " Did
you think I was on the other side ?"

" I s'posed you'd back the Gray Eagle."

" Well, I don't. I told pa, as soon as I thought about
—about—well, about the colt—I can't remember his new
name—that he'd be beat, and he'd better back down.
I've seen Pomp run in ' Number Two.' "

" He didn't take your advice ?"

" No ; and I made a bet with him that he'd lose.
I've got four or five other bets, too. You see, everybody's laying on the Gray Eagle, because he's won so
many races, but I don't believe in him much. Ma says
she hopes pa'll lose, and that'll stop him from throwing
away money on horses."

" Stop him !" exclaimed Uncle Horace, throwing back
his head and laughing in a way to wake the echoes.

" That's what she said," continued the child, evidently
abashed at the effect of her revelation ; " and I guess it
will. It appears to take a good deal to get the old
Eagle ready, anyway ; they've had to burn his legs."

" Fire him, you mean ?"

" Well, isn't that burning?"

" Of course. Is he lame ?"

"Well—he was," sagely. " But he does get over the ground when he's once limbered up," she added, doubtfully. " Pa says it'll take a lively nag to get away with him ; and if you should see him run once, you'd think so."

" There ain't any doubt about that. I suppose you told your father your suspicions about—about the colt ?"

" Indeed I didn't. Didn't I say I wanted you to win ? Ma said she wishes pa would get beat so bad he wouldn't dare look a horse in the face for the rest of his life ; it would be the best thing that could happen to him, and if he must lose, she'd rather you won his money than any one else, for you'll help Jack's father with it."

" That's a fact, little one," exclaimed the uncle, warmly.

"Oh, I know some things, if I am little," was the arch reply.

Uncle Horace turned, and put his gun back on the hooks inside the cabin-door.

" I thought you were going out to shoot squirrels ?"

" I guess I'd better wait and get dinner."

" Oh, do ; and I'll stay and eat it with you."

" Won't your folks be uneasy if you don't come home ?"

" I always stay to dinner when I go to Aunt Susan's ; don't I, Jack ?"

" Of course—that is—most always," answered the boy, doubtful whether he ought to favor or discourage her project.

Horace Goodwin was greatly puzzled by the turn affairs had taken, but concluded that it was better to trust this child, wise beyond her years and yet so apparently simple and transparent, than to show any suspicion of her. If she was a spy, she already knew all that could be of detriment to them, and it might be well to have her carry away an impression of confidence on their part rather than of doubt. Next to beating the Gray Eagle out and out, the best thing for the colt would be to have that horse pay forfeit to him. So he said, cheerfully :

"Give the pony a bait, Jack, and bring the colt out and let the young lady look him over while I set about dinner. We don't often have company, you know. You come at the wrong time to see him move, Deely," he added, with a meaning look at the boy.

The girl's surprise and delight at the condition and beauty of the colt, with which she had been acquainted' since he was a foal, was unbounded.

When she had concluded her inspection and the newly christened nag had been returned to his stall, the boy and girl wandered up the little valley to visit some of the quiet nooks where the lad had been accustomed to pass his unoccupied hours during their long seclusion.

"Oh, Jack !" she exclaimed in rapture, when they reached a pretty bower made by a leafy dogwood which had grown up among the branches of a fallen forest monarch and umbel-like shut out the light on every side. A broken limb of the great tree made a convenient seat, wherein she was installed. The giant trunk rose behind her, and the boy stood in the little open space before her, leaning against the bent trunk of the dogwood. It was his favorite haunt.

"Oh, Jack," she repeated, "isn't this nice ?"

"It's most like being in a house, isn't it ?" he said, pleased with her approval.

"Yes, only nicer. What good times you must have here. I do hope you'll win !"

Her face beamed with unconcealed pleasure.

"You want to win your bets ?"

"Oh, I don't care for them, Jack !" she exclaimed with gleeful abandon. " I only made them because I was sure it was your colt that was going to run."

" We thought perhaps you were on the other side."

"Uncle Horace thought so ; you didn't," she said, positively.

" I s'posed of course, you'd—" stammered the lad.

" No you didn't ; don't you ever say so !"

She threatened him with upraised finger.   The boy laughed.   It was very pleasant to have her play the tyrant.

" It was natural you should want your father to win," he protested.

"Oh, pa's all right," she said, with a sublime confidence in her father's ability to care for himself.   " He says he stands to make something out of the race, whether he wins or loses.   I guess he's been betting on the other side," she added, sagely.

" I don't know," said the boy, wondering how she had learned so much.   Betting was almost as much a mystery to him as the hereafter.   The son of Seth Goodwin had known a different environment from that of King Marsh's daughter.

" Nor I ; I only guess.   But he says if your uncle Horace wins the race, he'll make enough to pay off the mortgage and send you to college, too."

" I don't want to go to college," said the boy, doggedly.

" But you must," asserted the girl.

" I don't see why."

"Because, if you don't," answered the little lady, smoothing her gown over her knees as she spoke, " I shall get ahead of you.   You know I am going to school

—oh, ever so many years—until I learn as much as I can."

" S'pose you do ?"

" Why, I couldn't marry you if you didn't know as much as I."

The child spoke as if their marriage was as much a matter of course as any every-day event.

" Will you marry me if I go to college, Deely ?"

" Why, of course."

" Really and truly ?"

" Really and truly. You don't think I'd marry anybody else, do you ?"

There was a quaver of reproachful protest in her voice.

" S'pose your folks wouldn't let you ?"

" I'd run away."

" They might make you marry somebody else while I was gone !"

" Then I'd run away from him when you came back."

" And will you be my wife always ?" asked the boy, incredulously.

" Of course. Ain't that what they promise, ' forever and ever, amen ?' I've heard people married lots of times. Haven't you ever seen a wedding ?"

The boy shook his head.

" Well," said the girl, " the next time anybody gets married at our house, I'll let you know—if I have time, that is—they're most always in an awful hurry. You ought to see a wedding," she added, sagely, " so's to know how. You'll have to promise to love me always, you know, and take good care of me, too."

" Oh, I'll do that," said the boy, readily. " I always did think you were the nicest girl that ever lived."

He had edged towards her while they talked, and

finally sat down beside her. Then he put his arm about her neck and kissed her, shyly.

"But you'll have to go to college," she insisted, diplomatically drawing herself backward, as if to avoid his advances.

"I'll do that, too," said the lad recklessly, kissing her again.

"Oh, Jack, how good you are !" she exclaimed, throwing off all reserve, now that her point was gained, flinging her arms about his neck and putting up her sweet child-mouth to kiss and be kissed as much as he might desire.

"Won't it be nice ?" she sighed, when their caresses began to pall.

"What ?" asked the duller-witted boy, from whom life's supremest rapture was yet farther away than from the prescient girl-nature, which already felt its promptings.

"Oh, just to love each other always—always," she repeated ; and then, more solemnly—" forever and ever, amen."

Her tone awed the boy, and they sat silent, her head resting on his shoulder and her bright tresses flecking his brown "warm-us." It was the old, old story on the lips of babes. He was poor and sturdy ; she, rich and wordly-wise for her years, but tender and clinging as the woman-nature always is.

It was an odd betrothal, with the summer woods and babbling brook for witnesses. There was no false modesty or shame-facedness about it. The young souls had felt no touch of passion. It was merely the natural result of that instinctive pleasure in each other which had grown out of comradeship. The boy never forgot it. From that hour he counted himself bound as if by the marriage vow. From that day forth he never thought of himself alone. His plans and dreams included always the golden-haired girl whose great earnest eyes met his then with such unquestioning faith.

"Jack," she said, suddenly, releasing herself from his embrace and turning on him a look of serious concern, "who's going to ride the colt?"

"Why, I am ; who did you think?"

"I didn't know but—but Uncle Horace might."

"He's too heavy."

"You might get somebody, then—a jockey, you know."

"The colt'll do more for me than for any one else."

"I wish you wouldn't, Jack. Aren't you afraid?"

The light had gone out of her eyes.

"There will be so many people there," she added, hesitantly.

"I shan't see any of them," confidently ; "nothing but the horse—and the track."

"But something might—might happen to you."

"What?" in surprise.

"Well, he might bolt, or—"

"Not with me."

"But some one might—might get in the way, you know."

She cast down her eyes as she spoke.

"Oh, no fear of that ; they'll keep the track clear."

"But it's a mile long."

"Well, there'll be enough there to watch it," he continued, carelessly.

The girl sighed.

"Do you ever go—go to—to the house, Jack?" she asked, at length, her eyes still downcast.

"Sometimes," answered the boy, cautiously.

"I wouldn't—any more, I mean."

"Why not?"

"Somebody—might—might see you."

"No danger of that ; it's always dark when we go."

"But somebody might be watching."

"What for?"

"Well, they might want to know—don't you see?"
Her head was bent down and her cheeks burned.

"Is anybody watching for us, Deely?"
The bent head fell lower.

"And that is the reason you came here?"
Another nod. The boy saw a tear fall upon the little
hands which worked nervously in her lap.

"I understand," he said, gravely. He remembered
what his uncle had said about the danger of discovery.

"I—I didn't want to tell Uncle Horace," sobbed the
girl.

"He sha'n't ever know," answered the boy, manfully.

"You *will* be careful, won't you, Jack?" she pleaded.

"There won't nothing happen to me, Deely ; don't
you be afraid," he said, stoutly, though his lips were
white and his voice trembled a little. "I'm going to
win that race."

The boy had suddenly grown to be a man. The
nature which love could not awaken, danger and resolution had suddenly ripened.

"I believe you will," said the girl, looking at him
admiringly. The woman-nature pays tribute always to
courage.

The uncle whistled on his fingers to call them to dinner. They returned hand in hand.

"For all the world like a pair of old married folks,"
he said to himself, as they came near enough to enable
him to see their grave faces. "She's safe ; she won't blab
on him. That's often the way with girls. She's older
an' truer'n she's likely to be half a dozen years from now."

CHAPTER VII.

SCREENING THE COVEY.

The visit of Kincaid's daughter resulted in renewed precaution to secure privacy and divert suspicion in regard to the training-camp. From that time on, Chris Barclay spent the night there, bringing his dog Watch, who was better than a dozen sentinels. He passed the word to Horace Goodwin's friends, also, that they should bestir themselves to secure the attendance of people who would see to it that there was fair play on the day of the race.

It was the almost universal opinion that Horace Goodwin had undertaken a task quite impossible to perform. Every horse known to possess racing qualities in any of the adjoining counties had been canvassed by more than one jury of volunteer experts, and the result had been a practically unanimous concensus of opinion that no horse having the requisite conditions was to be found, nor, indeed, one of any sort capable of vanquishing the Gray Eagle. But the most puzzling fact of all was that not one of those most likely to succeed was in training. Under the circumstances, it was not strange that a report should obtain currency that Horace Goodwin had abandoned the attempt and gone East to avoid the ridicule certain to attend upon a failure to show that he had reasonable ground for the boast he had made. This rumor had gained strength from a repeated offer of Kincaid to bet that Horace Goodwin would not appear, nor any horse be entered to contest the race with the Gray Eagle on the day named.

Horace Goodwin's friends, who up to this time had seemed very apathetic, suddenly developed an unusual activity. Van Wyck posted a notice at every cross-roads for miles around that he was authorized by responsible parties to take bets in any sum from ten cents up to a thousand dollars that Horace Goodwin would appear and attempt *bona fide* to make good his challenge. Said bets to be conditioned only "that the said Goodwin and the horse he now has in train-ing shall be alive on the third day of July next." This authoritative challenge not only increased the popular excitement regarding the race, but tended to cast ridicule upon Kincaid's pretensions. It confirmed also the idea that Goodwin was training at some remote point. This was further strengthened by the assurance of a gentleman of undoubted character, living in an adjoining county, but more than fifty miles to the eastward of Ortonville, that he had "recently seen Mr. Horace Goodwin and received his personal assurance that he would be present on the day set for the race, and confidently expected to produce a horse answering all the conditions imposed and able to beat not only Gray Eagle but any horse he had ever run against." As this included some of the most famous horses of the day, the statement greatly enhanced the interest in the event.

The assurance that the race would positively come off brought with it a general conviction that no event of like importance had ever occurred in that region. People began to speak of it as the "Great Race," by which name it is still referred to by dwellers in that vicinity. With this came also the notion that an occasion of such importance required some unusual preparation for its due and orderly observance. At the " Quarterly Meeting " of the circuit including Ortonville, held two weeks before the race, notice was circulated that there would be a meeting the next Monday week to put the track in order and make other arrangements for the race. Everybody was invited to attend and bring such tools as might be useful in the work. No one objected to such notice being given at a religious meeting, and a good many worthy people openly approved the project, being convinced that " Brother " Goodwin, whose misfortunes were as well known as his character was respected, was likely to be greatly benefited by his brother's success.

Perhaps the general sentiment was best expressed by one of the stewards, who said :

" I don't approve of horse-racing, as a rule, though perhaps it's the things that go with it more'n the thing itself that I object to ; but if Hod Goodwin can't see any other way to help his brother out of a tight place—and I don't see that there is any other way—I don't think we ought to let his good intentions fail for want of a fair chance. As I'm an ' official member,' very probably I may not go to the race, but I don't see any harm in helping the folks that live along the ' measured mile ' to ' mend their ways ' a little about this time. So, I guess I'll go to the ' bee ' and let the boys go to the race —unless I find it necessary to go along to look after them, then, too."

The meeting to prepare the track was of unexpected proportions. Before nine o'clock more than five hundred men had assembled, armed with picks, shovels, hoes and other implements. Kincaid sent two teams with a plow and a roller. Chris Barclay was there with a new smoother of his own invention with backward curving knife-edged teeth, which was looked upon at first with derision, but which soon justified itself by its execution. A man was chosen by acclamation to super-intend the work, who, with that ready assumption of delegated authority which our American life has made habitual, at once appointed his assistants and began issuing orders. In twenty minutes every man was at work, the overseer being the only one who did not wield some implement, he riding up and down the line and giving directions, so as to secure uniformity and thoroughness of work.

It was a jolly gathering. The men worked as earn-estly as though in their own cornfields—some of them more industriously. The air was full of rough jests and loud laughter. The horses chafed at the unusual excitement. The drivers cracked their whips, shouted to their teams and took part also in the general jollity. The boys brought water for the men to drink from the wells along the route, in buckets with tin dippers float-ing in them. Nearly all were clothed in homespun ; many of them were barefoot. They wore palm-leaf hats, in the crowns of which many carried gaudily printed handkerchiefs. They were a wholesome, manly crowd, and their wit, if coarse, was seldom malicious.

There were not many people living along the " measured mile—"only three or four families—but they all felt honored by the great event which was to occur at their very doors, and gladly invited as many of the workers as they could accommodate to dinner. The limit of their capacity to "accommodate" was the ability of the " women folks " to cook and serve. Many of the men had brought their wives, who " turned in " and helped in this service.

It was expected that Horace Goodwin would make his

appearance during the day, but he did not. His brother Seth, sitting in his great arm-chair in the shade of a couple of giant elms which had somehow escaped the woodman's ax, and waved congratulatory greetings to each other standing at something more than their limbs' length apart, in front of his house, gazed composedly upon the busy scene, answered pleasantly the greetings and good wishes of his friends, and when asked about his brother, replied, without hesitation, that he had not seen him for more than a month. No one doubted his word. The man selected to supervise the repairs of the track consulted him in regard to arrangements for the race. It was agreed that there should be a strong force of special officers to preserve order, and that no liquor should be sold within half a mile of the grounds. These and other necessary regulations were to be submitted to a meeting to be held after the work was done, at the south end of the course. That the people of the vicinage might not have a legal right to make such proscriptive regulations did not seem to occur to any one.

When the hour of noon arrived, Susan Goodwin, standing on the horse-block beside the big front gate, blew a blast which was heard the whole length of the "measured mile," on a conch-shell, brought from the East among her household treasures, which had been in the family for at least three generations, having neatly pricked on its inner surface the initials of three housewives, who had successively joined their fortunes with the Goodwin stock. It was answered by the dinner-horns of all the neighborhood. The work ceased almost instantly. The horses instinctively stood still in their tracks on hearing the accustomed call. The men shouldered each the implement with which he had been working, and marching to the roadside, hung it on the

high "stake and rider" fence. Delia Kincaid, on her
pony, ran a race with the overseer down the half-fin-
ished track. The men stood aside and cheered as
they passed.

Some had brought their lunches and gathered in
the orchard opposite Seth Goodwin's house, or sat
around in the shadow of the trees and fence-corners or
beneath their wagons, to eat them. Others came to
partake of the provisions set forth by the Goodwins—
especially the barrel of hard cider, which flanked the
tables in the front yard. Many came to wash their
hands and faces at the big trough by the well, whose
stone-laden sweep had seldom made so many journeys
in a day.

As soon as they began to eat, the conversation turned
upon the weather. Men wiped their sweaty faces,
pushed back the damp hair from their foreheads, and
agreed that it was hot. The thermometer had not yet
become an instrument of universal discomfort, and none
knew that on the "measured mile" it would have regis-
tered "ninety in the shade" that sultry June day. The
general hope was expressed that it would be cooler on
the day of the race, though some knowing ones ventured the statement that the best time had generally
been made on hot days. A good many of Kincaid's
followers offered to lay odds on the Gray Eagle, but
it was not a betting crowd. They were interested in
the race, willing to give time and labor to prepare
for it ; but they had no notion of staking money on
the result. The boys bet jack-knives and other trink-
ets, and the women made foolish little wagers with
each other ; but the men generally contented themselves
with opinions and arguments. Their time for betting
had not arrived, since each wished to back his judgment
rather than his inclination.

The "State road," of which the "measured mile" was a part, was a notable highway. It had been a turnpike and the law had prescribed its dimensions—"a rod wide, clear of stumps and runners on each side ; the middle well piked up, thirty-two feet between the outer edges of the ditches on each side "—constituting two rods of border and two of roadway. The turfy borders were thus reserved for the accommodation of herds of stock, which were thereby enabled to pass along the road without interrupting the stream of wagons moving each way. The "measured mile" was an almost perfect level, that lay between two sharp depressions which cut the line of the great highway, and was marked at one end by a great beech, just in front of Seth Goodwin's house, and at the other by a big chestnut, a furlong to the southward of Chris Barclay's residence, the lines which marked the start and the finish being attached to staples on the north side of the beech and the south side of the chestnut, making a course, according to Squire Kendall's chain, of just one mile, three links and a half. It was the best piece of road in the whole region, but there were ruts and holes and sticks and stones here and there along its extent when the work of preparation began. Many willing hands soon changed its appearance, and the brown, springy surface being inspected by the overseer at four o'clock in the afternoon, was pronounced as good a track as any horse had ever struck a hoof on, though even then its condition was far enough from the modern race-course standard.

The proposed meeting was then held. The man who had been chosen to supervise the work, presided, standing on a work-bench under the great beech. He was unanimously elected marshal for the day of the race, and empowered to choose his assistants. The rules he suggested were adopted, and the sheriff of the county announced that he would make the marshal and his assistants special deputies for that day, so as to secure good order and fair play. The race was ordered to take place between eleven o'clock and three, so as to give time for people to return home before dark, and the marshal was authorized to stop all travel on the road during such time as might be necessary, and to make rules for the orderly egress of the crowd from the track after the race was over—a very necessary provision where each one was expected to come in his own vehicle.

After this spontaneous exhibition of the self-governing instinct of the American people, the crowd was about to disperse when Kincaid's groom appeared, mounted on Gray Eagle. He was a splendid horse, of that peculiar iron-gray which so often results from a commingling of the blood of Sir Archy and that Pilot stock so abundant in the Tennessee and Virginia mountains. A flaming eye and lordly crest, edged with flowing silver, gave him a peculiarly impressive aspect, while a tail, as white as that of the prophet's mare, proudly upreared in moments of excitement, had often flashed a baleful meteor in the eyes of defeated competitors. He was given an easy spurt over the soft track to the half-mile post and back, for the entertainment of the crowd, and Marshall Kincaid could not restrain a glow of satisfaction as he saw the depressing effect of the exhibition produced upon the friends of Horace Goodwin, who were somewhat comforted, however, by the confident, half-contemptuous words of Seth :

" He's a good horse, Mr. Kincaid. If it was a case of heads and tails he'd be pretty sure to win ; but he'll meet a horse next Tuesday week that hasn't much of an eye for flax, but will busy himself with eating up the ground instead of flourishing his tail."

He smiled with calm assurance as he spoke.

" Seth's a Goodwin, and knows a horse if he doesn't race," was the general verdict.

" Hurrah for the Gray Eagle !" shouted one of Kincaid's followers.

" Hurrah for Belmont's Abdallah !" exclaimed a gentlemanly-looking stranger who had ridden up a little while before. He took off his hat as he spoke to lead the cheers.

" Who's Belmont's Abdallah ?" asked Kincaid, brusquely.

" He's the horse that will have the honor of beating Gray Eagle," answered the stranger with quiet assurance.

" Why don't you trot him out and let us see him ?"

" You will see him soon enough. Hurrah !"

He swung his hat, and the crowd cheered good-naturedly. The stranger proved to be a resident of a county which touched the one in which Ortonville was situated, only at the extreme northwestern corner. The announcement of the name of the competing horse added greatly to the interest in the race, which was already at fever heat in the country round, and directed attention especially to the country from which the stranger came. So the cosy training camp in the woods, a mile away, remained unsuspected and undisturbed.

CHAPTER VIII.

THE SON OF ABDALLAH.

The day of the race was all that could be desired, and
the concourse of people greater even than had been
anticipated. Long before the hour of eleven, the
" measured mile " seemed merely a broad yellow ribbon
between two dark lines of vehicles ranged along the sides.
The horses were tethered in the fence-corners. The
men wandered back and forth, some along the roadway,
others trampling through the tall grass in the adjacent meadows. The marshals, with white sashes
across their shoulders, rode hither and thither, getting
the crowd in order and finding places for the wagons
still arriving. The trees in the orchard and along the
sides of the course were filled with boys. Men perched
on the fences or leaned against them, whittling as they
talked. Here and there were venders of cakes and
cider, ginger-beer and other harmless decoctions.
Numerous peddlers plied their trade up and down the
line or at stands where they displayed their wares.
There was much noise, little profanity, very few dis-
agreements, and absolutely no pocket-picking.

At each end there was an enclosure made by ropes
stretched from stake to stake for the horses and their
attendants. From these the public was rigidly excluded
by the marshals. The Gray Eagle occupied a spacious

marquee in the orchard, from which a flag gayly floated. The horse that was to compete with him was securely screened from prying eyes in a little tent erected in Seth Goodwin's yard, almost under the branches of the giant beech. It was carefully guarded by the friends of Horace Goodwin, none of whom seemed to know however, what manner of horse it was that stamped and whinnied when the brown mare was taken out, that her master might accompany Kincaid and the marshal on a tour of inspection up and down the track, to see that everything was in proper order and make the necessary arrangement at the other end. A great crowd had gathered at the south end of the course, where it was supposed the starts would be made.

Six judges had been appointed, who were divided by lot, three to officiate at each end of the course. At the southern terminus they were given seats on the work-bench under the great beech ; at the other end of the course they sat in a farm-wagon drawn up beside the chestnut-tree which marked the limit. Forty mounted marshals were stationed along the track, twenty on each side. Their duty was to prevent obstruction or interference with the race, and to observe and report any impropriety on the part of the riders when beyond the judges' view. They were provided with white and red flags with which to telegraph the result of each heat. There was to be an interval of twenty minutes between the heats, and the horses were to be called to the post by the beat of a drum. A gun was to be fired as soon as a start was made, to notify those along the course that a heat had begun, and at the end to announce the finish. The marshals rode back and forth in the narrow ditches, warning the crowd off from the track. Boys swarmed everywhere, and Delia Kincaid's black pony, white plumes and waving curls flashed in and out among the spectators in the most unexpected places.

When Horace Goodwin returned from the northern end of the track, he speeded the brown mare along the course, the rest of the cavalcade following at a sharp gallop. Everybody cheered the mare and her handsome rider, who was quite the gentleman in blue coat, with brass buttons and white bell-crowned hat. Everybody declared they had never seen a mile trotted in such short time and good form. This unexpected and gratuitous entertainment put the crowd in rare good humor.

When all the details were completed, the marshal, standing on the work-bench, commanded silence, ordered the track to be cleared and that no one should cross it until the race was ended. His deputies, sitting on their horses along each side of the track, waved their flags and repeated his announcement. Then the makers of the race were called on to name their horses, and Marshall Kincaid, standing on a chair on the west side of the track, named Gray Eagle, giving the name of his sire and dam and announcing himself as the owner. At the same moment, the sides of the marquee were thrown back, and the proud horse, with his wiry little colored jockey, clad in gray with shining boots and spurs, pranced out and took his place before the judges' stand. Their appearance was greeted with a loud cheer. Marshall Kincaid looked flushed and confident. People said it was a dangerous look—he felt too sure of winning. The rumor had gotten out that he would win by fair means if he could, but meant to win anyhow. It was more a deduction from his general character than an inference from any specific fact which had come to the public knowledge.

Nothing was yet known about the horse that was to contest the race with Gray Eagle. Kincaid's horse had been galloped along the track every day for a week. Twice in the dusk—morning and evening—two persons, so disguised as to be unrecognizable, had ridden horses equally well disguised along the track ; and once, on a moonlight night, a glimpse of two white forms and two straining steeds had met the startled eyes of neighbors, wakened by the clatter of hoofs. They had come twice from the north and once from the south, and, in each case, had disappeared at the first cross-roads beyond. That one of these was the horse which was to make the race with Gray Eagle every one believed. But all efforts to trace them failed, because no one thought of following the stony beds of the little rivulets, by which the riders had made their way into blocks of woodland, in the very middle of which the training stable was hidden. There was a breathless silence, therefore, when Horace Goodwin, standing jauntily on the shoulders of two friends, who jocosely offered him this support, took off his hat to the judges and announced :

" Belmont's Abdallah, son of Abdallah, by the Belmont Mare ; bay colt, four years old ; never entered for any race."

" Who owns him, and where was he foaled ?" interrupted Kincaid, imperiously.

" Seth Goodwin owns him, and he was foaled about forty rods from where he now stands !" answered Horace, with a ring of triumph in his voice.

The announcement was so unexpected that it was received at first in silence, then with shouts which were repeated over and over again, as the information made its way up the crowd-lined course.

" Do you want any proofs of these facts, Mr. Kincaid?" asked the marshal.

" Nothing but the horse," said Kincaid, incredulously.

"I've known him from a foal, and 'twon't be easy to fool me. Trot him out!"

Horace Goodwin placed two fingers of his left hand between his lips and gave a shrill whistle. The front of the tent was opened, and the son of Abdallah walked with steady, springing strides to the starting-place, looking wonderingly about upon the unaccustomed crowd. This quiet entry had been carefully planned to contrast with the expected flourish attending the production of the Gray Eagle. Jack had begged to be allowed to ride bare-back and bare-footed as he had trained, but his mother's pride had prevented the latter, and his uncle's fear of objection had vetoed the former. He was attired, therefore, in a white jacket and trowsers, with red stockings, tied above the knee with blue ribbons, without shoes, and wore a red cap. All were home-made. He carried a long, heavy whip strapped to his wrist and rode a narrow sheepskin pad with stirrups attached, which he hardly seemed to need.

There was another hush as every eye scanned the points of the new candidate for the honors of the turf, who stood quietly but fearlessly looking round on the assemblage. Some thought him lacking in spirit; others said he was too long in the back to endure continued exertion; one pronounced him too deep in the chest; another thought him too low in the withers; but all confessed that the trim, round body, slender limbs, lithe neck, lean head, quick-moving ears, shiny coat and glossy black points presented as nearly perfect a picture of the ideal horse as they had ever seen.

"A big little horse," said one expert to another, sententiously.

"May be a flyer and may be a stayer, or may be neither," was the cautious answer.

" Bound to be both," said a third, " with Hod Goodwin backing him. He's the horse for my money."
" I always bet on the horse, not on the owner,"
replied the other, in a sarcastic tone.

On the whole, the impression was favorable to the
colt. Marshall Kincaid saw it, and he knew it was
justified by the animal's appearance and Horace Goodwin's confidence in his ability. He wished to do something to counteract it ; not that public opinion makes
much difference with the outcome of a race, but the
man who bets always wants public opinion on the side
of his horse. There is a notion, too, that a horse knows
when he is winning applause and feels the force of
public favor.

" Do you have to ride him with an oxgad ?" asked the
owner of Gray Eagle, therefore, with a sneer, pointing
to the whip at Jack's wrist.

" Why, that's style, Marsh, don't you understand ?"
answered Horace, jocosely. " I couldn't afford to bor-
row a nigger and fit him out with gimcracks as you
have done ; but raw-hide's cheap, you know, and being
sure you'd got the longest purse, I thought I'd try and
have the longest whip."

This good-natured raillery was received with applause
by the crowd, especially the company of young men
who had gathered around Horace Goodwin and were
justly proud of his easy audacity.

" You are to determine where the start is to be made,
and have the choice of tracks, I believe, Mr. Goodwin,"
said the marshal.

" That's the bargain," confirmed Kincaid.

" The first heat will begin at the north end ; the
second at the south, and so on. I choose the west
track," Horace Goodwin proclaimed.

Both these announcements created some surprise,

but the marshal repeated them, at the same time cautioning the riders that if either crossed into the other's track with a lead of less than four lengths it would constitute a foul and forfeit the heat.

Two mounted marshals were sent to escort the horses to the starting-point. One rode in front followed by Gray Eagle, and the other after him followed by Abdallah. The veteran racer, catching the excitement of the admiring, shouting crowd, pranced and ambled along the whole course, his rider foolishly inducing him to sidle and curvet for the gratification of the beholders. Abdallah, as yet ignorant of what it meant, only looked from side to side in a mild, wondering way, which only tended to confuse the on-lookers as to his merits. Jack rode with a loose rein, allowing his horse to take the long, easy walk to which he had been accustomed in training, his head down and swinging from side to side, while his rider fixed his attention closely upon the track he was to use.

"I guess you're right," said the man, who had sneered at the idea of betting on the owner. "A trainer with as long a head as that move indicates, will do to bet on. Of course, if anything crooked is intended—and I can't help thinking something is in the wind—the trap has been set on the east side of the track, and it's too late to change it now. The idea of sending the horses through all this clamor to the other end of the course to begin is a splendid one, too. It'll take the wire edge off the old horse, who will be fretted by it, and just be a seasoning to the colt to whom it means nothing as yet Just see how he swings along there, as if he was plowing. I guess I'll try to learn something more about him."

He sauntered leisurely over to where Horace stood talking with his friends.

"A fine colt," he said, nodding toward the track.

" Some think so," was the careless reply.

" Did I understand you to say he is a foal of the Belmont Mare ?"

" Probably ; that's the case, anyhow."

" You said *the* Belmont Mare, I believe ?"

" That's what I meant."

" No chance for any mistake, I suppose ?"

" Got the evidence, bang-up."

" There's been a great deal of inquiry about her for the last two or three years, you know ?"

" That's what first put me on the track of her."

" Most people think she's dead."

" So she is."

" You know she has two of the fastest horses alive to her credit, I suppose ?"

" Yes ; and she'll have another before sundown," confidently.

" Your mount seems rather young ?" in a doubtful tone.

" He's a Goodwin," answered Horace, shrugging his shoulders.

The bystanders laughed. They understood the force of the allusion.

" Is he marked ?" asked one.

" He's got a red spur on his heel," was the confident reply.

" Then he's all right."

Again the little group of friends laughed.

" But something might happen," said the stranger. " The horse evidently has a temper."

Horace chuckled, quietly.

" See here, Mister," he said, glancing hastily around, and lowering his voice. " That whip wasn't meant for such as you. I'd back that boy to ride the colt with a

halter and win, without whip or spur.   You just watch
them."

"Is he for sale ?"

"The boy ?"

"No ; the horse."

"Will be after the race."

"Any bids up ?"

"One."

"Is it a secret ?"

"No ; two and a half."

"Hundreds ?"

"Thous."

"Conditional ?"

"As a winner—of course."

"If he wins, I'll double it," significantly.

"All right.   What's the name ?"

The stranger took a gold pencil-case from his pocket,
opened it and wrote his name on the leaf of a pass-book
which he tore out and handed to Goodwin.

The latter started in surprise as he glanced at it.

"So you owned—" he began.

"Never mind," interrupted the other, significantly.
"I've owned several things in my time."

"All right," with a laugh.   "Are you betting on the
colt ?"

"I will lay you fifty on the Gray Eagle—at, let me
see, what odds—well—say two to one."

He was a large man, with somewhat prominent brown
eyes.   As he uttered these words, he slowly closed one
eye as if going to sleep, and after a moment opened it
with equal deliberation.   It had none of the character
of a wink, but Horace Goodwin answered with a
chuckle :

"Very well ; I haven't much money, but if you see
anybody that wants to stake a little cash on those

terms, send him round and my friends will accommodate him."

" I will," answered the other, seriously.

Five minutes afterwards it was circulated about the course that the former owner of Gray Eagle, a man well known in the world of sport, was on the ground and backing his former possession at odds of two to one. This seemed all that was necessary to start the betting fever, and those of Goodwin's friends who had nerve enough to back his sagacity and luck took a good many small wagers on these terms.

Cris Barclay was the starter at the north end of the course. The gray was half a length ahead when the horses went under the string ; but Jack nodded to him and he gave the word. If the hindmost rider was satisfied it was none of his business. The starting-gun was fired, and before its echoes had died away the Gray Eagle had improved the advantage he had at the send-off, and was two, three—a half-dozen lengths ahead ! What was the matter with the colt ? At this rate he would be distanced in the first heat. The kind-hearted blacksmith shook his head and groaned. The people along the route were silent. The Gray Eagle's jockey glanced backward and spoke encouragingly to his horse. If he could keep his lead until the half-mile post he stood to win. But now the colt began to close the gap. The jockey touched the Eagle with his boot, not spurring him, but hinting at it as a possibility. Still the bay crept up. As they saw it the people cheered. Public sympathy was evidently with the boy and the home-bred colt. As they passed the half-mile maple, the black muzzle was even with the white flank. The Gray Eagle's rider urged him openly, and the veteran answered with a magnificent burst of speed. Still the colt did not lag. His ears were laid back, the

white teeth showed as he champed the bit, and his eyes
flashed wickedly ; but he neither gained nor lost.   The
boy patted his neck and spoke soothingly to him, his
hand bearing lightly on the rein.   They passed the
three-quarter post, and now the colt began to gain.
The rider of Gray Eagle is using the spur !   They are
twenty lengths away from the big beech, and the black
nose is on a line with the white one.   Now the boy leans
forward, shakes the reins and speaks sharply to the
colt.   The gray's jockey plies the whip.   The old horse
responds nobly, but in vain.   The colt is half a length
ahead as they pass under the string.

The gun is fired.   A shout goes up.   The marshals,
sitting on their horses along the course, wave their red
flags to show that the bay has won.   Then the shout
echoes back and forth.   Seth Goodwin smiles contentedly, and his wife, standing behind his chair in the
front doorway, waves a greeting to the boy, who glances
toward her before he jumps down and runs into the
tent, leaving the colt to be cared for by others.

"Well done ! Blamed well done ?" mutters the phleg-
matic stranger, as he saunters back to get a closer view
of the colt.

Kincaid gave some directions to his jockey, and
Horace Goodwin whispered a word in Jack's ear as he
tossed him to his seat for the second heat.   The boy
was pale and the set lips were white to their very edges.
There was some trouble about getting away, and again
the Gray Eagle got the lead and kept it all the way,
winning by a length and more.   The time, as near as it
could be computed, was nothing like as good as in the
first heat.   As soon as the result was announced, Goodwin's friends scattered themselves along the southern
part of the track.   Kincaid's followers cheered loudly,

but the shout lacked the volume that comes from numbers.

Seth Goodwin smiled composedly as he heard it. He did not doubt—he could not doubt. He had asked this one thing of God—the God he had served and loved— and he had no fear that his prayer would not be answered. So he only smiled when he saw the white flags waved and heard the shouts, "The Gray wins!" "Hurrah for the Gray Eagle!" His belief in the colt's success had become a part of his religion. It was a curious fact ; and the wife, who stood beside his chair, trembled lest his faith should be shattered as well as his hopes dashed by defeat. Fortunately, neither knew of the peril which confronted the lad, since no whisper of the warning received had been allowed to come to their ears. Indeed, the boy had given only the vaguest hint of it even to his uncle. When the gun was fired for the third heat the Gray was again in the lead and remained there, though evidently much distressed, for the first quarter. Then the colt closed up. At the half-mile they were neck to neck. Then the bay shot suddenly ahead, and at the third quarter there were a dozen lengths between them. A roar of triumph rolled before him down the line.

"No chance for a foul there," said Horace Goodwin, standing on the end of the work-bench, to the stranger at his side, in a tone of exultant satisfaction. Everybody was straining to see the finish and shouting in anticipation.

"Ah !" exclaimed the stranger, gazing with a look of horror up the track. What he saw froze his blood with terror ! Horace Goodwin's eyes followed his startled gaze. A man, brandishing a club above his head, had rushed out of the west line of spectators and was standing directly in the path of the rushing steed, threatening the colt and his rider. A cry of angry warning went up from the excited crowd. Even at that distance Horace knew him. He was, his enemy ; his brother's enemy, too. Dan Marvin meant revenge. The crowd thought so. Women shrieked and closed their eyes that they might not see the young lad's death.

"Get off the track ! Ride him down ! Kill him !" were cries heard amid the tumult. A dozen men started toward the intruder. It was too late ! The bay, with outstretched neck and gnashing teeth, was rushing down upon him. The man brandished his club and shouted. The boy's long whip went back over his head. He leaned forward, and it cut down into the man's face before he came in range of the brandished club. Marvin shrank back with a howl of agony. The colt rose to leap over him, hardly pausing in his stride. The bent knees struck the man in the breast and he was thrown down. The horse's feet cleared him by a yard, and the son of Abdallah came home a winner by some twenty lengths, not having swerved a hair's breadth from his course !

Horace Goodwin gasped, as he wiped the cold sweat from his brow and caught the boy in his arms. Marshall Kincaid cursed savagely under his breath. The crowd broke from its self-imposed restraint and swarmed about the winner. Dan Marvin would have been roughly dealt with by the angry multitude, but when taken up, he was found to be insensible. The concussion had been very severe, though no bones were broken, but the heavy rawhide had cut a deep gash across his face, the end striking an eye, and, it was thought, destroying the sight. He was said to have been half drunk, and his well-known spite against the Goodwins was thought a sufficient motive for his act. though some were suspicious of Kincaid. There was

a rumor which gained currency afterward that the
attack was expected and the whip loaded with shot
in anticipation of it. The blow was a severe one for
a boy to give, and left a mark time would never wholly
obliterate.

" Shows the effect of early training," said Horace to
the stranger, striving to recover his equanimity and
patting the colt's drooping neck as he spoke. " Jumping over logs and stumps in a woods pasture did that."

" Well, Hod," said Kincaid, jocularly, crossing the
track, when the result had been announced, " I believe
I've got the best of it, if you did win. A horse like
that is cheap at twenty-five hundred."

" Would be if you got him for that," answered Horace,
who stood at the colt's head, shaking hands and answering congratulations.

" If I got him ? Why, that was the bargain. I'm
ready to pay the money down."

" Not at all, Mr. Kincaid ; you agreed to pay that
sum for the colt if he beat the Gray Eagle, but nobody
agreed that you should *have* him for that."

" Why, that's what I bet on."

" Not much ; you staked that offer against my mare.
You didn't win the mare, and we don't accept your
offer."

" It's all he's worth, anyhow, and you ought to let me
have a chance to get my money back."

" Your money back ! You haven't lost any money,
except when you bought Gray Eagle—unless you have
been betting on him," he added, slyly.

" Well, give me a chance to make some, then. What'll
you take for the colt ?"

" We're offered twice what you agreed to pay, right
here on the ground, and aren't inclined to accept that.

You'll have to bid up pretty smart if you want to come
in, Mr. Kincaid."

The crowd laughed both at Horace's good fortune and
Kincaid's discomfiture.

The boy stole off during the excitement attending the
finish, and flung himself sobbing and unstrung upon his
father's breast.

"Oh, father," he cried, "you won't be troubled now ;
you will get well, won't you ?"

"John !" exclaimed the watchful wife, in a tone of
cautious remonstrance.

"You are a good boy, Hubert," said the father
solemnly, brushing back the damp locks and kissing the
white brow. "I don't think I'll ever have any more
trouble. God bless you, my son—and remember this :
What one does really and truly for another's happiness
is not likely to be very far wrong."

It was a generous notion, though a very doubtful
ethical principle. But Seth Goodwin's was not a critically
analytical mind. He had determined to countenance the
race for the sake of his wife and his child, even at the risk
of Divine disfavor, and was amazed and enraptured to
find that he felt no self-reproach for having done so ;
but, on the contrary, experienced a quiet exaltation,
which assured him that he had done well in laying
aside for once the scruples of a lifetime. It was thus
he formulated the lesson of his own heroism.

The mother led the weeping boy away, while scores
of people crowded about to congratulate their friend
and neighbor on the success of his colt. Not one who
saw Seth Goodwin at that time ever forgot the glow
that rested on his face, as he assured them that he had
never once doubted the result, because he had asked it
of God in faith, believing that his prayer would be
answered.

Before the morrow dawned, he had gone to meet the judgment of unerring wisdom of his acts. The cold clay wore the same beatific smile. People said he died happy because he was at peace with God. Horace Goodwin alone knew of the terrible determination he had expressed to secure his family from want, even at the hazard of his soul's salvation.

"I guess he's found that offering himself for others' good in this world is a pretty fair passport for the next," he said to himself, as he performed the last sad rites for the dead brother.

Strange as it may seem, the race added not less to the renown of the " child of Theophilus " for piety, than to the reputation of the "son of Old Harry " for shrewdness. No doubt both of these sentiments were enhanced by subsequent events.

PART SECOND—HUBERT.

CHAPTER I.

A BIT OF NEIGHBORLY GOSSIP.

"How's the Widow Goodwin's boy to-day, doctor?"

"He seems a little better, but it's hard to tell; he's had a good many set-backs."

"Do you think he'll weather it?"

"Well, I hope so," said Doctor Kelsey, turning so as to hang one leg over the side of his gig, and expectorating back over the wheel. "You see, he's young and sound as a nut. This last affair was pretty hard on him, but he seems to be getting the better of it now, and if nothing more happens, I guess he'll get along; though it's been a touch-and-go case from the first. He'd probably have had a mild attack of brain-fever after the race, anyhow. It seems he'd been expecting trouble—they had some hint of what was coming, I suppose—and then there was so much depending on the race, that with it all, and the danger he'd been through, the boy was all broke up when it was over. Then came old Ryther's sermon; that was enough of itself to frighten the lad into fits if he'd been well."

"That was too bad."

"Bad? It was the meanest thing I ever heard of, and that's saying a good deal."

Doctor Kelsey's black eyes flashed angrily, as he brought his leather-gloved hand down on his plump knee to emphasize his remark. He was the ideal country doctor, jolly and garrulous, who filled the gig in which he rode as full as the medicines he carried filled the plethoric saddle-bags that hung across the seat. He was active despite his weight, and, though given to gossip, never missed a call. He was autocratic within his sphere, as well he might be, for physicians of his skill were rare in that region, and the consciousness of power made him free to express opinions upon all subjects, especially those effecting the welfare of his patients.

" If I had imagined the old rascal would have been guilty of anything so outrageous, I would have forbid any service at the house. The boy wasn't able to go to the grave, you know, so he would have escaped that exposure, anyhow."

" What do you suppose possessed the Elder to go on so ?"

" Well, you see, he's one of the old-style circuit-rider's, who are beginning to feel that they are losing their grip and the world is kinder slipping out from under them. He has a spite at grammar, and realizes that people are getting a little tired of that sort of slang-whanging he's been used to all his life. Seth, you know, was careful of what he said—pretty particular, in fact— but he had a wonderful voice and a sort of natural fire, that always put the old man in the background when he spoke after the sermon, as he very often did when Ryther preached. This naturally didn't make the Elder love him any too well, and when he refused to say he was sorry for shoving that sledge-hammer fist of his into Dan Marvin's pumpkin face, why it followed just as matter of course, like night and day, that Ryther would take away his license to exhort, and then Seth had to leave the church or own up he'd been in the wrong. He wasn't the kind of man to do that, and when he took to going to the Congregational meetings and staying away from the Methodist services, it hurt them more'n it did him. He was so good a Christian, that he was at home in any sort of meeting, and people took sides with him on that account."

" 'Cause there wasn't any pretense about him—not a mite," said the blacksmith, sticking the knife-blade under the tire of the wheel. " You ought to have these tires set, doctor !"

"Been going to have it done this long time, but it hasn't come exactly handy. Well, you see, the people talked, and that made the Elder sour, so't when he came to preach the funeral sermon he thought he had a chance to get even with Seth by just sending him to hell out and out, by the short cut and slippery road."

"It was awful ; one could 'most smell the brimstone."

"Smell it ! It was so thick you could cut it up in chunks. I knew it would pretty near kill the boy to hear his father talked about that way and was actually glad when he jumped up and gave that yell, which I hope Ryther'll hear till his dying day. I don't know but he would have kept right on after they took the boy out, but I gave him a hint that the crowd wouldn't stand much more of that sort, and he kind of mellowed down."

" It's just as well that he did ; it was only respect for Seth's folks that prevented trouble as it was."

" Of course, and the old fool might have known it wouldn't do to say such things of a man that everybody believes is just about as sure of a good place in heaven as there are to be good places there. Ryther

did the church more harm that day than he's done it
good the whole year, and if the bishop don't take him
off the district when conference meets, there won't be
enough members left here at Ortonville to hold an
official meeting."

" It's too bad—too bad, ' said Barclay, sorrowfully.

" Well, I had a time, you may imagine, with that boy,
for a week after that. Couldn't leave him a minute
with any certainty how I'd find him when I got back.
I'd made up my mind to save him and I did. You may
guess how anxious I was by my going there three times
in one day and then staying all night. One don't often
do that with such a practice as I have."

" I s'pose not," answered the blacksmith.

" Then right on top of that came this matter about
Hod. I expected 'twould throw the boy clear down
again, but he don't seem to take it to heart as much as
I s'posed he would. He's only anxious to know what's
become of Hod, and don't seem to think he's done
anything to run away for."

" It's been rough on Hubert and the widow," said
Barclay, with a sigh, " and the rest of us, too, for that
matter. It's mighty disturbing to have such things
happen in the neighborhood."

He removed his foot from the step of the gig and
looked up into the doctor's face, irresolutely.

" That's so," rejoined the other, sympathetically.
" You haven't heard any news, I suppose ?"

The question was asked in a cautious tone, and with
an almost imperceptible inclination of the head and eye
toward the residence of the Goodwins.

The conversation took place in front of Chris Barclay's shop early one morning a week after the
great race. The blacksmith had hailed the doctor as he
drove past, and drawing his stiff leather-apron to one

side, had stood with one foot on the step attached to the shaft of the gig while he talked. His arms were bare to the elbow and his hands only lightly smutched, for he had just started a fire in the forge preparatory to beginning his day's work. His face was pale and his look one of sorrowful anxiety.

"Wal—not to say news," answered Barclay, hesitantly.

"Lots of surmises, no doubt?" with an approach to a sneer."

"Of course; one couldn't help surmisin'."

"'Tain't a bit of use; ain't nothing to build on, you see."

"Perhaps not, but it's a sort of comfort, after all."

"Mighty poor—might almost as well guess at the weather." He looked at the sky as he spoke, and added: "Are we going to get a shower to-day?"

"Don't see any signs of it," replied the smith, carelessly glancing around the horizon. "How's Dan?"

"He's alive, that's about all; though that's a good deal in such a case. The longer a man lives after a whack like that the better the chance of his getting well. The great danger is that he'll sink right off without any reaction. Of course, he just lives on brandy; but that's been a good part of his subsistence for quite a while."

"Any chance for him?"

"Well, yes; I shouldn't wonder if he pulled through. You see he ain't of any such grain as the boy. His brain don't make any trouble on its own account any more than a steer's. If he once gets over the shock, he'll be up and around almost before you know it."

"You don't think his skull's broke, then?"

"There may be a fracture, but there don't seem to be

any depression ; and as long as there isn't he's likely to get well, if we can keep up his strength."

" He isn't rational, I s'pose—hasn't said anything, I mean ?"

" O, bless your soul, no ; as soon as he becomes conscious he'll be practically out of danger."

" And you think that—that Hod did it ?"

" Not a doubt about it ; if he didn't, who did ?"

" But how did he come to be there—way long in the night, too ?"

" Don't ask me to account for Hod Goodwin's whereabouts. Where was he for six weeks before the race ?"

" Sure enough," said Barclay, with a start. " Why didn't I think of that afore ?"

The suggestion evidently brought something to the blacksmith's mind which did not occur to the physician, for he smiled quietly as the doctor responded in a confident tone.

" If you didn't think of it, everybody else did. There isn't any doubt, though, about where he was night before last. Matthews swears he heard his whistle—you know one who has heard it once couldn't ever mistake it afterward—along about one or two o'clock, over and over again, as if he was calling that mare of his. Then he heard voices down by the mouth of his lane ; then a pistol was fired, and he heard Hod's mare beating the devil's tattoo up the road toward home. In the morning there was his pistol lying in the road right beside of Dan, with the smoke-stain in the muzzle as fresh as if it hadn't been more'n an hour since it was fired off. Dan Marvin was lying there with his head broke, and halfway between Matthews's and Seth Goodwin's place was the very same rawhide the boy had the day of the race, all covered with blood. Horace Goodwin, the mare and saddle aren't to be found. What more do you want ?"

" But Hod sat up with the boy till near midnight ; and there was his coat and vest and hat on the chair in his room. You don't imagine he went off naked, do you ?"

" I s'pose Hod Goodwin's got more'n one suit of clothes, hasn't he ?"

" Of course ; but how'd he come to be off down the road a half-mile away at that time of night ?"

" Who says it was midnight when he left the house ?" asked the doctor, sharply.

" Why, Mis' Goodwin. She says he called her just before twelve to set up the rest of the night with the boy."

" Exactly ; and she says he stepped out doors then and hasn't been back since, don't she ?"

" Jest so."

" 'Tain't a very likely story, is it ?"

" You don't think Mis' Goodwin would lie, doctor ?"

" Not ordinarily, and perhaps not straight out at any time ; but when you come to know women as well as I do, you'll find there aren't many of them that won't dodge the truth for the sake of those they love."

" But Hod Goodwin ain't nothin' to her," incredulously.

" Nothing to her ! Why, man alive, he's her husband's brother and the boy's uncle. He's a Goodwin, too, and a woman that marries into such a family as that, kind of marries the whole tribe, you know."

" Susan Goodwin's an honest woman, doctor," said the blacksmith, sternly.

" Who said a word against her honesty ? Don't you know, Chris Barclay, that the better a woman is the more she'll suffer for those she loves ?"

" I s'pose so."

" Don't you know that woman would cut off her right arm to save Hod Goodwin from State's prison or the gallows, and her husband's and son's name from disgrace?"

"I s'pose she would," admitted Barclay.

"Well, then, do you suppose she'd mind twisting the truth a little to accomplish that result?"

"I don't believe Susan Goodwin would lie—nor Hod Goodwin, either, doctor."

"Oh, Hod didn't lie; he cut and run. You've heard it said, no doubt, 'Flight is confession.' Hod confessed when he ran away."

"Confessed what?" inquired the loyal neighbor.

"Why the shooting and beating of Dan Marvin?"

"But Dan wasn't shot, was he?"

"Well—not as we know of."

"I guess you'd have found it out if he had been, wouldn't you, doctor?"

"Yes—I guess so; but Hod probably thought he was, and concluded he might as well finish him off with the butt of the whip."

"Was there more'n one blow struck?"

"Oh, the whole side of his head is a perfect pumice, and he bled from his nose and ears llke a stuck pig. That's what saved him. He must have been knocked down and picked right up bodily and jammed head first against that stump. Ain't many men could have done it. That's another point against Hod."

"But how did Dan Marvin come to be there at that time of night—more'n a mile away from home?"

"There you've got me, Chris. I can't make it out."

"You don't think Hod went and took him out of bed and dressed him and brought him way down there to kill him, do you?"

"Hardly," laughed the doctor. "But how do you account for those things? Come now, let me cross-question you a while."

"I don't account for them at all, doctor," answered the blacksmith, solemnly. "I can't. I only know a few things, but them I know as well as anybody."

"Let's hear them," jocularly.

"I know Hod Goodwin was at home close on to ten o'clock night before last, and that he had been sitting up with the boy more'n half the time for a week, besides all the other trouble he's had to go through with.

"Well?"

"A man ain't apt to go frolickin' 'round 'twixt midnight and day, under them circumstances, is he now?"

"Well, no—not as a rule."

"I should think not. Now there's another thing I know, and so do you; Horace Goodwin's been a little wild one time and another, but he's always been straight and square. Nobody ever knew him to do a mean thing, and there ain't a man in Roswell county whose word'll go farther than his—is there, now?"

"Not that I know of; up to this last affair, that is."

"Whatever else may be said of the Goodwins, they're proud as Lucifer; now, ain't they?"

"That they are, Chris; there's no denying that."

"And Dan Marvin's been right the other way—a mean, sneakin', lyin' cuss, hasn't he?"

"You're about right there, too," assented the Esculapian gossip.

"Well, now, admitting there'd been bad blood betwixt these two—though I don't believe Hod was ever the man to hold spite—what's likely to be the rights of this matter? We'll admit one of 'em is found in the road a mile from home, his head broken, t' other one's pistol beside him, the other fellow's whip a hundred rods away, covered with blood, and that Matthews says he heard a whistle and voices in that direction; heard a shot fired and a horse's step goin' up the road, 'tween

midnight and daybreak. We'll say the other man's
missin', too—horse, saddle, bridle ; his nephew is lyin'
just at the p'int of death ; his brother's been dead less
than a fortnight. Them's about the facts, I think ?"

" They'd had difficulties," suggested the physician,
cautiously.

He was a politic man, always found on the popular
side in all neighborhood affairs, whenever he knew
which was the popular one, and his opportunity for
ascertaining this was such that he rarely made a mistake. The public sympathy, which had been with the
Goodwins at the time of the race, had been greatly
strengthened by what had occurred afterward, until the
morning of the day before, when Dan Marvin had been
found lying by the roadside, half a mile south of Seth
Goodwin's house, unconscious, breathing stertorously,
and with his head resting in a pool of blood. Word
was immediately carried back to Kincaid's by one of the
drovers who made the discovery, and, either by accident or design, the rumor was at once set afloat that
Horace Goodwin had killed Dan Marvin. The horror
which such an event inspires in a peaceful country
neighborhood, was all that was needed to ripen this
absurd suspicion into actual belief, in the minds of
many, and even the wavering were staggered by the
subsequently developed fact that Horace Goodwin and
his mare were nowhere to be found. A warrant was at
once issued, and men were sent to follow him to the
northward and eastward, whither it was assumed that
he had fled.

The Marvins, a numerous and clannish family, were
naturally very much excited and clamorous for ven-
geance on the supposed aggressor. The whole region, ·
therefore, had been in a ferment the day before ; and
Doctor Kelsey, though he had just come from the bed-

side of the unconscious son, and the tearful eyes of the
widow of Seth Goodwin, had not yet observed any turn
in the tide of public sentiment and still reflected the
heat and rage of yesterday's excitement. Chris Barclay
had not slept since the terrible news was brought to him,
just as he opened his shop, the morning of the day
before. He was heavy-witted as men of great muscu-
lar capacity are apt to be, but true and loyal to his
friends. The popular resentment against Horace Goodwin had been so fierce and the circumstances so inscrutable that he could only stand dumb and helpless before
them. During the night he had laboriously turned the
matter over in his mind, walking back and forth up and
down the "measured mile" until the dawn. He could
not unravel the mystery, but he had determined to
stand by his friend. The doctor was the first who had
offered him opportunity to put his resolution into practice.

" I never heard that they had actually come to blows,
did you ?"

" Hod gave him a bad throw at the barn-raising at
Phinney's last year, you remember."

" That was ring-wrestling, and Dan got it up himself.
I was there and saw the whole thing. Hod threw him,
as everybody knew he would, and he made a fuss because
the ground was hard ; that's all there was of that. You
know yourself, doctor, a man can't always pick out a
soft place for one he's throwing over his head. One
has to catch a lock when he can, and the fellow that's
thrown must fall where he lights. That's wrestler's
luck, and a man that is a man won't whine over it."

" Well, you know there's been bad blood between
them both before and since."

" I know Dan Marvin has always been threatenin' to
do them harm—Hod and Seth, both ; I've heard him

and so have you ; and you know what he did the day of the race ?"

" O, he was drunk, then."

" Drunk ! Fudge ! People don't plan to murder folks when they're drunk."

" You don't think he meant to kill the boy ?"

" Don't I ? Do you know what kind of a club he had that day ? Jest wait a minute and I'll show you."

The smith went into his shop and soon returned with a large club, the bark of which had been cut off in short occasional cuts, forming a checkered spiral line which wound around it from end to end.

" There 'tis ; Hank Wilder picked it up and gave it to me that day. I told him not to say anything about it, and brought it home and laid it on the plate of the shop. Nobody else has set eyes on it from that day to this. Now, what do you think of a club like that ? Just heft it once."

" It's a deadly weapon," answered the doctor, with a grave look upon his face.

" I should think it was ! I'd just as soon be hit with my sledge-hammer. Why, doctor, that's three feet long, green blue-beech, an inch and a half through at one end, an inch and a quarter at the other and most as heavy as lead. I could break your gig all to smash with it."

He hit the wheel a resounding blow as he spoke.

" There, there ; don't try it on that ! It's a dangerous weapon, and goes to show the bad blood between them."

" On *his* part ; not on Hod's. There ain't no doubt but *he* had bad blood."

" The Goodwins have got a temper of their own," said the doctor, with a shrug. " Even the boy left a bad mark on Dan that day, in spite of his war-club."

"Hubert is a good boy," rejoined the blacksmith, gravely, "and as brave as Julius Cæsar. He knew what was comin' that day, or near enough to guess. Hod wanted him to carry a pistol, and I borrowed one for him to practice with."

"Why didn't Hod use his own?"

"Sure enough!" exclaimed the simple-minded blacksmith. "I remember now; he said he'd lent it or sold it, I don't remember which, more'n a year ago; but Hubert will know all about it when he gets well.".

It was curious how everybody called the boy by the name his father had used as soon as the father was dead.

"Did he have it the day of the race?"

"Hod gave it back to me two or three days before, and said that Hubert thought he'd rather not have it, for fear he might kill somebody."

"And you think Horace had no pistol at that time?"

"Don't believe he's had one for a year."

"Then this one that was found in the road," suggested the doctor, "wasn't his, perhaps?"

"I declare, doctor, how you do see things?" interrupted Barclay, gleefully. "I never thought of that!"

The other nodded complacently.

"Now, what's the sense of turnin' in all of a sudden without stoppin' to think, and gettin' out a warrant against Hod?"

"Knocking a man senseless on the highway is a pretty serious affair."

"Any worse'n killin' a man?"

"Killing a man? Who's killed?"

"It's my notion, Hod Goodwin is."

"Why, Chris Barclay! What's put that idea in your head? It—it—why, man, it's preposterous!"

"Maybe to you, but to a man who don't jump at his

conclusions like a grasshopper, it ain't so very absurd.
I don't blame you so much. A doctor's always got to
shoot off-hand, and is likely to miss his sights sometimes. But I pondered all one day and tramped pretty
much all night, afore I could make head or tail of this
matter."

" And what is your conclusion, Mr. Barclay?" asked
the doctor, with a deference he had not before manifested.

" Well, doctor," rejoined the smith, throwing his
apron back over his shoulder, so as to enable him to
take a plug of tobacco from his trowsers' pocket, " I've
concluded this : Dan Marvin wasn't there by Matthews's
Lane at that time of night for no good ; and he *was*
there for some sort of harm to Hod Goodwin. If that
was so, he wasn't there alone—he's too big a coward for
that—and it's my notion he and whoever it was with him
meant to steal Hod's mare, or do him some bodily
harm. They probably did both—killed him and run off
the mare. You know there's a desperate gang of horse-
thieves down towards Kentucky line. They didn't have
a chance to take Dan along, or else didn't care to, and
probably took Hod away just to prevent the body being
found and a hue and cry for murder raised before they
got out of the State."

" Why, Mr. Barclay, you don't think so !"

" That's just what I do think," replied the smith, cutting off a chew of tobacco and putting it in his mouth.
" And I don't ever expect to see Hod Goodwin alive
again."

" But there was no traces of any one else where the
body was found !"

"Now, doctor, that's too ridiculous. As if you didn't
know that a drove of two hundred mules and horses
came up from Kincaid's just at daylight, and the men

who were driving them were the first to find Marvin
What trace would there be after that herd had tramped
over the road? If they'd stopped the brutes and let
me gone along the road, I'd soon found where the mare
went to."

"Sure enough," replied the doctor, swinging his fat
leg back into the gig and taking up the reins, ready to
depart. "I hadn't looked at it in that light. But if
they came after horses, why didn't they take the colt?
He's worth more than the mare."

"So he is; but you seem to forget that he's about
the hardest horse to manage that was ever known in
this region—kind as a kitten to them he likes, but
worse'n the devil to one he takes a spite against."

"I ought to know that; he came at me once with his
mouth open, as if he'd eat me up, just because I cracked
my whip at him, going through the yard one day. He
never forgot it, either. He'll lay his ears back and
show his teeth at sight of me yet."

"Exactly; that's his way; been like a pet dog all his
life. I've always shod him, and he don't mind me. I've
never hurt nor angered him; but I wouldn't undertake to get him out of that box-stall of his, especially
at night, for a good deal; would you?"

"I? Not for a ten-acre lot full just like him."

"Now, I'll tell you a queer thing, doctor. I went up
to the barn at Goodwin's, yesterday morning, just to
look around a little, and I found the pin gone out of
that sliding-door and the horse had a halter on—a thing
he hasn't worn in the barn since he was a yearlin'. I
looked in, and found blood on the inside of the door.
The colt seemed glad to see somebody he knew, and I
took off the halter, and found there was blood on that,
too."

"You don't tell me!" exclaimed the doctor, excitedly. "What do you suppose it means?"

"I don't know."

"Well, I'm sure I don't. Really, we are getting to be a very mysterious community. First Hod and the boy are lost for a month; then the nigger Kincaid had borrowed disappears; and now one man's gone entirely and another's likely to go, and nobody knows anything about who did it or what it was done for."

He tightened his reins and clucked to his horse, which had been contentedly nodding while his master talked.

"Nothing been heard of the nigger, I suppose?" said Barclay, carelessly.

"Nor ever will be," was the answer. "He disappeared right here on the track the day of the races, just as if the earth had opened and swallowed him up. Kincaid'll have to pay a pretty sum for his loss. But he's able and he shouldn't race with a man that always has the very devil's luck with horses, like Hod Goodwin, if he didn't want to lose; that's what I tell him. I wouldn't risk a dollar against anything that Hod backed, if it was a brindle steer against Eclipse."

"Well, you couldn't lose anything if you didn't bet," laughed Barclay.

"Just what I tell Kincaid. He's got a lot of men out watching all the roads to catch that nigger; but I tell him it's no use. It's my opinion the Abolitionists had a hand in his disappearance anyhow. I should have suspected Seth, if he hadn't died that very night, and Ryther, if he hadn't been so savage on Seth. It's about the only thing they ever really agreed on. But, of course, that's out of the question. It's my notion somebody took him off in a wagon, and probably before Kincaid's men started out they got him half-way to Canada."

"Shouldn't wonder."

"Well, good morning."

The doctor whipped up his drowsy nag and drove off.

"Well," said Barclay, looking after him with a smile, " I've given him something to talk about, anyhow. He's just as sure to repeat what I've said in every house he goes into to-day, as he is to lie to his patients. He won't say a word about me or my notions either—they'll all be his ideas. That's his way—just as sly as a fox. Before noon he'll have told the story so often he'll actually think it's his own wares he's peddlin'. Well, it can't do no harm, and is just as likely to be true as any other guess. I'm goin' up to the camp though, to see what's there. Queer, I never thought of that before."

He drew out the fire he had started upon the forge, locked the shop, and crossing the ravine to his house, took down his gun and whistled to the dog. In response to his wife's inquiry, he said that he had heard a turkey gobbling " up in the clearing " and thought he would try and get a shot at it. He did not tell her he might not be back until late. When she saw him take his gun she knew that he would return either when he had secured the game he set out to take, or had given up all hope of doing so. She always expected him, she said—when he came.

CHAPTER II.

A BEATEN BULLY.

" Do you think I'll get well, doctor ?"
The voice was low, and the face that looked up at
Doctor Kelsey from the coarse pillow had a timid piti-
fulness which was rendered almost grotesque by the
bluish grayness of the close-shaved scalp above. Instead
of answering, the doctor rose and put aside the calico
curtain which was drawn across the window at the head
of the bed, and, returning, sat down by the bedside,
took the patient's wrist and narrowly scanned the coarse,
ashen-hued face with a livid mark running diagonally
across it.

"When did this change take place?" he asked of a
tall, blacked-haired woman who stood at the foot of the
bed.

The room was a small one—the ordinary family bedroom in a half-furnished farm-house. In length, it
exceeded, by perhaps two feet, the bedstead whose
stained, curled-maple posts were turned to represent a
series of spheres with variously beaded and decorated
intervals between them. There was a space of three or
four feet in front of the bed, which had a valance of
cheap, coarse-figured calico. The door opened into the
kitchen where the table was spread for breakfast, which
part of the family had eaten. The room was unfinished

—a convenient addition to the main building, being
neither ceiled or plastered. The inside of the lapped
poplar siding showed a creamy white between the
unplaned studding. Clothing for men and women was
hung indiscriminately on nails driven into the joists.
The room was rough but not uncomfortable. The
woman the doctor addressed stood leaning against
a bed-post, her head resting upon the ball on its top,
while her hand grasped the narrow post below.

"He seemed to wake up kind of sensible this morning," she said, apologetically, in answer to his demand,
"and begun to talk and ask questions ; but he didn't
get this blue, peaked look, nor seem shivery and low-
spirited till just a few minutes ago. Do you think he's
worse, doctor ?"

The anxious eyes in the pallid face upon the pillow
watched the physician eagerly, and the pale lips trembled as they waited his reply. The doctor knit his brow
and pursed his lips.

"He ought to get well without any difficulty, now he
has regained consciousness," said he, finally, "but this
doesn't look like it. What's he been doing ?"

"Do you think it's his—his mind, doctor ?" asked the
woman, tearfully.

"His mind ?" repeated the other, with a half-percepti-
ble chuckle. "I shouldn't expect that to trouble him
much."

"I mean—if—if there was anything on it."

"Eh ? What ?" queried the doctor, facing around and
turning his head sidewise upon his short, fat neck, to
look up at her.

"His—his conscience, you know !" she replied, putting a handkerchief to her eyes, and sobbing dis-
tractedly.

" You haven't been talking religion to him, I hope ?" the physician ejaculated, angrily.

" But, doctor," expostulated the woman.

" Don't talk to me," he interrupted. " I see what's the matter. These over-pious people kill more than sickness and fool-doctors both."

He caught up his saddle-bags, swung them angrily over one knee, and began to unbuckle them with the deftness which comes only from long practice.

" This boy of yours has been bad enough in all con-science, Mrs. Marvin," he continued, reprovingly, " but you ought to have had sense enough not to begin to talk religion to a man just out of a comatose condition. The very purpose of giving him a stimulant was to prevent this reaction that is just coming on. I don't know whether I'll be able to check it or not. If I don't, there's no chance, and he'll just die because his mother hadn't sense enough to let him live."

" But, doctor, it wasn't me," protested the woman ; "I didn't say anything—only begged him to keep still. It was himself ; he's got that on his mind won't let him rest, you see."

" Won't let him rest ?" asked the doctor, in surprise.

" He says he can't ever rest till he knows what's become of Hod Goodwin."

" Nobody knows ; you're the last one that's seen him, for he hasn't been about these parts since he came so near killing you," the doctor said, looking questioningly at the anxious face on the pillow.

" But it wasn't Hod—at all ; that hurt me, I mean."

" Wasn't him—who was it, then ?"

" It wasn't anybody," said the sick man, stubbornly.

" Wasn't anybody ? Don't tell me. You don't expect me to believe you did it yourself, do you ?"

" Better tell him, Dan," said the woman, resignedly ;

"you'll feel better afterward. I knew he'd been sort of wild, doctor," she added, "but I didn't ever think it would come to this."

She buried her face again in the handkerchief, and, leaning against the high post, shook the bed with her sobs.

"It—was—the—the horse," whispered the man, weakly.

"The horse?"

"Yes, doctor," said the woman, raising her head in desperation, "he's a thief—a horse-thief—my Dan is! Think of that! I wish I had died before I ever heard the words! He didn't get it from me, doctor. There wasn't never any thieves in the Russell family—nor from his father, either. He isn't as good as some men, but he never took nothin' that wasn't his—never!" she exclaimed, wildly.

"A thief! What do you mean?" asked the physician.

"Tell him all about it, ma," said the young man, his teeth chattering and the blue lips quivering.

"Here! You take this and keep still. Bring me some water and a spoon!" the doctor commanded, sharply.

He snatched a bottle from his saddle-bags, removed the cork, took out a portion of the white powder it contained on the point of his knife-blade, jogged it with his fore-finger and dropped it into the worn pewter spoon the woman brought. Then he drew the blade across his tongue and glanced again at the label with accustomed caution—testing both by sight and taste his accuracy—dipped up a little water in the spoon, stirred the powder into it with his knife-blade, and, while the woman raised her son's head, placed the spoon between the blue lips.

" There, you go to sleep now ! Everything will be all right. · I'll tend to it ; don't you worry."

" Tell him all about it, ma," repeated the young man, with weak compliance.

The mother smoothed the pillow ; the physician sat with his fingers on the patient's wrist, his glance riveted on the weazened, timorous face. For a while no one moved or spoke. Presently the eyes of the invalid closed, he drew a long breath and sank into a quiet slumber. The doctor waited a moment longer. Then he rose softly, dropped the curtain into place over the window, and, nodding to the woman, went out into the other room.

" Won't you have some breakfast, doctor ?" she asked, as she gently closed the door. " Everybody's eat and gone. You must have started early."

" I haven't much time, but I'll take a bite, while you tell me about this matter, if it's no trouble."

" Not a bit," said the woman as she took a plate of biscuits from a tin oven before the fire, also one of fried pork and some roasted potatoes. She did not tell him that it was her own breakfast which she had put aside untasted. The doctor's early morning ride had not impaired his appetite.

" Well ?" he said, inquiringly, looking up from his plate.

The woman sat opposite, her long figure clad in coarse, slatternly garments, her black uncombed hair half falling from its coil, and her great dark eyes filled with a pathetic hopelessness, while the tears ran silent and unheeded down her faded cheeks.

" I s'pose I've got t' tell you, doctor ; everybody'll have to know it, in fact. It wasn't young Goodwin at all. I don't bear him no good-will, for he led Dan into bad ways—at least I've always believed he did—I don't

know now ; perhaps I was mistaken. At any rate, he
didn't hurt Dan."

The tears fell on the dark wrinkled hands that lay in
her lap.

" Who did, then ?"

" It was the horse—the one that won the race, you
know. I might as well out with it ; he won't ever get
well unless I do ; I knew that as soon as he told me.
It's the Lord's will, and perhaps his soul'll be saved even
if his body does rot in jail. It was the horse, doctor,"
she repeated. " You see, some of them horse-thieves
down along the line—the Lewis gang—were up here
the day of the race, and somehow they managed to get
hold of Dan, and together they fixed it up finally, when
the lick he got that day had kind of healed up—to go
and steal the colt and the mare both. There was three
of them, Dan says, one on a horse who stayed down at
the road to watch while Dan and the other fellow went
to the barn for the horses. They got the mare out and
saddled her, and then Dan went in after the colt. He
knew just what a temper the critter's got, but he wasn't
ever afraid of anything. So he took a halter and went
into the stall and managed to get it on the beast's head ;
but when he started to lead him out, the colt reared up
and beat and pawed him till he hadn't a bit of sense left,
and he didn't know nothin' more till he came to himself this morning."

" Where's Horace Goodwin, then ?"

" That's what troubles him, doctor. As soon's I told
him what had happened, an' that Hod wasn't to be
found nowhere, high nor low, he said he was a murderer
as well as a thief. You see he's afraid them other fellows have made way with him and run off the mare."

" It does look that way, sure enough," said the doctor,
starting up. " But how'd Dan come to be found way

down below Matthews's place, if he got hurt at the stable ?"

" He don't know no more about it than a babe unborn," answered the mother, solemnly. " I've tried him every which way, and there's no doubt about that. He's a horse-thief, doctor, and may never get well—I most hope he won't ; but this I will say for him—he never lied to his mother—not that I know of, at least."

" How did it happen that he was not cut by the horse's hoofs ?"

" He says the colt must have reared up and kind of hit him on the top of the head. They had taken off his shoes after the race, when he grew so valuable all at once, it seems, and put on a sort of leather boots, coming up over the hoofs to keep 'em soft. That's what Dan says, at least."

" Exactly ; that explains what I couldn't account for."

The doctor walked the floor a moment in deep thought, stepped into the bedroom, came back and made up a half-dozen powders.

" He's doing well now," he said ; " sleeping, with a light sweat breaking out. Give him one of these powders every hour if he wakes, but don't wake him. He ate something this morning ?"

" Just a mouthful of gruel."

" You might have a bit of chicken-broth ready against he asks for it. And if I were you, Mrs. Marvin, I wouldn't say anything to anybody about—this matter, you know. There's no use of going out to meet trouble. It may pass over without amounting to much. He's paid pretty dear for what he's done already. I'll try and be round again in the afternoon, and may be able to advise you better then. At any rate, take care of Dan. It all depends, on care now—care and quiet—and freedom from worry."

"If we only knew about Hod Goodwin," said the troubled woman, anxiously.

"We know which way to look for him now, at any rate," answered the doctor, as he took up his saddle-bags and made his way to the gig beside the gate. What wonder that he drove away at a somewhat unusual pace? He was the wisest man in all the township, even if he did not know much about the matter he was burning to relate.

----·----

CHAPTER III.

A RUNAWAY'S NEST.

Chris Barclay drew near the place where the son of Abdallah had been trained, with all the caution an Indian uses in approaching the camp of an enemy. Just what he expected to find there he could not have told. Indeed, he could hardly be said to have expected to find anything. Perhaps the nearest approach to a distinct hypothesis which he had yet formed was that Horace Goodwin might have committed the act with which he was charged, been wounded in the struggle, and hidden away here to await recovery before making his escape. If this should prove to be true, what did he intend to do? He did not know. He was a law-abiding man. Though a friend and a most zealous and faithful friend of Horace Goodwin, he could not stand by him as a law-breaker. He doubted if he could conscientiously aid him to escape; but he was not bound to apprehend him or give information that would lead to his arrest. So he reasoned with himself, as he stole noiselessly along the wood paths with that instinctive avoidance of all that would betray his presence, which only the experienced woodsman ever acquires.

He had heard that one who aided another to escape the clutches of the law was guilty of a crime; but he assured himself that if he found his friend wounded and helpless, the law could not blame him for relieving his need. However, it was just as well that no one should know what sort of errand he was on. Perhaps his idea was a mere fancy. Probably all he would find would be the deserted sugar-camp and the cooking utensils left there by the trainers. He had been in the secret ; had shod the colt, and had spent several jolly nights there just before the great race. He knew that the death of the elder brother and the illness of the boy had prevented Horace from removing the things they had used. How chill and lonesome it would seem to find the cabin silent and deserted! There is nothing in the world so desolate as an abandoned camp. He thought it probable that the squirrels had made havoc with the clothing and provisions. It is queer what eager investigators the little rascals are. A camp seems to attract them as honey does flies. It cannot be the expectation of plunder, for they may never have seen one before. It must be the instinct of curiosity—a desire to satisfy themselves about unexpected things. They will wait and watch for days and take advantage of the first hour's absence to come and explore. Chris Barclay laughed to himself as he thought what a jolly time they would have at the deserted training-camp. Besides the ˙remnants of cooked food, there was plenty of meat—salt pork of which they are so ravenously fond—a bread-box they had no doubt found a way into, apples, potatoes, eggs and a keg of cider. He˙wondered if the rascally shadow-tails had tapped that and relished its contents. Almost before he knew it, he was at the edge of the little cleared space in which the camp stood.

He stopped and scrutinized it through the branches of an alder-bush that grew beside the stream. There was nothing stirring and everything about the place was as silent as the grave ; yet somehow the place did not seem deserted. There was a black squirrel hopping along an opening upon the hillside back of the cabin, and a gray one sitting on a stump across the stream, shaking his silver brush in the sunlight and chee-chee-ing to one hidden in the limbs of a chestnut, on the bank above. But there were none about the cabin or on the pile of wood against it. Chris Barclay knew by this that the camp was occupied as well as if he had the testimony of actual sight. But by whom ? He did not know ; somehow, now that it lay there before him, in the hot summer sunshine, he did not care to guess. He wished he had not come, and had serious thoughts of retracing his steps. While he waited, the neigh of a horse sounded on the still air.

"Old Queen," he said to himself. "I could almost swear to her voice ; I expect the critter has winded me."

He moistened his finger with his lips and held it up to find the direction of the wind, not otherwise appreciable.

"Yes," he continued, "that's it. Wind lays just as square to the camp as one could point a compass. She's got a mighty delicate nose, that mare has, and is as sharp as a watch-dog. Now, who's with her ? 'Tain't no use of askin'. Wherever she is, Hod Goodwin ain't very far away. If I thought he was well and hearty I'd turn around and go home, but there ain't no sense in thinking so. Hod ain't the man to sneak out of anything he's done. But then, what's he hid away here for ? I don't like it, I vow I don't."

He shook his head in perplexity, and let the stock of his gun rest on the ground while he took out his tobacco, opened his knife and very deliberately cut off a new supply of his favorite luxury. When he had done this, he turned his attention again to the camp.

" Well, by thunder ! What next ?" he exclaimed.

The sight that met his gaze was well-calculated to awaken surprise. In the door of the cabin appeared the diminutive form of the jockey who had ridden the Gray Eagle, still wearing the suit which had been so conspicuous on the day of the race. He was a light mulatto, of slender frame and bright, intelligent features. Glancing quickly up and down the narrow valley, he came forward a few steps, and scrutinized, with evident anxiety, his surroundings. The hot July sun beat down upon his head, unprotected save by the mass of hair that lay kinked and matted on his crown. Chris Barclay stood and watched him from his place of concealment, scarcely a hundred yards away. There was another whinny. The boy turned inquiringly and looked down the path, glanced quickly from side to side, held his breath to listen, and finally, shaking his head and muttering to himself, walked slowly back to the cabin. After a moment there came another whinny of apparent recognition.

" The old gal knows who 'tis she's winded," said the blacksmith, with a certain satisfaction. " She certainly is the most knowin' horse I ever run across in my life. I've known her to come to the shop of her own accord more'n once, and hold up her feet to be shod.* I

* This may seem an incredible statement, but some years ago the writer was the owner of a Mambrino-Morgan mare, who, being left unfastened, as was customary, before his office door, went not once but many times to the smith's shop around the

wonder what the nigger is going to do now?" This remark was caused by the reappearance of the boy, wearing his jockey cap and jacket, and coming straight down the path beside which the smith was standing.

"Hello!" he called, as the boy sprang across the narrow stream and stood almost within arm's length of him, stepping forward as he spoke. The boy's face grew pale, and he turned instinctively as if to fly. A single glance at the athletic blacksmith, however, appeared to change his purpose, and he looked up with an air of relief, and said, with real gratification in his tone :

"I 'clare, Marse Barclay, I's mighty glad ter see you. I war jes' gwine dewn ter your house arter you."

"You were?" incredulously.

"I war that, shore."

"Wanted me to take you back to Kaintuck, I s'pose?" said the blacksmith, with grim sarcasm.

"I warn't thinkin' 'bout that—at least, I'd quit thinkin' 'bout it jes' now. I wanted you for somebody else."

"What do you mean?" asked Barclay, with sudden alarm.

"Jes' you come an' see."

The boy turned and recrossed the brook, the smith following on a line of stepping-stones placed there for the purpose. The jockey went straight to the cabin, which he entered, and Barclay, coming close behind him, saw lying on the pile of hay which had served as their bed while training the colt, the form of Horace

corner where she was accustomed to be shod, and put up one foot after another for inspection, returning afterward of her own accord to her usual standing-place.

Goodwin, his face flushed, and his breathing dull and heavy. As he looked, the boy stooped down, and, uncovering the shoulder, showed a bloody bandage around it.

" Shot ?" said Barclay.

The boy nodded. The smith stared in dumb amazement at this unexpected confirmation of his surmise. He had never been accounted a wise man, nor even esteemed himself one, and that he should have guessed the truth, or even a part of the truth in regard to Horace Goodwin's disappearance, seemed to hopelessly confound his faculties. He watched the boy replace the covering, rise, and look inquiringly at him.

" How'd he come here ?" was the only question he could ask.

" Rode the mare."

" When ?"

" Night afore last. You see, I was a hidin' out here, and way 'long in de night I heard somebody jes' come a-chargin' up the path, an' see a hoss—it was bright moonlight, yer know— stop with head right in de doo' and the feet jes' a-trampin' in the rushes there. I was layin' low over the back part of de pile o' hay nex' to de rof, an' I could jes' see her head an' fore-shoulders ag'in't the light. I didn't know who 'twas on her, but I thought they'd tracked me, an' my time hed come."

" What were you doing here, anyhow ?" asked Barclay, suspiciously. Though he knew the boy was a runaway slave, the fact was such an unusual one to his mind, that it kept slipping away.

" It was my onliest chance, you know. Marse Mosely was dar on de groun', an' Miss Deely, she tole me dey was gwine ter start back with me fo' Kaintuck that night. I knew he'd be fractious' ca'se he'd lost, too, but law sakes, it warn't no use fer dat ole hoss ter try ter do nothin' wid dat colt.   He certain is a flyer from way back.   De little miss knew I wanted to get away where I'd be free, an' she tole me 'bout dis yere place. 'Twas all of a suddin, not a minit to think, an' while all de rousement an' hullabaloo was gwine on about de race I slipped off, an' 'fore anybody'd missed me, I s'pose, was hid in de big trof under de hay."

" What made you stay here so long ?"

" What else was I ter do?   Didn't everybody fer fifty miles round know dese clo'es ?"

He glanced at his jockey suit as he spoke.

" Sure enough," assented Barclay, with a nod.

" Wal, I des corncluded I'd bes' stay right here ez long as de provisions held out," the boy continued, with a grin.   " I thought people might fergit 'bout it after a while, er I might git somebody ter help me.   I'd 'bout made up ter come an' see you, Marse Barclay."

" You had ?"

" 'Deed I had, sah."

" What for ?"

" Didn't know but you might help me—or know somebody dat would.   You was always mighty kind when I come 'bout de shoein'."

" But I—well, I'm thundering glad you didn't.   My wife's down on the Abolitionists the worst way."

The honest fellow took off his palm-leaf hat and fanned himself to relieve the sudden heat induced by the thought of what might have been the result of such an appeal.

" I'd hev come ef it hadn't been fer—fer him," with a glance toward the sleeper.

" What did he say when he found you here ?"

" Say?   Lor' bless yer, he war done past sayin' ennythin', he war.   The mare she stood and whinnied once or twicet, jes' ez ef she was a-callin' somebody, you know, an' I thought I heard a sort of groan. After a long while I crawled out as keerful ez I could, that mare callin' ter me all de time ter hurry up an' come along, jes' ez plain ez ef she could talk almost, an' when I got to de doo' an' peeked out dere was somebody jes' a-layin' down on her an' hangin' onto her neck.

"Den I was wuss scart'n I'd been afore; but I thought I'd ez well do somethin' ez nuthin,' 'case de mare was pawin' an whinnyin' ez ef she thought I was des a stupid fool. So I went an' took hold of him an' tried to lif' him down; but I couldn't. So I led de mare in here, and after a while got his hands loose an' kind o' eased him down on de hay. The mare she went on into de stall as soon as I got him off an' began to eat ez ef she knew she'd done her part.

"I made up a light—I'd found some fire in de ashes an' kept it mighty keerful—an' got some water an washed his face. His shirt—he hadn't no coat on— was all covered wid blood. I was lookin' round fer de place he was hit, when he spoke up an' axed fer a drink. I giv' him some water, an' atter that his head was cla'r, but he was powerful weak—he'd bled so much, you see. As soon ez I'd found de place where he wuz hit, he made me tell him all 'bout it, whar it was an' how it looked, an' then tole me whar to git some cloth that I tore up an' wet in cold water an' bound on it. He said that was better'n nothin', an' in de mornin' he'd tell me what else ter do. When it come mornin', he said he guessed I'd better go an' see you when it come night again—though he hadn't quite decided. He seemed powerful anxious that I shouldn't go in de day- time, which suited me, too; but afore night he was out'n his head, though he tried his best ter keep up, an' I did all I could for him."

"Did he tell you how it happened?"

"Nary word," said the boy, cautiously.

"I 'lowed 'twas a 'difficulty betwixt gentlemen,' sah, dat de least said about de better. I thought he might be hidin' out, too, an' it wouldn't hurt my chances none ter have company, ef he once got well."

"That wasn't a bad idea, either," said Barclay, "but what's to be done, now?"

He stooped and put his hand on his friend's forehead, and then felt his wrist.

"Seems mighty fevery, don't he? Ought to have a doctor—but who knows if—if it would be safe to get one. Just let me try to think a while. 'Pears as if that darned race was goin' to break up the whole neighborhood."

The sturdy smith sat down upon the stump beside the door and fanned himself while he undertook the task more wearisome to him than the labor of the anvil— of trying to think out the puzzle which had so unexpectedly presented itself for solution.

CHAPTER IV.

"OUT OF THE EAST."

"Doctor, I wish you'd drive down into the pasture with me ; I want to show you something."

"I'd like to, Chris, but I'm in a great hurry ; so many folks sick, it keeps me riding all the time. Heard anything since morning?"

The doctor pulled up his gig in the open space before Barclay's shop. The cinders crunched beneath the wheels. The door of the shop stood open, and the fire

shone brightly upon the forge still blown into white, sparkling flame by the weight upon the bellows which the smith
had just quit working.   A hammer lay upon the glittering anvil.   A tub of water stood in the middle of the
shop with various forms of pincers hung around its sides.
Other tools were scattered on the forge.   His shoeing-
box, with its appropriate kit, stood beside the anvil.
Metallic scales, cinders and hoof-clippings littered the
earthen floor.

The shop was rough-boarded and unpainted.   The
weather and the sooty dust had given it that peculiar
brown which no other building ever acquires.   Over the
door was the modest sign,

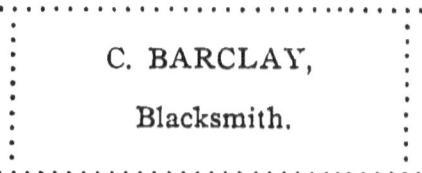

On one of the doors was burned the   form of a horse-
shoe ; on the other, a square and compass.   The outside
of these doors, and the whole front of the shop indeed,
were decorated with notices written and printed, of
various matters supposed to be of interest to the public.
Wagons and parts of wagons, in all stages of dilapida-
tion and repair, stood about the yard or leaned against
the shop.   A frame for the setting of wagon-tires stood
at one side, its surface curiously scarred by the hot rims
which had rested on it.   At one end of the shop was a
path deeply worn in the clayey soil that led to a spring
half-way down the bank.

Despite the incongruity of its surroundings, there was
a certain order in their arrangement and a sort of neat-

ness about the shop which at once impressed the
beholder. Chris Barclay was termed " fussy " about his
shop, and it was said to be not less his inclination than
the wish of his wife, who was a noted housekeeper, that
had separated the shop by the width of the sharp, narrow valley from the neat white house, with its green
blinds, and yard filled with blossoming shrubs and surrounded by a white picket-fence. That was his wife's
domain ; the shop upon the opposite hill was his. He
never crossed the valley between, with his apron on.
If his wife came to the shop, as she sometimes did, it
was always as a guest ; and if she sat for an hour or two
upon the end of the high forge away from the sparks and
watched her stalwart husband at his work, it was simply
because there was no other neighbor whom she cared to
visit at that time. She asked no questions about his
business, and never presumed to look into the smutty
dog-eared account-book in his desk, until he brought it
home at night and read to her while she posted the
entries in the ledger. It was said in the neighborhood
that it had been mutually agreed between the husband
and the wife that he should be the master upon one hill
and she the mistress on the other, and that the rugged
blacksmith, who was so dictatorial at the shop, was
meek enough in the domain of the sharp-tongued little
woman who looked after his earnings, and made his
home a model noted for miles around for its neatness.

It was four o'clock in the afternoon. Chris Barclay
had been working with tremendous energy all day. It
was yet early when he had returned from the camp,
and he at once begun a job of heavy forging which had
been waiting in the shop for some time. He had
slashed and pounded all day long, blowing the bellows
fiercely, and making the sparks fly and the anvil ring
beneath his blows as if he were doing to the death some

enemy whose overthrow was to be the price of his own salvation. So deeply had he been absorbed in his work, that he had only taken time to run across the hollow and bolt the excellent dinner his wife had prepared, without waiting for a moment's conversation afterward. It was his way of thinking. He was trying to determine what it was best to do, and how it had best be done; and when the doctor's gig came in sight, he had thought it all out and determined on the course he would pursue. The sweat was pouring down his face, and the long, black hairs upon his arms clung close to their damp surfaces, as he stood in the shop-door and hailed the passing physician. So intent was he upon his purpose, that he paid no attention to the doctor's protest or his inquiry.

"Just wait till I get some of the smut off," he said, glancing at his bare arms, "and I'll go with you."

"But really, Chris, I don't see—"

"You haven't got anything more important on hand— you couldn't have," the blacksmith interrupted, gravely.

"But what is it you want?" asked the doctor, impatiently.

"Do you see that, doctor?"

Barclay pointed to the square and compass burned into the door, upon his right, as he spoke. There was a sort of unconscious dignity, amounting almost to command, in the gesture, and a peculiar significance in the tone in which he directed attention to the rude hieroglyph.

"I see it—of course," the doctor answered, with a look of inquiry upon his face.

"Well, I want you should go with me, without asking any questions, and I want you to go *now*," said the smith, in the tone of one who had a right to demand consideration. "I'll take all the responsibility."

" Oh, if you put it on that ground—an order out of the East—why, I'll go, of course," responded the doctor, with a look of surprise and a half-shrug of his fat shoulders.

" Of course," repeated the smith, smiling significantly. " Well, you may just drive through the gate down there and go on up the lane. It's a good road and I'll overtake you in a jiffy—by the time you get to the bars, anyhow."

The doctor was evidently inclined to make further inquiry, but the blacksmith pointed again, with an emphatic gesture, to the mystic symbol, and with another shrug and a submissive " All right !" the physician turned his gig and drove down the hill. A moment after, Chris Barclay left the shop, his coat upon his arm and his gun upon his shoulder, and crossed the hollow to his house.

" What on earth have you and the doctor got on hand to-day ?" asked his wife, good-naturedly, as he entered the yard. " This morning you had a good hour's chat out in the road, and now you've got him hid away down there in the hollow. What are you going to do with him, anyhow ? 'Pears to me there's something mighty mysterious going on to-day."

" Just a bit of Masonic business," answered her husband, lifting his eyebrows meaningly. " The doctor's going to take another degree, you see, and I'm coaching him up a little."

" Where are you going to do it ? Is he coming here ?" asked the wife, apprehensively glancing back from the doorway where she stood, to see that the room was in order.

" We'll just step up into the edge of the clearing," was the reply ; " where there won't be no eavesdroppers, you know."

" Might just as well come here," urged the wife ; " there's the parlor that you can have all to yourselves, just as well as not. I shall be getting supper, and won't disturb you the least bit."

If there was one thing Melinda Barclay was prouder of than anything else, it was the fact that her husband was the brightest Mason in all the region round. The nearest lodge was ten miles away, but he had been the Master for years, and many mysterious conferences had been held at the house as well as at the shop, during that time. "Masonic business" was as sacred a thing in her eyes as it could have been in her husband's, and the wife of the Worshipful Master would have protected the mysteries of the craft from profanation with as much fidelity as the most devoted Tiler that ever guarded with drawn sword the approach to the lodge. She never objected to the waste of time or to her own careful exclusion from its secrets. The fact that it brought honor and recognition to her husband was enough for her. The truth is, that, though she was sharp-tongued, and so capable and positive that people said of her that "the gray mare " was the "better horse" in the domestic span, she was inordinately vain of her stalwart husband's strength and popularity. While she twisted him easily about her finger as to domestic matters, she knew, and it gave her pleasure to know, that there was a point beyond which she could not go. So she never questioned anything he did masonically, any more than if she had taken an obligation of secrecy and obedience herself.

" Might just as well have it as tramp way down to the clearing and back in the hot sun," she added, persuasively, seeing him hesitate.

The truth was, he was hunting for an excuse, and her words gave him the clue.

"It's too hot to sit in a close room, Melinda," he replied, "and of course, we'd have to keep the windows shut, though I know there wouldn't be no need with only you about ; but one can't be too careful about such things."

"I s'pose not," regretfully.

"Besides, the doctor has drove on down the lane and is waiting for me at the bars, I expect, right now."

He started off with long, hasty strides in the direction of the barn, smiling and winking to himself as soon as his back was turned.

"What are you going to do with your gun?" she called after him, banteringly, from the doorstep. He still had it on his shoulder, having forgotten to leave it at the house as he had intended.

"Keep off cowins and eavesdroppers," was the laughing reply.

"How long 'fore you'll be back?"

"'Bout an hour or an hour and a half, I should say ; the doctor's in a great hurry."

"Fudge! That's always his way ; well, I'll split the difference and have supper ready in an hour and a quarter. Tell him if he don't stop and take supper with us, I'll take the broomstick to him till he won't be able to ride the goat for a month."

"All right," the husband called back, jocularly, as he hastened down the path to the lane.

Once a day for a week afterward the doctor's gig turned in at Barclay's lane, usually at night, so that even the good wife was unaware of the fact ; and for a week, also, Chris Barclay was away from home the better part of every night and very frequently during the day, until even his wife's reverence for "Masonic business" began to grow weak.

"Well, I declare, Chris, I should think you were making a wholesale job of it this time, anyhow," she said, protestingly, one night, as he took his hat preparatory to his usual outing.

" There's a lot of fellows going out to Californy, 'cross the plains, you know," he answered, deprecatingly, "in a week or two, and they want to be finished off before they go. Might be worth a good deal to 'em out there, you see."

" I s'pose it might," said the good woman resignedly.

The blacksmith's eyes twinkled, but he showed no signs of regret for the deception he was practicing on his trustful spouse.

As the reader will have surmised, the doctor's mysterious. visits were made to the training-camp, where Horace Goodwin was slowly recovering from his hurt. In strict compliance with the blacksmith's injunction, he had asked no questions except such as pertained to the injury itself. He did this the more willingly because he felt satisfied that his own knowledge of the facts, if not more correct, was at least more definite than that of his friend, and he anticipated great pleasure in revealing the truth some time to a choice circle of cronies, to the confusion of the blacksmith, whose cumbrous shrewdness had, he thought, been so unnecessary. Day by day, as he pursued his accustomed round along the country roads, Doctor Kelsey chuckled to himself as he thought how, during some call from labor to refreshment, he would make the lodge-room echo with laughter at the Worshipful Master's expense, by relating to the appreciative craftsmen the story of this adventure.

During this interval, having seen nothing of Sam, the doctor did not suspect his presence, and naturally arrived at the conclusion that Chris had brought Goodwin to this place after he was wounded, simply from apprehension for his friend's safety, or else that Goodwin had fled here under the idea that he was pursued, and that Barclay had found him afterward. This impression had been strengthened by Barclay's statement that Horace had been delirious ever since he first saw him after his injury. The ball, entering the muscles of the back below the shoulder-blade, had passed around under the arm and torn its way out through the pectoral muscles. The wound was a serious one, therefore, not from primary but from secondary effects. Thanks to the vigor and health of the patient, the unpleasant symptoms had yielded readily to treatment, and as it was probable that Horace would soon be removed to other quarters, the doctor took occasion at the first visit he made unaccompanied by Barclay, to give his patient a statement of what he himself had learned in regard to his injury. He was seated upon a sap-bucket which he found bottom upward beside the couch of hay. His patient seemed rather more excited and feverish than he had expected to find him. This was but natural, since the doctor's unexpected arrival had allowed Sam only a moment to conceal himself. Half to soothe his patient's agitation and half to relieve his own sense of duty, the physician told him what the reader already knows of Dan Marvin's connection with the events of the night on which Goodwin had received his hurt.

CHAPTER V.

" That's the whole story," said the doctor in conclusion. " I haven't lisped a single word of it to a single
soul. You and I and his mother are the only ones that
know anything about it."

" I am afraid Kincaid had a hand in the matter," said
the other, half to himself.

" I don't know about that," responded the doctor,
cautiously. " I thought I ought to tell you about Dan ;
he's been punished pretty thoroughly."

" His mother's a good woman," said Horace, meditatively.

" She thinks'you led Dan into bad ways."

" He didn't need any leading."

" His father wasn't of much account."

" Not a bad man ; he taught me to play the violin.
Dan isn't a bit like him."

" Queer, isn't it," continued the doctor, musingly,
" how good lives generate bad ones, and bad lives give
forth good ones ? I suppose somewhere along the line
of his descent are to be found the qualities that go to
make up that bull-necked, sullen, revengeful cub. He
was probably lying hid somewhere in his parents'
natures, but nobody would imagine such a thing. You

can't guess the qualities of a man's offspring as you
do that of a horse."

" Perhaps because you don't know his pedigree as far
back, nor understand their qualities as well as you do
the horse's."

" There may be something in that, but it is not enough
to account for all that we see. Morally and physically
man is an anomaly among animals. The children of
the deaf hear, of the blind are clear-sighted ; the hunch-
back has straight children ; Apollo has crooked offspring ; but oftenest of all, the good have bad and the
bad good children.   I think it must be the surroundings
—what a child sees and hears and thinks—that give
prominence to inherited qualities and determine the
character of every life.   That's my hobby, you know ;
inheritance plus environment makes the man."

" Very probably you're right," said Horace, thinking
of the red spur on his heel.

" You and Seth, now," continued the doctor ; " just
as unlike as two men could be. I s'pose responsibility
—having to take a man's part when he was young—
sobered him ; and you never had anything to settle
you."

" Very likely."

" He married, too. That's what you ought to have
done. Queer, a man so fond of society should not have
even a sweetheart. I think I shall prescribe a wife for
you, as soon as you get over this."

The doctor spoke banteringly.

" No use," answered the other, smiling, and trying to
turn on his rude bed. " How's Susan getting along,
doctor ?" he asked, after a moment's silence.

" First-rate. It seems a queer thing to say, but I
believe the trouble that's come since her husband's
death has been a good thing for her—taken her mind

off her affliction, you know. Such things dull the edge
of grief—especially with women."

" And Hubert ?"

" O, he's all right. I should hardly go to see him any
more if it wasn't to let them know about you. They'll
be mighty glad to see you around once more, I can tell
you that."

Horace Goodwin laid with his eyes closed and made
no reply. He could hear the squirrels hopping about
in the dry leaves, and the bees droning in the verdant
stillness of the summer noon-tide about the camp.
Horace Goodwin was dimly conscious of these drowsy
delights, but it was the thought of his brother's wife
which brought the look of content the physician noted
on his face.

" The boy got out on the steps yesterday to pet the
colt," continued the doctor.

" The colt ? Who brought him out ?"

" It was that girl of Kincaid's. The hired man daren't
go into the stable ; but she said the colt wouldn't hurt
her ; and sure enough he didn't. She led him down to
the house, and it was curious to see the creature rub
and fuss about that boy. But he went back all right
when she started—swinging his head from side to side
in that queer, poky way of his, as if he never thought
of mischief."

" I'm glad she came to see Hubert."

" O, she's there about all the time, now he's getting
better. I never saw two young things so wrapt up in
each other. I believe it would about kill them to be
separated. He talked about her all the time he wah
delirious, and she wouldn't go to school, but just staid
at home to watch for me and ask how he was, till he got
well enough so that she could visit him."

" Deely certainly is a nice girl."

" There's another freak.   How'd she come to be what she is ?"

"Give it up.   I s'pose, as you say, it's somewhere in the blood, just as that colt's temper is ; but how it comes to crop out in just that form I don't know."

" Neither do I ; but she's a jewel, no mistake.   I must be going now.   What do you think about Dan ?"

" I s'pose if Kincaid was mixed up in the matter, it would all come out if there was a trial ?"

" Probably."

" That would just about kill Deely."

" It would be pretty bad for her."

" How's Dan getting on ?"

" He's able to sit up."

" If he'll tell who was with him—"

" He won't do that," interrupted the doctor.

" Well, I'm glad he's man enough not to ; that's some credit to him, anyhow."

" It might lead right up to Kincaid if he did," suggestively.

" You're right there," responded Horace, with a troubled look.

" King Marsh has been mighty subdued and anxious since Chris began to talk about getting out a warrant."

" A warrant—what for ?"

" Chris pretends to think you're dead, and that he's got a clue to them that killed you. He's quite a changed man lately—Chris, I mean.   His fire's out most of the time, his shop shut up, and he sits around the corners and talks and hints from morning till night almost.   He'll lose all his custom if he goes on this way much longer.   I shouldn't be surprised any day to hear there was a warrant out against Dan. Hank Welby, the constable, you know, spoke to me about it to-day.

He don't know much, but he's an awfully determined man."

"Are they hunting after Sam yet?" asked Horace, with an effort to appear unconcerned.

"Mosely's at Kincaid's."

"Come to close the trade for the colt?"

"I s'pose so. He wanted to talk with Susan about the matter, but she said she wouldn't do anything till you come back. He asked her if she thought you were alive, and she said she did ; and she guessed the time would come when some folks would wish you were dead, more'n they did now. He said he'd wait a couple of weeks ; and she agreed, if you weren't back by that time, she'd take out letters and 'tend to the matter herself· There's a great deal of talk about the matter, 'specially since Chris put a padlock on the stable-door and made the hired man sleep in the barn with a gun. It seems to worry Kincaid a good deal.

"Besides that, he and Mosely had a falling out about the nigger. It seems Kincaid gave a bond with security to take him back to Kentucky, but when Mosely draws it on him, and demands his nigger, or the money, Kincaid goes to a lawyer, and, after taking advice, tells Mosely his bond ain't good for anything."

"Ain't good?"

"That's what he said ; and when Mosely come back from Kentucky, where he took advice, too, he says the same thing. You see he consented to let the nigger go into a free State, and that, it seems, makes him free, if he chooses to take advantage of it, which it appears he did, and that, they say, invalidates the bond, it being a contract that a man shouldn't do what he'd a clear right to do under the law of the State. So Mosely said that, if he couldn't get it out of Kincaid by law, he'd have to get it some other way. He didn't say how, but just lay around and smoked in that lazy Southern fashion, winking his great big eyes as contentedly as a toad that has swallowed a lightning-bug, till Kincaid got real nervous. So yesterday they settled."

" King paid him off, I s'pose ?"

" Not exactly. I believe the bond was fifteen hun-dred dollars, which Mosely says is just about a fair price for the nigger. I'm sure I don't know. He don't look as if he'd weigh more'n a hundred, and fifteen dol-lars a pound seems a pretty good price for any sort of meat, as Hank Welby says ; but Mosely claims the boy'd bring it any day, under the hammer."

" A good jockey is worth 'most any money."

" So I s'pose ; but there was the chance of getting him back, and the bond not good—at any rate they set-tled—nobody knows just how. Mosely takes back the Gray Eagle, for one thing, and most people believe that Kincaid loses what he'd paid on him and gets back his notes for the balance."

"That wouldn't be a bad trade—for Mosely."

" Well, Kincaid says he don't ever want to see a crack horse again ; and some say he had to promise his wife never to own another or the old woman was going to desert. He'd be bad off without her, shrewd as he is."

" So Mosely has got pay for his nigger and still owns him ?"

" Oh, no ; he sold him after that."

" Sold him ? In a free State, too ! I'd like to know who bought him."

" You'd never guess."

" Anybody round here ?"

The doctor nodded.

Horace shook his head, after a moment's thought.

" Give it up, do you ? Thought you would. Well, it was nobody but Chris Barclay."

"Chris Barclay!" exclaimed Horace, attempting to rise in his excitement, and sinking back with a groan.

"Exactly. Chris was sitting on the counter when Mosely and Kincaid came out of the back room and said they'd settled. Kincaid showed the bond around, and after they'd all seen it, tore it up. Then some questions was asked about who owned the nigger, and Mosely said it still belonged to him. He s'posed the little cuss was in Canada by this time, but he held the title if he didn't ever see a hide or hair of him again. Then Chris asked, in his dry way, if he didn't want to sell him.

"'Do you want to buy?' asked Mosely, with one of his ten-minute winks.

"Chris said his old woman had always claimed she'd like to own a nigger, and if he could get one cheap, he thought 'he might like to buy. Of course, everybody laughed.

"'Take him running?' asked Mosely.

"'Of course,' said Chris. 'S'pose I'd have to.'

"'Won't ask to have him delivered?'

"'No.'

"'You take all risk for failure of title made in this State?'

"'I want a good title, whether I get the nigger or not,' says Chris.

"'I can't give that,' Mosely said. 'All I can give is a quit-claim.'

"'Well, what'll you take for that?'

"They bantered a while, and the upshot of it was that Chris gave him a hundred dollars, and took a deed to the nigger and a contract that Mosely should make out another when he got back to Kentucky."

"I'm glad of that," said Horace, with a sigh of relief.

" But wasn't it a queer thing for Chris to do ?"

" It would seem so," answered Horace, absently. " How long before I can be taken home, doctor ?" he asked, after a moment's silence.

"Oh, in the course of two or three days, I should think."

" Well, doctor—if Dan Marvin should take it into his head that—that he'd better go out west—to California or somewhere—before I get around I—well, I don't know as there'd be any harm done."

" I'm sure his mother would be glad ; she'd probably go with him."

" I don't want to know anything about it," said the sick man with a gesture of aversion. " I s'pose I'll have to tell all about the matter as soon as it's known I'm above ground, and the less I know about his getting away, the better."

" Naturally ; and for my part I'd like to know a little about how you got hurt, before I'd be willing to give any such hint. How did it happen, anyhow? How did you come to be down the road at that time of night ? How did you get there and how did you get here ?"

" You are sure Mosely made out a bill of sale for Sam to Barclay ?"

" O, perfectly sure ; saw it myself ; in fact, am one of the witnesses. Squire Kendall drew it up, and Mosely handed over the bill of sale he got of the man he bought the boy of when he was a baby. It's all square and straight. Barclay owns the nigger out and out—so far as Mosely's deed can give title in this State, that is."

" Sam !"

There was a rustling under the hay in the great store-trough, and the little jockey rose up before the astonished gaze of Doctor Kelsey.

" It's all right, Sam," said Horace. " You heard what

the doctor said. You are free now, though Barclay has got a bill of sale for you. Nobody can interfere with you, now, and Chris is the last man that would ever care to."

If any one had expected any clamorous demonstration from the man thus suddenly relieved from apprehension of a return to bondage, he would have been disappointed. It is a singular fact that liberty was so stupendous and overwhelming a fact to the African slave, that when it came, it seemed invariably to paralyze the power of immediate expression. Words were inadequate to voice the rapture of a newly freed bondman. What Sam Mosely did was neither to shout nor laugh ; but after gazing a moment at the doctor with a stare almost as incredulous as his own, his face grew pale, his limbs trembled, and, with a half-inarticulate moan, he sank down sobbing hysterically, upon his knees in the trough where he had been hidden.

" Well, I declare !" exclaimed the doctor, springing to his feet, " where did *you* come from ?"

" Now, you see, doctor," continued Horace, after he had enjoyed for a moment his friend's astonishment, " the reason so much caution was necessary in communicating with you. So far as I am concerned, the matter is very simple. I was watching with Hubert that night—had been doing so for several nights before, you know—and must have fallen asleep in my chair. After a time I heard the horses whinnying—I had heard them for some time, I suppose, but it had not fully roused me from the heavy sleep I was in. When I did finally wake I started up, fully aware that something was wrong. The colt in the barn was trumpeting like mad, and just as I got to the door, I heard the Queen answer from the hollow down near the road. I knew at once that somebody had stolen her, but could not imagine why

they had not taken the colt also. Then I thought it
was a trick of Kincaid's ; and calling Susan to stay with
the boy, I started out in my slippers with only a roundabout on, to see what could be done. As I went out of
the door, I caught up the heavy rawhide whip the boy
had carried in the race. It was the only weapon I could
lay hands on just then."

"Not a bad one, either," interposed the doctor.

"No ; it served well enough. I had a notion that
whoever had got the mare would not go very fast at
first, as it might attract attention to go running by the
three or four neighbors' houses just south of ours, and
thought if I could get near her and whistle, she would
make the one that rode her trouble enough, so that I
could get a chance to use the whip before he could sub-
due her. You know I am a pretty good runner,
and the slippers were light and made no noise. When
I got to the brow of the hill just below Matthews's, I
could see them about half way down the slope. The
moon had gone down, but it was bright starlight. To
my surprise there were two of them, and they were
walking their horses quite slowly. I jumped over into
the orchard and ran down the hill until I was nearly
opposite them. The mare called just then— I suppose
she winded me—and I heard one of them give her a
lick. She never would stand a blow, and I knew this
would be a good time to interfere. Climbing the fence
into the road, I put my fingers in my mouth and
whistled—not once, but a dozen times. You know how
far that whistle can be heard ?"

" I've heard it a mile or more, over and often."

"Well, the mare heard it, then, and there was evidently a squabble with her. The man who rode her
fell off—at least I heard something fall—and clutching
my whip I ran towards them. When I got near, I saw

there was a man on her and another hanging on to the bridle. I hadn't more than four or five rods to run, and in a minute I was among them hitting right and left, first one man and then the other, and finally laying the whip over the other horse. They've all got my mark on them yet, wherever they are. The horse reared when I struck him, which isn't any wonder, considering that there's nearly half a pound of shot braided into that cracker. This pulled his rider, who had hold of the mare's rein, out of the saddle. He let go and she turned towards me. I cut the fellow on her over the head and face once or twice—perhaps a few more times —literally beating him off the saddle ; caught a grip· in the mare's mane as she started past me up the hill, and after running a few steps beside her swung into the saddle with a whoop. Just then a shot was fired, and I felt the ball strike me under the shoulder blade. The mare was going like the wind by that time, making just lickity-click for home. I began to grow faint in a minute and fell over on her neck, just having sense enough left to take hold round it. The next I knew I was lying here and Sam was washing my face. I suppose the mare was so frightened that she kept right on past the stable up the lane to the camp where we have been so long. That is all the story I've got to tell, doctor."

"I see ! I see !" said the doctor musingly. "You mustn't talk any more now. I oughtn't to have let you say so much, but I wanted to know. Even a doctor has some curiosity."

Horace smiled. The doctor's curiosity was a thing well understood by all who knew him.

"Well, it was lucky for you she came here," continued the physician. "I could hardly have done better for you than the boy, and—well, other things might have been worse."

"Yes," answered Horace ; " and you see I couldn't betray him after that."

"Of course not ; and Chris knew all about it ? The rascal—he's sharper than I thought."

"He's a mighty good man, doctor," said Horace solemnly.

" Who? Chris ? Well, I should say ! And not half as stupid as you might imagine, either," responded the doctor, heartily.

The boy came out from his hiding place, and, crouching down beside the couch, took Horace's hand tenderly in his own.

"You'll be well taken care of," said the doctor, significantly, glancing at the boy. "Couldn't I drive up the lane past Seth's after dark, when I come the next time ?" he asked as he rose to go.

" Just as well as not. Tell Mosely I'll be out soon."

" All right ; keep quiet. Good-bye."

He nodded cheerfully to his patient, put on his wide-brimmed hat and started to walk through the woods to Barclay's lane, where he had left his horse. It was half a mile away—a long walk for a man of his build—and he was glad he would not have to make it any more. He had been very circumspect, and congratulated himself that he had saved the peace of the neighborhood by his sagacity. Years afterward, when he told of his adventures, he always laid stress on this fact.

" No, you don't, doctor," was the unexpected greeting that worthy received as he stepped outside the door of the camp. It came from the lips of Melinda Barclay, whose trim figure was advancing from the brook, with the massive form of the blacksmith coming leisurely behind her. She looked saucily at the doctor from the shadow of her stiff sun-bonnet as she spoke, and threatened him with an uplifted finger,

"Just you stand where you are, sir, and tell me if you are not ashamed to deceive a poor trusting woman as · you and Chris have been doing for a week back. I thought my husband was overdoing the Masonic business, and mistrusting just what was in. the wind, I charged him with it. I never allow him to tell fibs to me about anything but Masonry, and had no idea he lied to me about that before; so he had to own up, and I came right down here with him to see if it was true that you two heathen men, who talk so much about charity and the like, would leave a poor sick man to suffer and perhaps to die, without any woman to tend on him or look after him. Ain't you ashamed, now?"

"But he has been very comfortable," said Barclay. "You know he has Sam to wait on him."

"Sam! A little nigger that's fit only to wait on a sick horse. Comfortable! Much you know about it. Wait until you're sick yourself, and then see how you'd like to have a nigger boy to wait on you."

"Remember he's yours now," said the doctor mischievously. "I expect you'll keep him waiting on Chris all the time."

"Waiting on Chris? No, indeed. I've got better work for him than that."

"What are you going to have him do?"

"Watch the Masons, sir, and let their wives know how they're deceiving them. I guess that 'll keep him busy."

"I'm afraid he'll run away again, if you set him at that."

"I wouldn't blame him," was the reply. "He seems to be the only man around here that's got right good sense. He knew he didn't know enough to take care of a sick man. Just let me see how things are, anyhow."

She stepped inside the door and looked at Horace, with Sam, who had risen at her entrance, standing beside the

couch and fanning him with a green maple-bough.   The
bed was an ingenious contrivance of the blacksmith's—
a pile of hay over which was tightly drawn and staked
a piece of canvas.   Melinda recognized some of her own
bed-clothing,.also, about the form of the sick man.

"How do you do? This ain't so bad, after all ;"
glancing around as she spoke.   " I was afraid they were
just letting you lie on the ground, Mr. Goodwin, and
suffer like a brute.   I'm glad Chris had sense enough to
steal some of my pillows and coverlets for you.   Now I
know he's a liar, I don't mind his being a thief, you see.
I declare, I'm glad you're getting along so well.   And
this is Sam, I s'pose ? I'm 'fraid I'll never be able to get
him away from you, Mr. Horace.   He's taken such good
care of you, I think he's earned the right to stay with
you.   How would you like that, Sam ?"

" Suit me fust-rate, missus," said the boy with a grin,
ducking his head and scraping his foot.

" You'll let me have him now and then, to watch Chris
and the doctor, won't you ?"

" As often as you wish," laughed Horace.

" Well, that's settled then ; I'll give him to you.   I
can't keep him, you know, because my husband's an
Abolitionist.   I'm not ; I'd like to have a nigger to wait
on me, but I can't afford a fuss in the family.   So I'll
let you have him.   What do they give you to eat, Mr.
Goodwin ?" the bustling housewife continued.   " Really,
you look half-famished.   What do you suppose Susan
would say if she knew one of her family was being
starved right here under her nose ? Where do you keep
your things, anyhow ?"   .

In her eagerness to explore the domestic arrangements of the camp, the good woman opened the door in
the partition and found herself confronted with the
inquiring head of the Queen.   The consternation which

was pictured on her face drew roars of laughter from the beholders, including the wounded man, whose mirth, though evidently painful, seemed irrepressible.

"Well, I do declare ! In a stable !" was her ejaculation.

"See here, madam," said the doctor, with half-assumed gravity, "don't you see you are agitating my patient ? I must positively forbid such excitement."

"Well, Mr. Goodwin," answered the woman, who recognized the truth of the doctor's words, " I won't stay any longer now. You don't know how glad I am to see you doing so well. Chris shall bring you a supper, and, to-morrow, perhaps, I'll come and sit awhile with you. We'll soon have you out of this."

The jolly trio—the doctor, the blacksmith and his sprightly wife—went away ; their laughing banter coming back, softened by the leafy wood, seemed to Horace Goodwin the sweetest sound he had ever heard, and almost before it had died away he sank into that restful slumber which follows so swift upon the least exertion, with the hopeful convalescent.

-----◆-----

CHAPTER VI.

THE CLOUDS ROLL BY.

It was as the doctor had predicted. The return of Horace Goodwin was more like a festive occasion than the reunion of an afflicted family. Not only his safety but the consciousness of relief from financial difficulty, gave an air of contentment which had long been unknown to the members of the household. When the

dead was spoken of, it was always with tender regret
that he had not lived to share this unlooked-for prosperity. The will of the deceased, naming his brother
as executor, had to be admitted to probate before the
colt could be legally disposed of. It provided that
one-third of the purchase money, after paying off the
mortgage on the farm, should go to Horace, not as a
bequest, but as compensation for his skill in enhancing
the animal's value. The will was executed several days
before the race, but the testators seemed to have had
no doubt as to its result. It was evident from the
entire instrument that he fully understood his own
physical condition, and did not expect to survive the
excitement of that event. Only his strong will kept
him alive until it was over, and even this proved insuffi-
cient to sustain the enfeebled system, when the reaction
came and he knew that his estate was released from the
peril that had impended.

When the trade was completed, the money paid, and
the colt brought out to be delivered to his new owner,
Hubert, now quite recovered, after a last caress of the
animal which had so long been the pride of his heart,
fled to his room under the roof of the unfinished house
and flung himself upon his bed in a passion of tears.
He mourned his father and his pet. Who shall blame
him if the two were unconsciously joined in his thought ?
He lay there a long time. His tears finally ceased to
flow and his sobs died away.

Lying on his back looking straight upward, he
watched the wasps building their mud-nests along the
rafters and dreamed the curious day-dreams of boyhood—of " gay castles in the clouds that pass, forever
flushing round a summer sky." Already he had buried
his past and set his foot across the threshold of the
future. What a crude and narrow future his imagina-

tion painted! There were so few people in it! Himself and Deely were, of course, its central figures. He was too much a man to think of himself as acting anything but a leading part in his own life-drama, and too much of a boy to be ashamed of his thought. His mother and his uncle came next; then, not without some compunctions, Deely's father and mother, considerably retired from view, and then—the world! What a queer, misty, sun-tinted world it was! How easily he settled the somewhat vague relations of his little circle to it and to himself! Himself and Deely, rather—for what was his was to be hers, of thought, act and enjoyment, "forever and ever, Amen!" He repeated the words softly and solemnly, and wondered how long "forever" might be, and what the "Amen" meant.

"Jack!" a soft voice called, timidly, from the narrow stairway.

It hardly broke upon his day-dream, for it was Deely's.

"Yes," he answered, absently, still watching the mud-daubers at work beside the rafter.

"May I come up?"

"Oh, is it you, Deely?" rousing himself and sitting up on the bed. "Why, yes—of course."

There was a rush up the uncarpeted stair, and the girl leaped upon the bed and flung her arms about his neck.

"Oh, Jack!"

This was all she said—her tone told the rest. The tears came again to the boy's eyes, but he brushed them aside and said, stoutly:

"'Tain't no use to feel bad, Deely; it had to be—and I guess I'm glad of it."

"Of course; he brought a lot of money, didn't he? Pa says you'll soon be the richest folks around here, if your mother lets Uncle Hod manage for her, and then you can buy him back some day."

" I don't want to buy him back."

" Well, you can get another just as good," continued the little comforter.

"There ain't any just as good, Deely. Mr. Mosely says he's the best horse in the country, and he wouldn't take five thousand dollars for his bargain to-day ; but if he was twice as good, I don't want him, nor I don't ever want to see him again."

" Why, Jack !"

" I don't, Deely ! I'm never going to own a horse as long as I live, no matter how rich I may be."

" Why—Jack Goodwin !" exclaimed the girl, drawing back, and looking up at him with astonishment.

" I won't !" repeated the lad, stubbornly.

" Why not ?"

" 'Cause I'm going to be a minister."

" But you'll be rich ; pa says you will."

" I don't care if I am."

" Rich folks are never ministers," said the girl, in a positive, satisfied tone.

" I'm going to be one, anyway."

" Are you going to preach and holler like other minis-ters ?"

" I—I—s'pose so."

" It must be awful hard work."

The girl sighed, as if the thought of the exertion oppressed her.

" I 'spect it is," replied the boy, absently.

" But you'll need a horse to get to your preaching-places ?"

" I shall walk."

The girl burst into a laugh that echoed musically through the empty room. The mother, busy with her work below, heard it, and rejoiced that the sorrowing lad could so soon forget his grief.

"I don't see anything funny in that," said the boy half-resentfully. " You needn't go with me."

"I should think not," she rejoined, laughing still more heartily. " The idea of a minister walking to church and leaving his wife at home !"

"Perhaps I sha'n't have any wife," said the boy, sulkily.

"Oh, yes, you will," answered the girl, sobered at once by his anger. " You know I'm going to be your wife. Remember, we promised 'forever and ever, Amen !' I couldn't marry anybody else, after that ; it would be wicked."

The girl spoke in tones of grave reproach.

"I s'pose it would," said the boy, apologetically.

"What makes you think you will be a minister, Jack ?" she asked, after a moment of oppressive silence.

"Father said he wanted I should be if—if I got a call."

" What's that ?"

"I don't know ; something preachers have. I've heard them talk about it. Some say father had one once—a long time ago—and didn't listen to it, and that was the reason he had so much trouble."

"What did he have so much trouble about ? Was it because he was sick ?"

"Oh, no ; that's what made him sick ; 'cause he was in debt and was afraid he'd lose the farm, I s'pose."

"Couldn't he get another, if he did ?"

" I don't know ; never thought of that. I s'pose he'd set his heart on this one."

" If I had my way, there wouldn't be any trouble in the world—not the least little bit," said the child-woman, with quiet certainty.

"Oh, there has to be, Deely," said the boy, with reproachful earnestness. His religious education had made trouble so essential a part of the Divine dispensation, that to question its necessity seemed to him nothing less than sacrilege.

"Do you think we'll have any trouble, Jack—you and I?" solemnly.

"Why, of course."

"What do you suppose it'll be about?"

"I don't know."

"It won't be about money, will it? We'll both be rich."

The child spoke with gay assurance.

"It'll be something, if there has to be a new kind of trouble made just for us. Everybody has trouble, Deely —everybody—more or less."

"I s'pect they do," said the little lady, smoothing out her frock, as she sat upon the bed *à la* Turk, and folding her hands demurely in her lap. The boy, his legs dangling over the side of the bed leaned over upon his right hand and watched her contentedly.

"Do you suppose you'll have a 'call,' Jack?" she asked, at length, looking up at him with a sympathetic gaze.

"How can I tell? They don't ever get them till they are man-grown. Father said he wanted I should be ready to answer if one came."

"What will you have to do to get ready?"

"Oh, be very good—you know—and go to college— and—and—such."

"That's all right," cheerfully. "And if you don't get a 'call?'"

"Then I'll have to do something else, I s'pose."

"Of course ; and then you can have all the horses

you want. I don't believe you'll get any 'call,'" she added, brightly.

"Perhaps not ; but—but—I sha'n't ever own a horse if I don't."

The boy's lip quivered and his eyes filled with tears, as the memory of the happy days at the training-camp came to his mind, but he turned away his head and looked steadfastly out of the window to hide his weakness from his companion.

" Why not, Jack ?"

The girl laid her hand caressingly upon his shoulder and leaned forward to look into his face.

"'Cause—I can't," came brokenly from the lad's determined lips.

" Won't you tell your little Deely, Jack ?"

Unable to resist this appeal, the boy drew up his left foot, and removing the shoe and stocking, pointed to the red mark upon the heel. Either because the foot had lost its tan during his illness, or because the exciting events of the past few weeks had tended to promote its development, the mark, which had been barely traceable before, now showed red and angry.

"Why, how funny !" said the girl, scrutinizing it curiously, but afraid to touch it.

" That was only a little red mark that you could hardly see, when we were down in the camp," said the boy, with quivering lips. " Now look what it's like."

He turned up the foot to show that the red line crossed the sole, and then turned it back that she might see the branches almost meeting on the instep.

" That's where it's tied, I s'pose," said the boy explanatorily. "Uncle Horace says they used to tie 'em instead of buckling them."

" But what is it ?" asked the girl, in a hushed whisper.

" It's a sign, Deely."

"A sign? Sign of what?"

"If those two marks ever come together there," pointing to the instep and speaking very solemnly, "it's a sign the devil's got me hard and fast, and there's never any chance for me to get away. Until it gets clear round, though, he ain't ever sure of me; so I'll have all manner of good luck till that comes, just to keep me from breaking away and disappointing him, you see."

"Who told you about it, Jack?"

"Uncle Horace; he's got one, too; and it's quite a considerable bigger'n mine—oh, ever so big round under the foot here—but it hasn't got quite together on top; is just about half as far apart as mine. That's the reason he's so lucky—won the race, didn't get killed, and— oh, everything! That's the reason everybody likes him, too, and he can make money without trying whenever he's a mind to. The devil's just baiting him on, you see. But Uncle Horace says he'll give him the slip yet, and I hope he will."

"I'm sure he will," said the girl, cheerfully.

"It's a sign that runs in the Goodwin family; some have it and some don't. Them that does, have good luck, and are apt to have a bad end; them that don't, have bad luck but die happy. Father didn't have any; so he had trouble. Uncle Horace says I wouldn't ever have discovered Abdallah if it hadn't been for that mark. Father could see his points after we'd showed 'em to him, but he never would have found them out himself."

"I believe I'd rather have the mark," said the girl decisively. The spirit of King Marsh showed in her tones.

"But the dying, Deely," said the boy, solemnly.

"Ain't there any way to have the luck and die happy, too?"

" None—only just being a minister—a child of Theophilus."

" What's that ?" asked the girl, in wide-eyed wonder.

Then he told his little companion the story of Sir Harry and Theophilus Goodwin. When he had concluded, she looked timorously around the silent, unfinished chamber and said in a tremulous whisper :

" O, dear !"

" Hubert ! Deely ! Come, children—supper's ready."

His mother's voice sounded very cheerful. The boy started at once to put on his shoe and lace it up.

" What makes everybody call you Hubert, now ?" asked the girl, as she watched him weave the leather strings in and out through the uncased holes in the shoe.

" I don't know ; unless 'cause father did."

" Don't you think it's because you're going to be a minister ?"

" May be."

" You'll let me call you Jack, won't you ?"

" Of course."

" Always ?"

" To be sure !" straightening up and looking at her wonderingly. " I wouldn't have you call me anything else for the world ! 'Twouldn't seem natural."

She flung her arms about his neck, kissed him and pressed her cheek against his with unconscious fervor. The boy received her caress a little shamefacedly, but did not return it.

" Let me tie up my shoe," he said, after a moment.

Deely released her clasp of his neck and leaned her head upon his shoulder while he finished. Then they slid off the bed, ran a race to the stairway, went clattering down and burst open the door to find Uncle Horace propped up in the easy-chair, occupying his brother's accustomed place at the table, while Mrs. Goodwin sat opposite, smiling and cheerful. The girl ran to kiss the invalid, whose first appearance this was at the table, while the boy sat down in his wonted seat with a strange, indefinable apprehension tugging at his heart. Was his Uncle Horace going to take his father's place in everything? Another surprise awaited him. Mrs. Goodwin's face flushed as she cast a meaning look at her brother-in-law and bowed her head over her plate. Horace leaned forward and in stammering tones asked a blessing. In those days it was customary only for those who were termed " professors " to say grace before partaking of food, and the children felt that a very solemn and momentous change had taken place, which they could but half understand. The truth was that a new day had come. One king was dead and another had come to reign in his place. Would his rule be just and wise and tender? This was the unformulated question the young hearts were unconsciously striving to solve as they ate the first meal under the new dispensation.

CHAPTER VII.

HALCYON DAYS.

The days passed swiftly, and the sun shone brightly on the Goodwin household. Some were surprised, but everybody seemed gratified at the change in Uncle Horace. One of his first acts after complete recovery was to apply for admission to the church.

" I promised Seth when he was dying, and before, too, that I'd join the church when he was gone and take care

of those he left behind,and I'm ready to do my part,"
was the only satisfaction he gave the church officials
when they asked his motive for making such application.

He explained his choice of denomination, which had
awakened some surprise, in a like unique and matter-
of-fact way :

" You see, Seth didn't get along very well with the
Methodists, and as I am not half so good as he was, and
haven't any of his gift, I thought I'd better try the
Congregationalists, and see if I could not make a better
go with them. I s'pose it's all the same, anyhow ; all
bound for the same place, and so far as I can see, it
don't make much difference which road one takes.
Susan was a Congregationalist before she married Seth,
and I've a notion she feels a little more at home among
them yet. As I'll have to stay and look after things for
her till the boy grows up, I thought I might as well join
where she'd like best to go. It'll be better for the boy,
too. As for me, I never cared enough about either to
have any preference ; I just want to do what seems the
best thing for them."

It was a terribly prosaic view to take of a spiritual
matter. He did not seem to know anything about the
distinctive tenets of the church he had selected, or
rather, did not care to consider them. The cardinal
principles embraced in the declaration of faith presented to him he accepted without hesitation and with
evident sincerity. As to a change of heart, he candidly
avowed that he was not conscious of having experienced
any. He had promised his brother to join the church,
set a good example to the boy, aud see that he had a
religious training and a thorough education. This
promise he desired to fulfill, and wished the aid of the

church in doing so.   He expected the help of God as a
matter of course, because it was a good act.

This matter made a deal of talk in the neighborhood.
Everybody said it was just like Horace Goodwin, who
never did anything as anybody else did.   Some com-
plained of his apparent irreverence and lack of spiritu-
ality, but they all admitted that he meant what he said,
and nearly every one declared that he had done exactly
right.   Fireside theologians argued stoutly pro and con,
about a change of heart and the evidences of a saving
faith.   Being asked to pray, at a meeting of the pastor
and deacons called to consider his case, he complied in
such a simple, stammering, unconventional way, that
even those who smiled could not help weeping, yet
could not tell why they wept.   After some delay his
request was granted.   He soon became active in the
affairs of the church, not in spiritual things, of which he
professed to no knowledge, but in advancing its tem-
poral interests, and bringing into it many of his old
associates.

After a few months, Mrs. Goodwin joined the same
church by letter from the Methodist congregation with
which she had united in her husband's lifetime.   Little
more than a year afterward Hubert also united with it.
It was chiefly through his uncle's persuasion that he
did so.   "You know it was your father's wish," he said,
and the boy complied.   Deely Kincaid joined at the
same time.   Was it love of God or love of Jack, that
made her refuse to allow him to be separated from her
by any new relation?   Many remarked that it seemed
like a marriage of these two who were yet children, but
seemed to be one in all their aspirations.   There was a
rapt look upon the girl's face as they rose from their
knees with the water of baptism still sparkling upon
her pale, gold tresses, as she glanced at her companion

before turning to listen to the charge of the pastor. The boy hardly heard the words of the minister, so absorbed was he with the thoughts inspired by that look—a look he never forgot, and which came back to his memory in after years with a sting like that of a scorpion which he could neither slay nor escape. "Yours—for time and eternity, yours!"—was the language of her tear-dimmed eyes. How often was he to see them shining through the darkness when he could answer but with groans their unceasing appeal. O, child-bride and child-groom, who would have dreamed that only the grave could hide forever the shame of that glance of purity and love flashing from soul to soul, as you stood at God's altar! Terrible was the sacrifice you laid upon the shrine of love that day, oh, spotless soul, whom earth had no power to stain, and whom the Merciful Father at length found but one way to save from sin and secure from shame!

Horace Goodwin at once assumed charge of the family interests, and soon established a new era of prosperity. He came to the helm at a fortunate time. Balmy breezes were blowing and the foundations of many fortunes were laid in the next few years. The gold of California was just finding its way eastward, and enlivening business and production with the assurance of a stable medium. The Crimean War was on the horizon, and our agricultural products took a rebound from the depression of the previous decade, which put money in the pockets of all those who were wisely watchful of events. Among these was Horace Goodwin. The tide of public favor set strongly with him, too. People spoke of him with lavish praise, now that he had quit sowing his wild oats and settled down. He found no lack of means or opportunity to engage in any business he desired. Men believed him lucky and were anxious to join their fortunes with his.

The farm which his brother's industry and thrift had made to yield but a scanty profit, soon became a source of positive wealth. Horace violated all the maxims of the agricultural community in which he lived ; did many things they thought needed not to be done, and left undone others that were esteemed of prime importance. Especially did men predict failure because he would neither hold the plow nor drive. But he caught at new ideas, purchased new and improved breeds of stock, bought and sold with an appreciation of values that seemed instinctive, and paid wages that astounded his neighbors. If he did not labor himself, his eye saw all that was done or left undone, and neglect was sure to be followed by dismissal.

When an opportunity offered to enlarge the farm, he improved it. " Seth always wanted that piece to straighten his south line," he remarked. People smiled when he planted a double row of maples and elms along the State road from end to end of his possessions. " Seth always said he meant to do it if he ever got able," was his excuse. And so, for everything he did, he quoted the dead brother, until his neighbors laughed and his workmen jested with each other about it. But what he planted grew ; what he raised found a profitable market. He did not sell raw material, but turned corn into cattle and forage into flesh. He imported shorthorns, then just coming into favor ; raised horses, bought horses, trained them sometimes ; and from everything he touched realized some advantage.

Even the Queen, whom he kept from gratitude, yielded him a golden return. He had many offers for her, but he would accept none. He drove her sometimes, but never let the harness gall nor work tire her. He had

promised her, he said, that she should live with him and
have an easy time. Her progeny soon came to be worth
almost unheard-of prices. The blood of the Belmont
Mare grew more and more valuable as the achievements
of her descendants became more notable. Every year
some one of them lowered the record by seconds or
fractions of a second. Already she was known as "the
dam of trotters," when the Queen's first foal, a son of
Belmont's Abdallah, sold at three years old for a price
even greater than that paid for his sire. From that time
Horace Goodwin was known and recognized as one of
the most successful breeders in the country ; but he
would never race except to make a record. People
called his success luck and his abstinence superstition.
He did not talk about either except to Hubert—nobody
called him Jack now except Deely Kincaid. It was the
day of individuality in business, and Horace Goodwin's
individuality was the key-note of his success. Organization had not yet eradicated manhood.

For many reasons, the boy's relations with his uncle
were more intimate than he had ever sustained to his
father. Though the head of the family, Horace treated
him more as a companion than a child. He told him his
plans, encouraged him to make suggestions ; made him
his agent, sometimes his lieutenant ; but kept it always
before his mind that he must prepare for other work.

" You know your father wanted you to go to college,
and I promised that you should," he would say. " I
don't see how I am going to get along without you, but
you must go. I'll find the money and look after matters
here, and when you get through we'll just divide—share
and share alike. I guess that 'll be about right. I
really hadn't anything to begin with, and if Seth had been
alive it would all have been yours. But you must go to

college, and you must be getting ready for it. You needn't be in a hurry, but don't forget your books."

This lenient rule was too much for the boy's moral nature to endure without relaxation of his purpose. Life on the farm under his uncle's *regime* suited him exactly. He was not fond of study, and even his mother's persuasions were not sufficient to keep him up to his work. His attendance at school was irregular and his progress not creditable. The mark upon his heel seldom troubled him ; he felt at liberty to indulge his fondness for horses so long as they were not his own.

Deely Kincaid, still his chief companion, was glad to see him lose his morbid apprehension of the future, but began to grow alarmed when she found him falling behind in his studies. Her ambition for him was as keen as for herself, and for both it was insatiable. At sixteen he was not nearly ready for college, and his mother was suddenly alarmed by his persistent request to be allowed to go East with a drove of horses his uncle was about to send on. It was finally determined that in consideration of being allowed to do so, he should at once begin his work of preparation in earnest.

His mother met him on their arrival in New York with the horses and took him to one of the most celebrated schools of New England. She seemed very sad at parting with him ; and the boy, now fast growing to manhood, thinking only of her happiness, said impulsively :

" Ma, why don't you marry Uncle Horace ?"

He was somewhat taken aback when, blushing deeply, she told him that when he came home for the vacation he would find his wish fulfilled, adding that it was her desire, and Horace's also, that he should still call the latter " Uncle."

When she was gone, the knowledge of this fact seemed to put him very far away indeed from his past, and induced him to address himself more sedulously to the duties of the future than he otherwise would. He did not love study any better than before, but he had nothing to divert his attention from it, and made good progress. From that time until his graduation he had little thought of anything else. His mother's letters, his uncle's and Deeley's, sufficed to keep him in touch with his own world, and he did not desire any other.

Once a year, at the summer vacation, he returned home for a brief period of unmixed enjoyment. The evidences of prosperity multiplied so rapidly that at each visit he had to take account of new ones. The house had first been finished, and then had almost disappeared behind costlier additions. Barns and stables grew in number and value, and the young collegian found his old love for the horse returning as the best occupants of the stalls were placed at his disposal for long drives and rides with Deely Kincaid, now openly recognized as his betrothed, and growing even lovelier than the promise of her girlhood would have led one to expect. Even the birth of a little sister did not wean his mother's heart from him, nor affect his cordial relations with his uncle. He enjoyed their home no less than before, but he called it theirs, not his, any longer. He had begun to feel the impulse of separation which thrust the fledgeling out of the parent nest !

Marshall Kincaid and his wife softened somewhat as the years went by, but their pride in their daughter grew stronger· than ever. In her anxiety to justify their hopes, Deely had pursued a course of study as extensive as it was incongruous, which finally began to tell upon her strength. It was before the days of colleges for women.

There were only "female seminaries" then. This fact made the task of a woman seeking a liberal education far more difficult than that of the boy, since there was no prescribed curriculum, and she had to master both the solid work of the college course and the accomplishments then deemed far more essential to her sex than knowledge.

During her last vacation people began to talk about a decline, and hint at consumptive tendencies ; but her father and mother laughed at such forebodings.

"She's a little puny," said the stalwart King of the Corners with all his old willfulness, replying to such a suggestion by one of a group of customers, as he sat upon the counter one summer evening, just after Hubert and Deely dashed up to the old inn, their horses smoking and their tones full of the subtle gleefulness of young love, "but she's only got one more year. She's been working pretty hard for a good while, but she'll have a rest then. No consumption about her, and no fear of a decline. Do you hear that laugh? Clear as a bell. She's like her ma—there ain't much of her, but what there is is clear grit. No discount on her. She'll graduate next year, and she'll be away up at the head of her class, too, besides all she's done outside. She won't be like young Goodwin. I understand he graduated somewhere about the middle of his class. He's a smart fellow, but he ain't no such scholar as my Deely. She'll be top-notch, or she won't be nowhere. You mark my words. It's a pity she ain't a boy, so she could go to college sure enough, and just show 'em what can be done. Extras and all, she's done a deal more than the college course. Why, besides Latin and Greek, she's learned French an' German an' Italian, and what with her music and drawin' and paintin', I tell you she's got through with a heap more'n the boy. He looks kind o' tired an' washed out, too, as if he'd had about as much as he could stand up to. He don't learn as quick as Deely though, an', besides that, bein' mewed up in a house don't come natural to a man, nohow.

" They tell me they're goin' to send him back to the seminary—Theological Seminary—you know, where they polish off the college-made preachers—bound to make a minister of him, you see. But they won't ever do it ; he ain't that sort. That's what Deely thinks, an' I guess she knows him if anybody does. I'm glad he's goin' back to the city, this year, though, for Deely's sake—be a lot of company for her—but after that he'd better come back here and settle down. Now, that Horace has been 'lected to the Legislater, he needs some one to look after his affairs, anyhow.

" They'd made a team—he an' Deely. Needn't ever do a stroke o' work, or they might do anything they'd a mind to. He's got luck, an' Deely s got determination, an' they'd both have a good speck of money. Half of all the Goodwin property goes to him, you know, when he's twenty-one—that's this fall some time. That was the bargain when Horace married the widder—a good bargain on his part, too. You see, he got half the property and the widder besides. But he's kept it growin', no mistake about that. They had it all writ down in black an' white. Squire Kendall fixed it up, an' no lawyer has ever been able to drive a cart an' oxen through a paper he draw'd yet. So the young fellow's all right, so far as money goes.

" Will they get married ? Oh, of course, after a while. They've been sweet on each other for years and years. Deely could do a good deal better, no doubt about that. She's got style, you know—is one of them gals the fellers take to as nat'rally as bees to a pot of honey. She might just as well marry a hundred thousand as twenty—every bit. She knows it, too, as well as any-body, an' her ma gets real put out with her for her stubbornness. But she won't hear a word 'bout anybody else ; won't hardly treat a feller decent as soon's she sees he wants to make love to her. She's so wrapt up in Jack—that's what she always calls him, you know—that her ma an' I just quit tryin' to break it off any more'n if they was man an' wife.

"Of course, we haven't no objection to young Good-win—only this nonsense about his bein' a minister—an' if he *should* take a turn to business he'd be a clipper, an' no mistake. But if people keep fussin' round tryin' to make a silk puss out of a sow's ear, they're apt to spoil it for souse, an' then 'tain't wuth nothin'. There's a sort o' risk in it—always is in these people that are too religious. Many an' many a man has gone to the devil by tryin' to be too good ; insistin' on doin' somethin' the Lord didn't cut him out to do. That's what I'm afraid of with him. A man don't want too much conscience in this world. It's always standin' in his way, and henderin' him when he ought to be improvin' his oppor-tunities. For my part, I never seen a very rich man who had any more religion than he could afford to carry around wherever his interests demanded. If he's all the time inquirin' whether this or that or t' other thing's right, why, first he knows, he hain't got no time to make money ; an' in these days money's wuth more'n religion, and I've my 'pinion it's goin' to keep gittin' more an' more so right straight along.

"A certain amount of religion is well enough—pays in fact. I've been sorry sometimes I didn't take on a little myself. There's Hod Goodwin, now ; he's got just enough ; it's a great help to him sometimes, and ain't ever in the way. You couldn't get him to put a horse on the track an' bet he'd beat any other horse for any

money, I don't s'pose ; but he'll raise the horse an' hire
that little nigger, who is jest as full of tricks as Satan is
of sin, to train him, an' then he'll let him run or trot,
and others can bet on him if they want tb. Then, if he
wins, he'll sell him for a price, ten, twenty, fifty times
as big as he'd got if he hadn't won. For my part, I
don't see no difference 'twixt bettin' on a winner an'
raisin' a winner for others to bet on. But one's all right
for a church member an' t'other isn't.

" If I thought the young man wouldn't ever have any
more religion'n Hod, or would have that kind, I wouldn't
mind it. But you know his father wasn't that way.
I've never quite found out how 'twas that Hod managed
to get his permission to run that colt. There was some
sort of deception about it somewhere, an' I'm just as
well satisfied as if I'd seen it done, that it was his
conscience that killed Seth Goodwin. They say he'd
made up his mind 'twas all right for him to do it,
because he was so bad off and his family needed the
money ; but what kind o' reasoning is that ? It's my
'pinion he made up his mind to do it anyhow, an' just
died fightin' with his conscience, 'cause he thought 'twas
wrong. Now, if the boy should take after *him*, I
wouldn't have Deely marry him for anythin'. I don't
know as he will, but they tell me he's jest as hot an
Abolitionist as Seth was, an' after a man gets that far,
there's no knowin' where he'll stop. He's sure to want
to run the world his own way an' make everything over
on a ' higher law ' model—jest accordin' to his own
whim. I wouldn't trust an Abolitionist as far as I could
throw a bull by the tail, no matter how good he was. In
fact, the better such people are the worse they're likely
to get.

" I don't say 'tain't right for the niggers to be free ;
but what'd we do with 'em if they was ? An' what's the

sense of jest tearin' up the country an' cuttin' each
other's throats 'cause they aren't? An' that's what
we're comin' to jest as fast as these folks can push us on,
or I can't read writin'.

" An' the very worst kind of Abolitionist is an Abo-
lition minister. I'm afraid that's the sort o' preacher
they're goin' to make out of young Goodwin ; an' if he
does turn out that way, you can jest set it down as a fact
that I'll see that gal o' mine in her coffin 'fore she shall
marry him—with my consent, that is ; an' I promise
you that if she marries without my consent, she won't
ever see the color of my money afterward. I wouldn't
even give her the broken bank bills piled up in the
drawer there to save her from starvin' ! I wouldn't, by
the Eternal !"

Marshall Kincaid gave his thigh a resounding whack
as he made this declaration, and, leaping off the counter,
began making preparations to close the store for the
night.

CHAPTER VIII.

DUTY RUNS WITH INCLINATION.

Hubert Goodwin did not exactly fancy the notion of
entering the Theological Seminary. He not only did
not feel any call to preach, but he was not even what is
termed religiously inclined, without which, preparation
for the ministry as a profession is hardly regarded with
favor in this country. Not that he was at all irreligious ;
but he was neither inclined to metaphysical disquisition
nor had he that sympathetic nature which fits one for
counsel and monition. Organization, administration,

the adaption of means to specific ends—these constituted the decided bent of his mind. He felt that he would be out of place in the atmosphere of the seminary, not because it was religious, but because it was speculative, analytical, demonstrative. He did not care about the grounds of faith, either on his own account or for the sake of others. He believed ; that was enough for him. So, too, he did not care to speculate about spiritual matters. He had no curiosity about the plan of salvation, and no religious experiences worth mentioning. He was not given to self-dissection, nor fond of noting the operations of his own mind. He liked to do. He would have been willing to fight for his faith—would have been an unflinching martyr, if there had been any demand for martyrs ; but he was not worshipful by nature nor inclined to spiritual diagnosis. He believed, and was willing to do whatever was needful to be done, but he had no liking for the duty of persuading men to believe or to do. He did not even care to pray, since the act seemed to him often unnecessary, and at other times almost an impeachment of divine mercy.

He had talked with the president of the seminary before he left the city, telling him the circumstances as fully as he could and his own feelings in regard to the matter. As is usual with the strong nature that is induced to seek advice, he found himself more undecided afterwards than before. All this thoughtful and experienced man could do was to advise him to adopt whatever course seemed to him right. This was the very problem he was trying to solve—what was his duty. If he had been sure it was his duty to study for the ministry he would have done it without hesitation ; but this he could not decide.

If there had been any other profession to which he felt particuarly inclined he would not have hesitated to

embrace it, but there was none.   Had not a college bred
farmer in those days been an absurdity, he might have
turned to agriculture.   As a fact, though he did not
know it, his decided bent was for that sort of financial
adventure which we call speculation, aptitude for which
was the secret of his uncle's success.   He thought of
these things with that sort of unhappiness which comes
from indecision, but he spoke of them to no one.   His
was not a nature that clamored for advice.   Besides, he
knew the wishes of all whose opinions he cared anything about.

" Well, what are you going to do ?" asked his uncle
one day when the vacation was half over.

They were sitting under the great elm whose shadow
seemed especially imbued with his father's presence.
It was here that his father had sat day after day during that last summer when he was fighting with death
for the material triumph which had been the dream of
his life.   It was from this point that he had watched the
preparations for the Great Race and with unflinching
confidence awaited the result.   It was here that the boy
had heard his final words of approval when the struggle
had been won.

" I don't know," answered the young man, thoughtfully.

Time had made changes in the appearance of Hubert
Goodwin, but they were only the natural changes
which transforms the boy into the man.   He had been
a boy of ordinary appearance, and had grown into a
man without striking characteristics.   He was of
ordinary height, well built, showing endurance rather
than great strength, the heavy lines of his father's face
softened by the milder elements of his mother's visage,
but his full eye, blue as it was, shone dark under its
heavy brow, shaded with long lashes.   His face indi-

cated decision, and his uncle, looking at him as he leaned easily back in his chair, knew that, however much he might yield to the wishes of those interested in his welfare, the time would come when he would determine for himself what he would do, and when that time came, their advice would count for nothing in the balance against his will.

" That being the case," said Horace Goodwin, with a shrewd appreciation of the yet undeveloped manhood of his hearer, " I think you had better go to the seminary for a while at least. I believe I know something how you feel. You have been through a long course of preparation ; think that you ought to be able to do something ; perhaps think you might do any one of several things, but have no special inclination to any of them. Of course, you don't want to make any mistake by a wrong decision. Your father wished you to prepare yourself for the ministry. He was a wise man as well as a good one. You know the men of our family are always in danger of going to the bad unless some special strain is put on them. I can realize now that it may have been our father's death that saved Seth from making shipwreck of his life, just as his death, by devolving on me both responsibility and opportunity, showed my bent and gave scope to activities which were before either useless or harmful. The seminary seems to me a good place to wait till you are ready do decide as to your vocation. It will be a change of interests and associations, and from all I can learn, give you a chance to study other things as well as theology. You have not yet received a call ; perhaps you never will. Then, again, it may be that your surroundings and associations have not been such as to incline you to that work. I think you owe it to your father's memory to go a little beyond rather than stop

short of what you think he would require if he were
present instead of me. I am sure you won't lose anything by doing so.

"I wish you would go back and try it for a year or
two, anyhow. It can't hurt you, and I feel as if I'd
promised Seth that you should. Of course I didn't,
only in a general way, but I should hardly be content if
I didn't ask you to do that much, at least. Don't mind
the expense, we can afford it ; and then if you don't
wish to go on, you'll probably learn what you really
want to do. If you don't get a call, why I'm clear of
my promise and you of yours. Then—well, it'll be time
enough to plan when that happens."

" But Deely thinks—" the young man began to make
reply.

" Yes, I know ; she thinks you won't ever be a minister. She says you're too good. That's humbug, of
course, but I don't see why you're not good enough.
But if you don't ever preach, I s'pose the seminary
won't hurt you, and, as I understand it, you can study
about what you choose if you don't take a notion to
theology. They tell me there isn't any better place to
put a convenient addition to a college education than a
theological seminary. Of course, you know more about
that than I ; but it seems to me that there couldn't be
anything better for a colt that's been a little overtrained
than to turn him loose in a pasture and let him pick.
You've had to stick to the regular course in college.
Now why not go to the seminary and pick out your own
course ? If it don't lead to the ministry, it's dollars to
dimes that it will lead to the very place you ought to go.
Besides, you'll be right in the city with Deely. She
don't graduate until next summer, and I expect she'd be
lonesome enough if she didn't see you once or twice a

week. I guess she's seen you as often as that for the past two years, hasn't she ?"

"Well—yes," answered the young collegian, with a blush.

"Nothing to be ashamed of, my son. A man that's ashamed of honest love isn't fit to have a sweetheart ; and if there ever was a girl that was just as near perfection as womankind ever gets, her name is Delia Kincaid. Her love has been so much a matter of course, that I don't believe you half appreciate your good fortune. I never saw anything like it. I don't believe she's had a thought of the future since she was a dozen years old without putting you in the foreground of her dream. Suppose you should lose her ! I don't want to alarm you," he added hastily, seeing the pallor in the young man's face, " but she don't seem very well of late ; been studying too hard, I suppose. I've always told Kincaid he'd kill her, and I'm afraid he will, if you don't look sharp and prevent it."

" What can I do ?" Hubert asked, gazing earnestly into his uncle's face.

" Well, I'll tell you what I'd do in your place. Take a horse with you when you go back, and get an order from her mother to the president, or whatever they call the head of the school she is attending, for her to go out with you two or three times a week, or as often as you choose. That would be a good thing for both of you. It'll improve her health and make you contented. It will do you good, too. A young man can't be with a girl like her too often.

" It may be you haven't any call to preach. 'Tisn't every man that has, and it's lucky it's so ; but I wouldn't back out of anything I'd set in for until I knew for certain that wasn't my hold. There's plenty of places in the world for you to do a man's work outside of a pulpit ; but it always seems to me a young man ought to take a year or so after he's through college to loaf around, look the world in the face, and determine just how he'll tackle it. I think we are on the threshold of great events. Being in politics lately has given me a wider outlook than I used to have. No man has a right to live for himself in a republic. There are great questions coming on to be decided pretty soon. They are too big for me. Some of them I think I could determine after a fashion ; of others I cannot even guess at the solution. I have thought you might, perhaps, do something in this direction, if you shouldn't care to be a preacher. It will require manhood, courage, and brain ; of that I am sure. How they will be applied or where they will come from, I do not know. Of one thing you may be certain : the country, the American Republic, means more than we have ever thought—to the world, I mean. Up to this time it has been *our* country ; after this it will be the world's. Until now, we have followed the world ; have taken lessons from other countries, and counted ourselves successful just in proportion to our success in imitating their institutions or improving on them. After a little we are going to lead. You will live to see the time when our country will be the foremost nation of the world, and when the now almost unoccupied West will be the real seat of empire. At such a time it cannot be bad policy to wait a while, in the meantime studying the forces and conditions of our life, before determining just where you will make a plunge into the great conflict.

"Don't confine yourself to study. Stay at the seminary, and don't neglect study ; but mingle with people ; observe public affairs ; get out into the air and be a man among men.

"Here's my idea," continued the uncle, rising from

his chair and walking back and forth on the lawn:
"Whatever you are going to do you need variety and
extent of observation. Why not take a horse and sulky
and drive back to the city? Take your time for it; go
where you please; see whatever you have not seen that
lies along the way. It's not a very extended course of
travel; perhaps you will want a longer one some time.
You may want to go abroad next year. There isn't any
reason why you shouldn't, that I know of. Then you
would wish you knew your own country more thoroughly.
When you get back to the city keep the horse and drive
him every day. You've got the knack of training a nag—
getting the best out of him—and I don't see why you
shouldn't make some money, and at the same time give
yourself a little more color—put yourself in better condition than you are now. I think that's half what's the
matter; you need the open air, exercises and something
to interest you, outside of books."

"You remember, I've taken that trip once," said the
young man, with a smile.

"Yes; you went East with a drove and saw more of
life in forty days than you had ever seen before or have
seen since. Have you any notion how the world has
changed even in those few years? There are no more
droves crowding the roads eastward. We met the
locomotive just west of Buffalo, then. Do you remember that evening when you first saw its fiery eye headed
westward along the lake shore? There were small cities
of "paddy houses" built all along the track, where the
work was still going on. You wondered if it would ever
reach Ortonville. Two years afterward you came home
without doing a mile of staging. All the droves go on
the railroads now. In a few years, a man who has ridden
or driven from the East to the West, or from the West
to the East, will be a curiosity."

"It's a pretty long drive," said Hubert, rising and joining his uncle in his walk.

"You've got plenty of time, I'll tell you what I'll do. You've seen that big bay in the south barn?"

Hubert nodded.

"Ever paid any particular attention to him?"

"I noticed that he was big and homely, and I judged— old."

"There's where you are mistaken. I thought so, too, at first, and was never more surprised in my life than when I opened his jaws and saw as pretty a six-year old mouth as you ever looked at. I expect his dam must have been old when he was foaled. That sometimes makes a colt look like a patriarch, you know. Well, that horse's got something in him."

Hubert smiled significantly.

"You think he'll need a good deal in him, eh? Well, that's true, too; he's a big horse and a big eater, even for his size; but that ungainly fellow is going to disappoint heaps of people before he quits going up and down ' on this terrestrial ball.'

"Where'd I run across him? Over in Pennsylvania— Titusville. Went there to inquire into this rock-oil business; a friend of mine was interested in it. Looks as if it was going to be a big thing, but I don't see just how it's going to be handled. He was drawing barrels —the horse, I mean—backing his loads on to the boats without any driving to speak of. He took my eye by his intelligence and strength. One morning I saw the boys racing back to the stable after having ridden the horses to water. This big fellow was so far ahead that none of the rest were in it. Heavens! What a stride! What an arm! What a shoulder! What a thigh!"

"And what a foot?" interjected Hubert with a laugh.

"Yes, and what a foot!" assented the uncle. "That's

just what I said, 'What a foot!' Did one ever see its equal? Chris insists that he ought to have double price for shoeing him. But in spite of his feet, I saw at once that he was a great horse—or might have been. I thought he was old then. I sauntered around to the stable after breakfast, looked him over, learned his age, and bought him out of hand for what was thought a pretty stiff price. I wouldn't take ten times as much for him now. Yet nobody thinks him fast. I have jogged him a little, and taken him down to 'Number Two,' to try him once or twice. The way he handles those big feet would astonish you. I don't know his pedigree yet; he's evidently a Patchen or a brother of Patchen—I'm inclined to think a brother. His dam must have been a good one, though, for he certainly received that head as a direct inheritance from Rysdyk's Hambletonian—couldn't have got it anywhere else. I believe with good handling that horse can lower any record that's been made. Now, why not take him, use him as long as you need, and along in the spring sell him. You are in a good place to do it. There's a track there, and lots of men that want speed and are willing to pay for it. I'll make you a present of him, Hubert, if you'll do it. Let's go and have a look at him."

The two men sauntered off toward the stables.

Horace Goodwin was a shrewd man, and he had touched, in his remarks, the three strongest forces in the young man's nature—his reverence for his father, his love for his betrothed and his fondness for a horse—and had made through each a cogent appeal for the course he advised. It is hardly strange that the young man yielded to such urging.

CHAPTER IX.

It was early winter. Hubert Goodwin had been a student of theology for a whole term. He had determined to remain during the year, though a feeling strongly antipathetic to a farther continuance of the course marked out for him had already sprung up in his heart. The events of the year had been momentous. They had fixed his attention on other matters, and made the ministerial profession seem to him dull and insipid in comparison with a life of activity and tangible achievement. Added to this, he had had something approaching an estrangement with his betrothed. On his proposing weekly or semi-weekly rides, she had frankly pointed out the unseemliness of the proposal to one in her situation. The truth was that her ambition stood in the way of the weekly outings quite as much as her sense of propriety. She had fixed her heart on graduating first in her class, and she had many rivals in the Brainerd Classical Institute for Ladies, whose ambition was as keen as her own, and whom she had hitherto distanced only by the most unremitting application. Hubert did not take kindly to this check upon his carefully matured plans. He did not realize how dear her ambition was to her. He looked with all the manly scorn of one who has secured a Latin certificate of scholarship from a college duly authorized to confer degrees, upon the first honor of the Brainerd Classical Institute, and never once imagined that, saving her love for him, this was the one thing on which the daughter of Marshall Kincaid had set her fiery heart with inflexible purpose. The loss of love wôuld kill her, but she would rather not live than fail of her ambition. It was a foolish notion, but in those days, when high attainment was more difficult for women, it was a worthy ambition for one who had long before determined to be a co-worker with the man she loved. Hubert Goodwin did not understand these things, and felt himself seriously aggrieved by her refusal to adopt the plan he had marked out for their year's sojourn in the city. It made him moody and discontented, and though he did not neglect his studies he felt little interest in the life of the seminary.

The mark upon his heel began to annoy him, too. The horse which he had driven from home had shown such qualities as to awaken all his latent desire for equine association and admiration for equine excellence. He had placed him with a farmer, just outside the city, and thither he repaired on Wednesday and Friday afternoons of each week to give him exercise and training. He often remained over Saturday and sometimes until Monday. The farmer's daughter, a bright, spirited, intelligent girl, took great interest in the horse left in her father's care, and still greater interest in the young theologian who stole away from his seminary to speed and train him. She often rode with him and fully shared his confidence in the horse which he was secretly preparing to take a place among the noted steeds of his time. Her sympathy was very pleasant, and it was not

long before Hubert found himself counting on her welcome and confiding to her his hopes and difficulties.

He did not once think of loving any one but Delia
Kincaid, but, seeing little of her, he naturally appropri-
ated the sympathy and appreciation which were nearer
at hand. He had not hidden the fact of his engage-
ment from his new friend. Perhaps the very knowledge
of it had served to draw them closer together. At any
rate, it was with a curious feeling of unaccustomedness,
that one Saturday, in the early winter, he found himself
waiting on the platform beside the drive, which circled
in front of the Brainerd Classical Institute, at which the
guests were accustomed to dismount, holding the reins,
and awaiting the appearance of Delia Kincaid. He had
written fixing the hour and knew that she would be
expecting his arrival. He did not, therefore, hitch the
horse and climb the imposing steps to announce himself, but knocked his feet together and stamped back
and forth upon the platform to stir the blood during the
brief moments of waiting. The cold was not severe,
but an hour's ride had given him a sense of numbness
and chill.

At length the door opened, and Delia ran down the
steps, along the path with its heaped-up bank of snow
on either side, and stood beside him upon the platform.

"Isn't it jolly !" she exclaimed, giving him her hand,
and glancing from him to the sleigh, with undisguised
mirth. "Haven't I obeyed orders? But what does it
all mean? You ought to have seen Miss Brainerd when
I showed her your note. 'It is certainly a very strange
request,' she said, ' but Mr. Goodwin is so careful of you
there can be nó impropriety in complying. They are
probably going to have a masquerade sleigh-ride, or
something of that sort.' So I made bold to ask if she
had something that would do for the occasion, and she

hunted up this cloak which was out of fashion years before I was born, and offered me a bonnet of the time of 'Tippecanoe and Tyler, too,' but I thought that was a little too much, and so put on this hood. You know it is 'countrified,' for you've ridden with it before. That was what you wanted, I believe, ' countrified !' What impertinence ! To ask a young lady to make herself look 'countrified!' Do I look 'countrified' enough to please you, sir ?"

She pirouetted gracefully before him, as he stood with the reins in his hand, waiting to assist her into the sleigh, looking up archly as she concluded the movement, as if challenging his verdict.

" I guess you'll do," was the laconic answer, though, the young man's eyes sparkled with admiration as they took in the slight form snugly wrapped in a long, blue cloak of antique pattern surmounted by a quilted silk hood which matched the cloak in color, and was dotted over with white tufts like snow flakes, while underneath its cape rippled down upon the cloak a cataract of pale golden curls.

" Don't you dare look around," she continued, banteringly. " Every girl in Brainerd Institute is watching us, and I'm sure every last one of them would fall in love with you, if they should get a fair view of that costume. And how terrible that would be ! Think of three hundred and twenty-one girls, besides a score of more or less experienced teachers, all in love with the same fellow !"

Of course, Hubert stole a glance at the windows of the Institute, and found that each one framed a group of smiling faces.

" They're all agog to see us off," said the girl, in a low, confidential tone, as she gathered her skirts about her knees, and taking his hand, sprang lightly into the

sleigh. "I don't wonder, either," she continued, as he
tucked the great buffalo robe about her, and then standing on the rave, knocked one foot after the other against
it to remove the snow. "You and Henlopen and this
old sleigh do make a picture. Henlopen is no beauty
at any time, but with that harness and that cutter, he's
better than a circus. Just look at him! I thought I
should have died of laughing when they called me to
see you coming up the drive."

The horse of which she spoke was a dead, blood-bay,
high in the withers, seemingly raw-boned, though a
second glance showed him to be in fine condition ; so
deep in the chest as to convey the impression that he
was light behind, though the close observer would have
seen that, while finely gathered at the loin, there was
an unusual length and harmonious slope of thigh which
indicated great propelling power. A long tail, fine and
silky, carried with a swaying droop, tended to enhance
the false impression as to the strength of the quarters,
while the thin, light mane, which fell half-way down
the long straight neck, held always upon the level of
the withers, increased the impression of its length and
thickness. From the end of this a great lean head
depended, with large mobile ears and a muzzle singularly
full and heavy. Big bony legs supported this unattrac-
tive superstructure, ending in hoofs of apparently
unusual size, though, when the weight of the animal
was taken into consideration, one found that it was the
fine-drawn lines of the strong flat legs rather than the
size of the hoof itself which gave this impression.

"Why *do* you insist on driving such a horse, Jack?"
asked the young lady, as the great animal strode lazily
down the drive to the street.

"You haven't seen him move lately."

"How should I?"

"That's what I brought him on here for ; I wanted to take you out once or twice every week."

" But you know, Jack, Miss Brainerd did not approve of—of such frequent rides."

" You have your mother's permission."

" But she did not know, and Miss Brainerd has to consider so many things. She was willing we should go once in two weeks—a whole half-day, if we chose. I think she was very reasonable."

" You know your health demands fresh air, and a good deal of it."

" O, I have been very careful, because I knew you were anxious," she said, stealing a glance at her companion. He was looking straight forward at his horse, with evident traces of displeasure on his countenance. " I thought we would have such nice times, but you haven't come—not near as often as you might."

" I thought you were getting tired of me."

" Now, Jack—" There was a tremor in the fresh young voice, and the girl looked off over the snowy level to hide the tears that crept out on the silken lashes despite her determination to keep them back.

The Brainerd Classical Institute for Ladies stood just outside the city. The first heavy snow of the season lay soft and smooth upon the ground, showing steel-blue shadows along the fences and under the edges of the few drifts which had formed as it fell. It had been beaten down into level tracks before the weather became severe, and now the dry, cold snow, creaking under the runners but not crumbling with the weight of the horse, formed the very perfection of a sleighing track. They were driving toward the city, the great bay consuming the space with long, swinging strides whose beauty was then unnoticed but which were destined very soon to be the admiration of many,

" Where did you get this rig, Jack ?"

" Out in the country."

" Did you get that hat and coat there, too ?"

" Yes ; ain't they stunning ?"

" That depends ; if we had a basket or two I think we would make a very good country couple going to market."

" Or returning from it. By Jove, Dee, you've struck it!" exclaimed the young man, with enthusiasm. " I'll stop at the very next grocery and get them."

" But what does it mean ? Is it a masquerade ?"

" Rather," with a quizzical smile. " Henlopen makes his *debut* to-day."

" What *do* you mean ?"

" Wait until I get those baskets and I'll tell you."

He drew up before a grocery store, and sprang out. The grocer stared at the curious figure that entered, and still more at the order he gave. An old russet-brown overcoat, with a cape, and high, fur-lined collar, a wide-brimmed, high-crowned white fur hat, and red woolen mittens, having separate forefingers, the thumb and forefinger lined with soft buckskin, were the salient points of the costume. Whether the man was young or old, required a second glance to determine. He ordered a couple of market-baskets to be filled with eggs and vegetables, which he placed in the sleigh so as to be in plain sight, though apparently intended to be covered by the robe. Having paid for his purchases, he took his place beside his surprised companion.

" Do tell me, Jack, what all this means ?" pleaded the young lady, as they drove off.

" Well, you know, Dee, I brought Henlopen on here, just to ride with you—Uncle Horace gave him to me for that express purpose. I expected to keep him until spring, and then get him into shape and sell him. Of course, that wouldn't be much trouble if we drove him once or twice a week all winter. Such a horse needs work and lots of it, and that's all he does need. When I found you didn't care about riding after him—"

" But I did, Jack."

" Well "—with an expressive shrug—" once a fortnight isn't enough to count. It was no use to keep a horse for that ; so I put him out in the country with a farmer I happened to know, and went out to drive him every Wednesday and Friday afternoons."

" Is that where you have been Saturdays ?"

" Mostly. I made up my mind, you see, that I might as well sell the horse this winter as next summer. There's a lot of fancy horsemen here in the city who are fond of speeding their nags out on the Bay Road when the sleighing is good. There's Mr. Sedley, with that span of blacks which he thinks will lay over any straight trotter in this region ; and Tom Burton, with his gray pacer, which has all he can do to keep even step with them ; and a dozen more, real ' goers,' that are sure to be out on a day like this."

He glanced up at the dull, leaden sky as he spoke, and continued :

" You see it's a perfect day ; no wind or sun, not cool enough to be uncomfortable, nor soft enough to make a horse ball up. Oh, they're sure to be out !"

" Well, what if they are ?"

" What if they are ? Why, I'm going to introduce them to Henlopen, and show 'em how to trot ; that's all."

" In this rig ?"

" Nothing else. Don't you be afraid ; this isn't as bad a ' rig' as you might think. The harness is a little heavy, but it fits him and he's used to it. The sleigh looks heavy, too, but the runners are hard cast-iron and have

a smooth, glassy surface that does not stick or cling to
stones or sand like the lighter wrought-iron casing of
the modern sleigh.   So, on the whole, we're not so badly
fixed.   Besides, Henlopen is as strong as an elephant."

" But—can he trot ?" asked the girl, incredulously.
" Oh, of course he can !   I might have known," she
added, hastily.

" Trust a Goodwin to know a horse," Hubert answered,
almost bitterly.   "I haven't got a red spur on my heel
for nothing.   Did you think I brought him all the way
from home for his beauty ?"

" I didn't know—you didn't tell me—" apologetically.

" I wanted to surprise you, but—no matter.   Here we
are at the Bay Road, and there's Sedley with his blacks.
Now you'll see some fun.   I hope Parker is somewhere
about ; it will do him a world of good."

" Who is he ?"

" The farmer who looks after Henlopen."

The Bay Road was a lively scene at that moment.
Gay costumes, beautiful equipages and fine horses filled
the broad, gently curving avenue, which was renowned
as the best winter trotting course in the world.   It was
in splendid condition, and the fashion and fancy of the
city were out in force to enjoy it.   Bells tinkled, whips
cracked, shouts and laughter prevailed ; everything
testified to the keen enjoyment of the drivers, spectators,
and even the sleek, finely trained beasts themselves,
from whose flying feet flew backward a hail of beaten
snow under the high-perched sleighs.

A portion of this course was especially reserved for
trials of speed.   On one side of this there was an open
space where both foot-passengers and sleighs might
stand and see the frequently recurring contests, while
on the other side, the stream of gay equipages flowed
steadily on without interrupting the sport.   As if by

accident, Hubert drove into the space reserved for trials of speed, in the very track of a pair of glossy blacks, gayly caparisoned, and attached to a sleigh which, although containing four persons, seemed formed of spider-webs in comparison with the clumsy affair which Henlopen was steadily and unconcernedly dragging along.

A chorus of warnings and objurgations greeted this piece of awkwardness on the part of the supposed countryman.

"Get out of the way !" called out the driver of the blacks, who were just settling down to accept the challenge of a slender limbed chestnut, which had stolen noiselessly up, and now threatened to slip by the champion trotters of the Bay Road.

"Get out of the way !" roared the crowd, anxious to see the trial of speed between the renowned roadsters and their bold challenger.

"Tip him over !"

"Pitch him out !"

"Drive over him !"

"Come out, Country !"

"What have you got to sell ?"

These were some of the cries that greeted the apparently unconscious driver of Henlopen.

"What's the matter?" he asked, looking around in well-assumed surprise. "Want to go by us, mister?" glancing over his shoulder at the driver of the blacks.

"Get out of the way !" was the angry rejoinder.

In an instant, the heads of the blacks were even with the dash-board of the old-fashioned cutter. In another second, the black hoofs were throwing a shower of crisp snow into the cutter, which forced Delia to hide her head under the robe.

"Gee-whillikins !" exclaimed Hubert, snatching

awkwardly at his reins. The crowd laughed at the countryman's comical plight.

"Tsst—tsst—tsst—tsst!" A sharp, broken sibilation came from Hubert's slightly parted lips. The big bay gathered his feet under him ; his driver leaned back, pulling wildly upon the reins ; but the sharp recurring sibilation continued. The trim blacks were already at the bay's head. Then the long ears dropped back upon the neck, the great coarse muzzle was outstretched, and side by side with the crack roadsters, Henlopen, with easy, magnificent strides, swept over the fancy course. The crowd laughed and cheered. Of course, it was only a spurt ; the old bay would break in a moment.

But he did not break. For a while, the mocking cheers were hushed in surprise, only to break out again in genuine admiration. The driver of the blacks loosened the reins and gave his horses a cluck of encouragement. They shrank closer to the ground, and the polished ebon legs flew back and forth as if impelled by electric force. But still the great coarse muzzle held its place, half open now, with two rows of ivory shining between the back-drawn lips, while an angry eye shone over the brown, cracked blinker, which fell backward when the driver pulled the reins.

And how he did pull ! He leaned back in his seat and braced his feet against the front of the sleigh, knocking out, one after another, the baskets, whose contents rolled and scattered about the smooth track, adding by their heterogeneous character very greatly to the amusement of the spectators. Delia nestled her head against her lover's shoulder, to hide her laughter, leaving only a peep-hole underneath the hood through which she could see the sport. Every one took this for evidence of fright, and it added greatly to the realism of the performance.

Still it was counted only a spurt, though such a
remarkable one as to be a good joke on Sedley. But
now the bay began to draw away from the quick-step-
ping blacks. The big horse showed no sign of breaking. The great hoofs rose and fell with the regularity
of a walking-beam. The silky tail, half-raised, swayed
back and forth like a triumphing banner. The mighty
arms and steaming quarters assumed unexpected lines
of beauty. The heads of the blacks fell steadily backward. Now they were opposite the dashboard ! Soon
the spray of the off one's gleaming nostril fell on the
cheek of the spirited girl, who, sitting bolt upright now,
was gazing with rapt admiration at the splendid action
of the horse before her. The countryman, with his
white hat pushed back upon his head, held the reins
steadily, while from his lips came now and then the
keen, encouraging sibilation :

" Tsst—tsst—tsst—tsst !"

The driver of the blacks plied the whip. One of them
broke, and for an instant they passed the bay's quarter
and lapped his shoulder. The great muzzle went lower,
the black eyes flashed more wickedly, the great white
teeth snapped angrily together, and the blacks fell back
again—past the sleigh !—a length !—another !

Then the waiting multitude awoke to the fact that
they had seen a remarkable performance—a wonderful
horse, who, coming out of obscurity, had distanced at
the very first trial the best of all known competitors.
They cheered the big bay and his driver as they flew
past, and continued cheering until they passed the
second mile-post and disappeared beyond the limits of
the drive, going on down the Bay Road toward the
country. The crowd stared after them in amazement.
The owners of fancy-steppers walked their smoking
steeds back and forth and talked of the remarkable

event. It is not often that an attempted surprise of this kind is a success. In these days, the horses that can do great things are usually known and named, though even now a phenomenon is sometimes found in a butcher's cart. At that day such things were much less infrequent. The reduction of the best time made by a trotting-team from two minutes thirty-six seconds to two minutes fourteen seconds makes an amazing difference in the conditions of what is termed a " flam " of that sort.

" Who is he ?" asked the driver of the blacks in an irritated tone, as he drew in his team at the end of the accustomed course.

" Ask me something easy," said one whose rig showed him to be familiar with such matters. " I thought I knew every horse and horseman in these parts, but I don't either of them."

" Better telegraph and find out, Colonel," said another, not unwilling to jeer the beaten horseman.

" Pretty good horse that, Sedley," said the driver of the chestnut, who had fallen out of the race as soon as he saw the struggle begin with the countryman.

" Good !" exclaimed Sedley, half-angrily ; " he's the best horse that ever struck a hoof on the Bay Road. Why, he went away from me as if I were standing still ; and the blacks were going at better than a two-forty clip, too. It's my opinion the time of that horse hasn't been beaten on any track—not often, anyhow."

" The girl was mighty scared."

" Scared ? Not much. She was just enjoying it."

" Well, she'd good reason to ; no other woman ever rode two miles in as short time."

" Who'd have thought that old countryman would prove such a Tartar ?"

" Countryman ! There isn't a better driver than he

ever pulled strings on the Bay Road," said Sedley, irritably. "It's some professional who has made a guy of himself and the girl just to put up a job on us."

"You must admit he did it well ; sold you out clean and fair."

"So he did," admitted Sedley, with a laugh.

"Want to try it again, Colonel?"

"No ; I'm satisfied. But where'd he get that horse?"

"Like to buy him, perhaps?"

"That depends. But if he's not too old and is sound, he's worth a lot of money."

"Suppose he was about seven now," said a pleasant-faced man with a bit of gray whisker under his chin, who stood beside the railing.

"Seven? He's fifteen if he's a day," said the driver of the chestnut. "I saw him when he came on the track."

"So did I," responded Sedley ; "and when he went off, too !"

"I thought you were out of sight, then !"

"Oh, no ! I was near enough to see that he wasn't half as old as when he came on—and I tell you if that horse is under ten and sound, he's worth more than any two that ever trotted on the Bay Road."

"How much did you give for the blacks, Colonel?" asked one of his friends, quizzingly.

"No matter ; I stand by what I say."

The man with the gray whiskers under his chin turned away with a smile upon his face, and took his seat beside a girl with bright black eyes and glowing cheeks who sat in a sleigh a little way off.

"Oh, papa !" exclaimed the girl, trembling with excitement, "wasn't it splendid !"

"Don't say a word, Kitty, or I shall explode !"

Twenty minutes afterward, Farmer Parker drove

into his barn, where Hubert was rubbing down the big bay, the whole family,.with Delia added to their number, standing by. The story of the race had already been told, but Farmer Parker, after throwing himself upon a pile of hay and giving vent to his long-repressed laughter, had to tell it over again with many interruptions and much uproarious mirth.

"You are Miss Kincaid, I suppose ?" said the black-eyed girl, approaching Delia and offering her hand. "I am Kitty Parker ; Mr. Goodwin is too busy to introduce us, but I know all about you. I've ridden after Henlopen over the Bay Road many a time—after dark, you know—and just envied you to-day."

Delia Kincaid felt an instinctive heart-twinge as she gazed at the pretty girl beside her, and wondered if there had been any other attraction for her Jack at Farmer Parker's besides Henlopen, during the months when he had been so assiduous in his attention to his favorite.

Naturally enough the facts in regard to the affair on the Bay Road leaked out, and people were greatly scandalized that a pupil of the Brainerd Classical Institute and a student of the Theological seminary should be mixed up in such an escapade. Just what there was about the matter to render it discreditable, it would be difficult to say ; but the faculties of both institutions were greatly disturbed by it. Delia was sharply censured for her conduct, despite the fact that the principal of the institute had assented to the masquerade. and was informed that her previously immaculate record, on which her hope of receiving the first honor at commencement depended had received a serious stain. Hubert was notified, in terms more vigorous than polite, that for the sake of the good name of the institution, the principal was compelled to request him to abstain from visiting the institute or communicating with any of its inmates in the future. In a letter stained with her tears, Delia Kincaid begged him for her sake to comply with this harsh request. She was still determined to win the first honor of her class. " I could not meet my father and mother if I should fail of that," she wrote. " They have dreamed of it every day since I entered the Institute."

Hubert was called before the faculty of the seminary also, some of the members of which were seriously shocked that he manifested no regret for his conduct, and refused to admit that it was in any degree reprehensible. Some proposed his expulsion, others his suspension ; but as he had violated no rule of the institution, and as his competitors on the Bay Road had been Deacon Sedley, one of the most prominent members of the church, and a very liberal patron of the seminary, there seemed a sort of inconsistency in disciplining the theologian for what was not blamable in the deacon. The matter was all the more difficult from the fact that the young man's conduct had been in other respects irreproachable. He was not at all "fast." He had entered the seminary from a sense of duty merely. He did not claim to have either a "call" or an inclination for the ministerial profession, but was there in fulfillment of a promise made to a dying father. The horse was his own, and there seemed to be no good reason why he should not use his hours of relaxation to enhance the value of his own property. Indeed, the president bluntly asserted that it would be a good thing if some of the other students employed their leisure in as healthy and profitable ways. The lady who was with him at the time was his promised wife, and the harmless masquerade was fully understood and approved of by the principal of the school she was attending.

There seemed, indeed, to be "Nothing morally wrong about Mr. Goodwin's conduct," the president shrewdly said, in summing up the matter, "except that his horse was a better one than Deacon Sedley's." The president was not only a sagacious man, but liked a good horse himself, and facetiously remarked that he did not think there would be any serious objections to Mr. Goodwin's driving on the Bay Road every Saturday, if he took one of the faculty with him now and then.

When next Henlopen appeared on the Bay Road, President Neuman sat beside the driver. There were several brushes, and the big bay easily kept the place he had won on his *debut.*

"What are you going to do with him?" asked the president, as they drove home one day, some weeks later, after a very pleasant outing.

"Sell him."

"What do you consider him worth?"

"That depends upon his record."

"How fast he will go, you mean?"

"Yes; an official record of time actually made upon a public track."

"He has never been timed, I think you told me?"

"Well, he has never made a record."

"What do you think he will do?"

"A good deal better than you have seen him."

"Have you had any offers for him?"

"Colonel Sedley has made a bid for him on condition that he beats two twenty-four."

"Do you think he can do it?"

"I would not have accepted it if I had not thought so."

"When will the trial come off?"

"Some time in the spring."

"Will it be public or private?"

" Private—for Colonel Sedley's satisfaction only."
" I should like to see it."
" You can ; I have a right to have one friend on the stand, and you shall be that one, if you like."
" Well, we will see about it when the time comes," laughed the president.

From that hour Hubert Goodwin felt that he had a friend in Dr. Neuman, and there was no lack of interest on his part in the studies of the seminary. The principal of the Brainerd Institute modified her order of exclusion after learning that the young man was so staunchly supported by the president, and he visited his betrothed once a fortnight during the pleasant months that followed, while Destiny was silently shaping for him the web of an adverse fate.

CHAPTER X.

"THE CALL."

Hubert Goodwin heard at length the "call" for which he had waited. In one instant all thought of hesitation and indecision vanished. War had broken out! The sound of battle echoed through the Sabbath stillness! The Confederate forces had opened fire on Fort Sumter! At the first thrill which followed, he knew that there was an end of doubt. He had found, if not his vocation, at least his duty. He would be a soldier. He did not stop to ask questions. He solicited no one's advice ; he did not need advice. His whole nature was aflame. There was no questioning whether war were right or wrong. His logic was strangely

elliptical.   The defense of the flag—the maintenance of
the Union—such a cause must be right.   Behind it, too,
was the thought of liberty.   The Confederacy represented slavery ; that was its corner-stone, one of its cham-
pions had said, and slavery was wrong—must be
wrong—so Hubert Goodwin thought, or felt, rather.

He did not reason very profoundly about the matter.
He did not know how the question presented itself to
the Southern man ; perhaps he did not care very
much.   When the moment for action comes, the time
for argument is past.   He did not doubt that the South
was wrong, any more than they who mustered under
her banner doubted that she was right.   He was ready
to fight for liberty and union—the union his fathers had
established and the liberty he had been taught to
believe the holiest gift of. God.   He was all the more
ardent because it was not his own liberty, nor the liberty of his kindred, but of a despised and feeble race
who had been for centuries the buffeted foot-ball of
Fate.   The knightly impulse is hidden in every uncor-
rupted nature, and the love of self-sacrifice lies side by
side with the love of strife and glory, in every manly
heart.

Besides this, Hubert Goodwin came of manful stock.
The spirit of Theophilus had not diluted the blood of
Sir Harry.   How the mark upon his heel burned at the
thought of conflict !   The tumult of Naseby and Pres-
ton Pans was in his veins !   The Puritan would stand
once more against the cavalier !   New entries in the
long accounting between right and wrong would be
made in blood.   And he would feel the shock of battle !
He knew now it was of this that he had dreamed
through all the peaceful years of youth.   Would war be
as his fancy had painted it ?   No matter ; the worse it
might be, the better !   His whole nature panted with

exultation. He burned to do, to suffer, to achieve, to
endure—to die if need be! It was for his country, he
said—his country and his God!

Those upon the other side said the same thing. Two
moieties of a great people prayed to the same God that
Sabbath morning—the first of a new epoch—for victory
—the one with the bells of initial triumph clanging in
their ears, the other with the presage of a primal defeat
impending over their prescient consciousness.

There were hushed tones and solemn faces when the
students of the seminary met in the chapel that Sabbath
morning for prayer. These young men, who had dedicated themselves to the Master's service, were looking,
awed and trembling, upon the opening scene of one of
those great passion-plays of history by which the Most
Holy teaches to the world the highest truths. But
Hubert Goodwin was content—flushed and silent, but
peaceful; one might say happy, but for the seeming
harshness. Doubt was gone; duty was clear; danger
he did not count. The venerable president, despite the
agony that rung his own soul, marked the demeanor of
the young man, in whom he had come to take a peculiar
interest, with some curiosity.

" Well, Goodwin," he asked, as he returned the student's greeting and walked beside him along the
strangely hushed and resonant corridor, " what do you
think of this?"

" I guess I have got my ' call,' sir," the young man
answered, in a tone from which he could not keep back
the exultation which he felt.

" Perhaps you are right," said the old man, a faint
flush rising to his cheeks. As he looked into the flashing eyes, he wished that he might lay aside the burden
of years and feel the fervid glow and hot, fierce love of
peril and adventure which showed in the young face.

We are all born fighters, with the clamor of a thousand battle-fields echoing in our ears when the trumpet calls to strife. Nevertheless, he counseled prudence ; but the young man's lip curled in scorn.

How war quickens a people's pulses ! Before another day had elapsed the streets were echoing with the tread of mustering legions. Hubert Goodwin did not believe it was to be a holiday excursion, and felt that he must bid adieu to his old life before he began a new one. He must write to his mother ; wait until he had heard from his uncle ; say good-bye to his sweetheart, and conclude the sale of his horse. It would not require many days, but his heart ached when he saw the first company rushed on board the cars and hurried away to receive their equipments and fly to the defense of the beleagured capital.

Those were busy days. How full of life ! Years were crowded betwixt sun and sun. Yet he did nothing. The dust gathered on his books. He could not listen to lectures. He did not study ; he did not think. He only tramped the streets and felt. Once he went to the Brainerd Institute. Delia was trembling, fearful, awed. They talked of commonplaces ; wondered if there would be war. He said nothing of himself, and she intimated nothing of what she feared. He wrote to his mother a brief, unsatisfactory letter, not to ask her permission, but to announce his determination. He knew the letter had been received, for a telegram had come from his uncle :

" Hold on ; do nothing until you hear from me again."

What did it mean ? Did they think to keep him until the war was over ? If it were to be so brief he did not care to go ; but believing it to be long, he was all the

more anxious to begin to do his part. He had heard the
"call" and was ready to answer. He wondered what
his father would have said could he have foreseen this
time. He did not question what he would say if alive.

He met Sedley one day upon the street. The colonel
was very busy. He had been in the army in his young
days—was a graduate of West Point. He was hardly
too old for the service, but the demands of a great business prevented him from going to the front at once. But
he gave his time to the work of organizing—time and
money.

"I cannot go," he said to Hubert; "at least not yet.
It would take months to get my business in shape to
leave it. If it keeps on, I shall have to go, I suppose.
Doctor Neuman tells me you intend to enlist. There
will be no difficulty in your getting a commission, I
suppose?"

Hubert said he did not expect one.

"But you ought to have one. It is such men as you,
young, intelligent, resolute, who ought to constitute the
subalterns of our army. You think you have not
experience? You will get it fast enough. The field-
officers should have experience, of course—old army
men, so far as we can get them; but young men,
enthusiastic, clear-headed, ambitious, should have the
companies. That's my idea—no politicians—no drones.

"I have just applied for permission to raise a cavalry
regiment—myself and a few others—at our own expense,
you know. You see, there is no cavalry called for—
only infantry and artillery. It is all folly. An army
without cavalry is blind and deaf. It cannot help but
meet defeat, because its commander knows nothing
about where he is going or what he has to meet. I used
to be in the cavalry—the dragoons, you know. Jeff
Davis had a troop in the same regiment; that was before

my time, though. I've picked out a man to command it—an old West Pointer ; best man in my class, though he hasn't got on very well—so far as rank is concerned. No chance for a man to show himself in our army, except with the Indians, and that don't count.

" How about our trade ? Woodrow tells me the horse is as sound as a nut and in prime condition. Under seven, too, he says, though I'd swear he was twelve, at least. Thinks he'll fill the bill, too, but I don't. There aren't two horses in the country that can reliably trot under two twenty-four. The little mare is said to have beat twenty somewhere out West last year ; but that was a scratch. There's talk about the track being short, too. She's a marvel, anyhow, but she'll never do it again. The war will spoil sport, of course, but if the bay can come to time he's worth the money, war or no war.

"When can we have the trial ? Any time? How'll to-morrow afternoon do—say about four o'clock—if it's fair ? All right ! That's settled, then. O, by the way, who's your man ? Doctor Neuman ? All right again ; no harm in it, as there is to be no betting in it and no record. By the way, I'd like to have it understood that the time is to be a secret ; if he wins, that is. If he loses, of course you don't want it known. Woodrow's as silent as the grave. You might caution the doctor. I suppose you'll drive yourself ?"

" I'd rather Woodrow did, sir."

"Well, that's satisfactory. He'll do the fair thing. Nobody ever accused him of any crookedness. I'll take Jones ; he's the regular 'starter,' anyhow, and knows how to keep still."

When Hubert returned to his room, after this con-versation, he found a dispatch from his uncle awaiting him :

" Don't join elsewhere. The governor will send you a commission as lieutenant."

It was a complete surprise. A lieutenant! It was an honor, a privilege greater than he had expected. He was glad he had talked with Colonel Sedley. He showed the dispatch to Doctor Neuman as they drove out to the course next day.

Colonel Sedley was late, owing to numerous and exacting engagements. The president was full of the new honor that had been conferred upon his pupil, and lost no time in mentioning it. The colonel congratulated the young man heartily.

It was a warm spring afternoon. Woodrow announced the track to be in fine order. Watches were compared as the big bay was jogged back and forth and finally given a breather around the course. The little group of men upon the judge's stand commented upon his action and jested about the result. A few spectators strolled in and watched the proceedings curiously. A group of boys, with the gamin's instinct for the unusual, clambered about the empty benches.

" When do you expect to leave, Lieutenant ?" asked Sedley, to pass the time while they waited. Already the war filled all the intervals of life.

Hubert flushed at this first sound of the new title on another's lips, but answered as quietly as he could :

" As soon as my commission arrives."

" That's right. Better have your uniform made while you wait. It's well to be ready for duty when you report ; makes a good impression on your superiors, you know. I brought a check so that our matter can be settled up in a second, if the horse comes under the wire in time. I'm satisfied as to his age and soundness. Here it is, doctor. I put it in your hands. If he makes a mile in two twenty-four you will give that check to the lieutenant and I will take the horse. Here they come! Heavens, what a stride!"

The big bay was coming down the home-stretch with an even, steady stroke which fully justified the admiration of the prospective purchaser. As they neared the wire Woodrow nodded to the starter, and just as the dark muzzle lapped the mark Jones shouted "Go!" Three pairs of eyes noted the time, and were lifted now and then to watch the progress made.

"The fastest half ever made without a break!" said Jones, as they passed the stand again. The others stood silent in admiration and expectancy. The seconds crept by, and the horse entered on the last quarter.

"A great performance!" whispered Sedley, excitedly, to the starter.

" Pity it will not be a record," was the regretful reply.

"Time enough for that," said the buyer, contentedly.

Down the homestretch came Henlopen, swifter than before. The driver urged him, but he did not break. Under the wire he flashed as if shot from a catapult.

Three fingers touched the springs, and the starter, pale with excitement, whispered the time.

"Gentlemen," called out Woodrow from the track below as he turned back and walked beside the steaming horse to the stand, "that's the fastest mile I ever rode!"

"And the fastest anybody ever rode!" said Jones, excitedly.

"What!"

The veteran driver tossed the reins to an attendant, scrambled over the railing, and ran up the steps into the stand.

"What was the time?" he asked.

The gamins and the few spectators were gathering around, eager to learn the result.

" Take care," whispered Sedley, with a glance toward these seekers for knowledge.

The starter whispered to the driver.

"What! It can't be ! Why wasn't it a record?"

" Never mind ; you shall drive him when he beats it," Sedley hastened to say.

" He'll never beat it, Colonel," said the old horseman, sadly. " No horse ever will. And nobody would believe it if you told it. Oh, if it had only been a record !"

" Will you please let us know the time ?" called out one of a group of spectators, who were discussing the performance a little way off.

" It was under two twenty-four," answered Sedley evasively.

" Thank you. My friend, here," pointing to one who held a watch in his hand, "has been offering to bet that it was under two-ten, but, of course, we knew that could not be."

"O Lord, if it had only been a record !" moaned Woodrow. " It would be worth everything to be able to tell of that, and have it official, you know. I'd have it put on my tombstone—I would I vow !"

" I suppose I'm to give this to Mr. Goodwin, then ?" said Doctor Neuman, holding up the check inquiringly.

"Certainly. Haven't you delivered it yet? Give it to him, quick, before he backs out," said Sedley glee-fully. " I'm sorry for you, Lieutenant," he added, as Hubert took the bit of paper, " but that horse is worth double the money I paid for him, this very minute."

" Not a doubt of it," interrupted Jones.

Doctor Neuman looked from one to the other, wonderingly. "Do you know, gentlemen," he said, with impressive simplicity, "that check represents more money than I ever earned in ten years."

Hubert Goodwin felt very rich as he folded the check and put it in his pocket. There was more conversation, reminiscent and speculative. Other horses were discussed, and the career of the new marvel—what horses he would have to meet and what events he might be entered for. The sun was getting low when they started to go down the stairs. It had been a very exciting affair, and each one congratulated himself upon his good fortune in having witnessed the race.

The attendant who had been walking Henlopen up and down the track, now called to Woodrow. The driver climbed down from the stand and approached the horse's head, where the attendant was standing. The loiterers had moved away, and the little company followed slowly, going around the end of the stand.

"Mr. Sedley, will you please step here a moment?"

There was no mistaking the anxiety in Woodrow's voice. They walked quickly down the track to where he stood. With his left hand he lifted up the great brown muzzle, while with the right one he drew back the inflexible cap of the left nostril, showing the red, glistening membrane within.

"What is it?" asked Sedley, looking down at the dark spot on the track under the horse's head.

"Do you see that?" said Woodrow, nodding toward the horse's nose.

A little red stream was trickling down the membrane and through the stiff short hairs of the upper lip. Henlopen thrust out his tongue now and then to lick off the falling drops. While they looked he shook his head and coughed, scattering bright fresh blood drops upon them.

" Hemorrhage ?" inquired Sedley.

Woodrow nodded affirmatively.

" When did it come on ?" Sedley asked the attendant.

"Just a minute ago," was the reply. "I gave him a sup of water. He coughed, and then I noticed this."

" Might have been bleeding for half an hour, I suppose."

" No, sir. We have sponged his nose and mouth three or four times since the heat was over, and there wasn't a trace of blood till that moment."

" Any chance for him ?" to Woodrow.

The trainer shook his head sadly :

" It is red blood, you observe."

He wiped his hands upon the horse's mane as he spoke.

" I see—an artery."

Woodrow signed to the attendant to remove the sulky and harness. Hubert placed his ear at the horse's chest. He heard a curious gurgling sound.

" Poor old fellow !" he said, putting his arm over the drooping neck and caressing tenderly the broad forehead. The horse gave a low neigh of recognition and coughed again. Instantly a red stream burst from his nostrils. He raised his head and gazed from one to another with an almost human look of startled inquiry. All the little company, except Hubert, sprang back to avoid the red torrent that spouted from the black, quivering muzzle.

" Poor fellow !" said Hubert again, still clasping the neck and patting the upraised head. With a sharp neigh of alarm, the horse rubbed the side of his head against the young man's breast, as if begging for aid. His breath came chokingly. His mouth opened, and the blood gushed from it also. His neighing became one choking shriek for help. He kept turning toward his master, as if imploring him to give relief. The great brown eyes were full of agonized entreaty. Hubert moved backward to avoid the stream of blood, still holding the neck, stroking the outstretched head, and speaking tenderly to the doomed beast.

His voice choked, and there were tears in his eyes. The others wept, too—all but Sedley. He stood dry-eyed, indeed, but with his firm jaws set and a look upon his face that attested the emotion which he felt. Wheeling round and round in the vain endeavor to confront the one whom he had learned to love and to whom he turned instinctively in mute entreaty for aid, the streaming blood from the horse's mouth described a red circle partly on the white graveled track and partly on the fresh-springing grass beside it. He moved slower and slower every moment, while his neighing sank at length to a faint moan. He began to paw, but only with his off-foot, as if even in death he remembered not to harm the master he loved. A shiver went through his limbs. His body swayed back and forth.

" Look out !" cried Woodrow.

Hubert did not heed this warning, but kept his clasp upon the quivering neck and strove to hold up the drooping head. There was a long, low moan of mortal agony ; the head was turned suddenly, the great nostrils distended ; the brown eyes looked into the brimming ones beside them. The trembling limbs slowly gave way and the vast hulk sank slowly and easily to the ground. Hubert laid the brown head tenderly upon the green turf—there was a sob—a tremor of the mighty limbs, and the great horse was dead.

Hubert rose and brushed the blood from the sleeve of his coat, turning shamefacedly away to hide his tears. The others regarded him with that kindly commiseration we bestow upon those who stand by the death-bed of friends.

"He was a good one," said Woodrow, speaking of the dead. It was the highest praise the old trainer could give.

"He deserves a monument," said Sedley, "and he shall have one, too—right here beside the track where he died."

Hubert answered with a grateful look. He could not trust his voice. The great, homely bay had grown much dearer to him than he thought. He recalled his virtues, which had been regarded as a matter of course while he lived—his steadiness, kindness and sagacity, as well as his amazing fortitude and determination.

"'We ne'er shall look upon his like again,'" said Jones, with an attempt at levity.

"It is strange," said Doctor Neuman, solemnly. "He seemed to know his end was approaching almost as well as if he had been human."

Hubert walked back toward the stand to conceal his emotion. The others stood a moment in the soft, spring sunset gazing on the stiffening limbs of the great horse who had died in the very hour when he had outdone all his race, but whose name would never appear among the list of those who have triumphed on the track which was moistened with his blood. Then they started toward the sheds where their horses stood.

"Well, Lieutenant," said Sedley, cheerfully, as they overtook the young man, who walked on with them, "I'm sorry now we didn't let the big horse make a record. It seems that you were the one that was in luck, after all ; though I did think I was getting him cheap. There are not many who win on such a narrow margin as that."

He gazed keenly at the young man as he spoke.

"I hope you do not think—" began Hubert, confusedly.

"Oh, that's all right," interrupted Sedley. "He's my horse just as much as if he had died of old age. He was worth the money when I bought him, and more, too. All the same, you are lucky. The doctor here, don't believe in luck ; I do. It's worth everything to a man in this world, too. Some have it and others don't ; and some have it for a time and then lose it. Some win with all the chances against them—against their own expectations even ; others will lose with ninety-nine clear chances in their favor, though they exercise the utmost prudence and caution. There's no accounting for luck ; and you've got it, no mistake about that. You'd have been expelled from the seminary for your escapade last winter if it hadn't been for your luck. Instead of that, here's the doctor come with you to see you win on a dead horse. He would have expelled any one else for proposing such a thing. From what he tells me I find it isn't the first time your luck has served you well. There's nothing like it, and there's no sense in trying to give any reason for it. I don't blame you ; I just envy you. I'm probably better able to lose what I paid than you the price of an ordinary horse. I've had pretty fair luck myself, but I envy yours. You are not only lucky, but every one believes in your luck—expects you to succeed, don't you see. Be grateful for it, young man, but don't abuse it. Let it cover mistakes, but don't strain it by advertising for impossibilities. If you ever want a partner—especially in anything connected with a horse—just let me know. I'd stake a good deal on your judgment, and a lot more on your luck. Good-bye. I expect to see you come out of the war with a star on your shoulder. It's a great chance for a man with your luck."

" Mr. Sedley—I—I wish you would take this back,"
said Hubert, taking the check from his pocket.

"Young man," responded the sturdy capitalist, with
some show of anger, "don't be foolish. More people
spoil their luck in that way than in any other. Take
what belongs to you without stopping to consider
whether the man who loses is sorry he risked or not. If
the horse had lived, I should have doubled my money
and not given a thought to the chance you lost. The
money is yours ; do what you choose with it, but don't
think of returning it to me. That is not only folly, it is
almost an insult. There is one thing you can do to
oblige me : keep the matter still for the present—the
time he made, I mean. I don't care to have people
pitying me. Come on, Jones."

The colonel strode stiffly away without further adieu.

It was a very silent ride back over the paved streets in
the echoing twilight, to Doctor Neuman and his pupil.
The day's experience had been a rare one to the good
divine. He had seen a side of life with which he had
no little sympathy, but at which he could not but
wonder. He was not only fond of a good horse, but he
liked also brave, adventurous men—men who could win
or lose with equanimity. He had always wanted to see
a race, but regard for his profession had kept him
away from the track ; and now he had witnessed an
event sure to be among the most memorable in the
annals of the turf, though it would be but a tradition—
a tradition like that of Flying Childer's yet unrivaled
achievement. Only half a dozen pairs of eyes, it is said,
watched that marvel of equine tradition. One of them,
he had read somewhere, belonged to a dignitary of the
church. For a hundred years nobody doubted the
great racer's achievement, or, at least, dared express a

doubt. Since then nobody has believed it. Would it be the same with the marvel he had witnessed?

He had been taught that day to use a stop-watch. He had held one of the three by which the time was marked. They all agreed within a fraction of a second. He had held his up for examination by the others before reading the result himself. He had seen both the others. Had his eyes deceived him, and his hand also? He was glad he had witnessed the trial, and glad, also, that the result was to be kept secret. His conscience was easy, too. There had been no betting; not a cent had been staked on the result. Yet the young man beside him had been, if not exactly poor, at the least not rich when they went out; now he had a fortune in his pocket. Was this quite a true statement of the case? When they went out, the young man was the owner of the most valuable horse in the world; the check in his pocket was not more than half as much as the best judges declared the horse to be worth. He had not made a very good sale, after all, though the buyer had nothing to show for his money. The good doctor mentioned this view of the matter to the young man beside him, who answered with a curious incredulity of tone which set the elder man to wondering what his future would be like—what he would do with the money he had received or what it would do with him.

"Will you let me come into the library a moment, doctor?" Hubert asked, as they stopped before the gate.

"Certainly. Will you not stay to supper with us? It must be ready now."

"Thank you; I don't think I can—to-night, I will only detain you a moment."

He fastened the horse and they walked up the path

together, the elder wondering at the younger man's request. Ushering him into the library, he renewed his invitation ; but the other persisted in declining it. Asking permission, he seated himself at the writing-table, dropping his hat upon the floor beside him, and taking the check from his pocket, he indorsed it to the other's order.

" Please use it to help equip the regiment Sedley is raising," he said, raising and handing it to the other.

The doctor put on his glasses, and read the indorsement.

" But—had you not better wait and—think this over ?"

The young man smiled.

The doctor knew it was useless to give advice, but could not help saying :

" This is a great deal ; you are not rich. Can you afford to give so much for—for such a purpose ?"

" But, doctor, I have already offered my life for the cause it will aid."

" True, true, my son," answered the old man. " May God bless you and your gift."

He raised his eyes as he spoke. The young man looked down and twirled his hat in an embarrassed way. Then he stretched out his hand.

" Good-bye," he said.

" We shall see you again ?"

" I am afraid not ; I expect to go to-morrow."

" So soon ? Write me when you can. I have no doubt I shall hear of your success without it, but shall be glad to receive your own report. Good-bye."

When he was gone, the doctor spread out the check and read it again before putting it in his pocket.

" Come," said his wife, from the door, " you know you are expected at the meeting to-night."

"Meeting? What meeting?"

"Why, about the regiment Colonel Sedley is raising."

"Ah, yes; I had forgotten."

The wife smiled. She had been her husband's calendar for years, and was not surprised at his absent-mindedness during the meal which followed.

*   *   *   *   *   *   *

"So Henlopen will never make a record," was Hubert Goodwin's regretful comment, as he told the story of the day's happenings to Delia Kincaid that night, and informed her of the disposition he had made of the check.

"And you gave all that money—to—to—"

"The country," he interrupted, laughingly. "Why not? I may have to give—a great deal more, you know."

The girl shuddered and her cheeks grew pale.

"Don't you think this is enough—as much as you ought to do?"

"Why, Dee! You wouldn't have me stay at home?"

"Oh, Jack, if you only would! Please do! Let us go away—let's go abroad, where we will know nothing of this dreadful war. We might be married and go to-morrow. I will give up the school—anything—if you will. O, Jack! I know I shall lose you! There will never be any happiness for me in the world if you go. You know you promised me, Jack, 'Forever and ever, Amen!' And now you are going away to be shot—to be killed! You are breaking your promise! You do not love me—if you go!"

"Forever and ever, Amen!" What visions the words recalled. All his life he had loved this girl—this woman—who now would persuade him to turn back

from his duty—to be deaf to the "call" he had
received. "Forever and ever, Amen!" The sun shone
through the sheltering leaves, and the sounds of the
summer woods were about him again. He heard the
droning of the wasps, and saw again their nests of tem-
pered mortar beside the rafters in the old home which
was then new. And now she offered him her beauty as
the price for his manhood! His brain reeled.

"But, Dee—" he exclaimed, confusedly, entreatingly.

She broke in passionately, angrily, on his remonstrance:

"Don't talk to me! What do I care for the country?
I want *you*. And you promised me; you know you did.
I know I am not brave. I am tired and sick. I want
to go away—to Italy—Switzerland—Venice! O, Jack,
why can't we go to Venice and dream away the days of
strife? Everybody is not called upon to fight, and you
have done enough. They can get a hundred men with
what you have given."

"I suppose they might—" thoughtfully.

"Of course they can—and we!"

She nestled close to him with rapturous suggestion.

"But every one would call me a coward—"

"Suppose they should?"

"I don't think I could stand that, Dee."

"But it wouldn't be *you*—not your wish, that is, but
mine. You could tell them I was sick. And I am sick,
Jack—oh, *so* sick! You don't know how sick!"

She cast herself upon his breast weeping passionately.
He smoothed her silken curls with a loving hand, and
soothed her, hardly knowing what he did. At length
his face lightened.

"Dee," he exclaimed, eagerly, "I think you *are* sick;
you have been studying too hard. Why not get
married, anyhow?"

"And then?" She did not raise her head.

"You can go with me; officers often take their wives. It will probably be a good while before there is any fighting—before they are ready to fight, I mean."

"No! No! No!" She shook her head and shuddered. "I can't do it! I can't do it! I can't tell you why, either. Only go away—leave the country—and I will go with you to-morrow—to-night—this very minute!"

She raised her head and looked at him with almost frantic appeal.

"And Jack," she continued, "if you do not, you will lose me—we shall lose each other—forever and ever!"

"You would not forget me, Dee?"

"I shall love you always, Jack, always—but—but if you do not consent—oh, I cannot tell you! We shall never be happy again."

"Poor little girl," he said, soothingly; "you are tired to-night. It will seem different to-morrow."

She shook her head, hopelessly.

"Oh, yes, it will; you are nervous and worn-out to-night. I shall tell Miss Brainerd you need a rest, and take you home with me."

"Home!" with a start. "When are you going there?"

"O, in a day or two."

"And you will not go away—with me?"

"Abroad, do you mean?"

She nodded.

"I will—think about it. There's the bell; I must go."

The bell of the Brainerd Institute rang at nine o'clock for the departure of guests, if any chanced to be within its portals at that hour. They were sitting in the private parlor of the principal—a privilege accorded to but few. They knew that lady would enter soon. Delia started

up, hastily smoothing her hair. Her lover caught her in his arms and kissed her passionately

" You will go ? " she entreated.

" O—do not ask me. I cannot promise—just now—at least."

" Then—good-bye !"

She stood on tiptoe, her pale, agonized face upturned for his kisses.

" O, Jack—dear Jack ! Remember, whatever happens —I shall love you ' forever and ever !' "

There was a knock upon the door.

" I am very sorry to disturb you, young people," said the kindly-faced principal, " but the bell has rung. Why, what does this mean ?" as the young girl threw herself upon her teacher's breast, weeping hysterically. " No lover's quarrel, I hope ?"

" She dreads to have me go—into the service—you know,"answered Hubert, stammeringly.

" Poor girl !" said the lady, tenderly patting her pupil's head. " That is part of our woman's lot—to lose those we love."

There was a far-away look in her eyes as she spoke. Hubert bowed himself out, and went back to his lodging with a burdened heart. He found the uniform he had ordered awaiting him and tried it on. The new life it represented quickly chased away the memory of love's tears.

CHAPTER XI.

The newspapers of the day succeeding Henlopen's death contained a curious account of that event. The world of sport was not what it is now, nor was the reporter so absolutely ubiquitous. Not only this, but one great central thought then occupied the public mind, and other events had a singular fictitious value according to their relation to it. The most remote connection with the conflict which was then impending, rather than actually begun, lifted the most trivial matters in the realm of news to a plane of prime importance as compared with matters having no relation to it. Wrecks, accidents, the death of sovereigns, the opening of new gold fields, even scandal fell to a second place in public estimation in comparison with things relating to the progress of the war. It is not strange that the death of Henlopen, an event which would now command universal attention, was then regarded as worthy of mention chiefly because of the circumstances connected with it. These, however, gave it a place on the editorial page, where it appeared the next morning, under the title of

"A MANLY ACT PROMPTLY REWARDED.

" We noted in our issue of yesterday that one of the students of the Theological Seminary had been commissioned a lieutenant. To-day, it is our privilege to record an act of chivalrous generosity on the part of Lieutenant Goodwin, which shows that the governor of his native State made no mistake in conferring upon him that honor. He is known to many of our citizens as having been the owner of the trotting-horse, Henlopen, which played such havoc among the crack turnouts on the Bay Road last winter. At that time an offer of twenty-five thousand dollars was made for the horse by Colonel Sedley, on condition that he should beat two twenty-four. This was accepted, and the big horse has been in training with Woodrow ever since for his match against time. It came off yesterday on the Park Course. It was a private affair, only half a dozen friends being present, and they were sworn to secrecy. The price is said to be the largest, with one exception, perhaps, ever offered for a horse in the United States ; yet it is generally admitted that if able to make the time required, the big bay was well worth it. Woodrow held the reins, and expressed the opinion that the horse could do all that was asked of him, and more too.

" It was nearly five o'clock when he got the word, and those present witnessed a performance they will not soon forget. The mile was trotted without a break. The exact time cannot be given, but it is ascertained that it was several seconds less than has ever been done before or than most horsemen supposed possible. The horse finished the heat in prime condition, and Mr. Sedley handed over the check for the amount agreed on with the utmost cheerfulness.

" Shortly afterward, as the party were leaving the

grounds, they were called back to witness the death of the noble animal which had just won such distinguished honor. While being walked about to cool off, he was startled by a dog which attempted to run across the track, and took three or four of his enormous strides before the driver could bring him down. A moment afterward, it was found that he had burst a blood-vessel, and in a short time he was dead.

"No doubt Colonel Sedley felt some chagrin at having only a dead horse to show for his money, but those who know him do not need to be told that he evinced none. It was an ordinary business risk, and he had lost ; that is the way he looked at it. Lieutenant Goodwin, however, refused to retain the price paid for the horse, and handed the check to President Neuman with a request that the money be applied to the equipment of the regiment of cavalry which Colonel Sedley proposes to raise. The colonel received it on his way to the meeting reported elsewhere, to consider whether our citizens should not join with him in tendering the government a regiment of cavalry, armed, uniformed and mounted ready for the field.

" Colonel Sedley repeated at this meeting his proposition to give $100,000 for the purpose indicated. He understood, he said, that the government had a sufficient supply of sabers of good quality, and he believed the sum named would furnish the uniforms and complete the equipment of the men. He thought it would require $200,000 more to provide the mount and general equipment. As a first subscription toward this, he had received, he said, the sum of $25,000 from a young man who probably had not as much more in the world ; perhaps not half as much ; and who, in addition to this, had already offered his services, and was ready to give his life, if need be, for his country—Lieutenant Hubert Goodwin, of the Theological Seminary.

" After the applause which greeted this announce- ment had died away, he stated in response to calls for Goodwin, that the lieutenant was not present and knew nothing of what was taking place. He had sent a check for the sum named, by Doctor Neuman, whom he had authorized to apply it in this manner. He was, prob- ably, at that moment making preparations to leave the city, to join his regiment.

" This statement aroused the wildest enthusiasm. It was immediately voted to raise the sum required, and subscriptions for the full amount, with pledges for as much more, if necessary, were made in a few minutes. Colonel Sedley stated that a distinguished officer of the regular Army had signified a willingness to accept the command of the regiment, and moved that the meeting request the President to detail him for that duty.

" When this had been adopted, the venerable Doctor Neuman arose, and in a speech of unusual eloquence told the story of young Goodwin's life, and moved that the President be requested to appoint him the lieuten- ant-colonel of the regiment. The proposition took like wildfire, and Doctor Neuman's speech was punctuated with applause. It seems that the young man has not only fighting blood in his veins, but, so to speak, cav- alry blood, also. A distinguished cavalry officer of Cromwell's army and a captain of dragoons who fell at Trenton, were among his ancestors, and the doctor pre- dicted for him a brilliant future.

" Colonel Sedley seconded the motion in the most earnest and emphatic terms. As one having some knowledge of the requirements of the office, he did not hesitate to indorse the doctor's prediction.

" One of Goodwin's classmates pledged himself to

raise a company and go with them himself, if Goodwin received the appointment. There was no dissent, and the proposition was carried with a rush. Colonel Sedley was directed to telegraph the President requesting immediate action in the matter. It was proposed to call the regiment the 'Sedley Legion,' and, despite the colonel's demurrer, the suggestion was unanimously adopted, and we have no doubt the corps will be an honor to the city and the State, as well as to the patriotic citizen whose name it bears. Only the best men will be accepted, and service in its ranks will be an honor any man might covet.

"After the adjournment, it was proposed to serenade the young colonel. The crowd formed in line and marched to the seminary building, the band leading the way. The young man had just donned his lieutenant's uniform, and his astonishment as he listened to Colonel Sedley's statement of what had occurred showed how little he had expected any such recognition of his generous act He was hustled down to make his acknowledgment to the crowd, which he did, or rather tried to do. If his words were somewhat incoherent, the applause was vociferous. He is not a man of striking appearance, but there was something in his demeanor, as he shook hands with this clamorous company of new-found friends, which satisfied every one that no mistake had been made in selecting him for such a responsible position. The Sedley Legion are sure to be proud of the second in command before the war is over. It is expected that Colonel Craft will report for duty in about a week. In the meantime, recruiting will proceed under charge of Colonel Goodwin at the Sedley Block, the large hall of which will be used for drilling."

It is strange how things were done in that first fever heat of war ! The next day was a wild one for Hubert Goodwin ; so were those that followed. He was no longer his own master, but the slave of his good fortune—the servant of the regiment. It was not that he had so much to do ; Sedley and his committee, with a hundred other willing helpers, did much of the work ; but he had to seem to direct, to approve, to encourage to suggest. It was a strange task for one so inexperienced. Fortunately, he had Sedley at his elbow, more fortunately still, others were as inexperienced as himself. A uniform went for a great deal ; a title was a badge of authority then. Courtesy in hearing and promptness in deciding were the chief qualities that were necessary in his new field of duty, and these he had.

He learned afterward that if he had been a trained soldier he probably would not have succeeded as well as he did in his new *rôle*. He would not then have dared attempt what he did not now hesitate to undertake. The new uniform, no longer suitable to his rank, did service with its one row of buttons just as well as if there had been two. He worked night and day, and at high pressure all the time. Everybody wondered at his success. He wondered himself more than any one else. He knew that the days seemed years, but he felt that the " call " for which he had been waiting had come—he had found what there was for him to do.

Saturday came, and with it the colonel ; a sturdy, chestnut-bearded man, beginning to show gray threads among his close-cropped hair. Hubert was ready to report. Seven troops were complete, the others nearly so ; the ranks of the Legion would be full before Monday night. Sedley reported that he would have the camp ready by Wednesday. It was to be on the racecourse where Henlopen was buried.

The colonel commended what had been done. He wondered, indeed, that so much had been accomplished in so short a time. It is not strange. The civilian always excels the soldier in the preliminary work of organization ; he is not hampered by habitual fear of disapproval. But the time was ripe for the military mind to assume control. There were men enough ; they must be transformed into soldiers. Drill, discipline, subordination, confidence in things unseen, these things must be taught the ardent recruits. The colonel's eyes flashed with pleasant anticipation as he contemplated the task. He had hardly expected ever to hold so important a command. A regiment of cavalry ! It had been the dream of his life ! He would make it the best in the service. Sedley promised that he would attend to the equipment, and Hubert rejoiced at an opportunity to learn the duties of his new station under one of the brightest examples the time afforded. It was with a sigh of relief that he laid aside the responsibility of command and assumed the station of a subordinate.

Relieved of the burdens which had been so suddenly cast upon him, Hubert Goodwin returned to his old room in the seminary building to take a final leave of his old life. He had not visited it for a whole week. It seemed as if a lifetime had elapsed since he crossed its threshold. How shrunken and unfamiliar it looked—as if he had gone back into some other state of existence ! A heap of letters lay upon the table. He smiled as he thought of the contrast with the formidable official missives to which he had become accustomed during those eventful days. It was curious that what he had done appeared as nothing to him now, yet a week before it would have seemed impossible. He did not feel tired exactly ; he felt old. He was a new man ; the one who had occupied that room a week before was dead—buried under a new life.

He had not forgotten the old life, however. Every day he had sent a brief note to Delia, telling how hurried he was, and promising to come and see her on Saturday. And now Saturday was here, and he suddenly remembered that he had neither seen her nor heard anything from her. What did it mean ? Many ladies had called at the headquarters. Even Kitty Parker had come to congratulate him on his new title, and condole with him on the sad fate of Henlopen. It was strange she had not written. He had not thought she would carry her opposition to his enlistment to such lengths. He would soon cure her of that, he said to himself with quiet confidence. Perhaps—he caught his breath, and a flush of rapture lighted up his face as the thought flashed through his mind—perhaps he might even persuade her to redeem her oft-repeated pledge and become his " forever and ever " before he marched away into the vortex of war.

How sweet the quaint words of the child-betrothal seemed as his lips whispered them ! He was sure she would see that they need not wait longer ; that she ought to be his wife before he went out to battle. Why not go home and be married at once? He could get a week, perhaps two. It would be a short honeymoon, but at such times love must stand in abeyance. Duty is the soldier's watchword, and he was a soldier. He felt that the transition was complete. The red spur on his heel burned hotly, but its glow gave him only pleasure. He was a son of Old Harry now ; and Theophilus ? Pshaw ! What did he care for doom or dole ?

He picked up the letters. The first was directed in his uncle's hand. He laid the others down, and opened it with a smile. A flush of pleasure came to his face as he read the hearty congratulations, and the smile deepened as he found that his future was to be linked with another horse—one of proud enough descent to be worthy of his high destiny. He wondered if the glare of battle would bring him closer still to that noble beast with whom his fate seemed to be irrevocably linked.

"It's a pity about the big bay," wrote Horace Goodwin, "I always knew he was a good one, though I can't quite believe he did a mile in the time you mention. You did just right about the money, and deserve the luck it brought—every bit of it. Come and see us before you go. Your mother is dying to show you off, and we are all very proud of you. I am sorry your regiment is not from this State, but, of course, you couldn't miss such a chance as that. I am very busy helping raise and equip troops. If it was not for your mother and the babies I should have to go, too. I know how you feel, for the old mark burns like fire every time I think of it.

"Now that you are going in the cavalry, you will want a horse that will be a credit to the regiment, and I have decided to let you have Damon, out of Queen, by Gray Eagle—five years old, with all the good qualities of both stocks. You can hardly imagine how he has come out since you saw him. You know he has the lofty crest and proud carriage of the Eagle, with the soft, seal-brown coat and silver mane and tail of old Diomed. He has even that curious mark that comes out now and then on one of that grand old horse's progeny, and never yet seen where his blood was absent— a white spot as big as a dime, an inch above the crown of the right hoof. He is the very ideal of an officer's horse—proud, bold, full of fire and determination, and as tough as a whip-cord. If you go to Virginia, you will probably find a good many who will recognize him as a descendant of one of the proudest sires of the Old Dominion. If he has any fault of form, it is that he is a little too long bodied—if that is a fault. I am inclined to think it an excellence. He gets it through the Belmont Mare—all her descendants have it. You won't find anything that will outshine or outstep or outlast him, though, North or South. That's my notion at least.

"Susan and I had planned to make Delia a present of the colt on her wedding day—he is so fine under the saddle, you know—but we feel sure she would not want him, under the circumstances. Poor girl! How does she bear her trouble? It must be terrible to one so high-spirited. Everybody had a sort of distrust of Kincaid, but no one thought he was such a rascal. It would probably never have come out if it had not been for that whelp, Marvin. It seems he has been bleeding Kincaid for years on account of some connection with that old gang of horse-thieves. Marsh got tired of paying, and the scamp threatened to blow on him—did begin to let out hints of what he could tell—and the first thing anybody knew, Kincaid was gone. He left a power of attorney with Kendall, to sell everything and send him the money. His wife followed him two or three days afterward. I don't think he had done anything very bad—probably getting me shot was the worst—and, if he had, it was outlawed ; but he has been getting proud and trying to be respectable of late years, and was so fond of Deely that he couldn't stand it to meet disgrace. So he broke and run. I'm inclined to think it the best thing he could do. I don't suppose Dee will want to come back here now—though everybody would be just as kind to her as ever ; but if you don't marry her and keep her with you until you are ordered to the front, you're not the man I take you to be. After that, if she will come and stay with us while you are gone, we will give her just as warm a place as there is in our hearts.

"Some pretend to think that Marsh has gone South, but I don't believe it. It's my notion he'll turn up somewhere with the army. He's got plenty of money and is just the kind of a man to make it count at such a time. You might keep an eye out for him."

What did it mean? What had Delia suffered while he had been so happy? He glanced hastily over the other letters—all but one at the bottom of the pile, directed in her familiar hand to "Mr." J. H. Goodwin. She had not learned of his preferment then—or was she angry? She did not know how thoroughly "Jack" had been expunged ; even the initial was gone now. His commission was addressed to "Hubert" Goodwin, and as such he had been mustered in. He had eliminated even the suggestion of that name whose grotesque equivalent his love had chosen for a pet name. No one else would ever call him that again. He tore it open hastily. It was dated the very night he had seen her last :

"JACK : I couldn't tell you what you will probably know before you read this. I wanted to go away—to hide from it, but you would not. You were right. My place is not with you, but with those who suffer shame. I shall go to them before you are awake to-morrow. Do not try to follow or find me. If the time ever comes when I can be your wife without stain to your good name, I will let you know. I will write—sometimes, and, wherever I am, will read the *Standard.* If you insert an advertisement 'To Dee,' I shall see it and will answer it, if—if I can. I shall love you 'forever and ever.'   DEE."

While he had been so busy about other things his love had fled out of his life ! How barren his honors seemed now that he had lost her ! All else was ashes ! But he had hope. He hastened to the Brainerd Institute and learned nothing more than he already knew.

He sat down and wrote an advertisement, which he sent to the office of the *Standard*.

" To DEE : I shall wait 'forever and ever !'
." JACK."

It did not seem an extravagant statement, though the advertising clerk smiled incredulously when he read it.

He enclosed a bank-note to pay for the advertising, and asked that whatever remained might be credited to " Jack."

Then he went out and walked the streets until nearly night, trying to decide what he ought to do, and finally doing the very thing he ought not to have done. He went to see Kitty Parker.

Perhaps what afterward happened would have happened anyhow, but it is a dangerous thing for a man to seek the presence of one attractive woman when his heart is sore, even though it be full to bursting, with love for another. And Kitty Parker was not only a pretty girl, but bright and intelligent, too, and had unfortunately a very tender regard for Colonel Hubert Goodwin—a regard that antedated by many months that officer's commission.

The month which followed was called by Colonel Craft a month of idleness. It was that rugged veteran's belief that the best way to make soldiers out of raw levies was to set them at once to doing a soldier's duty —marching and fighting. From the very day he assumed command, therefore, he was clamorous for the arms and equipment, and tireless in drill. To the men, and especially to the officers of the Legion, these were very far from being idle days. It takes a deal of brain, as well as patience, to transform a thousand men who have never had an hour's training of hand or eye into efficient soldiers, especially when they who teach must themselves be taught. If the days were busy ones for the soldiers, they were overcrowded ones for the officers. Drill, tactics, reports—all the infinity of detail which distinguishes military from civil life—these had to be learned at high pressure, a year's work crowded into a month. Under these circumstances, Hubert had little time for regret. Now and then, when the thought of his lost love seemed likely to overpower him, he would get leave of absence from the camp for a few hours and ride out along the road which had become so familiar to him when Henlopen was in Farmer Parker's care. He did not talk with Kitty about Delia Kincaid. He could not tell her all, and foolishly concluded to say nothing. She knew, of course, that there was something wrong between the lovers. Whether she was glad or not, who shall say? That she sympathized with Hubert there could be no doubt, and her sympathy comforted him. How should she know that every day his eyes scanned the columns of the *Standard* for an answer to his advertisement? How should she know that he was the " Jack " who had directed the advertisement to be marked " itwtf "—once a week until forbidden ? She did not even recall that his name was " Jack." She had met Miss Kincaid, but she had never heard of " Dee." It is not surprising, therefore, that she journeyed to the Western city near which the Legion were to receive their mount, under pretense of visiting a cousin, but really that she might see the regiment when it passed through on its way to the front.

That was a proud day for the young lieutenant-
colonel. He knew that his mother, his uncle and Kitty
Parker were among the spectators; yet though he
responded gayly to the greetings of these friends, there
was a weight on his heart that the one face dearer to
him than all others was missing. The regiment presented a fine appearance despite the inexperience of the
men. It was but three days since they had received
their saddles. The better part of them had never been
on horseback a dozen times in their lives. The horses
were fresh and spirited. Sedley had attended to their
purchase, and in each troop they were all of the same
color—black, brown, bay, chestnut. Taken as a whole,
they were probably the best lot of horses that ever bore
the brand " U. S." upon shoulder and flank.

There were some fine mounts among the officers, but
Damon eclipsed them all, quite fulfilling his owner's
expectation. His bright eye, swelling nostril, high-flung
silver crest and splendid action attracted attention not
only to himself but to his graceful, self-possessed rider
as well. The sturdy colonel smiled grimly as he
listened to the cheers which greeted his dashing subordinate and thought of the thirty-mile march which
lay before the regiment on the other side of the river
ere it would go into camp. He meant to give men
and horses a jaunt that would test their mettle, and
expected to see his lieutenant-colonel droop as well as
the others. How proudly erect the experienced soldier
sat in his saddle! Firmly braced up, he knew men
would have before them all day long one model, at
least, of soldierly form and fortitude. He thought there
would be only one; but when the sun dropped to the
edge of the horizon, and he sat by the way-side to
observe the regiment file past as it went into camp, he
found, to his surprise, that his young subordinate sat

his horse as firmly and unweariedly as himself, though
during all that first long march Damon had not con-
descended to abandon the proud amble with which he
set out and come down to a staid and quiet walk.   He
gave the horse and rider a look of admiration as they
went by, and when next morning he found both as
ready for duty as himself, he counted it fortunate that
his immediate subordinate would do credit to his
tutelage and example.   From that hour the old soldier
and the young one were sworn friends.   The luck of
Old Harry still clung to his descendant.   If Venus
mocked his desire, grim-visaged Mars smiled fondly
upon him.

CHAPTER XII.

HOW HISTORY IS MADE.

It was nearly two years after the storm of war began.
The troopers of the Sedley Legion had long since
become veteran campaigners.   Their guidons had
known both victory and defeat.   They had marched,
scouted, fought and fled.   They had stubbornly impeded
the advance of a triumphant enemy, and fallen savagely
upon his rear in retreat.   They had been the eyes and
ears of commanding generals ; had guarded communi-
cations and protected trains, and sometimes acted as
body-guards and servitors of those carrion-birds of our
army, the cotton speculators who coined gold out of
brave men's blood.   The gleam and glitter of their
bright array had long since paled.   War had ceased to
be a holiday to them.   The horses of the various troops
had lost their uniformity.   Beardless boys who went out

as private soldiers wore soldier-straps as complacently
as their mustaches, now. Men who had never mounted
a horse until mustered in, sat their saddles now as easily
as a *vaquero*. The brilliant officer who first commanded
them had won a star before he had been three months
in the field, and Hubert Goodwin had been promoted
with the hearty approval of his superior. The blood
of the old cavalier served him well, and not only the
regiment he commanded, but a whole army were proud
of the dashing young soldier. He was not alone. All
around him there were men who had leaped from the
desk to the saddle, and were striving in noble compe-
tition for coruscating stars—the priceless rewards of
valor—with which the firmament of war was full. It
was the day of miracles, which were so common that
men hardly wondered at them.

A great battle was in progress. The Sedley Legion
—now a "legion" no more, but only Nth Cavalry—
was scattered here and there—a troop at headquarters,
others with the trains, two more upon a scout, and three
with the young colonel in command, watching Sigsby's
Bridge upon the extreme left, with orders to prevent a
crossing if attempted in force, but not to attack unless
absolutely necessary.

All day long the battle had roared and surged away
to the right, swelling down to the center, pushing back
the left, but still the troopers of the Nth Cavalry waited
unengaged behind the wooded crest that hid them from
the enemy beyond the bridge. The day had been cold
and lowering. The rain had swollen the narrow stream
until it overflowed its banks and spread half across the
bottoms on which the unpicked cotton stood, the snowy
bolls flecking the rows of frost-browned plants. Along
the stream was a narrow belt of timber, and through it
a single opening, with a weather-beaten bridge across

it, and the turbid water touching the stringers on either
side. The green leaves and red berries of the holly
dotted the hedgerows, while the mistletoe hung from
the branches of the few ancient giants which marked
the course of the stream. Above the second growth of
the low-ground could be seen the enemy's picket-line
upon the hills beyond, and now and then a couple of
guns, posted on the highest of them, sent a shell shriek-
ing through the oaks beneath which the troopers stood.
The side and crest of the hill behind which the troopers
lay were covered with dark, clinging cedars, through
which the road leading down to the bridge showed red
and steep.

Colonel Goodwin, pacing back and forth in the edge
of the cedar thicket, watched and waited. Toward
night, his scouts brought word that troops were mass-
ing beyond the river, preparing to cross in force. He
reported the fact to the commanding general, and asked
for help. Not a regiment or a gun could be taken from
its place in the beleaguered front. The reports became
more positive ; his appeal more urgent. Not a man
could be spared ; so came the reply, but the Nth Cavalry must prevent the crossing ; an attack from that
quarter would be fatal. If they could delay the enemy
an hour, a brigade coming up from the rear would
relieve them. This was the response of the general in
command. The enemy was preparing to cross.
Hubert Goodwin sent back three troopers to find and
guide the relieving force, and placed himself at the
head of his men. A brigade had already crossed the
bridge and formed in line on each side the road. They
were evidently intended to support the crossing of a
larger force which had not yet appeared, and for the
coming of which they waited. They outnumbered him
three or four to one, but for the moment they were at

his mercy. The ground was in his favor. If he could beat these back, it might delay the intended movement —probably would. There was no hope of doing it by any other means. He rode along the ranks and spoke a few words to his men. His horse tossed its silver mane as proudly and pranced as daintily as if on review. He knew his men, and they knew him. The hard, tanned faces, the firm-set lips and down-drawn brows answered his appeal even more satisfactorily than the cheer that went up from their throats. They were old soldiers, and, consequently, not anxious for battle ; but not one of them would flinch at any odds.

Then he returned to his post. The bugle sounded ; some needless orders flew from lip to lip ; sabers rattled from their iron scabbards, and their curving backs were pressed against the firm broad shoulders. Every man settled himself doggedly in his saddle. There was a quick trot to the brow of the hill. Then the bugle sounded the charge. Every lip repeated the expected command, and with the silver-maned son of Gray Eagle in the lead, the Nth Cavalry swept down the sharp incline, in the face of shot and shell, upon the thin infantry line in the bottom. These made a brave stand ; but, knowing that the ground was firm, the cavalry wheeled to the right and left, and before they could reload or even fix their bayonets, were upon them. They were forced back into the overflowed skirt of timber. Most of them threw away their arms and swam and scrambled for the other side ; but many recognizing, with a soldier's quick intuition, the advantage of this position, though the water was almost to their waists, halted and fired from behind the trees at their pursuers. At the same time, a section of artillery wheeling into position on the road beyond the bridge, sent a perfect hailstorm of shot along the way by which the cavalry had come.

It was over in an instant ; the retreat sounded, and the few who were left put their horses at the sharp, shot-gashed ridge and dashed back to form again under its shelter.

The silver-maned charger was in his accustomed place, his eyes flashing, white tail waving proudly and nostrils showing red and hot in the quivering seal-brown muzzle.   But the wooden stirrups with the splashed leather shields hung empty at his side.

———•———

CHAPTER XIII.

A LESSON IN ORNITHOLOGY.

" Say, Bill ; did you ever hear a whipper-will in Christmas week before ?"

" Can't say ez I ever did, Jim, an' I ain't dead sure I hear one now."

A couple of Confederate pickets crouching in the cedar thicket above Sigsby's Bridge were talking in low tones, while the plaintive note of the night-bird came with startling clearness from the narrow bottom beyond.   The day's battle had been a drawn one, and the two armies bivouacked within hearing of each other. In many places the pickets were hardly fifty yards apart, and a fitful fire ran up and down the lines at intervals all night long.   Each army could see the glare of the other's camp-fires reflected from the trees and the lowing sky.   Each could hear the sound of preparation, too, and the low, plaintive cadence of the moans that went up from the wounded and dying who lay between the lines—that saddest of all the grim incidents of war.

" Don't yer hear that one down thar on the bottom ?"

" I'm a-hearin' of it straight enough, but I ain't exactly sure 'bout it's bein' a whipper. Ef hit wer' June, now, instead of December, I probably wouldn't think nothin' of it, but jest at this time hit do sound suspicious-like."

" Seems ter be right across the run, whar the cavalry charged on us, don't it ?"

" That's just whar it is. I've been a-hearin' of it quite a little time now by spells. I thought at first hit mought be some sort of a sign, and have hed my eyes and ears open to see ef thar wer' anythin' goin' on tharabouts. Ye know the Yankee pickets is jest in the edge of the wood on the brow of the hill 'cross thar, an' I didn't know but they might be tryin' for the bridge again. 'Tain't likely though, fer they must know thet ef they couldn't get through thar by daylight it ain't anyway probable they'd be able to at night. I 'low it's some poor fellow thet's got hurt a-whistling fer his mate to come and help him off. Of co'se it's orders to fire at anything we see a-stirrin' toward the front, but I ain't gwine ter shoot at no whipper-wills, ner nobody thet comes ter help 'em, either. It's too dark to make out anything clear an' good down in the shadder on the bottom anyhow, an' ef the clouds should break away, an' I should see anythin' movin' round thar, I couldn't make out whether it wer' a man er a mule—unless thar wer' a good many of 'em. That ain't orders, but it's sense."

" So hit ar, Bill. I 'low ther's many a poor fellow over thar—ours ez well ez their'n—that's jest a-prayin' fer somebody ter come an' take him off, or, perhaps, even give em one drink of water 'fore he dies. Of co'se, orders is orders, an has ter be, but sojers knows 'bout sech things, an' the feller that goes ter shootin' cause one of the t'other side crawls out ter find his pardner, ain't fit ter be on picket at sech a time. Hark! Thar 'tis ag'in! Wal, now, ef that ain't a whipper then I don't know one when I hears it."

"Hit do sound powerful like one—that's a fact."

"That were a mighty purty charge the Yanks made thar, jest about sundown, Bill?"

"The cavalry? Never seed the like! It were all nonsense, though ; ef they'd got the bridge they couldn't er held it."

"Not a minit."

"An' all our folks hed ter do was jest ter fall back inter the edge of the swamp, an' they was ez safe ez ef they'd been inside the rock of Gibraltar."

"Edzactly ; arter all, 'twere jest foolbizness, puttin' a line over thar at all. We'd no bizness a-crossin' the run till enough on us went over ter do something."

"That's so ; but we emptied the saddles lively when they started back! I don't b'leeve more'n half on 'em got over the hill. Did you see the kunnel?"

"The one on the hoss with the white mane?"

"Edzactly."

"Who could help seein' of him?"

"Wasn't it splendid! There he was, with not more'n three or four hundred men at his back, chargin' a line four times as strong, an' tryin' ter take a bridge in p'int blank range of two twelve-pounders, that wasn't served by men asleep, by no manner of means! He must have knowed thar warn't any chance for 'em ter do nothin', and not much chance of many of 'em gettin' back ; but ter see him come down the big road thar, ahead of the line, his sword over his head, an' a-lookin' back every now an' then ter see if his men was all right—with the shell drappin' all about him, an' tearin' up the dirt in front of 'em—I tell you it was grand!"

"Our fellers didn't stop ter have no argyment with 'em," said the other, laughing softly. "They jest turned an' took ter to the water like so many frogs in a mill-pond."

"No use of doin' anything else."

"Co'se not; thar war the critter-fellers comin' right down on 'em, an' the creek way over its banks behind 'em, an no chance ter get across only that narrer bridge. An' we couldn't help 'em a mite till the Yanks war plum down to the bridge. I s'pose they thought too many of us was crossin' ter the'r side."

The dry, quaint humor of the Southern countryman showed in the words and tones of the speakers.

"Of co'se; an' ef it hadn't been fer that charge, I s'pose we'd all been all over that bridge pretty soon a-tearin' up the hill, an' like as not rollin' up the'r flank with a yell jest ez we did the other wing in the mornin'."

"I wouldn't wonder. They say that was the gineral's plan, an' that's why our folks hed been so mighty keerful not to make any show round here all day—jest keepin' a little gyard down at the bridge, ez ef the'r wasn't only a handful in the neighborhood. But the'r was some mis-connection; nobody were on hand ter foller them two regiments across, an' they hadn't fairly got inter line each side the bridge, afore the cavalry was onto 'em—an' they were a-comin' back without waitin' for no pontoons."

"I s'pect the Yankee kunnel seed what was in the wind, an' charged jest ter break it up."

"More'n likely; he did it, too. Yer see, 'twouldn't do ter try ter steal across ag'in, an' it were so late afore the

artillery got up ter cover the crossin' thet ther' warn'
no use ter start afore nightfall."

"I s'pect we'll have ter try it in the mornin'."

"I doubt it. Yer see, 'tain't no fit place ter cross
nohow, unless we could steal across unbeknownst.
Our fellers ought to have charged up the hill yonder
as soon as they struck the dirt, instid of spreadin' out
on the bottom like a fan, an' waitin' ter be rid down."

There is no keener military critic than the observant
veteran in the ranks.

"Of co'se; but I s'pose they hed their orders, same as
we 'uns."

"Likely; but I don't believe there was anything but
the leetle squad of cavalry to stop 'em then; an' that
wouldn't have been anythin' ef they hadn't squatted like
an ole har' in her form an' waited ter be rid down; but
there'll be infantry an' artillery thar afore mornin'. I
wonder ef the Yankee kunnel were killed?"

"I seed his hoss go back without him."

"Yes, I seed that, too; when the bugle sounded he
fell inter his place an' went up the hill with stirrups
flyin' loose, ez proud an' stiddy ez ef his master war on
his back."

"Which he ain't ever likely ter be ag'in."

"Prob'ly not. That were a powerful unhealthy
place down by the bridge when our folks was once out
of the way, an' not a sign of cover goin' back up the
hill. Thar's the bird ag'in! Yer see that ain't no
whipper."

"I s'pect yer right; but the feller's playin' it fer all
it's wuth this time, no mistake. What's that?"

There was the sound of a scuffle at the rear; cries of
"Whoa!" and the shouted command, "Stop him!"

"Reckon somebody's hoss is loose," said the other,
carelessly.

" Here he comes !"

The sound of a horse's hoofs splashing down the clayey road toward their post was now plainly heard.

" Looks ez ef he were desartin' to the enemy, don't it? Shall I shoot ?"

" Tain't no use, but—here he is !"

Both discharged their guns, instinctively, as a horse dashed by them along the road by which they were posted. They began at once to reload.

" Was there anybody on him, Jim ?"

" I don't believe there was—it was so dark I couldn't see—but the stirrups was a-flyin' ; I heerd them. Thar he goes across the bridge !"

" Looks like it war a deserter, don't hit ?"

" Listen."

The horse had stopped on the other side of the bridge and gave an inquiring neigh.

" Jest listen at the whipper, Bill—ain't he a-goin' it ?"

" An' the hoss is answerin' him, Jim."

" 'Pon my soul, I b'leeve he is !"

The horse was evidently retracing his steps, whinnying from time to time with startled inquiry. The whip-poor-will call was rapidly repeated with an unmistakably persuasive emphasis.

" It's some feller callin' his hoss, Bill."

" But this one come from our side."

" Hit must be one o' their'n thet didn't git back. Yer know ther war a number of 'em come cl'ar acrost the bridge."

" So they did—the kunnel among 'em. I wonder how any of 'em got back."

" This one didn't, ye see ; an' hearin' his master a callin' of him, he's answered. That's the way on't, Bill."

" Wal, don't that beat anythin'? I tell ye, Jim, a hoss knows 'most ez much ez a man—ef he's treated right."

"Sometimes more. Yer couldn't fool a hoss with no whipper-will song, 'specially of a New Year's Eve."

"Thet's so."

The soldiers laughed under their breath.

"Who's there?"

Footsteps were hurriedly approaching from the rear.

"All right," answered an officer, in a low tone, as he joined them from the reserve.

"What was it, Capting?"

"The colonel's horse has deserted to the enemy," answered the officer, unable to repress his laughter.

"Anybody on him?"

"Not a soul; but he's taken the colonel's kit—saddle-bags, holsters and all."

The captain chuckled again over his superior's misfortune.

"Which hoss was it?" asked Bill.

"The bay he got up in Kentucky."

"How did it happen?"

"He's been a-fretting for half an hour, biting and kicking like mad. The boy couldn't do anything with him, and the colonel, who always thinks he can do everything better'n anybody else, went to try his hand. He no sooner got hold of the bridle than he was pitched on his head in the mud, and the horse started full tilt for the Yankee lines. I s'pose he was crazy, but it's a good joke on the colonel all the same."

"Capting, that hoss has found his old master over thar. Jest listen at him now."

Short neighs of recognition came up to their ears out of the darkness in the valley, and the whip-poor-will call was repeated softly and quickly.

"I believe you're right," said the captain, after listening a moment. "There he goes," he added, as he heard the sound of the horse's footsteps walking away from them along the road. Almost instantly there was a commotion among the pickets on the crest of the hill beyond the river. Shots were fired and a general alarm seemed to be given.

" The durn fools 'll shoot ther own man !" said Jim, in a tone of disgust.

" An' the hoss too," added Bill, regretfully.

" If he'd jest charge on 'em, I reckon he'd stampede the post," said the officer. " And that's what he's doin' too !" he added, excitedly. " There he goes, by thunder !"

The rush of galloping hoofs was heard dashing up the opposite hillside ; there were a half-dozen shots, shouts, a drumbeat, and all the vague clamor of a night-alarm in an army lying upon its arms in constant apprehension of an attack.

" Well," said the officer, with quiet humor, " the colonel has lost a mighty good horse and the Yankees have lost some sleep. We needn't be afraid they'll disturb us any more to-night, but I hope it won't be our turn to be in the lead if our folks try to cross that bridge in the morning. The Yankees'll have twenty guns ready to play on it by that time. Good-bye."

The officer turned back toward the reserve, and left the picket quiet and watchful, waiting impatiently for the relief.

" Jim," said Bill, after a while, " I wouldn't wonder if the story got out in the newspapers an' worked its way along into books, an' so finally come to be believed, that a whipper-will was heard a-singin' atween the lines of these two armies this very night, cold an' dark an' the last day of December ez it is. Yer see them Yankee newspaper chaps don't know a whipper-will from a water-rat, and don't know but they're just as likely ter sing New Year's Eve ez May-day night. Bet ye what ye dare, Jim, the No'th'n papers'll hev a big splurge over that thar whipper's singin' ter the dead an' dyin' down where the Yankee cavalry got cut up."

" Shouldn't wonder," answered Jim, sagely.

And, sure enough, they did. It is thus that history is made. The mid-winter whip-poor-will of Stone River still lives, a splendid example of the force of human credulity. Science is not less powerful against the supernatural than truth against sentiment. Bill Sykes and Jim Blaisdell guessed out the truth ; but they were not newspaper correspondents, and the world never got their version of the marvel that happened between the picket lines at Sigsby's Bridge that night.

CHAPTER XIV.

OUT OF THE DARKNESS.

" You've had a close call, Colonel."

The man who spoke wore the uniform of an army surgeon. The one he addressed sat in a rude reclining chair, on the porch of a hospital, which stood upon a bluff overlooking a noble river, which was covered with gunboats and transports. There was a hint of spring in the air and sunshine. Forts and earth-works showed red against the brown hill-sides. A half-mile away was a city. Lines of white tents were visible here and there. Flags dotted the landscape with color. The invalid, who was wrapped in an army blanket, with a soft red rug thrown over it, looked up inquiringly from his pillow.

"You see, it was a good while before you had any proper care, and that bullet, which only made a new parting in your hair, played the mischief with the brain under it. It seemed to touch the very centre of volition. Involuntary action was not much impaired ; that's what saved you. Liquids placed in your mouth were swallowed, and, fortunately, assimilated. The straps on your shoulders showed your rank, but it was a good while before we were able to learn who you were. There didn't seem to be any scarcity of colonels, and we couldn't learn of any who were unaccounted for."

The doctor laughed quietly at his own humor.

"How long has it been since the battle ?" asked the invalid, weakly.

"Do you see that hint of color in the orchards across the river ?"

The young man looked languidly in the direction indicated, and signified assent by a movement of the eyelids rather than a nod of the head.

"What do you think it is ?"

"Peach-blossoms ?"

"Exactly. They are a little late this year, they tell me. This is the last day of February, and the battle, or your part of it, at least, was the last day of December."

"That—is ?" glancing toward the city.

"Nashville."

"We won—I suppose ?"

"Naturally, or you would hardly be here in my care."

"And my regiment ?"

"It is at the front."

"When can I join it ?"

"Can you bear the truth ?"

The officer's lips quivered, but he nodded affirmatively.

"I believe you can," said the surgeon, with a satisfied smile, "and it is better for you to know the truth at once than be finding it out by degrees. Well, then, I suppose you will hardly go back to the regiment at all."

A spasm of pain passed over the young man's face.

" Is it as bad as that, doctor ?"

"Well—yes and no. A man who has had your luck should not speak of anything as bad. Let me give you a stimulant and light a cigar, and I will see if I can get you back into the world, so that you will know where you stand."

The doctor poured some spirits into a glass upon a stand near by, and gave the other a sip. Lighting a cigar, he seated himself upon a camp-stool facing the couch, and after a few whiffs, said :

" I have been expecting these questions for a week and been fearful that something might happen to shock you before you were prepared for it. You must understand that I think you are all right—that you only need care and rest and attention to be as good as you ever were ; but my associates of the medical staff do not agree with me. They say it is possible, but not probable. You must understand, therefore, that your recovery depends very largely upon yourself, and just now the most important thing is that you should not suffer any sudden shock. I will tell you all I know, and the rest you must gather up little by little, never allowing yourself to get excited about anything. Can you do it ?"

"I will try."

" That is it—just put on the brakes and I don't believe you will be in any sort of danger. Now, what is the last thing you remember ?"

" I think it is—Was there a charge ?"

" Down a hill—toward a bridge," suggested ne surgeon.

" Yes ; I remember they had crossed the bridge. It was a wicked thing ; but it had to be done."

The speaker closed his eyes and shuddered.

"No doubt about that; and it was well done—splendidly done. Everybody is proud of it. They say the charge saved us from an attack on the left flank that would probably have been fatal, hard-pressed as we were on the right."

"We didn't get the bridge?"

"No, but you threw the troops which had already crossed into inextricable confusion, and there was no time to supply their places with others before dark."

The officer nodded.

"There were a few reached the bridge and some say you went clean across it."

"I believe I did," with a flush.

"The next in command, thinking you were lost and satisfied that all had been done that could be accomplished, ordered the retreat to be sounded. Your horse returned to his place, but you were not with him."

"I seem to remember falling off."

"Do you remember anything more?"

The other shook his head.

"Some time during the night you came charging into our lines, half-unconscious, clinging to a strange horse—a Confederate officer's horse, in fact. Do you know how you got it?"

He shook his head again.

"I had a curiosity to know, for it seemed to me most probable that the shot you received was fired by our pickets. You might have been stunned by your fall?"

"I seem to have a remembrance of being down—afraid I would be trampled on, you know—and then getting up—on a horse—but it is like a dream. I seem to have been dreaming ever since."

"Well, you have been. Your regiment was sent to the rear—what was left of it, at least—"

" There were only three companies," interrupted the other.

" I know—the rest were detached. Well, there weren't many left—men nor horses—and they were sent back after the charge. A new brigade which had just come to the field was ordered into position there. They, of course, did not know you—a good many thought you were a Confederate, indeed, but you were sent to a field hospital, and after awhile brought to the city—not exactly unconscious, but curiously out of joint "—the surgeon tapped his head to explain his meaning. " Nobody expected you to get well, and an army hospital is a poor place for such cases as yours. I happened to be down at the church where you were, and was attracted to you by a singular circumstance. You did not seem to know anything that went on about you. You could see—for you flinched from a blow if your eyes were open—and could hear, for the calls which were sounded at a battery on the hill above the hospital seemed to start some train of thought in your mind. But the thing that struck my attention was that you kept repeating over and over again exactly the same expression that a patient of mine whose case interested me greatly had used in something the same way."

" What was that ?"

" Oh, it wasn't anything of importance," answered the doctor, evasively. " I'll tell you about it some time. You've had about enough for the present. What I want to tell you now is that I had you brought here, and after a while learned who you were. You mustn't let it disturb you, but your friends supposed you to be dead. Somebody had taken everything from your pockets before you reached the hospital—perhaps while you were on the field—and so you were reported dead or missing."

" And some one has been put in my place ?" asked the young man, chokingly.

" Don't let that trouble you. The day before you were shot, you were nominated a brigadier-general ; and when the story of your gallant conduct was received, though you were then missing and might be dead, the Senate confirmed the appointment and the President signed the commission. There, there ! Don't let your good luck break you down now. There's many a man would be willing to change places with you, even if you were as dead as everybody thinks you, for such honor as that."

The tears were running over the sunken cheeks down into the brown beard. The doctor handed him the glass and required him to take more of the stimulant.

" Now, I am going to have you taken back to your room," he said, " give you an opiate, and you must go to sleep. In the morning you must tell me what word I am to send to your people. I have let no one know, as yet, that you are alive."

The next day Hubert Goodwin was decidedly better. The languor and apathy which had previously affected him had perceptibly diminished, and he was already beginning to make plans for the future. The first thing to be done was to re-introduce himself to the world who believed him dead. He thought it would have been pleasant to have remained incognito awhile longer—to have watched the world until the weariness he felt passed entirely away. But then he would lose his share in the great events that were happening—that share already so brilliant. He determined to announce his return to life, or consciousness, at least, by a letter to the President, thanking him for the promotion he had received.

The surgeon wrote the few lines necessary, at his dictation, which he signed with difficulty.

"And you must telegraph to my mother !"

"Of course," answered the surgeon, dryly.   "We will have her here in no time.   You think you could stand it to see her—and anybody else, I suppose?"

"I guess so," answered the young man, thoughtfully.

"You know you are not—very strong yet—and have to be watched all the time when you are asleep, lest you should do yourself harm."

"What do you mean?" asked the patient, a little irritably.

"Well, you see, one of the queer things about your case is that you had all the time a sort of semi-conscious-ness of the depression of the skull and its pressure on the brain.   This consciousness showed itself in sleep, and you were all the time trying to dig it out of the way.   So you kept the wound torn open all the time, and we have had to keep it bandaged and plastered and your hands tied, too, until—well, until we concluded to have you watched while you slept."

The truth was that the young officer had undergone that most delicate of surgical operations, trepanning, with the difference that in his case a portion of the skull had been taken from the head of a less fortunate sufferer, and carefully fitted to the opening.   As death had just occurred, and the subject from which the portion was taken was of about the same age, it soon began to grow into its place, but the irritation of the swiftly knitting edges gave such annoyance to the patient that he was in constant danger of displacing it. The surgeon did not think it wise to let him know this fact, and yet felt that he must offer some explanation of the constant watch-care exercised over him, both while sleeping and awake.

" I heard that your uncle—your stepfather, I believe," continued the surgeon, " came and got your horse. He had a bullet through the fore-arm, I think, but was doing well. They say the regiment was almost as proud of him as of their colors."

Tears showed under the young officer's lashes as he closed his eyes and whistled softly to himself to hide his agitation.

" Do you know what they call you in the hospital ?" asked the surgeon, with a smile.

" What ?"

" They call you the Whip-poor-will—because every now and then you take to whistling, as you did just now, only sometimes you whistle a great deal louder and keep it up by the hour at a time."

" It is the way my uncle always teaches his horses."

" By the way, I remember seeing in the papers that a whip-poor-will was heard singing between the lines the night of the battle, despite the fact that it was midwinter and freezing cold. I suspect it was you instead of the bird."

" Likely as not."

" You've been at it ever since, anyhow. You haven't asked me who identified you."

" Some of the men ?"

" No, indeed !"

" Perhaps I told you myself ?" with a smile.

" Oh, but you didn't know yourself. If you had told us we shouldn't have believed a word you said. Give it up ?"

The other bowed assent indifferently.

" See if you can't guess. Who would be most apt to hunt you up ?"

" Sam ?"

" Who is Sam ?"

"My boy—my servant."

"Pshaw! no. Think, now—a woman."

"What—who? A woman?"

Was it—could it be? Alas! he knew it was not. Memory had come back, and with it the recollection of a letter received from his mother three months before :

"Horace says I must write and tell you," it had said, "that he has traced the Kincaids finally. They are prospering under another name. Dee was sick for a long time after she left school—in an asylum for several months. She was discharged as cured, and married a short time after. Horace went to see her, so that there should be no doubt about the matter. He says he never saw her looking better. She pretended not to know him, and, he says, carried it out splendidly. When he asked her if she had forgotten you—Jack—she said : 'Jack? Jack?' 'Yes; Jack Goodwin,' he said— angrily enough, I do not doubt. 'Jack Goodwin?' she repeated, smiling in his face as bold as brass. "Seems as if I had heard the name, but I cannot recall the person.' When he told her he had come on purpose to see her because you wished to know how she was, and asked her if she had any word to send to you, she professed great surprise, but said, in her sweetest way : 'Tell him I am sorry I do not remember him, but I am glad he does not forget me.'

"And this is all there is of it, my son. I know it will almost break your heart, but she was not worthy of you. I received a paper containing her marriage notice. I do not send it to you, judging that you will prefer to know nothing more about her. We feel as if we had lost a daughter. I believe Horace thought almost as much of her as you did. We cannot understand it, but, as he says, 'seeing is believing.' Of course, we have got to forget her, too, and I suppose the easiest way will be to say nothing more about her."

"And she promised to be mine 'forever and ever, the young man said, as he bowed his head upon his hands after reading the letter. All the rest of it had faded from his memory. These words seemed etched forever on his consciousness.

"You haven't guessed yet," said the surgeon, desiring to interrupt what he judged to be an unpleasant reverie.

"Not my mother?"

The other shook his head.

"There is no one else."

"Did you not know a lady—a young lady—black hair —dark eyes—red cheeks?" naming each attribute separately and suggestively.

The young man shook his head with blank negation. There was no woman in the world for him but Dee; and Dee was no longer his; married, months ago— another's! His face grew pale; he was sick at heart. He did not wish to hear of any other.

"Never knew a young lady named—named—Kitty?" the doctor suggested.

The young man smiled languidly.

"Ah! I thought so. It really frightened me when you guessed everybody else and said nothing of her. Such a splendid girl, too! But when one's head has been out of gear for a while, it takes some time to get his bearings again. Well, sir—she came, this Miss Kitty—what's her other name?"

"Parker."

"That's it; you are getting along finely—well, she came about six weeks ago, maybe more—and just began a systematic search for you. You see, the trouble was that nobody could be found to correspond with your 'descriptive list.' There was very little fighting just at that point, except the charge you made, and no one having your rank or of your description was found there. There were two theories : one, that you had been captured, and the other that you had wandered off and died on some other part of the line. Miss Kitty determined to find out the truth. She is a very decided girl, or she would never have done what she did. She thought you were dead, of course, and went and hunted up all the "burying details" and showed them your picture, hoping to learn where you had been buried. She had copies of it made, too, and sent to the Confederate surgeons, but could get no trace of you.

"Finally, she happened to run across the surgeon who examined you when first brought in, and so traced you to my hands. Of course, I knew the portrait as soon as I set eyes on it, and she has been here ever since and has taken the best kind of care of you. There's no nurse so good for a man as a woman who loves him."

"She must have taken a great deal for granted," said the other petulantly.

"Now, see here, young man," interposed the surgeon, jocularly, "don't you go to breaking the poor girl's heart by talking in that way. You owe her a good deal more than you think—more than you will ever owe anybody else."

There was an impatient movement from the couch.

"There aren't many girls that would have been as faithful and persistent," continued the surgeon ; "and now she is frightened nearly to death lest you should be displeased with her. If you don't treat her right, I shall wish I had left you to your fate instead of bringing you here and making your case special."

"Why didn't you?" asked the patient wearily, half-turning his head away and gazing at the rough board partition.

"As I told you, I should have done so if it had not been for a peculiarity of your case which interested me. I was down at McKendree—that's the name of the church where the hospital was—one day, and heard you whistle. 'Hellow, doctor,' I said to my friend; 'have you got an aviary here?'

"'O, that's our whip-poor-will,' he replied. "By the way, you are interested in such things, suppose you come and have a look at the fellow? Nobody here thinks he has a ghost of a chance, but he persists in living; and, well, there can be no harm in looking at him.'

"You see he knew that alienism was my specialty. I had been assistant-superintendent of an insane asylum for years before I entered the service, and would have been superintendent if I had not been a better medical man than politician.

"Well, we went into the body of the church and found you in one of the pews they had transformed into cots, whistling away for dear life, greatly to the annoyance of the other patients, who were, however, very lenient and kindly to your infirmity. The nurse said you had been worse than usual that day, meaning that you had whistled more. While I was looking at you, you stopped. The expression of your face suddenly changed, and it seemed to me that you had received a new mental impression, either from sound or touch. You did not open your eyes ; but when I pressed back the lids the orbs rolled about in their sockets uneasily, showing an uncomfortable sensitiveness to light. Finally, the expression of your countenance softened and you said, solemnly :

"' Forever and ever, Amen.' "

The officer started.

"You are surprised? Well, I don't wonder. Of course, if I had known that you had been a divinity student, it would not have seemed quite so strange ; but the fact is that this very sentence was the keynote, or, rather, the insoluble puzzle of one of the most interest- ing cases I have ever known. So, when you repeated it over and over again, I naturally took an intersst in you, and the result is—well, I have added quite a little to my reputation, or shall, when you make me the medical officer on your staff, as I shall expect you to do as soon as you get the stars on your shoulders."

"And I'll do it, doctor," said the young man, heartily. "You may count on that."

"All right," answered the surgeon, jestingly. "Here's my card ; so there will be no excuse or delay about the matter."

He handed the young officer a card as he spoke, on which was printed :

```
....................................
:                                  :
:        EDWARD TALCOTT,           :
:                        Surgeon,  :
:     39th I. V.                   :
:                                  :
....................................
```

" I'll not forget it, and only hope you will not refuse to come on my demand. But—what was the other case you refer to ?"

" The other case ? O, yes—the ' forever-and-ever- amen,' case. Well, it was a curious one. Let me see," he continued, taking out his watch. " I've only got a few minutes, but I can give you the main points of it

It was while I was at the Institution, you know, just about the beginning of the war, a young lady was brought there who had only two thoughts left in her mind. She would speak—sometimes, not very often—but the only word she uttered was 'Jack.' "

There was a groan from the cot.

"It was hard. I suppose you can sympathize with her. I don't think the word meant anything to her, though. She just repeated it mechanically. She had been at school for years and had overworked herself, so that the brain all gave out—was completely disorganized, so far as thought was concerned. She was very quiet and gentle ; never made any trouble ; did whatever she was set to doing, but did it entirely mechanically. She would feed herself if she saw others eating, but left her food untouched if she did not. She would sew if given a needle and saw a few stitches taken, but she sewed right on, whether there was a thread in the needle or not.

" She had been a remarkably fine scholar, I was told, but she had forgotten every word in the language except ' Jack,' and every letter. She did not understand any thing that was told her ; would answer no questions and did not know her own name or anything else. As she improved in health, we tried every means we could devise to awaken the slumbering intellect, but all to no purpose. We brought her a dog, a cat, a piano, books, but nothing could awaken the least sign of recognition or interest, and I should have given up the case as utterly incurable, but for the fact that we began to find scribbled on the books and papers in her room the very sentence you kept repeating, ' Forever and ever, Amen.'

" At first I did not think she did it. I had requested her mother to bring me some specimens of her writing. It was a fine, sloping, Italian hand, while these sen-

tences were written in a strong, heavy, almost masculine, back-hand. We had left pencils about the room,
for she was so quiet and lady-like, that she had a nice
room to herself, just to tempt her memory, so to speak.
She never touched one while awake, but when asleep,
as we found by watching, she would get up and write
these sentences, and very often hide them somewhere
about the room or bed. Queer, wasn't it ?"

"Very," answered the young man, hoarsely. The
surgeon did not notice the pallor of the face now wholly
turned toward the wall.

"That is the curious thing about the insane. No two
of them are alike. Each one is an independent puzzle
that has to be solved on its own combination, if at all.
Well, I tried for weeks to get a clue—find the key to
that girl's intelligence—but I couldn't do it. Finally I
concluded that her mind was just a blank. All the
impressions that had been made on it had been rubbed
off. It was still receptive—weakly so it is true, and not
at all retentive—but after awhile she learned to repeat
words ; forgetting them, however, in a moment. Then
she began to notice what happened about her ; a change
of nurses annoyed her—and one thing after another was
done to awaken, not her former life and thought—that
was dead—irretrievably dead—but to establish a new
intelligence. Curiously enough, the first word she
repeated with any show of comprehension was 'horse.'
She was very fond of being driven and even riding
horseback, for which she seemed to have a natural aptitude. Almost the first thing she did showing connected
thought was to don her riding-habit, when she saw a
horse with a side-saddle on it, standing at the gate.
After a while she spent half her time almost in the saddle, and for that matter, does so to this day, I am told.
It made no difference who rode with her so long as he

was well-dressed and had a good horse. If he had not, she would attach herself to the first gentleman rider she met possessing these qualities. It seemed to make her angry to meet another lady riding with a gentleman, and she sometimes behaved badly on such occasions.

" As soon as we found this key to her intelligence, however, she improved very rapidly. She learned to speak and to write in a few weeks, speaking and writing exactly like her preceptors. After six months she was discharged, cured ; that is, she was reasonably intelligent and fairly sane, but she had not recovered, and never will recover, any hint of her former life. She learned to say ' father' and ' mother,' for instance, but has never showed any affection for either. Instead of that, I and my wife are the real parents of her new life —her new intelligence. She has had one or two partial relapses—probably always will have them, now and then—but a week or a fortnight at the institution fully restores her.

" She was married along in the fall—last fall, that is. I went home to the wedding. She was very glad to see me, took me all over the new house her father had built for her, and appeared to be fond of her husband ; but it seemed to me to be rather as a toy than anything else. I am afraid she has no clear comprehension of the relations between them. I advised against the marriage, but my wife favored it. She was afraid something might happen to her, you know, and I suppose it was best. I should be afraid of trouble if that old life should ever come back—but it never will. Her husband is a very good man, considerably older than she, and as gentle with her as if she were a child. Well, I must go."

" What—did you say her name was ?"

" Cyvelia King—but she named herself ' Wecly,' after

she began to talk, just as a child often does, and is always called so by her friends. By the way, her father, Marshall King—is with the army here. He is a very pushing man, and has done an enormous business buying cotton. Perhaps you have met him, being in the cavalry—they say he keeps about half the cavalry of this army scouting after cotton. You know there is one regiment they call ' King's body-guard.' "

"Yes ; I've heard of it. What kind of a looking girl —lady, I mean—was this—your patient ?"

" Can't help thinking about her, eh ? Well, I'm glad to give you something to think about, besides yourself, and this was a queer case. Lucky I've got her picture, for I couldn't ever make any headway describing a woman. My wife says, that if she should ever get lost I would have to get somebody to write out a description, if I wanted to advertise her. There she is—don't look as if she had lost any of her wits, does she ?"

He opened a small ambrotype case, which he took from his pocket, as he spoke, brushed the dust off it and handed it to his patient. The young man raised himself on his elbow to look at it, but instantly fell back, and the case would have fallen to the floor had not the surgeon caught it.

" Hellow ! You musn't risk such sudden changes of position," he exclaimed. " Here, take this." He pressed a glass to the chattering teeth and white lips of the young man. " That was too much exertion after my long talk. I must go now, and you must keep very quiet. Shall I send Miss Parker to you ?"

"I suppose you may as well," came faintly from the pallid lips.

" You—you will be quiet and—and kind to her ?"

" Certainly—of course."

" That's right."

The surgeon bustled away, and after a few moments Kitty Parker entered. Tears sprang to her eyes as she saw a look of recognition in his eyes, and clasping the hand he feebly raised from the coverlet in both her own, she knelt beside the couch and covered it with tender kisses.

CHAPTER XV.

IN THE TOILS OF DESTINY.

What a mocker is Fate! Hubert Goodwin would willingly have doomed himself to celibacy, with only the memory of love to cheer his loneliness. He was not romantic or sentimental. It was with him as much a matter of course that he should love Delia Kincaid as that he should live; and having once loved her, he could never cease to love her. Until this moment, it had never once crossed his mind that he could ever seem to love another; but he was human, and in a sense fond of the charming girl who knelt beside his couch. He had written to her, now and then, bright, breezy letters full of the camp and the march—the glamour and the charm of the soldier's life. He had not thought of love, nor dreamed that he had inspired it. Kitty Parker was bright, piquant, ardent; not so intellectual as his old playmate, but intelligent and accomplished—fitted to adorn any position. That was his estimate of her character. In appearance she was not less attractive, if estimated by ordinary standards. He had never thought of instituting a comparison between them.

The one he loved; the other he liked. That was all there was of the matter.

What is it that makes one nature or one type harmonize so unmistakably with another? With Delia Kincaid, Hubert Goodwin always felt himself at ease. She seemed a part of himself. But this other, not less beautiful, whose attractions he confessed, whom he respected and admired and whose love had unwittingly revealed itself—this woman to whom he owed so much —it was very different with her. The touch of her lips upon his hand was unfamiliar. Her kisses were hot and tremulous; her tears annoyed him. He confessed that the bowed head was shapely, but could he ever fondle those dark shining locks? How the pale golden tresses blinded his eyes! This flushed cheek, the shell-like ear, the slender neck, round and firm, with its graceful arch—they were all beautiful—but they were not his. He would have felt no pang in yielding them to another; nay, he would have deemed another fortunate in their possession. He even counted it a misfortune that Fate had mocked him, in the very hour of his bereavement, with a love so pure in a shrine so fair.

He knew it was Fate, however. His love was not only his no more, but his very image had been blotted from her memory. She had repeated his name—only mechanically, however; it brought no picture to her consciousness. She was lost—dead. He was glad it was so, if he must lose her. It would have killed him to think that she was false. "Forever and ever" had been no light vow to him. Why had she been given to another? Even if the soul had fled, he would have cherished the precious casket it once informed, with a love as tender as when he sealed it with boy-kisses on her child-lips. He flushed hot with anger at the thought that another hand had profaned its sanctuary with caresses. But why should he dwell upon it ? Her love was dead—its very ashes scattered on the winds of oblivion. And life, harsh and real, was before him. Fate was inexorable. Honor and gratitude alike demanded that he should not spurn the precious spike-nard this fair girl had lavished on his insensate form. He could not shame the love which had thus unwittingly revealed itself. He knew that his fate was sealed even while he rebelled against it.

" You will forgive me—won't you ?" she asked at length, lifting her eyes to his face.

" For what ? For saving my life ?"

" Oh, I didn't save it ; Doctor Talcott did that ; for not sending for your mother sooner ?"

" Why should you ?"

" Oh, I ought ; I know I ought. What will she think of me ? But I—I did not want to go away. It seemed as if I had a right to stay—when I found you after everybody else had given you up."

" So you had," solemnly.

The girl hushed her sobbing, and her breath came in short, quick gasps. What did his words mean—no, not the words, the tone ?

She turned her cheek away, that he should not see the hot blood leap up in joyful answer to his summons.

" Kitty !"

" Well ?" softly, doubtfully. She held her breath for his response.

" You will not go away ?"

Not go away ? Did he mean—much or little ? Did he want a wife—or a nurse ? She could not tell. What did it matter ? She had shown this man her love. She had broken the alabaster box upon his feet and wiped them with her hair. He was her lord by open confes-sion. Why should she question whether he asked much

or little? If he desired her life, it was his; if only her
services, why should she refuse a part, having freely
given the whole? So the hot, flushed face was lifted,
the tearful eyes sought his, and she answered, with bitter but entire self-abnegation :

" Not if you wish me to remain."

" I do."

It was like an order given to one of his soldiers, and
like a soldier—none was ever braver—she bowed her
head in acquiescence ; bowed it upon the hand she held,
her face turned away from his gaze. Who shall tell her
disappointment? She had hoped—ah, for what had she
not hoped? Love—passion? Why not? She had
deserved all that man might give. Gratitude was the
least she could expect. And he was cold—so cold!
The hand she held lay inert as death in her fervid
clasp. He had asked her to remain—to sacrifice herself—her maiden pride for him—almost as if perform-
ing an unpleasant task. When she looked into his face
there was no more trace of emotion there than in the
sculptured features of the Sphinx. But he was not
himself; he was sick, weak. No matter. She had
given all when she hoped for no return ; why should
she shrink now that her expectations were but half fulfilled? She would stay ; she would at least be near him
until his mother came. That would be one, two—perhaps three days. After that—

It was needless to formulate the alternative. Even
while she knelt beside him Fate was busy forging the
links that were to bind them together. A press correspondent, one of that host of imaginative news-gatherers
who follow in an army's track, easily wormed out of the
elate and kindly surgeon the story of his favorite patient's recovery, to which he added a pretty tale of

woman's love—a story which outlives all other phases of human experience in universal and perennial charm.

The correspondent did not, of course, reveal the lady's name, but in announcing the discovery and convalescence of a gallant officer who had been mourned as dead, he painted as sweet a romance as was ever hung on the ferruginous front of war. The news of Hubert Goodwin's recovery, and of the devotion of the young lady whose love would not let her believe him dead, went out to the world together. There was no longer any other course for him to pursue. If Delia Kincaid were to come to-morrow, an unwed maiden, to ask fulfillment of his vow, he must in honor offer name and hand to the woman whose heart would not rest upon uncertainties in respect to his fate. His love he could not give her—he had none to bestow. He did not hesitate—but told her the truth, and asked her to be his wife. As before, she answered his request with the lifeless formula of self-surrender :

" If you wish it—to be so."

There was no elation, no tender exultation in her tone. She had longed for love, and her hunger was unappeased. Under other circumstances, she would not have accepted an empty hand—a hand without a heart—but she, too, was bound by Fate. Her secret had been wrung from her and published to the world. To refuse was not only to proclaim herself discarded, but to stain the name of one whose honor was dearer to her than life. So, on the heels of the story of their love, came the announcement of their marriage.

Three months' leave of absence was granted the young soldier. When it had expired, he was ready for duty in his new station. Just before his departure, his uncle said to him one morning, as they sat under the great elm in front of the new mansion, which had replaced the old house :

" Do you know, I believe I have solved the mystery of your getting off the field that night ? It flashed into my head as soon as I heard the doctor tell about your whistling my old call. What is my theory ? You read this, I suppose, when it came out ?"

He handed his listener a newspaper clipping, worn and soiled, as he spoke :

"The lovers of good horse-flesh will regret to learn that the noted horse, Belmont's Abdallah, was stolen from the premises of his owner, Mr. James Mosely, on Wednesday night, by a squad of men claiming to be Confederate soldiers. As Mr. Mosely's Union proclivities are well known, this claim would naturally be made by any company of bushwhackers who might see fit to plunder his stables. He has often been warned that it was folly to keep such valuable stock on disputed territory, but until the present advance of Bragg's forces, his property has been undisturbed."

"Yes, I saw it," answered the young officer ; " and during Bragg's retreat, while we were scouting in his rear, I kept my ears open for any rumor as to Abdallah's whereabouts. In fact, I rode twenty miles one night on a false report that he was ' hidden out ' at a place in the ' knob country,' east of Lebanon, but found no trace of him."

" Well, I have, or rather Lieutenant Barclay has," answered the uncle. " By the way, I am glad you promoted Chris. I tried to keep him from going as an enlisted man at all. He might have had a commission at the start as well as not ; but he was over-modest, and besides, had his heart set on going with you. He wanted to be a farrier, too. He is proud of his ability to shoe a horse, you know, and really thought he could do the country more good by using that knowledge than in any other way."

" With good reason, too. I hesitated about promoting him on that account, but it has proved to be sound policy. Half the efficiency of the regiment is due to the fact that he has been permanently detailed to look after the horses' hoofs. We rarely have one go lame on the march now. There was some murmuring when I gave him a first lieutenancy and detailed him as inspector of horses, but every one soon recognized its wisdom. If I get a cavalry brigade, as I hope I may, I shall take him with me."

"Well, as I was saying, Chris got word from some prisoners that a horse of Abdallah's description, belonging to the colonel of the Second Kentucky Confederate Infantry, which was one of the regiments guarding the bridge where you made your charge, broke away and came over to our side that night. They spoke of it as a good joke on the colonel, who had bought the horse of some bushwhackers up in Kentucky. They said he evidently disliked the Rebel service, and made a break for the Union lines. Now you see how it all happened ; you were delirious and took to whistling our old call ; he heard it and answered ; you clambered up on him and he brought you inside the lines."

" Seems very probable."

" Oh, there's no doubt about it. Tne horse that brought you in was a bay—that's about all that could be learned about him from the regiment whose lines you entered, except that he was taken possession of by an officer who was shot the next day."

" And that was the last of him ?"

" Hardly ; just after the battle there was a big cock-

and-bull story in the papers about Mr. Marshall King—
that's the new name of our old friend of the Corners,
you know—who was acting as a volunteer *aide* on somebody's staff, being taken prisoner during the second
day's fight, and getting away and coming back into our
lines on a Confederate officer's horse, which he had captured. Of course, King Marsh or Marsh King, which-
ever he calls himself, is a good deal of a man, there's no
mistake about that, and under such circumstances
would probably take considerable risk. The Confeder-
ates are not partial to men of his stamp—cotton-thieves,
as they call them—but such a feat is easier imagined
than performed, I fancy, and we know he has a very
able-bodied imagination. Of course, if it was a fact, I
take it he'd have got a commission before this time—
though, perhaps, he don't want it—more money in cotton, I s'pose. But I ran across something this morning
which shed some new light on the matter."

He handed the other a newspaper, and pointed to a
brief paragraph as he spoke :

" The splendid stallion which was captured by Mr.
Marshall King at Stone River has been sold to Mr.
Stokes, of St. Louis, who will put him on a horse ranch
he is just starting in Colorado. The price paid is said
to have been a fancy one, it being the general belief
that the horse is one of the most noted of trotting sires.
The West is to be congratulated upon his accession, and
it is quite possible that it may fall to the lot of his
progeny to justify the prediction so often made by horsemen, that the greatest trotters of the world will be bred
in a high altitude and a dry climate."

" It's my notion that's our old Abdallah."
" I rather think it is."

"Kincaid got him after all, it seems, if he did have to steal him twice. I was mighty sorry for you, of course," continued the uncle, with an affectionate look at his companion, "but I'm glad now you didn't marry into that family. Dee was well enough, but—why, what's the matter?"

The young man had grown suddenly pale, reeled in his chair, and muttered brokenly :

"Forever and ever !"

"I declare, it's his old hurt ! Susan ! Kitty ! Come here, quick !"

They found Horace Goodwin supporting his nephew's head, while the young soldier's eyes glared wildly down the road, and his white lips repeated over and over : "Forever and ever, amen !" But no one thought of connecting these words with the vision of a girlish figure on a black pony, which had flashed across his memory and made the man a boy again.

CHAPTER XVI.

CAUGHT BY THE UNDERTOW.

The close of the war left Hubert Goodwin, like many others, in a most unpleasant position. Before reaching his prime he had won high honors in a profession he must now renounce. What should he do? The American had not then learned to loiter. The impulse to achieve was then the controlling force in every life, and the young soldier felt the full strength of that restless desire for achievement which has built up an empire within a possible lifetime. Strangely enough, he found the avenues of business almost closed against him. He was not only a distinguished soldier, but a young one. People thought the qualities which had given him success in the field would militate against him in civil life. He had no aptitude for politics, no desire for a professional career. He had capital, energy, confidence, luck, so it was said, so the past had proved, but no one wished to venture with him. Even Sedley seemed to have forgotten his old offer. Perhaps there was something of envy in it. It was not pleasant to know that the " Sedley Legion " had been almost forgotten, and that the young soldier, whose feet he had set so high upon the ladder of preferment at the outset, had gone on climbing up without his assistance until his fame overshadowed his patron's. He had hardly grown a fair mustache when a colonel's eagles graced his shoulders, and the corps, which Sedley had created, began to be known as " Goodwin's regiment." Nobody thought of it as anything else, now. It was known only by that and its number. Only by a careful scrutiny of the records could one learn who had organized and equipped it.

Hubert Goodwin had seen little of the wife whom Fate had given him since their marriage, but he had given her the key of his purse and she had used her privilege thriftily in his absence. A charming home awaited him on his return. His family had taken the brave young wife into especial favor. His mother, resenting, as any mother would, what she considered the perfidy of his first love, had given even more than a daughter's place to the wife whom she realized instinctively had less than her due share of a husband's affection. She felt that in his years of service her son had thought more of the love he had lost than of the wife he had won ; but she did not know how, in the strange seclusion which the camp brings, he had turned again toward that dream of the past. Closely associated with Doctor Talcott, he had learned through the letters of the surgeon's wife everything that had happened to her ; how she had grown petulant, morose, and finally so violently antipathetic to both her husband and her parents that she had come to the physician's house and refused to return or hold any communication with her relatives. She was quieter there, but took no interest in public affairs and showed no memory of her former life. She wandered in the grove near the house, rode her horse, and seemed to have no thought of the present and no care for the future. She would allow herself to be called by no name except "Weely," which she often repeated over and over to herself for some minutes at a time, with a vague, puzzled expression that was new to her. The only attention she paid to the announcement that her husband had been elected to Congress was to remark that she was glad of it, if it would keep him away from her.

Dr. Talcott would say, after each of these letters :
"Strange as it may seem, I am afraid she will recover. That would make trouble. You see, her marriage was not really an act of her volition. The woman who assented to the marital obligation was quite another person—a different consciousness from that which once dominated her nature. It seems as if the brain was slowly drifting back to its normal condition. If it ever reaches it, all that has intervened will be as blank to her as her former life is now."

The kind surgeon did not know that this was rank poison to the soul which had pledged itself, "Forever and ever," to that clouded consciousness.

Each day since his return had driven home to the heart of Hubert Goodwin, more clearly than ever before, the terrible fact that he did not love his own wife, but did love another's with a fervency which time could not abate nor absence dull. Long before, he had arrived at the conclusion that his marriage was wrong, a sin, almost a crime—not against her he had married, but against the other, whom he might not marry—that love who was dead and yet alive. He had even begun to consider whether there was not some way by which he might remedy the wrong. If he could only take the poor, stricken life he loved away from her cruel surroundings, he was sure he could make her happy. He did not wish to do wrong, and he would not sully her white, half consciousness even with the shadow of shame. If he could only be with her, soothe, protect, cheer her as if she were his sister ! Ah, he would willingly subordinate himself—eliminate, eradicate himself—to give happiness, repose, content to the shattered life he loved ! It was a dangerous mood for such a compound of conscience and recklessness as the son of Theophilus and Old Harry.

For a brief time the bright, sunny home dissipated such fancies. Kittie Goodwin did not understand her husband. Why should she ? He did not understand himself. She feared he would be lonely after the turmoil of the camp, not knowing that among the multitude of other men· the individual man is lonelier than anywhere else. He has then no one to come near his heart ; no one to share his life and thought. A man dwells always in a zone which only a woman can enter. Mother, sister, sweetheart, wife, daughter, friend—some relation there must be which brings the complement of manhood to his side, or man lives essentially alone. Only rarely do two men become so attached that each desires the constant companionship of the other. They are naturally repellant poles. Cast away upon a desert island or frozen in upon a polar sea, they become suspicious, resentful, hostile. If one is strong and the other weak ; if one demands and the other affords protection and support, the mutual aversion may be subordinated to this need ; but if both are strong, safety can be found only in separation—mutual isolation

It is not so with woman. Isolation is death to her. Left alone, she loses her womanhood ; becomes coarse and masculine in appearance and character. Thrown near another life, she gravitates toward it by irresistible attraction. If any insurmountable barrier prevents intimate association with man, she turns to her own sex for companionship. She is never recluse from preference. She does not think out the puzzles of life alone, but feels them out with another, or with another submits to them. So this young wife, to cure her husband's loneliness, as she thought, surrounded him with cheerful society. For this she had planned during his absence ; on this she relied to keep him near her and win him nearer. The new home was full of light and revelry. The famous young soldier and his beautiful bride made a center around which society in those days of triumph and rejoicing clustered as naturally as filings about a magnet. She was trying to please, to divert him—to keep him from thinking of himself or that shadow which she knew hung over his consciousness, the result of his wound. It was a sweet, womanly effort. She endeavored to make his wealth, his fame, her beauty and attractiveness minister to his happiness, and hoped thereby to win his love.

Ah, if she had only known—what woman can never know—the heart of man, she would have taken a different course. She would have realized that the gratification of all a man's desires is the surest road to discontent ; that it is only struggle and the need for struggle that keep him on an even keel. He must be doing for

himself or another, or he rusts, retrogrades, becomes de-
moralized. If she had applied the torch to the beautiful
home ; if, instead of self-helpfulness, she had shown de-
pendency and demanded care, the result might have
been different—nay, it would have been.

This is not said in blame. Save himself and his fate,
Hubert Goodwin had no one to blame for his acts or
their consequences ; it may, perhaps, be said in mitiga-
tion of the condemnation heaped upon him that he
blamed no one. If he had known his wife's thought, it
might have been better or it might have been worse,
As it was, he said to himself, when he saw the sparkle
in her eye, the flush upon her cheek and the thrill of
happiness echoing through her tones :

"This is her life. How happy she is ! I am the
only blot on the white page. I am deceiving her.
These things give me no pleasure ; but she thinks I
enjoy them. I am wronging her by the pretense of
happiness. She thinks me content ; she believes that I
love her as she deserves to be loved. I do not ; I cannot !"

Ah, if there had come to him then the need of great
exertion ! But Fate will not be cheated. While he
waited, heart-sick and wistful, seeking opportunity, his
strength panting for demand upon its potency, the day
of subtle and irresistible temptation was approaching.

At the close of the war, Horace Goodwin, with justi-
fiable pride in his success, had said to his nephew :

"There is no need for you to take any thought for
the morrow. Here is the result of our joint venture."

Then he made a report of his acquisition, and apprais-
ing everything at a just value, divided it in twain, and
deducting only what he had paid on the other's account,
he handed to the silent partner in his enterprise—one

moiety of the proceeds. It was a tin box full of government securities. The young man turned them over curiously. He had known little of the financial struggle by which the armies were supplied and the nation saved ; so that these crackling sheets of paper, with their green lettering, intricately ruled ornamentation and plentitude of blood-red seals, as if a soldier's life were the guarantee of each promise which the nation made to pay for her deliverance, were to him a strange mystery.

"All you have to do," continued the proud uncle, as he showed the result of his sagacious foresight, "is to turn the key on those bonds—make a special deposit where they will be safe ; use the interest as you may desire, and their appreciation alone will give you a greater profit than most business ventures can be made to yield. I hope you are satisfied with my stewardship ?"

"Satisfied !" was the hearty response, "I should be most unreasonable if I were not. But you are unjust ; you have taken nothing for your expense—your care and watchfulness."

"There you are wrong. Do you not see that what we have expended is not in the aggregate ; it has been consumed. I have charged you with your expenses up to the time you entered the service, and thought, as they then ceased, I ought to charge myself with our own, but your mother said she was sure you would not allow it."

"Nor would I."

"Well, I am satisfied if you are ; there is enough for all of us ; though I expect to make something more for the little ones now and then, as opportunity offers. Making money has become a habit, you see. You do not think I have been so bad a step-father, Hubert ?"

The young man silently reached forth his hand.

" I am glad you are not sorry for having followed my advice. I was not at all sure I was right, but I tried to do what I thought Seth would approve. I only thought of you and your mother ; and she only thought of you. I don't think you at all realize how closely she has followed your steps, and how proud she is of you. You were her first child, and all she had to pet and care for, until you were almost man-grown. Seth didn't give her any chance to show her love for him. We are a hard set in that way, we Goodwins ; we like to give, but will not take. When you went off to school, I thought she would cry her eyes out ; but you never seemed to think she could be unhappy. I don't believe your letters had a word of sympathy in them."

" But she had you, uncle."

" Me ! A nice pet I was, to be sure ! Of course, I loved her—always had, for that matter, I believe—but she would as soon have thought of loving a polar bear. She wanted somebody to whose existence her love was a necessity. She thought it was to you, until you went away from her so contentedly. Of course, the children have helped to console her, but they haven't taken your place—never will. You are *her* child, her pride. I really believe it would kill her if anything should happen to you ; if you should go to the bad, you know, as we're both likely to, having the mark."

Horace Goodwin spoke with a prescient apprehension which startled his listener.

"What are you going to do ?" he asked after a moment.

" I don't—know," came the hesitant answer.

"You must not be idle ; it is death to a Goodwin. Why don't you go West and look around ?"

" I think I will," meditatively.

Ah, watchful guardian, it was a cruel thing for Fate
to make you the instrument of woe !

The blow came very soon. The wife had no premoni-
tion.

One morning, she found on her dressing-table a note :

"KITTY :   I am going away. I do not know where
nor when I shall return, if ever. There is no excuse
for the course I have taken, and I cannot hope for your
forgiveness nor to retain your respect. Not to soften
your resentment but to testify my regard, I give you the
major part of my estate.

"Trusting that you will forget me, and be happier
than you could hope to be if I remained, I bid you good-
bye.   "HUBERT GOODWIN."

It was the last time but one that he ever subscribed
his name. These two signatures transformed an honorable patronymic into a blazon of eternal shame.

Upon her husband's desk, Kitty Goodwin found the
key of his strong-box and a deed to its contents. He
had taken with him one-third of the capital. The house
was hers. The deserted wife was rich, young and fair.
She did not know how soon she was also to be a widow.
She did not know that two days before there came a letter from Doctor Talcott, saying : "The poor lady whom
you wot of is no better. She wanders about, calling
with plaintive eagerness for 'Jack ! Jack ! Jack !'—a
word which is the one remembered fact of a past she
will never find again."

CHAPTER XVII.

A FORSWORN KNIGHT.

The life I have depicted lies so far away from that which followed, that its events seem to have occurred to another. For this reason, I have told them in the third person. Even now, when my mind has dwelt for weeks upon the retrospect, I can hardly realize that it was I who bore the name of Hubert Goodwin, and my wife that was abandoned in the pleasant home while I sped westward with only one thought in my heart—to answer that yearning cry for my lost love. It had been ringing in my ears ever since I read my friend's letter : "Jack ! Jack !" I heard it every moment, night and day —for I could not sleep—the throbbing engine called me and the singing rails echoed the cry, " Jack ! Jack !"

I had no plan, no purpose, only to get to her side. I had acted deliberately from a dull, stolid conviction that the course I was taking would separate me finally from my wife. I did not greatly care, if it did. For myself I had no feeling except a certain sense of humiliation. I knew I was doing her injustice and bringing discredit on myself. These things I felt keenly. The old Goodwin pride was not dead, though the terrible throbbing pain in my head—the pain which had always marked the spot where the operation had been performed—almost drove it from my mind. It was a

strange delusion, but all the time I had the thought
that if I could only find Dee—if I could once touch her
hand and look into her eyes, she would know me ; her
old life would come back and this terrible depressing
pain would disappear. And then—but I did not go
any farther. I did not care to imagine what might happen then. So I fled, sullen and desperate, but never
once relenting in my purpose, from honor to shame—
from life to death.

I did not need to ask the way to Doctor Talcott's
when I left the train at Wiswall Station. I knew he
lived five miles out on the road to Good Cheer, which
was as far on the other side. His place was called
Heart's Ease, and embraced a beautiful lake with a
romantic wooded outlet, called the Glen. This property
he intended to convert into a summer resort and sani-
tarium. Lying between two great lines of railroad, in
a region where the eternal sunshine of the prairie makes
the relief of shade and the music of falling water especially grateful to overworn nerves, the good doctor
believed that in this bit of shaded waterfall and quiet
stretch of willow-bordered lake, he had not only health
and comfort, but that inevitable fortune of which every
American dreams. Over and over again I had listened
to his plans for its development. I am glad to say his
dreams have all been fulfilled.

I merely asked the livery-keeper, from whom I hired
a rig, the road to Good Cheer. As God is my judge, I
had no thought of what would happen on that eventful
day. I intended merely to get a glimpse of *her*—and
then go away. I will not deny that I hoped she would
recognize me, or that I confidently expected her to do
so ; but I had no thought of anything more. I wished
to let her know that she had my sympathy—that I still
loved her. I did not conceal from myself that I had

no right to do even this. I was another woman's husband, she another man's wife. The double barrier between us I fully recognized. If I were willing to plunge myself into shame, I had no right to drag her down with me, and did not mean to do so.

It was a bright day in October. The dark, hard road lay straight and level between brown, dry fields, bordered with struggling osage orange hedges. Country homes, bursting cribs, eastward-sloping windbreaks, black cornfields with ripe ears hanging down and gatherers at work in them, or sleek flocks browsing among the broken stalks for neglected ears, hardly relieved its flat monotony. The horse was one of those even-going, hard-hoofed roadsters, with which a prairie country always abounds. His pace did not seem rapid, and I was surprised to find in half an hour the dun, stunted grove of the Glen rising just before me, and catch a glint of the little lake through the half-bare branches. On the other side of the Glen, and a half-mile above, I could see the unpainted roof of the new building I had been told the doctor was erecting at Heart's Ease.

The sun was very warm, but not warm enough to account for the perspiration that poured down my face. My heel burned as if in a clamp of red-hot iron. I felt that I was going to my doom, yet I was powerless to turn back. In truth, I did not wish to if it were possible that I might give *her* any pleasure. I was willing to endure anything for *her* sake, but this did not make the agony I suffered any less. I drew up at the top of the bank where the road slopes down into the narrow gorge, and thought of all these things. The bright blue sky was without a cloud.

I could hear the hammers of the men at work on the new building across the ravine. The strong-limbed chestnut pulled upon the rein and pawed the ground impatiently. Should I go on or return?

I did not know what would happen. I had formed no plans, except that I would see *her*. But suppose she recognized me ; suppose she appealed to my love—implored my protection ? I knew that if she did I would trample honor under my feet and become, from that moment, an outcast among men. Should I go forward or back—back to the wife I had abandoned or forward to the love who had been torn from my arms? I thought it all over—my father's hope, my mother's trust, my uncle's loving pride, my wife's happiness—it was strange I did not think of her love. I realize now that I had never gotten over a sort of resentment at the fate which bound us together. I knew she loved me, but had never comprehended the depth of her devotion. It had never occurred to me that, even as I loved another, so did she love me ; that knowledge was yet to come. The hot blood mounted to my face, and I put my hands over my eyes to shut out the sunlight, as I thought how, only a week before, my old friend, Doctor Neuman, had asked me if I felt no inclination to return to the profession I had abandoned—had told me of the good I might do, of the need of reapers in the great white harvest-fields, of my father's aspiration, of the prayers which had gone up for me in the days of battle, and the joy of many hearts that, from the midst of temptation, I had come forth unscathed.

How these thoughts stung and blistered and shriveled my heart ! But all about me in the golden sunshine, echoing from the blue vault above, from the russet-lined gorge below, in the strokes of the workmen, in the roar of the waterfall, came the imploring, abjuring cry, " Forever and ever, Amen !" A white face swam before my close-shut eyes, white and wan and appealing, with golden tresses, wax-like, wraith-like, drooping with the unutterable agony of helplessness and despair. A fresh breeze came over the flat, pitiless prairie, rustled the yellow corn-husks on the one side and the brown oak-leaves upon the other, and each one whispered and wailed : " Forever !   Forever !"

How the patched place upon my skull throbbed and beat !   The whole world seemed pressing down upon my brain.   My head was full of phosphorescent light. And the Goodwins were proud—so proud of their good name !   My life had been honorable, and I had had the devil's luck.   Now I must pay the devil's price.

I caught the whip from the socket and gave the horse a savage cut.   He dashed madly down the sharp incline. The swift motion pleased me.   I laughed at the bank and the trees as they flew backward.   Would the buggy upset and dash me down—down to death on the rocks below?   I hoped so.   I struck the horse again ; the buggy balanced on two wheels as we turned toward the narrow bridge that spanned the white torrent-bed which the shallow water spread itself lazily half-way across. The frail structure swayed beneath the spurning feet, and the rattling echoes raced up and down the Glen as we flew over it.   The road turned sharply to the right and climbed up the other side of the gorge at a grade even heavier than that which we had descended.   There was a wall upon the left, somewhat higher than the wheels of the carriage—a parapet built to restrain the slaty earth above.   The rush had calmed my excitement. Something seemed to have given way in my brain. The wild, throbbing, desperate pain which marked the location of the trephine was gone—gone forever, as I learned—and I felt strangely light, exultant, free ; reckless, perhaps, I might better say.   The past was not forgotten, but seemed dim and remote.   The steep

A GRAY FIGURE SPRANG FROM THE GROUND.—*See Page 327.*

grade was telling on the horse ; his pace fell first to a trot, and then to a labored, wheezing walk. His flanks were covered with foam. The sun beat down fierce and hot in the windless ravine.

" Jack ! Jack !"

A gray figure sprang from the ground a dozen steps away, and in an instant stood balanced on the wall by the roadside. I checked the horse in amazement. There was a rush of garments, and a woman lighted like a bird in the buggy by my side. The horse started, but was too much fagged to run, and, after a few steps, resumed his hurried, frightened walk.

" I'm all right," she whispered, seating herself composedly. " Let him go."

I hastily soothed the horse with my voice.

" Jack ?" she said, inquiringly, turning her head toward me. " Jack ! Jack !" she repeated wildly, flinging her arms about my neck.

Ah ! How they choked me ! Or was it the heart-beats? I knew I had met my doom. Nay ! I was already in perdition ! Yet I had no wish to turn back.

We were approaching the top of the gorge. I remembered having heard that the road to Good Cheer ran along the " section-line " a considerable distance from the house. I put up the carriage-top, drew the dust-cloth over her lap and took the right-hand road.

The die was cast ! I no longer felt sorrow, shame or dread. *She* was with me !

" Jack ! Jack !" she continued to repeat, as she sobbed hysterically on my shoulder.

" Dee," I said tenderly, when we had passed the house and had only the open prairie before us again—" poor little Dee !"

I heard the workmen's hammers ring behind us as I

spoke. I took the reins in my right hand and clasped my left arm about her.

"Don't scold Weely," she said, shrinking away and looking half-timorously, half-reproachfully up into my face. My excited tone had frightened her.

What was it made the cold sweat start out from every pore? This was not she whom I sought. The features were the same, the eyes the same, but another, a different intelligence was in them. The voice had changed, too ; there were the same tones, but of a different quality. It seemed as if another being looked through the shallow, wavering eyes ; some soulless automaton moved the lips that used to smile upon me when they spoke. The hair, too—it had partly fallen down, and had that visibly snaky look so characteristic of the insane.

"Deely ! Dee ! Dee ! Don't you know me ? Don't you remember Jack ?" I cried, in agony, striving to awaken the consciousness I would not believe could be dead to my entreaty.

A troubled expression came upon her face. She seemed to be listening to something very far away—a voice she could dimly hear or was unable to recognize.

"Jack ?" she cried, with pathetic inquiry, looking not into my face but past it. "Jack ! Jack !" she repeated ; but there was no hint of recognition in her tones.

I bowed my head in shame and horror. What had I done? For what had I bartered manhood—honor—the esteem of all? A crazy woman's senseless cry had dragged me down to perdition. Strange enough, it did not once occur to me that what had been done might easily be undone, that I might drive back to Heart's Ease, and by telling only the truth, hide forever all suspicion of the truth. I had set out to give my life for her happiness. I did not think it material whether her desire was rational or insane. So when she asked in that

horrible, mechanical tone, but with a bright, interested
look : " Are we going to Good Cheer ?" I nodded affirmatively.

" How good ! It is five miles," she said, contentedly.
" Shall we take the cars ?"

I looked at my watch. A train would pass there in an
hour going east.

" Would you like to ?" I asked.

She started at the sound of my voice, and looked at
me with curious inquiry.

" Jack !" she moaned, plaintively. " Jack ! Jack !
Jack!"

The last words sank to a whisper.

" Where would you like to go ?"

" Anywhere," she answered brightly again—"anywhere. How good !"

Then her eyes became dreamy, and she repeated,
softly : " Jack ! Jack ! Jack !"

" To Dubuque ?" I asked.

It was there her husband lived.

"No !" she exclaimed, excitedly. Her brows knotted,
and she turned and spat angrily toward the roadside.
" No ! No !" she repeated.

There was a moment's silence, and then came again
the plaintive cry :

" Jack ! Jack ! Jack !"

How my heart ached ! Had she been calling me day
and night for all these years ? What were honor, rank,
esteem in comparison with her poor heart's content?
Hereafter she should never call for me in vain. But
what should I do with her ? She would attract the attention of every one we met. Thinking perhaps my
voice had stirred her memory and made her unusually
excited, I tried to disguise it, and said, in a very different tone :

"If you go on the train you must be very quiet.''

She looked inquiringly at me an instant, as if a little disturbed by my presence, and then answered, lightly: "Oh, I will; you know I always am. I do like to travel. Shall we go in a sleeper? I never was in a sleeper—but once. How good!"

The childish sentences pained me not less than the eager look which accompanied them, but most of all the senseless phrase of acknowledgment. Presently I noticed that her lips were moving, and heard her saying, below her breath:

"Jack! Jack! Jack!"

How many times had she called me in the silent years since we parted? I vowed then again to remain with her "Forever and ever!" I did not say until she was dead, for I knew I could never go back to the life I had abandoned.

It was ten minutes of train-time when we reached the station. At my suggestion she had put up her hair with all her old grace and deftness. I could not touch it. It was like the locks of the dead to me. I assisted her from the buggy, gave the driver of a waiting omnibus the price he asked to return the horse to Wiswall Station, and taking my overcoat, umbrella and gripsack entered the station with Dee at my side. I gave her the light overcoat to carry—a woman looks strangely uncomfortable with nothing in her hands when traveling. I bought tickets to Chicago. The seats in the sleeping-car were all occupied except the state-room; so I took that. She was full of childish wonder at everything she saw, asking the same questions often over and over again.

It was nearly dark when we reached a station where the train stopped for supper. It was a junction with another great trunk line leading southwestward. As we steamed into the depot I saw a train upon the track beyond the station headed the other way. My plan was taken in an instant. I did not know where it was going ; I did not care. When our train slowed up, I took my companion by the hand and started to get off. She followed me gladly. There was a great crowd rushing back and forth. The gong was sounding ; parties were shouting ; the station-lamps glared ; the steam hissed, and all was confusion. The porter said, as he helped us from the train, that it would wait twenty minutes for supper. He advised that we should leave our luggage in the car. I pretended not to hear him. There was a good reason why I should not. Dee's eyes were roving about the unaccustomed scene, not wildly, but with that uncomprehending eagerness which more surely tells of a brain diseased. Tucking her hand under my arm, I hurried through the crowded station and secured seats on the other train. Then I went back, procured tickets to the western terminus of the road, ordered a porter to bring us refreshments, and while she ate, indited a note to Doctor Talcott informing him of what had occurred. I thought it only just that I should relieve him both from anxiety and imputation. It was well I did so. That letter was the last vestige of my old life. Since I dropped it in the letter-box of the Junction no hint or trace of Hubert Goodwin has been found by any one who knew him while alive. The tree of my first life had grown thriftily and straight, its branches decked with honorable deeds and rare good fortune. It had flowered and fruited with golden promise. Alas! they were apples of Sodom—ashes and doom.

All night long she leaned her golden head against my breast and slept, while the train rumbled on into the darkness. A storm raged without ; one more terrible still raged in my bosom. She was ignorant of both.

The train was crowded. The great Eastern hive was swarming out on the yet unoccupied Western plains. As the night crept on, the strange silence which never prevails where the habitations of man are frequent settled down upon us. We were passing over the almost unsettled prairies, which were so soon to become the seat of empire. The engine throbbed, the wheels rolled on through the silence while I thought out my destiny. The past was dead—how dead I did not know. The future had no ray of light. Even love was dead. I thought I could not love the woman who slept in my arms so peacefully. The fiercest passion could not look into her eyes and live. Pity was the strongest sentiment she could evoke, and I did pity her tenderly and truly. As I caught sight of her sleeping face, now and then, by the light of the flickering car-lamp, I knew that destiny had linked me with her doom irrevocably. Fate had made her my sister ; shame and folly, perhaps sin, had made me her protector. Whatever I had been before, I recognized the fact that thereafter I could be only the wind-break of this shadowy existence. I might shield her from the storms of life ; beyond that I had no future.

Had it been possible, I think I might even then have been tempted to retrace my steps. Strange as it may seem, for the first time I thought that night regretfully of my wife in her deserted home, and of the life I had voluntarily broken in twain. The pain in my head, which had hardly left me since consciousness returned after my wound, was gone. I had felt none of it since that mad ride through the gorge at Heart's Ease. Yet the suffering of that night it is impossible to describe. While she slept I bent above her, my hat drawn down over my eyes, my face burning and chill by turns, but wet with drops of unutterable agony. It was as if I

had just waked out of a fevered dream, to know that by
my own frenzied act in that half-conscious state I had
cut myself off forever from all hope of happiness.

I had strange dreams in those fevered hours. At one
time I thought I would return next day, deliver her
to her husband and go back again to my old life;
perhaps I might wire Doctor Talcott and the escape o_
his patient thus be kept secret. Could I do it? Would her
husband receive her back from my hands? She was as
spotless as when I first kissed her child-lips so long ago.
I could not kiss her lips now. In all the long hours of
that terrible night I felt no inclination to once touch the
parted leaflets which smiled and quivered as she slept
and dreamed upon my breast. I had no wish to possess
what I had so long yearned to enjoy. I knew it could
not be. The world would not permit either the
wronged husband or the deserted wife to forgive. My
story would be laughed at. Why should it not be? It
now seemed incredible even to me. So, I beat around
the cruel circle of my Fate, coming always to the same
conclusion ; no backward step was possible ; we must
go forward, she and I, and hand in hand.

Before the morning dawned, I had decided what
should be done. I would bury the dead past and we
two would live alone, a new life in a new world. She
should be my sister. I would live for her, care for her,
acquire for her. She should have comfort, tenderness,
love—such love as one gives to things unconscious or
superhuman. I would live by her side, and when the
end came to her, would bury the rest of my shattered
life in oblivion. But I determined that I would never
wear the old name. No future act should add to the
infamy I had already heaped upon it—the dear old name
of which I had been so proud ! I bent and kissed the
fair brow of the sleeper as I reached this conclusion,

little dreaming how Fate had joined hands with my purpose and wrought for me in those bitter hours of darkness.

The sun was shining over the gray shimmering autumn prairies as we steamed into an infant metropolis of the plains.

"Paper? *Morning News?*" cried an enterprising lad who boarded the train before it reached the station. "All about the big cyclone !"

I bought a copy and ran my eyes hastily over the news columns, trembling lest my shame had already become public. Sure enough, there it was in glaring capitals :

"General Goodwin, the Brilliant Cavalry Leader who left his home in the East so mysteriously a few days ago, Steals the Wife of the Hon. Ransom Howe from a Private Asylum for the Insane !"

"The Guilty Couple take Passage for Chicago on a Train which is Wrecked by a Cyclone, and are Both Killed !"

"Terrible Cyclone in Iowa, Sweeping Through into Northern Illinois !"

My brain was in a whirl as I read. The train on which we had taken passage for Chicago had run into the cyclone which devastated three States that sultry autumn night ; the sleeper attached to it had been blown from the track and caught fire and burned, with all on board. It was known that we had taken this train, and *not* known that we had left it. We were indeed dead—dead to all the world except ourselves.

Nay, to all except myself ; the fair creature who, waking from undisturbed repose, was watching with childish eagerness all that went on about her, did not count. She had died before. And now we were alone—the dead with his dead.

It flashed upon me in an instant. I had only to accept the boon that Fate held out—enter the grave that had been prepared for me—and the tide of shame would sweep harmlessly above me. There would be need of such shelter, as I well knew. The very journal in my trembling hands reeked with denunciation of my infamy. How I pitied the poor wife who alone would be left to meet its force ! And the Goodwins—the Goodwins who were so proud ! My brain reeled !

But I knew I must act quickly. Already it seemed as if a score of suspicious glances were fixed upon me. I fancied that I heard my name bandied from one to another—the name I loved—of which I was so proud ! I must never answer to it again, never show any interest should it be mentioned in my presence ! I must have another. Where should I get it ? What should I call myself ? A thousand names flashed through my brain. Which should I choose ?

But first we must leave the train. It would not do to risk detection by traveling longer with those who had been our fellow-passengers from the Junction.

"Come !" I said hurriedly to my companion, gathering up our things.

"Are we going to stop here?" she asked in pleased surprise. "How good,! Jack ! Jack !" she began in her low, wailing cry.

I turned and looked at her sharply, reprovingly.

"How good ! How good !" she murmured apologetically.

As we rode from the station she kept repeating these words alternately in half-audible whispers.

"Jack! Jack! How good! How good!"

I was busy with my thoughts, and paid no heed to her words.

When we reached the hotel and I stood pen in hand before the register, they flashed upon my consciousness and I wrote :

"John Howgood and sister."

I could not help smiling at the contrast between the name I had assumed and the one the world had given me that morning. When I glanced in the mirror in the hotel parlor where I left *her*, I saw that my hair was streaked with gray. In a week, it was almost white. I let my beard grow. It was white also. I gave out that I had brought my sister to the city for treatment, and was fortunate in finding a quiet lodging and securing a bright, strong-armed French girl, whom the ebb of fortune had just then cast adrift in the city, to attend upon her. She was faithful, tender-hearted, and spoke so little English that there was small danger that she would tell what she might learn, or guess at what she did not know. There was not much to fear. We were new beings in a new world ; nameless but for the pseudonym the irony of her unconscious repetition bestowed. Yet into this new world love entered, and with it hope. I determined to attempt her restoration, and began very soon to people a possible future with bright visions of a love no past should disturb.

It seemed an easy task. There was only a little way between her sprightly consciousness and that strange sequence of ideas which we call sanity, and I wondered that those who had had her in charge had not long ago found a way over the impalpable barrier which separated them. But I soon found that her poor brain was like the sands of the seashore. However fair and plain a thought might be written on it to-day, it was a blank upon the morrow. A few every-day facts seemed weakly impressed upon it.

She was quiet, modest, docile, and ever anxious to please. She was very fond of having one read aloud to her, but cared little what the book might be, only preferring poetry or prose of a metric or sonorous character. Like a little child, she was vain of her ability to read ; an act which consisted of a ready and correct pronunciation of the words upon a printed page without the least comprehension of their significance, or rather without any coherent sense of the succession of ideas presented by them. This verbal recollection I had often heard Doctor Talcott refer to as one of the strange phases of her ailment. He connected it somehow with her previous linguistic ability, which had been very noticeable, and thought this had created a sort of instinctive mechanical aptitude for verbal forms, just as persons of weak minds sometimes possess remarkable arithmetical powers without any comprehension of the problems they solve or the significance even of the numbers they use. While she pronounced most words correctly, her enunciation showed that she had no comprehension of their import—she pronounced rather than read, and never opened a book except to display this faculty.

I did not murmur at the task I had assumed, counting no penance too great for the wrong I had done. Besides that, she was all alone in the world. There was no one else to whom her darkened soul could appeal, for I alone knew that she lived. Her mother had died a year after her daughter's marriage, and her father married again and entered upon a new life in which she was hardly included. He was one of the great army of speculators who seized upon the opportunities of that wonderful West which sprang into existence with the return of peace after the turmoil of civil war. I do not doubt that her supposed death was a matter of relief rather than of sorrow to him ; not that he failed in affection for her, but he was one of those men whose schemes absorb all their thought.

In seeking to effect her restoration, my conversations with Doctor Talcott in the old days proved to be of the greatest service. Absolute seclusion from all exciting association, good health, fresh air, absence of restraint, and the constant presence of a sympathetic nature, offered, he was accustomed to say, the only ameliorating influences in such cases as hers. If one could manage to start the long unused intellectual machinery without shock, the probability was that it would continue to work on without future aberration. Relapse, I had often heard him declare, was almost sure to prove fatal or result in absolute hopeless amenia ; and there was nothing so likely to produce such a relapse as a too sudden or too complete knowledge of what her condition had been, and what had occurred in the interval of unconsciousness.

Never before had I been especially grateful for the abundance which had fallen to my lot. Now I dedicated it to her, and determined to spare no effort to effect her restoration. I could not yet abandon the idea that she would some time recognize my presence and respond to my prayer ; for I forgot all else in the impenetrable oblivion which had fallen upon us, and looked forward only to life and love with her. For a time I fancied I perceived signs of amendment. She had readily associated my name with my presence, and called me Jack in the same careless tone with which she spoke to others who were frequently with her, and

though she seemed to half forget the name during my
absences, she recalled it, as she did not any other, without assistance. I spent as much time with her as I
could, but soon became aware that something more than
temporary arrangements must be made for her care and
exclusion from sights and sounds which diverted her
attention and rendered my best efforts abortive.

PART THIRD—JOHN HOWGOOD.

CHAPTER I.

BY FORCE OF LAW.

" Away back in the sixties," as the phrase is in the
" Centennial " State, John H. Howgood bought property
in Denver.

The Queen City of the Plains was hardly more than
a possibility then. It was a hopeful possibility, however. The reaction had set in after the subsidence of
the Pike's Peak "boom." The close of the war and the
fact that three great railroads were already looking
toward it as the rallying-point of prospective prosperity
made its great expectations seem wonderfully near to
the elastic-spirited adventurers who had staked out a
desert-Venice—a metropolis unique in character and in
insularity—under the shadow of the white mountain-
peaks, where the Platte debouches from its granite
gorge and bravely begins its doubtful journey over the
shimmering plains. The cloudless air of the high pla-
teau plays curious freaks, not only with the eyes but
with the imagination also, discounting time as well as
distance, and bringing the future as well as the mountain very close to the hopeful observer. So while the
embryo metropolis was at that time hardly more than
staked out, it was staked out a great way and in imagin-

ation built up to the very limit of the map which dazzled the eyes of the incredulous " tenderfoot." Still, a little money went a good way then, even in the purchase of corner-lots, and John Howgood—" Old Howgood," as he soon came to be called—seemed to have a fancy for corner-lots, and a confidence in the future of the undeveloped Queen City which staggered the enthusiasm of even the " oldest settlers." It soon became apparent that he had "struck the thin edge" of a new " boom." The mere accession of adventurous spirits whom the end of the war had set free to find new homes and build new empires, would, no doubt, of itself have proved sufficient to have entitled the Territory to a place in the galaxy of States a decade later ; but the general belief in her yet almost undeveloped mineral resources was doing very much to revive the depression which followed upon the exhaustion of the original " Pike's Peak " gulches.

Even in this infant city, however, there were few who could boast any personal knowledge of the new investor. He had boarded for a time at a hotel and had a box at the post-office. That was about as near a location as he made. All negotiations with him were by letter, or, after a time, with his agent, who lived in a modest one-story house on what it was expected would some time be a corner, to be bounded by streets yet undiscoverable, except with the aid of a map and a surveyor's compass. Whenever an agreement was reached with him in regard to any particular property, the matter was referred to his attorney to examine the title, and a draft given payable to his order, to conclude the purchase.

Other things as well as his invisibility aided to establish for Mr. Howgood a reputation for eccentricity. He never gave more than he first offered for property, and

never made a second proffer for the same premises.
Nobody knew where he was from, what were his ante-
cedents, or how much he was worth. To tell the exact
truth, nobody cared much except as to the latter. The
people of the new territory were very lenient about
some things. No man was asked for a certificate of
character. Individuals, like money, passed at their face
value. If they chose to "bank" upon the past, it added
little to their credit. A man's name was of no more
consequence than the house he lived in, and this no
more important than the coat he wore. If he chose to
make acquaintances, well and good ; if he chose to " live
in his hole," nobody intruded on his privacy. There
were too many failures and too many shaky reputations
in the budding metropolis to make society especially
heedful of the character of its new accessions. Every
" tenderfoot" counted one, and was welcome. If he
grew too troublesome, he was given a hint to move on.
If he obeyed, well and good ; if he did not—well, there
was always "the bridge." And there was, also, always
an overwhelming majority on the side of the public interest, if not of public morals. It would not do for a
town to be too bad, any more than it would do to have
it too—too nice.

Assimilation was easy with such a population, and
Howgood, despite his whimsicalities, was soon recognized as an enterprising citizen, against whom, as nothing was known, nothing was said. Estimated by the
market value of the lots standing in his name, he was
soon accounted rich. The fact that no mortgage was
recorded against him greatly enhanced his reputation.
Time passes quickly in such communities, and the "tenderfoot" becomes an "old resident" almost before he
knows it. "Old Howgood" was a "well-known citizen"

in a few months, and after the lapse of a year or so, was estecmed one of the " substantial men " of the city.

About this time an incident occurred which for a day or two drew on him the attention of the town. The "very oldest" residents still speak of it as "the fight over an initial." There was another John H. Howgood, it appears, who was known to live in a very unpretentious house away out on the bluffs, where the streets were then quite undiscoverable. He was a quiet, inoffensive young man who did nothing ; owned only the place he lived on, and supported a feeble-minded sister and her attendant—nobody knew how. He paid for what he got, and was devoted to the sister, who was never seen abroad except on horseback in his company. "Old Howgood" quarreled with this man on account of his name.

Of course, letters directed to John H. Howgood or to J. H. Howgood were as likely to fall into the possession of the one as the other ; and, equally, of course, each one was likely to open the letters he received, and so become possessed of the other's secrets. The modest dweller on what has since become famous as Capitol Hill made no objection to this, but "Old Howgood" raised a row. He wrote to the postmaster, to the department, to his namesake and to the newspapers about it. But the young John H. Howgood was as stubborn as the old one. The whole city laughed, and the confusion continued. At length the capitalist had his name changed, by special act of the Territorial Legislature, to plain John Howgood, giving due notice of the same. The transaction created some amusement, but was looked upon as one of "Old Howgood's" whims. An attested copy of the act was filed in all the public offices, and made a matter of record in every county of the Territory.

Soon after this, the owner of the humble dwelling on the hill sold the premises to his disgruntled namesake and disappeared. People said he got a fancy price to move away and leave the original Howgood the sole use of the name. Be that as it may, John Howgood had thus become a legal existence of the most indisputable character, a clause in the act having annulled and extinguished all other names and *aliases*, by which it might at any previous time be known. Nobody dreamed that the whole controversy was simulated—a studied ruse, by which what seemed like two identities had been merged into one, and a name which was a mere cloak had been given substantial verity.

As "prospecting" went on in the Territory, "Old Howgood" acquired an interest in various mining properties, most of which were so successful that it came to be laughingly spoken of as a fortunate thing to have him as a partner in such ventures. He always paid cash for such interests, and never let go until he sold at an advance. So matters stood when his lawyer received directions to purchase for him, from the government, a large tract of land in one of the most inaccessible and barren portions of the Territory.

"Well, Old Howgood has done it now," the attorney said to his partner, as he read these instructions.

"How so?" asked the other, looking up from the brief over which he was poring.

"Why, I haven't heard a word from him for months. His agent said he was out of town, and he had no idea where he was or when he would return, but here he sends an order for me to buy for him both sides the river for five miles up and down one of the worst canyons in the Rockies, lying a hundred miles from nowhere and inaccessible to anyone not blessed with wings. I declare, it is a pity to waste money in that way! With such chances as there are here, too—lots of splendid property changing hands every day."

" What does he expect to do with the gorge ?"

" That's the funniest part of it—says he's going to start a horse-ranch."

" The devil ! Well, he can afford to amuse himself ; but it does seem a queer thing to dump Denver corner-lots into a canyon a thousand feet deep. Hadn't you better get out an *inquisition de lunatico inquirendo* and have a guardian appointed ?"

" How would I go at it ?" queried the partner, jocu-larly. " I've never set eyes on the old scoundrel, and wouldn't know whom to have the papers served on. Queer, isn't it ? How do I manage to do his business ? Well, I'll tell you. He picked up old man Van Wyck, who had failed somewhere back East, and came out here hoping to get a new start. He was a good business man, but utterly broken in health and spirits as well as in estate. He was working as bookkeeper in the hotel where Howgood stopped when he 'first landed,' it seems ; just dragging along on nothing and anxious for the end. Howgood offered him a house rent-free and a salary twice as big as he was getting to look after his affairs. It was exactly the thing the old man was best fitted for. The job was an easy one, and he was grate-ful as well as faithful. I suppose that was about the best investment Howgood ever made, and he has made some cracking good ones. After a while he made Van Wyck's wife a present of the house they lived in, and ever since the old man has been getting along, with Howgood's help, of course, mighty well. He has settled with his creditors and is considered fairly well off now. He says he knows no more about his employer than any one else. Howgood stays with them, I believe, when in the city, which is only now and then, but has never

said a word to him about any business except what he
leaves in his charge. If the old man knows anything
more, you couldn't draw it out of him with wild horses ;
and I don't blame him. But your plan wouldn't work
anyhow. ' Old Howgood ' could give us both odds in
the line of hard sense and have enough left to ' bank '
on for the rest of his life. No ; the only thing to do is
to go and buy the land according to orders and charge
him for the service."

" With commissions, of course," added the partner,
with a laugh.

" Not any commissions with him ; I tried that once."

" Didn't it work ?"

" Not much. Van Wyck brought me a sealed note
from his principal, which stated that he had observed a
charge for commissions in my last account—he requires
a separate account for each transaction—that while willing to pay reasonable fees, he declined to pay commissions ; and if I did not wish to attend to his business on
those terms, he would find another attorney. Of course,
I couldn't let him slip, and it would be folly to try to
work any fancy charges on him."

" I guess it wouldn't pay, that's a fact. Is that the
reason you are so close about his business ?"

" Oh, no ; Van Wyck stipulated, when he employed
me, that I should always attend to his business myself.
He said Mr. Howgood did not wish to employ a firm,
and if I was not at liberty to engage myself individually,
preferred not to retain me. I thought it was a mere
notion and so agreed to it. As you know, he has
made it profitable for us."

" That he has. Oh, it is evident that no court would
listen to a charge of incapacity against such a man ; he
is a little too sane, if anything."

The partners laughed good-naturedly, and each went on with the work he had in hand.

Thus John Howgood secured a legal status. "Old Howgood" was only an insignificant incident in the curiously indifferent life of the Queen City of the Plains. The sun kissed the snowy mountains ; the sparkling river dashed quickly past ; the water trickled along the open ditches ; the sand beat against the panes, and the muffled hum of her busy life went up from her unecho-ing streets. Nobody asked who John Howgood had been. Everybody knew who "Old Howgood" was. He was accounted an honorable man ; a worthy citizen ; a man hard to entrap ; apt to succeed in what he undertook ; having the devil's luck in speculation, and attending strictly to his own business. A new civilization spreads the mantle of charity over the mistakes of an old one with amazing facility and unfeigned kindliness, and "strict attention to one's own affairs" becomes a not unimportant element of good repute in such a community.

CHAPTER II.

TETE DE LOUP.

Tete de Loup was one of those surprises abounding in the great table-land out of which the Rocky Mountains rise. It was a basin with sheer, precipitous sides, half-way down the narrow clefts in which the scraggly pines crept here and there in pointed phalanxes, as if seeking to reach the black waving crests that stretched upward from the bottom in a vain attempt to hide the gray, scarred rocks. Seen from above, Tete de Loup was only a curious widening of the canyon's walls, with a stunted forest growing around the edges and a mad river dashing through it. Seen from the bottom, it was a valley five miles long, and half as wide, with a narrow gorge at either end ; a belt of pines about the sides, and rich pasture on either bank. Except for one narrow and difficult trail it was inaccessible, save by the river, and only a few daring explorers had ever chosen that dangerous route. When the region was surveyed it was declared inaccessible ; its length and breadth were determined by triangulation, and it was duly made a part of two townships of Range Eight of the N*th* Meridian West, on the map of the national domain. In those days, it was almost a hundred miles from the edge of civilization as the crow flies, and much more by any practical route, though a broad road, which connected two great " parks," as the rifts between the mountain-ranges are termed, ran through a picturesque pass, only a score of miles away.

The surrounding region was too barren even for the Indian to care to dispute its possession seriously. Down the one possible path into the sequestered valley, years before—just after the wild rush to Pike's Peak— a man had found his way, bringing a mare and foal, and here he had remained. Afterward, he had added to his stock a couple of calves, carrying them down the narrow path, one at a time, slung across his shoulders. How he became possessed of them he never thought it necessary to explain. He built a rude house and shelter for his stock against the face of the rock, deftly concealing them with shrubs and vines, which he planted for the purpose. Back under the cliff stretched a roomy cavern, along which a mighty torrent had some time flowed, now dwindled to a tiny rill. Here the stock was hidden whenever concealment was necessary.

He called the valley—his valley—Tete de Loup, from some fancied resemblance of outline to a wolf's head. His stock had increased to a small herd, though he took care that it should not grow large enough to awaken the cupidity of any beholder. He had little need for caution. In all the time he had been there, it had been visited but thrice. A little band of Indians, a couple of prospectors and a party of explorers, were the only intruders on his solitude. None of these tarried long, nor found anything to induce them to return.

It was a curious life the owner led, going and coming at pleasure, his stock his only companions. He did not seem to have any special care for the animals he raised. He had never sold any, and had little use for them in that remote narrow valley. The cattle indeed furnished him with milk and meat, but not one of the horses had ever been up the difficult trail. Indeed, it was not absolutely certain they could get up it.

One day the owner of Tete de Loup found a stranger lying by the road-side in the pass, fevered and delirious. His horse was grazing quietly a few steps away. After some hesitation he secured the animal, and without any attempt to learn the identity of the stranger, placed him in the saddle, and mounting behind, brought him to his ranch. It was a case of that form of typhoid, known in the region as "mountain-fever." It was a remarkable thing for one like the Hermit of Tete de Loup to do. Probably the stranger's white hair won upon his sympathy.

Three weeks afterward, the man had so far recovered as to comprehend his surroundings and question his rescuer. He found the latter to be a recluse of that curious French type, which seeks the wilderness, not merely for the love of adventure or greed of possession, but as a refuge from misfortune, disgrace or disappointment. In lieu of society, he had made the animals he reared his companions. They knew him, and flocked around him at his call. By accident he had become possessed of a stallion wounded in one of the engagements with the Indians, and left to die of his hurt. Brought here with difficulty, the high-bred animal had left his stamp upon· the herd, giving it a quality which the owner fully appreciated, and of which he was very proud. It was one of those rare instances in which the blood of the thoroughbred mingles harmoniously with that of the desert-born, the offspring showing the form and action of the sire, without losing the toughness and endurance of the wiry dam, the product of centuries of wildness and hardship with the blood of the Castilian barb as its starting-point. Already a half-dozen youngsters attested the excellence of the new type.

One day, the owner called his little herd about the door of his cabin, where the stranger, yet pale and weak, wrapped in robes and blankets, sat drinking in long draughts of the bracing air—absorbing, as the convalescent seems to do, the sunshine—and, while the horses bit and kicked in jealous rivalry for his favor, told his guest their story.

The stranger smiled as his eye fell upon the stallion, a long, round-barreled bay, who, despite some stiffness, the result of wounds and age, was yet a horse of splendid style, with an eye full of fire—a masterful patriarch who showed no sign of yielding his place even to the best of his offspring. He listened to the owner's estimate of the value of the youngsters with a twinkle in his eye, and when, finally, the horses had wandered off, obedient to their master's words and gesture of dismissal, began to whistle—a soft, quick-recurring repetition of a familiar night-bird's call. The owner of the ranch turned and looked at him with a smile. The notes evidently awakened pleasant memories. The old horse, a hundred yards away, halted, threw up his head, and uttered a shrill, piercing neigh. Still the quick, even call came from the cabin-door, echoing sharply from side to side across the canyon. Suddenly the horse wheeled and dashed back to the hut, uttering joyful neighs of recognition.

The stranger extended his hand familiarly, and the horse, after one sniff of inquiry, stretched out his dark muzzle, now plentifully streaked with gray, to receive the proffered caress.

" Knows you !" said the owner, his black eyes sparkling under the beetling brows with astonishment and delight. " Great horse!"

His companion smiled. Withdrawing his hand from the drooping head, he. snapped his fingers and a hard black hoof was laid in his extended palm.

" Good ! Good !" cried the owner, clapping his hands. " Great horse ! Great horse !"

" What will you take for him ?"

" Your horse—your horse !" answered the recluse. " Not mine."

" What do you think he is worth ?"

" Old horse—not worth much. How old ?"

" He has seen twenty, but he is worth a hundred for every year."

" Two thousan' dollar !" exclaimed the owner, in amazement.

" All of that. He is known all over the country as one of the greatest horses that ever lived. That is Belmont's Abdallah."

" I never heard of him," said the other, dubiously.

Then the stranger told the horse's history, and descanted upon the probable value of his progeny. The eyes of the recluse flashed ; he threw back his head and ran his thick, stumpy fingers through his hair as he listened.

"You—you will take him—away?" nodding his head at the horse, which was licking the stranger's hand.

"O no ; he is yours."

"I s'ould be reech, vare reech—now I know he is so —so great."

"But you are rich," with a gesture which included the valley.

"No, no," answered the other, shaking his head. "I no keep him. Give him up—go away—away!"

The stranger eyed him keenly for an instant, and then sent the horse away with an impatient word.

"What is your name?" he asked, abruptly.

"*Mon nom?*" repeated the recluse, with a start. "Jacques—Jacques—Combien," he added with a twinkle of the deep-set eyes.

The stranger laughed good-humoredly.

"And you—" he asked, "what name have you?"

"Jack, too—Jack Howgood."

"How-good?—Com-bien? Good!" said the other, significantly. "Vare good!"

Then they both laughed. They understood each other without exchanging confidences. That is the way with men. They had liked each other from the first. Now they were friends. Never since he had come to Tete de Loup had the recluse felt loneliness until the stranger manifested a desire to depart. His one fear had been that others would come and dispossess him, or seek to take from him a part of the little rock-ribbed valley—not that he was greedy, but he wished to be alone—and he loved Tete de Loup. The explorers, the prospectors, even the Indians, he had regarded with keen jealousy—the latter less than the others, because the inaccessibility of the valley had unfitted it for their

purposes. The prospectors he had watched unceasingly
while they dug and washed, studying the seams in the
rocks, and the pebbles in the river-bed. If they had
discovered anything worth their while—if they had
driven a single stake, or showed any inclination to return,
he would have killed them. Since the government survey had been made he had been in mortal terror lest
some one should "enter" the land, and so bar him from
the enjoyment of his valley. And now, strange enough,
he wished this white-haired, white-bearded man, who
was yet young—much younger than himself, he judged,
to stay with him. Civilization was crowding upon him.
He was afraid of its forms. He knew nothing of his
rights and had a vague terror that he would be driven
out. Perhaps this man might help him.

"But you will come again ?" he asked.

The other shook his head.

The owner scowled. He was not angry, only trying
to think. He was a man of powerful physique, not tall,
but compact and strong. His face was swarthy ; his
beard and hair dark and stiff. It did not curl, neither
was it straight, but lay in a close, wavy mat on brow
and cheek. There were white threads in it here and
there. His forehead bulged over the eyes, as is so frequently the case with men of his descent, and the heavy
brows so shaded the great, black eyes as to give them
almost a sinister appearance. He spoke English fairly
well, but with a trace of the Canadian *patois* in his tones,
something in his phrasing also. He had said nothing
about the reasons which induced him to hide away in
Tete de Loup. The other had not asked, neither had
he spoken of himself or his circumstances.

"See here," the owner of the ranch broke out, after a
long silence ; "you got money ?"

"A little," smiling. "I was about to ask what I should pay you?"

"Pay *me?* Nothing—not a cent! That would be insult!" seeing the other put his hand in his pocket. " This is what I mean : you see this?"

He waved his short arm and strong, grimy fingers toward the plain.

" The gov'ment want it; the surveyor come to take it. I see 'em up yonder measure—squint. I know Jacques Combien have to get out some time. He hold one hundred sixty acres—that's all. That what ze Denver lawyer say. How many here?"

"A thousand or more."

"More—more! Two thousand—more yet! Now, how many come in? Five—ten—hundred people! Sh! *Sacre!* Who live here, then? Where my horses—my cattle—my—?" He shrugged his shoulders and thrust his open palm away from him with a gesture of infinite aversion. "What 'come of Jacques, then?"

" Well?"

" How much it cost to buy it all?"

" Probably five or six thousand dollars."

" Desso—desso! Where Jacques Combien get five thousand dollars?"

" It is quite a sum."

" Desso! Well, dis what I say. You buy—buy it all —then I give you half. No! Two-thirds—three-quarters the stock! You come here ; we raise horses ; sell —grow rich, have good time—all 'lone. No? Don't say no!"

And this man wanted to be rich! It did not seem strange when he told the reason. He had sworn never to go back to his native village until he was richer than any man in it. He had been unfortunate ; had lost his little property—and had hidden here in despair. He did not doubt that the girl to whom he had made this boast had married another. Nevertheless, he wished to return—to show that his boast had not been vain. Perhaps he thought there might be another ; he did not say so.

So John Howgood and Jacques Combien became partners in Tete de Loup—the one to have the east side of the river, the other the west, and the stock to be owned in common. John Howgood ordered his lawyer to secure the title, and Jacques Combien, whose squatter's right he had bought for a sum which made that worthy feel himself rich already, started to redeem his boast. But he never reached his native village. No doubt his heart had grown tender in the long sojourn in the wilderness, or the sound of his native tongue was too great a temptation to be resisted. At any rate, travelling with his new friend, he made the acquaintance of Louise, the sprightly French maid who waited upon the unfortunate sister of John Howgood, and when he returned to Tete de Loup, she came with him as his wife.

In the meantime, the little valley had been transformed. A road of easy grade had been blasted out of the sheer wall. A bridge spanned the river. A comfortable house stood on the site of the old cabin ; a more pretentious one on the other side of the river. Stalls and paddocks were prepared, and quarters provided for grooms and laborers. Some new stock had made its appearance, too. Brood-mares, brought over the plains from the blue-grass pastures of Kentucky, whose fine lines and high spirits attested the correctness of the pedigrees, which avouched their descent from great names of the turf. The Tete de Loup Stock Ranch was established. Its appointments were not luxurious, but they were serviceable. Its advantages were abundance of the best pasturage, water, shelter, and a rare, dry atmosphere. No wonder a type, celebrated not only for its performances, but for temper and endurance, has sprung from that sunny mountain cove.

" Ah, money can do anything !" said Jacques Combien, as he surveyed the result.

It had not required very much money, but from that hour the simple-hearted fellow strove for riches, not meanly, but honestly and manfully—and fortune smiled upon his efforts. The ranch has been profitable—more profitable than many of the ventures which lured men into the mountains by thousands, a few years later, with the glittering promise of boundless argentiferous reward.

CHAPTER III.

THE BALM OF SOLITUDE.

It was to Tete de Loup that I brought *her*, and began in more serious fashion the task to which I had devoted myself, of joining, if I might, the edges of her dual consciousness, or, more properly, the restoration of that consciousness of which the key had been lost. It was no light or agreeable undertaking. My very love made it all the more distressing. She was in the fullness of a beauty always rare, and in this case the more trans-cendant, because the weakened brain had relieved her from] everything like care, and prevented any of that exhaustion of nervous energy which, quicker than any-thing else, brings age. Her hair was of that tint which lies midway between the silver's whiteness and the gleam of beaten gold ; her face, calm and peaceful, had the innocent glow of girlhood with the fullness of ripened womanhood. Her form, developed without restraint, had the suppleness and grace we are accustomed to attribute to tropical climes.

The task seemed hopeless. None of the eminent specialists I consulted gave me any encouragement. Yet I did hope. A thousand times I despaired, yet never ceased to hope again on the morrow. I had learned that life in town was not good for her. New faces troubled her. Varied surroundings seemed to make her fancy more flighty and her thought less coherent. Somehow it seemed to me as if the sameness of Tete de Loup would be restful and healing to her. There was only the sky, the level, silent valley, the gray, circling walls with the dark, woody fringe above, the flashing river and the white mountain peaks in the distance. There would be horses, it is true, but they would be the same ones all the time ; and of human beings there would be only myself, Jacques and his wife, to whom she was much attached in her fickle way, and the grooms and laborers, of whom she would only now and then get a glimpse. This was to be our world, and from its unvarying sameness, its silence, seclusion and restfulness, I hoped for much—or, rather, I tried to hope.

I did not conceal from myself that, whatever the result might be, my life—my new life, and all that it might give of comfort, attention and entertainment belonged to *her.* No matter whether she appreciated my efforts, comprehended my devotion, or even recognized my presence or not ; I was bound to her by a tie stronger than even love could forge—the obligation to care for this frail consciousness which I had torn from its moorings and assumed the sole responsibility of its direction. Already nearly two years had elapsed since Fate had thrown her into my arms and sealed the deed of wrongful appropriation by hurling us both into oblivion. Not only was she lost to the world, but the world was lost to her. Already she had forgotten her husband's existence. Allusion to him no longer provoked any show of resentment, but only a glance of uncomprehending surprise. Doctor Talcott's name had long since ceased to awaken any sign of recognition. A change of attendants made her uneasy for a day or two ; in a few days, or weeks at farthest, their names were forgotten. If they returned she showed no signs of recognition. New surroundings seemed to excite her wonder, but she expressed no regret for those she had left. If she saw them again she had no remembrance of them. There seemed, therefore, little room for hope —whether I did hope I hardly know. At any rate, I determined to devote myself unreservedly to her. I thought it my plain duty. It seems strange that one like me should talk of duty, and surely it was not so great a thing to consecrate a useless life to enlivening one to whom each day's trifles were all there was of joy or sorrow, that it need have so grave a designation ; but I was unable to find any other name for the impulse.

This is why I bought Tete de Loup and brought *her* there. If I could not restore the lost consciousness, I judged that I could there better bestow upon her that care which did so much to make her simple life peaceful and contented. There was no doubt that she enjoyed my companionship more than that of any other person. She remembered me after long absences, or perhaps it would be more correct to say, became acquainted with me after such absences more readily than with any one else. She called me Jack—sometimes Jack Howgood,

seeming to take a childish pleasure in linking my
name with the phrase of acknowledgment from which
it was really derived.

" Jack !" she would say—" Jack, how *good*—Jack *Howgood* !"

Then she would laugh gleefully at the dimly comprehended ambiguity, and repeat it over and over again
with the peculiar tendency to iteration which characterizes persons of weak intellect. Still it was apparent
from her tone and manner that she did not consciously
associate me with that other " Jack " of whom her
errant fancy was always full. There was something
very touching in her reiteration of this name in varying
tones under different conditions. When she was brightest and happiest she repeated it hardly above her
breath, in the intervals of conversation or sitting alone
in calm content.

" Jack, Jack, Jack !" she would whisper rapidly to
herself ; then aloud : " What a pleasant day !" Then
in a whisper again : " Jack, Jack, Jack !"

But when she was ill, or anything had gone wrong
with her, or one of those dark days was on her which
come periodically to the insane, the word became a wail
whose sadness pierced the dullest heart. I have often
seen a groom fling up his hands and flee beyond hearing
of her voice when on such occasions the plaintive
" Jack ! Jack !" echoed through the sequestered valley.
I noticed after a time that these gloomy intervals
became less frequent, while the cheerful, chattering
whisper was almost constant with her, as if " Jack "
was becoming the echo of a hidden but pleasant consciousness instead of a sad and despairing one. There
was recompense if not encouragement in this. It was
more than my broken life was worth if my presence
could make cheerful rather than sad the void in which

she seemed to live—for there was all the time a seeming consciousness, a something vainly struggling for expression, of which the weak and fleeting intelligence she displayed was only a glimmer, like the corona which in a total eclipse tells of the sun's presence, though the luminary itself is hid.

The idea that there was a latent consciousness beneath this external, superficial one, capable of receiving intense and lasting impressions was confirmed, in my opinion at least, by the fact that she seemed to have as just an apprehension of natural laws as any one. She was careful in approaching the edge of a precipice ; she clearly understood the fact that it would be perilous to fall into the river, and, though fond of watching it carry away what was thrown in, was extremely cautious in approaching its banks. So, too, while she loved to watch the firelight, she never manifested any inclination to trifle with combustion. The same was true in reference both as to propriety and taste in dress. Though she seemed to have no idea about increasing or repairing her wardrobe, yet she was very positive in her preferences, both as to color and texture, and was not only able to clothe herself but did so becomingly and tastefully, according to seasons and conditions.

Of course, some of these things may be said to have been instinctive, and others were no doubt due to the excellent training to which she had been subjected immediately after recovering from her first aberration of mind. But an incident occurred during our removal to Tete de Loup which strongly confirmed my view of her condition, though it gave no hint of any practicable method of reaching or awakening this dormant consciousness. The horses attached to our carriage took fright while we were descending a narrow gorge, and

ran with great violence to the bottom. A dozen times
we were in the greatest peril of being thrown over the
precipice, but by good fortune we escaped without serious injury. She was utterly unstrung with terror when
I lifted her out, and from that moment had an almost
unconquerable aversion, not for a horse, but for a carriage. Indeed, she never afterward entered one without a shudder. It seems a cruel thing to say, but this
discovery gave me great pleasure. She made the rest
of the journey on horseback, and her enjoyment of the
mountain scenery and the quiet loveliness of our evening
camps had the effect of transforming our trip into a
loitering stroll along the winding mountain trails.

At Tete de Loup we were together all day long. We
rode, talked, sang. I remembered her old favorites, and
read over and over again to her the same books. She
was especially fond of the Bible, and never tired of
listening to portions of it. The thought of eternity
—endless duration—seemed to be the one abstract idea
which continued to hold a place in her consciousness.
She had no conception of death. The fact that a bird,
which I shot, would not fly when she tossed it up,
troubled her so much that I took care that she should
not again witness anything of the kind. Immensity
however—boundlessness, whether in space or time,
though said to be an incomprehensible idea, evidently
impressed her consciousness very deeply. The sky, the
mountains, the mystical boundlessness of the starlit
night, all soothed and hushed, but at the same time exalted her. The idea of interminable duration seemed to
have the same effect. It was evident that it touched a
deeper, more responsive chord of her hidden nature
than any other. "Forever and forever, amen," she
would whisper with solemn ecstasy, whenever a word
importing endless duration occurred in our reading. I

tried a thousand times to enlarge this crevice, through which a beam of light from her past seemed to find its way, but in vain.

I suppose there must have been other indications of improvement during the years that followed, but I had long since lost hope, and so failed to note them. I had almost forgotten to repine, and came to regard the devotion of my time and energies to securing the comfort of this pitiful half-life, not merely as a deserved penance, but a not altogether disagreeable duty.

It was a peaceful, quiet life we led upon our ranch. The horses and their care were the only things we had to break the uneventful days' monotony. It would be difficult to say which derived most pleasure from our occupation, Jacques Combien, myself, or the lovely woman who was always a looker-on and often a participant. It did not once occur to me that the eagerness with which she waited for the time to come when she might mount each colt in turn was of itself evidence of an improved mental condition.

We trained the Tete de Loup horses naturally. They were never broken ; we found nothing to break. They inherited docility, good temper, the desire to do what was required of them, to outdo each other and to win favor by excelling. That these qualities characterize the well-bred horse, and are both heritable and cultivatable, there can be no doubt.

The history of the horse is full of suggestions to the owner who desires to promote his excellence and secure further development. There is doubtless much in soil, climate, food, and what is called training.

The soil, climate and rich food of the British Islands unquestionably contribute largely to the early development of the English thoroughbred, as also for his early decay. So the desert air and scanty vegetation are largely responsible for the lack of size and the remarkable endurance of the Arabian. But the influences which make the Arab horse, after all our boasted scientific methods, unapproachable in the most desirable qualities a horse can possess, are not dependent upon climate, food, or what we term care. He is but poorly fed, badly groomed—and never broken. From the day he is foaled until he dies, at an age the English thoroughbred rarely attains, he is the associate of man. His master pets him ; the children play with him ; the women fondle him. He is to the Arab tent what a pet dog is to his master's apartments—a privileged character who, if not invited in, watches the portal in perfect confidence that whoever may come out will be a friend and familiar.

The English thoroughbred is a wild brute, tamed and broken—compelled to serve through fear. This, indeed, is the general relation of the Anglo-Saxon toward inferiors, whether brute or human. Power is the scepter of his dominion. He never persuades, but breaks or kills. It matters not whether it be a man, a people, a race or a brute—the method is always the same. The French, by treatment approaching the Arab's in gentleness, have developed the intelligent and reliable Norman, which in the hands of our American breeders is fast retrograding again into savagery. So everywhere it will be seen that what may be termed the moral qualities of the horse depend almost entirely upon the moral qualities of those who rear and train him.

The broncho of the plains is undoubtedly of gentle blood, being descended from the Spanish barb, which approached nearer to his master in familiar association than did the horse of any other European nation of that time. His transportation to this country in their little crowded caravels for use in conquest is evidence of this. Only a people accustomed to intimate association with the horse could have transported him successfully in this manner. Yet the broncho has lost all trace of confidence in man, not merely by generations of wildness and unrestraint, but by the barbarity of successive generations of Indian masters.

The brutality of the English groom and the formality of the English gentleman are reflected in the viciousness and stiffness of the English horse. Neither groom nor master usually cares anything for the temper, comfort or intelligence of the horse, but is only desirous that he should be amenable to orders and perform the tasks he is assigned. Fortunately for the American horse, we are, so far as this noblest of our dumb animals is concerned, growing away from our English inheritance. The horse is more his master's friend and less the mere instrument of his pleasure in America than in England. Consequently, American horses of the better class are less frequently vicious, more docile and longer-lived than the denizens of English stables.

These things are especially true of the southern part of the country, and particularly of the blue-grass region of Kentucky, where the kindness shown the foal is quite as important an element of their future achievements as the quality of the food they eat. For the moral quality is almost as important in a horse as in a man. In the breeding of trotters especially it is necessary that this fact should be kept in mind, since with them not only speed but the faculty of self-restraint are essential to the highest success—nerve as well as muscle. Of the great names on the trotting turf to-day, almost every one of the greatest has been the daily companion of a man or of a family, who not only prized but loved the proud and happy recipient of their attentions.

We are learning—not as fast as we might, but surely —that the most valuable qualities of the horse—those

which will always command the best and readiest market—can only be developed by constant care, gentleness and appreciative familiarity. It is safe to say that
such treatment has been an appreciable element of the
value at least of nine-tenths of the horses which have
brought ten thousand dollars or upward, and of ninety-
nine-hundredths of those who have doubled that sum
for their owners.

There is little doubt that the finest type of horse in
America, like the finest type in the old world, will come
from the plains. Sand, sunshine and a certain degree
of aridness give the best hoofs, the best muscles, greater
endurance and greater longevity. But the perfect
American horse will be developed, not by the wholesale breeder with the costly training-stables, but by the
American boy who feeds and fondles his weanling, and
prizes him not merely for his money value but for his
moral qualities—when we become not a nation of fast
drivers and race-goers but of horse lovers. The horse
needs not to be broken ; he is no longer *ferax naturæ ;*
he needs to be civilized and taught to believe in the civilization of his owner.

These were the principles applied at Tete de Loup.
Every colt felt the touch of some kindly hand every
day from the time he was foaled until he left our possession, and learned to submit himself to human direction and control, not because of fear, but because he
knew it was kindly. A horse so trained may, indeed,
forget his training and break away from restraint, if he
loses confidence in the decision or capacity of his driver.
So, too, he may be made wild with fear or pain, or the
mere love of rivalry may make him oblivious to
attempted restraint, as in the case of those who were
the unconscious cause of my present condition ; but he
will be many times less liable to any of these defects

than a horse which has been "broken" and taught to yield through fear. "Rareyism" was a scientific method of teaching vicious animals that man is their superior in power. As long as we rely on fear as the controlling impulse of the horse-nature, this method is, perhaps, better than any other ; but even observant horse-men, who believe in the doctrine of force as devoutly as any, have noted that the resultant condition of absolute submissiveness is not favorable to the best achievement. The truth is that hopelessness, the consciousness that he is purely and solely the creature of another's will, is just as bad for a horse as for a man. If well trained he is willing to obey, but to obtain the best results his work must always be an act of conscious, willing obedience, not of passive submissiveness.

The horse should yield himself to his driver's will because he has confidence in him, not because he knows he cannot successfully resist him. The mares which the Prophet selected for his stud because they turned back from the water's edge despite their long depriva-tion, at the sound of the trumpet, did not do it because they feared to disobey, but because their love of the wild route of battle was stronger even than their rag-ing thirst. That there are horses—just as there are men—who are not susceptible to influences of this char-acter, I do not deny. There are no doubt some that are inherently vicious, though I do not happen to have known one which, if properly treated while young, might not have been rendered easily subservient by a master who had himself been properly trained, unless the animal inherited distrust from a long line of wild ancestors, or came of a stock imbruted by the savagery of their possessors. There are, no doubt, horses lack-ing in intelligence—horses which, as has been well said of a certain stock, "have to learn everything afresh every time they go upon the road." Such, like the asinine hybrid, may be valuable merely as controllable masses of tractionary muscles, but they are not worth reproducing. The best horse is always an animal of rare intelligence, and equine intelligence is stimulated always by human associations, and whether it shall be trustful or distrustful depends very largely upon the character of the human associate. A man whom other men cannot trust rarely trains a horse on which any one can rely.

I need not say how congenial this occupation was to me. A man may become a good rider or driver without any love for the horse, but only one born with that love in his veins can ever properly train one or care for one. After a while, we brought a couple of colored grooms from Kentucky. Their wives came with them and served as our domestics. They were not faultless. They were sometimes harsh and often neglectful, but they had a decided fondness for the animals they cared for, and their vices were easily modified, if never wholly eliminated. I was fortunate, too, in having as an associate, Jacques, with his ancestral Breton tendencies, and his wife, who had memories of her own of the Côte du Cher, and the inherited love of the peasant-farmer for a petted weanling. They had charge of the foals, and saw that they were gently taught to submit to being handled and restrained, to lead, to follow, to start and stop at the word, to bear light burdens, face unusual sights and sounds, and made to acquire that most difficult and unusual of equine accomplishments—a fast and steady walk. When the colts were two years old they crossed the river and came under my especial supervision.

It is not my purpose here to give an account of our method. Indeed, there was no inflexible method. The efficient trainer, like the wise schoolmaster, must be a man of brain and sagacity enough to adapt his tuition to the intelligence and character of his pupil. Suffice it to say that no actual force was employed nor any show of force more tangible than insurmountable inclosures. I do not mean that the whip was discarded, but it was used more as a symbol of authority and a means for communicating orders to the eye like the officer's sword than as an instrument of punishment. In rare cases, it is very true, it was used for that purpose, but only on my own judgment and in extreme necessity. I am not sure that its primitive use, with a colt having sufficient intelligence to be worth training, is not always a mistake.

During the period of actual training each colt received a lesson every day of sufficient length to make an impression upon his memory and not long enough to produce weariness or discouragement. After that time, exercise, practice, trials followed, both to harden the muscles and to crystallize the lessons into habits of action and obedience. As we had no intention of breeding for the turf and no desire to secure the patronage of the gambling fraternity, which delights only in extraordinary and destructive performances by half-developed colts, there was no inducement to rush our stock into market before their powers were fully matured and their qualities firmly established. Our purpose was to breed horses, not mere gambling materials. By adopting this policy, Tete de Loup Ranch was enabled to send out every year a string of thoroughly trained animals, every one of which was brave, intelligent, trustful, obedient and reliable, of matured powers, and of a quality to fully gratify the owner's pride, though they might not minister to the gambler's greed. Their quality was at once appreciated—the more readily

as we refused to part with them on any terms, until
they had had a few months of careful handling on the
lower levels of the East to accustom them to a moister
climate and a denser atmosphere.

The prices received have been as satisfactory as their
performances. The only case in which they have
proved refractory—if that could be called refractoriness
—being the one in which the stupidity of an awkward
driver resulted in the destruction of the splendid pair,
whose impetuosity was the cause of my present injury.
I did not need to seek pecuniary profit from this venture. The enhancement of values and the development
of new properties in the beautiful metropolis of the
plains made me quite able to gratify my inclination,
even at a much greater expense ; but no success I have
ever achieved has been more satisfactory than the
material results of Tete de Loup Ranch.

As I have said, our life was very simple, and to me,
in a sense, most congenial. I am almost surprised to
think how I enjoyed *her* presence during this period
when hope was dead, and I looked forward to a future
in all respects like the present which I lived.

I occupied the new house on the east side of the river ;
the others lived in the enlarged old one upon the west
side. Every night I escorted *her* across the narrow
bridge and bade her good-night at Jacques's door,
and every morning she waked me with her impatient
demand for my appearance. All day long she hardly
left my side. I loved her, and her stunted intelligence,
little by little, ceased to jar upon my consciousness. I
came to accept her as she was, thinking less of what
she had been and not at all of what I had hoped she
might become. I had at first been somewhat encouraged by the fact that she seemed to remember
Abdallah, but neither the name nor the horse appeared

to awaken any other memories of her early life. Except
that she remained fonder of the battered old veteran
than of any other horse at the ranch, I could hardly
regard this preference as the result of any indistinct
recollection. But the fact that to the very last she
would rather ride him than any other horse at the
ranch seems quite unaccountable, in so good a horsewoman, on any other hypothesis. Considering his age
and the fact that she rode in turn almost every one of
our colts in those daily trips which were a regular part
of our system of training, this continued fondness for
the infirm old veteran seems so strange a thing that it
is little wonder it gave me hope that memory might yet
recover its sway.

Especially will it seem impossible to account for this
preference on any other ground, when we recall the
fact that the silver-maned son of Gray Eagle, peerless
in all those qualities which make up the perfect saddle-
horse, was always at her disposal, and indeed her customary mount. Some months before our coming to
Tete de Loup, I had learned from a paragraph floating
through the press, that my wife, being about to dispose
of her establishment, the horse would be for sale upon
a certain day. The time was very limited, but I
hastened Van Wyck East to buy the horse for me. The
price he paid was not so large as I expected ; whether
the favor of his master's notoriety detracted from his
value, or his qualities were not fully appreciated, I
never knew.

I was very glad to have him in my possession once
more, and glad also to learn incidentally that my wife
was not taking my abandonment seriously to heart, but
contemplating, as Van Wyck told me, a trip abroad.
Of course, I asked few questions about her ; but I was
sorely tempted, as I had been many times before, to

write to her, not to excuse, but in part, perhaps, to extenuate my fault, and more especially to prevent her from being led into difficulty by a re-marriage. Believing me dead, she would, of course, naturally suppose herself free to marry again without the formality of a divorce.

I saw, however, that such a course was impossible, without involving other and still more serious and embarrassing consequences. It was more than probable that she would consider such action as adding insult to injury. Besides, I was responsible for the good name as well as the creature comforts of the woman whose destiny I had taken into my hands, and I could not subject *her* to any of the reproaches which would be sure to be evoked by such a revelation. Fortunately, the good sense of my wife afterward relieved me from such apprehension. She applied for a divorce, and a newspaper containing a notice of the application found its way into my hands. I was puzzled to account for its being sent to me, at the time, but concluded that the fact of Van Wyck's having acted for me in the purchase of Damon accounted for its having been mailed to me in his care. As the application was made in a Western State, and the husband's name was stated to be J. H. Goodwin, it attacted no attention ; and even when the decree was finally granted, as I suppose it must have been soon afterward, there was no mention made in the press even of the fact that the husband from whom she sought separation had ever been a man of any note. I suppose the divorce was only a precautionary measure, owing to the fact that my death was not absolutely provable. It was a very wise thing for her to do, and I felt really proud of the sagacity with which she had acted in the matter, being sure that her chief motive in so doing was to avoid casting any unnecessary odium on my name.

It was terrible—this utter, irremediable eradication of the past; having but one to love and none to love me; being a stranger in the land I had fought to save; my fame dust and ashes—its very mention bitterness! I suppose even my comrades in their reunions avoid mention of my name as far as possible. I have never attended one. I dare not. I am afraid my emotion might betray me or some accident make my woe unbearable.

Even the poor tribute of a headstone is denied me. No one will ever point out my grave. The car was burned; the bodies destroyed. It seemed terrible then. Now I am glad it so happened. In time, perhaps, while the good of my life is yet remembered, the evil may be forgotten. I am surprised when I look back upon it now, that when I came to realize my position I did not seek refuge in the death I had so miraculously escaped. But for my obligations to *her*, I should have done so, I am sure. So we lived on, together, yet separated by an insurmountable wall. Mounted upon Damon, she accompanied me everywhere about the surrounding country in the lessons which I gave the younglings under the saddle—a portion of their training which I reserved especially for myself, and in which she took the utmost delight.

Thus five years had elapsed since Hubert Goodwin's death. The anniversary of our last meeting before the darkness fell between us had come again. The bright spring sunshine flooded the little valley with that peculiar white light which characterizes the clear atmosphere and cloudless skies of our mid-continental Italy. At this season of the year she had always been more restless than at others. She was lying curled up on a lounge in the kittenish way peculiar to her, in the sitting-room of my house. I was reading to her for the thousandth time, perhaps, a poem we had read together just before the evil days came—a pleasant story of that New England life now quite forgotten by the newer life which has succeeded it—Holland's "Bitter Sweet," which has already grown almost as unfamiliar to American readers as the Norse legends ; far more so, indeed, than Ibsen's cynicism, or Tolstoi's degrading speculation. Perhaps it was because I had first read this book with her that it still held a tender place in my heart, and I read it over and over to ears to which it was always new, with less of weariness than I felt in re-reading other more notable works. Perhaps I found in it a hint of something in harmony with my own sin. Be that as it may, it always set me dreaming of the past. On this particular day, the page vanished from my sight ; I forgot the lithe figure upon the sofa, the great gray eyes that watched me and the shining hair which gave back the silvery light with a softened glow like that of the mountain twilight. My thoughts were busy with the past.

"Jack !"

What was there in the tone that made my heart stand still ? Was it memory that played me false ? It was not the voice to which I had lately been accustomed, but that which I had heard when I first read the volume in my hand. I dare not look around or move, lest I should destroy the sweet illusion ; for I did not doubt that it was illusion.

"Jack !"

There was no mistaking it now. It was not the simple, trustful, half-comprehending "Weely " who was calling me, but the old, old love so long dead and buried in shame and misfortune. The sweat burst out upon my brow ; my whole frame shook with the tremor of unexpected rapture. I did not move or speak—I could not.

"Jack !"

There was a touch of impatience in the tone quite characteristic of her old self. Never shall I hear again anything half so sweet. The music of the Seraphim will be dull to my ears in comparison with that voice.

"Well ?" I answered, as composedly as I might, not turning my eyes, lest I should betray my agitation.

"Jack, what makes your hair so white? It didn't use to be."

It was my lost one's voice ! The dead soul was speaking ! The puzzled, half-querulous tone showed that the blind eyes saw again, and that the clouded brain was struggling to the light.

I could control myself no longer. Rising hastily but not abruptly, I went to her ; lifted her in my arms ; kissed her face, and, while the tears rained down my own, and the agony of those long years burst out in sobs, I cried :

"Dee ! Dee ! Dee !"

That was all I could say.

"Dee? Dee ?" she repeated, inquiringly. "Why, Jack ! Jack !"

There was none of the accustomed plaintive inquiry in her tones, but positive, up-gushing gladness. She threw her arms about my neck, and I felt her slight form thrill with the rapture of recognition. Our tears and kisses mingled while the bright sun sparkled on the dashing stream, and afar off the white peaks rested, clear and soft, against the infinite blue depth.

> " Like spirits that lie in the azure sky,
>   When they love but live no more,"

"JACK, WHAT MAKES YOUR HAIR SO WHITE?"—See Page 371.

I murmured, as I saw Dee's gaze turned toward the dis.
tant peaks, inquiringly.

"Oh, Jack!" she cried, as she clung to me with a
thrill of apprehension. "What is it? Are we dead?
What has happened? Where are we, Jack? Tell me—
tell me truly!"

I recovered myself with a sudden wrench. Could she
stand the shock? Was I not likely to lose the one only
treasure earth could hold for me? Could the poor,
weak brain throw off the gloom of years and live? Had
I found my love only to lose her again!

"Dee," I said, firmly, as I laid her down and smoothed
the soft bands upon her brow caressingly; "Dee, it is
all right; I am Jack—your Jack; and I will take care of
you—always."

"Forever and ever?" she asked, with a smile.

"Forever and ever, amen!" I answered, solemnly.
"But you must not ask any more questions now. You
have been very ill. You must lie still, very still, and
go to sleep. Will you do as I wish?"

"If—if I can," with a sigh of apprehension. "But you
will not leave me, Jack—again?"

"I will sit by you and hold your hand. You need not
fear. Wait a moment while I get you something."

I stepped across the room, opened a cabinet, took from
it a sedative, poured a strong dose of it into a glass of
water, returned and held it to her lips.

"Drink this, dear," I said; "and when you waken and
are stronger I will tell you everything. Now go to
sleep."

I sat down by her, took her hand and stroked her hair.
It was terrible to send the newly-wakened soul back
into oblivion. Would it return again and be itself? I
did not know, but I *did* know it could ˉot survive the
shock of this new birth without rest.

Thus I sat and watched her while she slept. When the twilight fell and the maid came to call me to the evening meal I held up a finger warningly, and told her to send Louise. When the latter came, with hurrying steps and pallid cheeks, I said, chokingly :

" She must not be disturbed ; she—she is—*herself !*"

" Ah, *le bon Dieu !*" exclaimed the tender-hearted woman who had served her so long and so faithfully. She sank into a chair, buried her face in the white apron she wore and sobbed silently.

" She must not be disturbed," I repeated. " Put some food in the adjoining room. If she wakens I will feed her. She must not see anybody she does not know."

" Does not know !" exclaimed the faithful creature. " Not know her Louise ?"

" But you forget," I answered. " She will not be the —the same."

" Ah, true," she said, rising with plaintive dignity ; " I did forget. She will not be the same. She will be one I do not know ; and she will not know her Louise. Why should she ? She will be dead, and this—this will be another. *Dieu*, it is strange ! It is terrible ! It gives me fear ! It is like a miracle—like the resurrection ! I—I think I shall be sorry to lose *her*."

She rose and went softly away, her dark eyes shining in the dim light, with a wondering awe which brought a thrill of fear.

Who would *she* be when she awoke ? I almost wished she might not waken at all, but that the sweet soul might exhale—might flee into the infinite void before the sunlight came to make visible the world's realities:

CHAPTER IV.

Hour after hour I watched beside her, holding her hand, noting every breath, counting the pulse—hardly daring to breathe, myself. Louise came and arranged her clothing that she might sleep comfortably, without waking her. We heaped soft coverlets upon her, for the nights are chill in the mountains. I had bought them, thinking the gay colors would please her childish fancy, and had not been disappointed. After a time I drew the curtains, so as to shut out the moonlight. Then I could hear her breathing softly. I sat silent, hour after hour, wondering what the morrow would bring, and the days which were to follow. It was a long time since I had thought of the future—since I had dared to think of it. Who would *she* be when she awoke? Would she be Dee or "Weely?" How I hated the name which was the badge of her infirmity! If Dee, what should I do? If "Weely," of course the old life must go on.

Tired of the dull agony of doubt, I went out and walked up and down beside the dashing stream in the bright moonlight, with the wondrous stillness of the mountain night about me. I seemed to be in the very center of eternity. The snowy peaks in the distance were, to my questioning heart, the crystal pillars of the throne of God. I knelt on the river-bank and prayed with my

face toward them. It was a long time since I had dared
to pray. Even then, I asked nothing for myself. I did
not expect to be forgiven the wrong I had done—did
not think I could be forgiven. I had regretted the
wrong, but had not repented of it. I was not sure that
under like conditions I would not repeat it, terrible as
its consequences had been. I only prayed for *her*—that
her white soul might not be stained by my sin. In the
infinite stillness of that primeval sanctuary, I asked the
Eternal to take from me my one joy—the hope of meeting recognition in her waking eyes—if thereby only she
might be saved from stain. It was a fearful request to
make of Omnipotence.

Suddenly the earth seemed whirling aimlessly in radi-
ant, gusty, freezing space. The river-bank, the work of
unnumbered ages of erosion, crumbled beneath my trembling knees. Instinctively, I scrambled up the falling
mass, with difficulty escaping engulfment in the dashing
torrent. The moon was swaying in the firmament.
The earth was throbbing with an angry roar. The
mountain peaks were rocking in their places. The cold
sweat stood upon my brow when I secured once more a
firm foothold. What was the significance of this con-
vulsion, following swift upon my prayer? Did the
Almighty mean to indicate a way in which it might
receive fulfilment? Had "the canon 'gainst self-
slaughter" been intermitted in my case? It seemed
so to me, and I accepted the omen without murmuring.
I suppose all men are more or less superstitious, and
both my long seclusion and my recent exultation had
endowed me with that peculiar egotism which counts a
single soul the center of the universe and regards nature's
manifestations as designed for individual warning and
behoof. At least, this was the construction I put upon
what then occurred. It was too slight a shock to be

termed an earthquake—just one of those angry roars by which Nature seems to assert her sentiency. Not willing to act under excitement, however, I walked down to the paddock and whistled to Abdallah. The old horse came at my call. I petted his grizzled muzzle, took the foot he lifted up in customary greeting, shook it as if he had been a man and bade him farewell. Then I went to where Damon was kept. He was the one visible token of a past blazoned with honor ; I remembered how proudly I had ridden him through the city's streets, when we celebrated the jubilee of peace—the grand review. How long ago it seemed ! Only *she* had ridden him since. The gallant troop-horse seemed older than the bay, who was his senior by some years. Was it because the service had told on him, or had the Gray Eagle strain detracted from the vigor of the Belmont mare ? The children of Diomed are not long-lived like the offspring of Messenger. I thought of these things as he came obedient to my call. His silver crest was held as high and proudly as ever, but there were white hairs scattered thickly in the seal-brown coat.

It was a sad parting. He was the ghost of my buried life. I had never ridden him since he had returned to my possession. Only honor and pride and good repute had ever sat upon his withers. I would permit none but *her* to mount him. My only quarrel with Jacques had been when I found him once with his foot in the stirrup ready to spring upon Damon's back. I should have killed him if he had done so. He shrank away from me white and terrified at my unreasoning wrath. He had no purpose to offend. In explanation of my act, I took him into the house and showed him a photograph of myself at the head of my command. It was the only relic of the past I had retained. The honest-hearted fellow looked at it a moment, the tears coming into his eyes.

" I understand," he said.

Then I tore the picture in twain and threw the pieces into the fire. Terror came over his face again as he looked up at me and softly withdrew, leaving me alone with the ashes of my past.

I bade good-bye to my old war-horse, and turned back toward the house. There was no one else to whom I needed to say farewell. The child of Old Harry was beyond the pale of human friendship. The devil's luck had worn itself out at last. Not one in all the world knew of his existence. Only one weak soul had had a dream that he still lived. There were no preparations to be made. My will had long since been prepared. My estate would insure *her* comfort ; after that my sisters, should they require it, and the family of Hubert Goodwin's wife Kitty, according to their propinquity to her. Poor Kitty ! What would she say to me when we met across the river ? " Across the river !" I even smiled at the double significance of the phrase. What would she say when we met ? I laughed aloud at the thought. We should *not meet !* I recognized that as an immutable truth. And echo even came back from my old, old life : " Where I go ye cannot come !"

My old life ! When I was waiting for a " call !" And *I* had thought to proclaim the Word of Life to dying souls ! I shuddered at the remembrance. Yet I had not been a hypocrite, and had never meant to do any wrong ; I had only been unable to see what was right. It was well that the struggle was so nearly over. I felt really glad to think that being dead I should at least be harmless. I had never seriously contemplated suicide before, and found the thought really pleasing. The idea that one might end responsibility for even unintended harm to others was very consoling. There are a few who do evil purposely, but a thousand times as many who cause suffering by inadvertance, ignorance and folly. I wonder if the Christ hated the wicked as much as he pitied the weak?

I would not go into the house, lest proximity to *her* might unman me, but looked long and tenderly at it in the white silent moonlight, and breathed a prayer for her who slept within its quiet walls. Then I walked toward the river-bank, feeling happy and peaceful. The mystery of my life would be forever hidden in the rushing stream. No one would find my body or know my fate. Perhaps the shelving bank would give a clue; no matter; the miles of foaming water below would hide it forever.

Then occurred a most wonderful thing. I had approached within ten steps of the river. I was not at all excited. What I was about to do seemed altogether right and proper. I was even grateful to the kind Omniscience which had sent so unmistakable an omen in answer to my prayer. I was walking firmly and briskly toward the bridge, deeming it better to leap from the middle of the span, where the full force of the current would surely carry me down. I was not thinking of anything but the business in hand. At this moment I heard a voice say:

"Hubert?"

I was not surprised or alarmed and could not have been mistaken. The word was uttered clearly and distinctly; the tone was familiar. There was neither entreaty nor command in it. It was merely an accustomed call—nothing more. I turned my head inquiringly, and saw a woman standing on the porch, which was flooded with moonlight from end to end. It was not ten minutes since I had been within five yards of that very spot. She was clad in white, not ghost-like, but apparently a morning-gown of some soft material, and there were roses on her bosom. I did not need to ask her name. I knew it was my wife—Kitty !

" Hubert !" she repeated.

I did not doubt that she was dead. Whether her presence meant pity or punishment, I did not know. So far as I was concerned, I did not care. My only thought was of *her*—a vague, wild fear that harm had befallen her.

I walked hastily back to the porch. She held out her hand. I went up the steps and took it, my eyes falling beneath her calm, steady gaze. We passed into the house and along the hall into the room where *the other* lay. When I went out it had been dark. Now there was a light in the room adjoining which I had fitted up as a bedroom years before, in the wild hope that *she* would some time occupy it. It was a dainty affair—for the wilderness, that is. No one had ever slept there. Indeed, the door had hardly been opened a dozen times since it was furnished. I had shown it to *her* once—in an hour of weakness. The door was open now and a lamp burning within. The light shone upon the placid face of the sleeper. She led me close beside the sofa, and after a moment said :

" Hubert, you must never desert *her*."

She tone was reproachful, but very tender. I bowed humbly without looking up. .

" Take her away," she continued, " as soon as she is able to travel, and never let her know what has happened in the past."

There was nothing unnatural about this apparition. Her face was white, indeed, and her voice a little tremulous. The touch of her hand was as it used to be—

except that it, too, trembled in my listless clasp. I was overwhelmed with confusion and could not answer.

" Remember," she said, " I have forgiven your unfaithfulness to *me* because of your faithfulness to *her*."

Somehow, I had expected ever since I had heard her summons to find a corpse upon the sofa. I stooped and touched the hand that lay outside the coverlet ; it was soft and warm. I felt her pulse ; it was beating calmly. I was stupefied with amazement.

" She will live," said the other, assuringly. I was overwhelmed with gratitude at her unexpected magnanimity. I think I must have fainted then, for the next thing I recall she was holding a glass to my lips containing the same decoction I had given *her*. I swallowed it in obedience to her dictation. I noted its bitterness, and wondered dumbly if she had given me an overdose—if that was to be her revenge, the penalty for my unfaithfulness. I did not seem to mind very greatly if it were. Then she led me into the bedroom, and drew the coverlet over me when I had fallen stupidly upon the unused couch.

She was standing by the bedside when I fell asleep. I thought she kissed me and that I heard her sobbing as she stole away.

I suppose it must have been a dream ; but it was so real that for months I did not go to sleep without living it all over again. If it had not been for a landslide on the river-bank opposite the house, the marks of my scramble up it and the evidence of my exertion to save myself, which were all evident enough when the morning came, I should have thought the whole thing a delusion. But there was no such thing as doubting the fall of the bank the waters had undermined, my scarred hands or torn clothes. How I managed to escape I cannot conceive. The exertion must have wearied me very greatly, though I did not notice it, probably because of the exalted mood I was in at that particular time. Feeling the necessity of rest, I must have gone into the house, lighted the lamp, and taken the opiate, from the effect of which, no doubt, the dream resulted.

It is possible, however, that I fell asleep lying beside the stream, after the exertion to escape engulfment by the crumbling bank, and dreamed all that seemed to have happened afterwards. There was one thing I could never account for, however. When I awoke, just as the dawn was coming on, and tumbling out of the luxurious bed whose spotless linen was flecked with the sand and gravel which had fallen from my clothes, and went into the other room, I found *her* sleeping peacefully with a bunch of white roses on her bosom—the same I had dreamed that Kitty wore the night before. *She* evidently had not moved. I suppose I must have picked them from our little conservatory where they were blooming, while in a somnambulistic state, and placed them there. I felt very weak, as was but natural after a night of such excitement. Nevertheless, I knelt down beside the couch where *she* lay slumbering so peacefully, and uttered a prayer of thankfulness for the vision I had seen. My heart was lightened by the assurance that Kitty, though dead, had forgiven me.

When *she* awoke, I saw at once the old light in her eyes.

" Why, Jack !" she cried—and the remembered tones echoed like heavenly music out of the desert of the past —what are you doing here ?"

" Hush ! Hush !" I exclaimed, bending over and kissing the lips I had not touched in all these years. " You must not ask me any more questions—you must not think—only trust me. Will you not, darling ?"

" Why, of course I will, Jack, ' forever and ever,' "

she answered, with a bright smile ; "only I wish you would tell me what has changed you so. I should not know you—if—if it were not *you.*"

She passed her hand tenderly over my hair and beard as she spoke, but there was none of the old pitiful uncertainty in her tone and manner.

" Wait !" I said. " Let me bring you something to eat, and then I will allow you to ask—let me see—three questions—not any more to-day."

I shook my finger at her with assumed imperiousness and went into the other room. A lamp was burning under the coffee-urn. It was evident that Louise had been early astir to provide fresh nourishment against her awakening. I took her a cup of the steaming beverage, some slices of bread and butter and a glass of milk. What rapture it was to see her eat !

" Why, Jack," she said, noticing my delight, " one would think you never saw me eat before."

I answered her exclamation only with a loving smile.

" Now," she said, when she had finished her light repast, " for my three questions. I think you are very mean to restrict me to three when you know I want to ask so many. Of course, I want to know where I am and how I came here ; how long I have been ill and what has been the matter, and—why, Jack, I could ask questions all day !"

"Yes, I know ; and that is why you must ask but three. There are days enough coming, dear, and you will have nothing else to do."

" Well, then—where am I ?"

" In my house."

"Your house?" she said, surveying it critically. " I don't think I ever saw such a one before."

It had not occurred to me how strange the house, made chiefly of hewn logs, must seem to her.

"How long have you lived here?" she asked, turning to me after a moment.

"Oh—a good while," carelessly.

"How long have I been—sick, Jack?"

There was a troubled look upon her face. I dreaded the effect of answering the inquiry, yet judged it best not to avoid it.

"What is the last thing you remember?"

"Oh, you know, Jack. There was war, and you said you were going—and—"

"That was in 1861."

"Of course—I know that."

"And now it is—"

I paused to let her think a moment and then held up before her a calendar which I took from my pocket.

A grave look of wonder and incredulity came into the gray eyes as they scanned the figures. I answered the appeal with a confirmatory nod.

"I see," she said at length, with a sigh. "I see."

It was the only allusion ever made by either of us as to what her condition had been.

"And you have taken care of me? How good!"

I trembled at this lapse into the language of her other life.

"How good!" she repeated—"*How* good? Isn't your name *How*good, now?"

I bowed affirmatively

"Just so; I remember—Jack Howgood. It used to be Jack—Jack— What was it?"

"I have forgotten."

"You mean you wish me to forget."

"It might be as well."

"Well, I will not try to remember; for, Jack,"—her voice became grave and tender—"I am never going to do what you do not wish me to again. You don't know what I suffered for—for *that*."

"There, there," I said, soothingly, "don't think of it! That is all over now."

"Yes, it's all over—all over," she added, meditatively. "Jack, I must be an old woman!"

I rose and handed her a mirror, smiling at the response it would make to her inquiry.

"I don't look so *very* old, do I?" she asked, with a touch of her old coquettishness.

"I don't think you are any older than you were—then," I said, stopping to kiss her.

"Ah, that is because you love me," archly. "You do love me, don't you, Jack?"

She stretched out her hands imploringly, letting the mirror fall upon the couch beside her. I took her in my arms and answered her question with an embrace more assuring than any words. Presently she disengaged herself, pushed me gently away, and, looking searchingly in my face, said:

"Am I—are we—married, Jack?"

A soft flush mounted to her cheeks as she made the inquiry.

"Not yet, dear," I answered, gently.

"Ah, I—I thought we had been."

She was silent for a moment.

"But we shall be? You are not married, Jack?"

"You shall be my wife, dear, just as soon as you are well enough."

"And until then?"

"You will remain as you have been, my sister. But you must not ask any more questions now."

"I understand," she answered, gravely, after a moment's silence. "And you will take care of me.

Then—" she added with a merry laugh, " I think I will
go to sleep again."

It was curious how easily she became fatigued. She
would wake up bright and cheery, and after a few minutes drop off again to sleep. Her physical health
was of the best, but her brain seemed incapable of
anything more than the most trivial exertion. Little
things did not worry her, but serious matters seemed
beyond her capacity   She was a child although a woman.

The attendant who had been with her for more
than a year was ill the next morning. She was a
very intelligent and faithful woman, who had been
sent to us by Van Wyck, when Louise's domestic duties
made it necessary for her to relax her attention. I had
never observed her very closely, though, of course, as
her attendant, she had the run of my house as well as
the other. Indeed, there were no bolts or bars at Tete
de Loup, there being no need for any. There was but
one thing to be concealed, and that was hidden in my
heart. As I said, I had never given any thought to the
presence of this attendant. She was kindly, attentive and
a lady. That was enough. I do not think I am as generally observant of women as many, and since I had *her*
in my charge I naturally thought only of her. The
woman had fallen easily into our life, though *she* never
manifested the same affection for her as she had displayed to the red-cheeked, wholesome and demonstrative Louise. This woman had often predicted *her* recovery, and expressed a desire that she might never see her
afterward, as she would be so unlike the loving, tender-
hearted child she had known.

Louise took her old place as maid, and, at my suggestion, spoke only French to her new mistress. The arti-
fice not only diverted her attention from her environment, but prevented troublesome inquiries. She began

at once to recall her vocabulary of French words, and, as I had hoped might be the case, did not recognize her attendant as one she had ever seen before. This cost Louise some tears, though she protested her joy at the fact, since it meant recovery.

In a day or two *she* began visibly to droop. I had not allowed her to go out of the house, and at my request she had refrained from looking out of the window. I remembered Doctor Talcott's assurance that the most dangerous of all things in such cases was a too sudden joinder of the old and new consciousness, and feared the effect of recognition of her old surroundings. " Different environments, variety of scene, but few faces," he had declared to be the conditions most favorable to recovery. " Many a feeble brain," he once said, "lapses again into insanity from being constantly confronted with the surroundings of his diseased condition."

So I decided to take her away. It was a long journey to civilization then ; but there were settlements here and there, and the mountains and prairies were in the glow of early summer. I dreaded her antipathy to travelling in a carriage, but thought if we could once get her beyond familiar scenes the conditions would be favorable, and she could make the rest of the journey on horseback. The silence, the distance and the soft surprises of the plains, it seemed to me, would be exactly what she required. We started at night. She was sleeping soundly from the effects of an opiate when I placed her in the carriage. Jacques and Louise were with me, and one of the grooms had gone forward to our first camping-place, with a string of led-horses. Never have I been so grateful for the horses of Tete de Loup as on that journey. Before she woke we had made the first stage, and when morning came her delight in

everything was almost pitiful to witness. When I lifted
her into the saddle after our morning meal, she was
more like herself than she had been at any time before.
How rapturous was that first day's ride with the newly-
wakened soul who did not know that her eyes had ever
witnessed before the beauties which now delighted
them. We did not hasten our journey. It would have
been folly to do so. Each day found her brighter,
stronger, more fully restored. When we finally bade
our faithful attendants farewell, it was to hasten to a
quiet nook by the seashore, and after loitering there a
few months, to make that journey abroad for which she
had pleaded in vain so many years before.

CHAPTER V.

SUNSHINE AND SHADOW.

It is wonderful how readily we made our transition
back into the world's life on returning from abroad.
Already we had become known in more than one
European capital as *the* Howgoods. As my bank
account was ample we were sometimes referred to as
the rich Howgoods, and, as we were indifferent to patronage and favor, the fair woman and white-bearded
man, who loitered where they listed in the ways of
foreign travel, found themselves regarded first as somewhat eccentric and finally as quite the thing among
their countrymen. It was curious thus to come into
the swirl of life again. It was with no set purpose that
we thus made our advent in the society of our native
land by way of Sandy Hook. Had it been deeply

planned, however, no better scheme could have been devised. So many had met us abroad that we found ourselves already well known at home. A civilization always ready to assimilate anything that stands on a gold basis opened its doors to us without hesitation. No one questioned who we were because so many knew already what we were.

There was, no doubt, the flavor of Western origin about us. " Old Howgood " was still a reminiscence in Denver, but so few had known him that he was little more than that. It is doubtful if any one really thought the connection between us anything closer than comes by inheritance. Whether I was a brother or son of the eccentric financier nobody seemed quite able to determine, but I think few accepted my denial of relationship with him, and, so far as I am aware, none suspected my identity.

How easily we fitted into the life of the great metropolis ! A luxurious home, a stable income and a luck which rarely failed to add something to the sum total of my holdings, whatever the turn of the market—they were enough had there been even less of personal merit than the Howgoods might justly claim. But *she* won all hearts by simple, unaffected kindliness. It was amazing how humble she was and how solicitous of others' happiness. We did not go into society much, but society came to us—to *her* rather—for I do not think it cared so much for me. But *she* was a magnet that drew all natures. She was not gay and yet the butterflies loved her ; nor sad, yet the bereaved sought her. The rich admired her without envy, and the poor blessed her for her benefactions. We did not embark upon the stream of pleasure nor give entertainments. There was always a feeling, though we never spoke of it, that she could not endure such excitement ; but the world streamed in and out at our door, asking only leave to come.

Yet we were curiously alone. She called me Jack. That was the only thing that linked us with the past. In the years that followed there was little worth recording, save the fact of our love ; unless, indeed, my success in that wild game of chance, which we call business, may be thought worthy of mention. I played it only for the pleasure I derived from it, and enjoyed to the full the delights of loss and gain. The old luck has been with me, and the mark of Old Harry would not let me rest.

So far as I am aware, no one ever suspected my identity with the disgraced and forgotten man whose name I once bore. As for *her*, I told her the story so far as was necessary. Of course, the shadow rested always over us—or rather over me—the strange haunting fear of discovery. With this fear *she* seemed to sympathize. It drew us closer together, and, despite our station in life, kept us apart from other lives. We had troops of acquaintances, but made no friends. The past was dead : we had trodden it under our feet ; but we could not ask others to tread upon its ashes also. Until the young nurse came, I doubt if *she* ever met a woman whom she felt inclined to trust. At the very last the old trouble came very near to her again. She seemed for a while to have a double consciousness, but through them both shot one ray of light—her unvarying love and trust in "Jack." I doubt if she really understood that I had ever been anything else or even had been other than what I was. I have often thought she never fully recalled the names under which we once knew each other or the events of our early life. We never spoke of the past except once or twice, and then only vaguely and briefly. I thought sometimes that she had a strange antipathy to the name we bore ; but thought it only a fancy until the very last. There was no reason why she should so regard it. It is a good name—my name, her name. Mine by creation, mine by right, mine by law—and by me legally and lovingly bestowed upon her. It is the symbol of a loyalty as perfect as the stanchest type of steadfastness. Never once while she lived did I feel any desire to go back and be what I was before.

It is a good name—so good that it will make a draft of seven figures worth its face in gold in any market of the world. It is an honorable name, too ; a name of which I am proud because I made it both good and honorable. It came to me unspotted with evil, unlightened with good—out of darkness, void, oblivion. It brought no heritage of honor or dishonor, success or failure. It brought no moral or intellectual bias, no attainder of blood, no obligation of kinship. It is mine by creation, mine by adoption, mine by the law's confirmation, mine by the ineradicable brand of sin and shame. In all the world there is not one who can claim affiliation through it. I alone have worn it—I and she —and with me it will disappear. As it was born of love for her, I made it honorable and kept it clean for her sake. Our name ! How proud I was of it when I inscribed it upon the register of the hotel of which I was to remain so long a guest !

" John Howgood and wife, } New York."
Miss Katherine Parks. }

That was the record of our advent. How obsequious the landlord became when he had read it. Why should he not be ? He who can command any service he desires honors him whose service he accepts. I engaged rooms for a day. She was not well ; that is why she traveled with an attendant; why we stopped here; why we traveled at all, indeed. All places were alike irksome and hateful to me while the cloud rested over her. Yet the name does not adorn her tombstone. It was her desire, and that is more potent than man's law or even God's command to me. I think I would willingly break all laws to fulfill the slightest wish of hers.

It was no light affliction to me that I might not carve upon her tomb the name I had made for her and shared with her so long. I loved it and could not bear to think that it would drop back into unnoted oblivion when I should die. It is known almost the world over. It has been at the fore in good deeds and bears the stain of no evil purpose upon it. Yet if she must sleep without it, so will I. I wonder if I could persuade the nurse to wear it. She was very fond of *her*, and during the days which have since elapsed has been very kind to me. Somehow, I feel as if it would please *her* to have one whom she loved bear our name. I would have proposed it and made the nurse my heir long ago if she would have consented; but she is proud—very proud and very unjust, I think also. Pray God she may not be mercenary! Yet why should I blame her if she be? Who am I that I should cavil at another's imperfections? Why should I care anything about her indeed? Yet I do care and am in constant fear lest she should go away and leave me. I do not understand the feeling. Perhaps it is because *she* commended her to my care so earnestly.

To my care! It would have been more to the purpose had she commended me to her care. I am alone now, helpless and unloved, unless, perchance, the nurse has some little compassion for me. Money can buy service; but it cannot buy tenderness—love. And I am hungry for love—not such as *she* gave me, but for the love that crowns the close of life—a child's love. The lust of possession is dead—I desire now only to be possessed, claimed, prized—to be for a little while the centre of some life's thought, and afterward cherished as a pleasant memory. Ah, if the nurse were my child —if she would only be my daughter! Yet until that day—that saddest of all days—I had hardly noted her existence. Perhaps it is because she came to me out of the cloud that she seems now so resplendent to my thought.

How everything has changed! Only two short months ago my life was at the zenith. The love which had shone steadily through so many years was to the last unclouded. Then came the night! How swift it fell! How impenetrable its darkness! I, that was so much, am less than nothing! The world does not count me even a potentiality—only the shadow of what was once a power. Yet I am not unhappy. I am even glad that *she* did not have to bear the burden of isolation which now presses down on me. I am sure it would have been more than she could have endured. She might even have fallen back into the abyss from which my love had rescued her. I am glad, too, that she knew no lingering, wasting woe. It was as she had always wished—as she was in life so she smiled in death.

When they thought all was over—when they told me *she* was dead, I was like one rent with mortal agony. She must have heard me and come back from the dread unknown in answer to my cry. The life-light came once more into her eyes; the bloom of youth glowed one moment more upon her cheeks. Her hair shone like spun gold in the sunshine. "Jack," she said. Then while the glory faded from her face, we heard her lips repeating the lines with which she had answered

my prayer for love in that other life which lay beyond
the verge of one long night :

<blockquote>

" If I should fade
Into those mystic realms where light is made,
And you should long once more my face to see ;
I would come forth upon the hills of night,
And gather stars like faggots, till thy sight
Led by the beacon-blaze fell full on me."
</blockquote>

It was enough.   I never looked upon her face again.
Why should I regard the mold while the rose was yet
fresh in my memory ?

Two days afterward, we bore her to the grave.   Poor
dear.   It was the first carriage-ride she had taken in
many years without moaning and trembling with fear.
I was full of terror lest even the cold heart should throb
with agony as the nicely balanced hearse swung to and
fro under the weight of the heavy casket.   It was an
imposing procession that followed it, though we were
strangers in the city.   The rich never lack for sympathy.   It is only those who need assistance to whom we
forget to offer it.   A leading citizen had begged to be
allowed to place his private carriage at my disposal.   I
feared there was a sinister purpose behind the offer—
the rich must always be suspicious—but I accepted, and
asked the young nurse who had closed *her* eyes to share
it with me.   I was afraid the minister who was to officiate would be forced upon my privacy and might seek
to offer consolation.   She seemed surprised at my
request.   I had hardly noticed before how young and
attractive she was, nor how like one of us she had
grown in the long months during which we had watchen
together the fading life.   For *she* had not sickened and
died ; she had only faded and exhaled.

" There will be no other mourners," I explained.

" No relatives ?

I shook my head. " There are none."

" None ?"

" None who—no, none—not one," I answered, irritably.

She asked no more questions. I was 'afraid she would refuse. I knew that *she* had come to love the gentle girl who had attended her so faithfully in those last days. Besides, I shrank from being the sole mourner at her grave. It seemed as if it would appear like a reproach to *her* purity if no woman bent above her resting-place wearing the habiliments of grief. I had not realized before how terribly *she* had been cursed by my act—by a past which, though dead, was yet potent to doom. Of friends we had no lack, but of those to whom nature gives the right to mourn there were none who would know of her death—or, knowing, would have cared. The nurse still hesitated, or seemed to hesitate.

" I thought you loved her," I said, with unreasoning bitterness.

" Oh, I did—as if I were her daughter !" she exclaimed, in passionate protest.

Her daughter ! How the words startled me ! If she only had been !

" Will you not be ?" I asked, impulsively.

She looked up at me incredulous—reproachful, I thought,

" Not *my* daughter," I said, humbly—" *hers.*"

She smiled sadly.

" For a few days, if—if you desire it to be so."

Her voice trembled ; it was low and sweet. I think it comforted me. I was seized with an overwhelming desire to keep her near me.

" Why not forever ?" I asked, earnestly.

" I am very sorry—for you," she replied, seeming not to heed my question.

"*She* loved you," I said, apologetically. I was not even angry that she should doubt me.

Tears came into the beautiful eyes. She bowed her head, but made no reply.

I construed the gesture to mean assent, and told those in charge of the preparations that I had adopted her. She gazed up at me in surprise when she heard the words. I would have provided mourning for her, but she would not permit. The black gown she wore was not new. I wondered for whom it had been worn before. I was glad she was to be my companion. She would at least ask no questions. Ah, me ! it was a sad thing for her. Yet many envied her, no doubt, as she took my arm and walked beside me to the carriage. It is a nice thing to be heir-presumptive of a man whose wealth is a matter of common knowledge to the whole country. I could not but note the envious glances cast upon her by the assembled company as we followed our dead through the long corridor. They made my thoughts bitterer and the world lonelier. She seemed to understand it all. How kind she was in that last ride ! I do not think I can ever forget her tenderness. Was it disinterested ? Would she have shrunk from me had she known the truth ?

It was a splendid span which drew our carriage. My eye noted that unconsciously when it came back from following the casket as it was placed carefully in the hearse. I wondered if the insensate clay perchance felt any jar, and reproached myself for not having per-sonally examined the vehicle which was to bear *her* to the grave. It would be cruel to jostle even her dead dust. There was no embalming. I would allow no

stranger's hand to touch her. The faithful nurse and I
had placed her in the casket. It was a soft, white
couch, and the iron case was a safe receptacle. The
undertaker had screwed down the lid, and I myself had
locked it at head and foot. It was a notion of mine.
Even in the grave I would not yield possession of her.
She was mine—still mine !

Our coachman had a mourning band upon his hat.
As we came down the steps I noticed that the close-
clipped browns were restless. I could see the muscles
twitching under their silky hides, and one stretched out
a lithe fore-leg and daintily but impatiently scraped the
pavement with his toe-calk, as if to hint that the springing tendons could not long be denied opportunity for
action. Despite my grief I sympathized with him, and
involuntarily glanced again at him and his mate. I
knew them in an instant, though I had never seen them
before. They were too distinguished in ancestry and
achievement not to be recognizable by one having any
knowledge of the quick-steppers whose records illumin-
ated the trotting register. I comprehended at once
why they had been sent me and was grateful. There
was no footman, but the owner himself held open the
door, hat in hand. He was a stranger, but I gave him
a glance which he must have understood. He knew I
was a lover of horses, and had sent his matchless span
out of respect for my bereavement. It was a little
thing, but it touched me. One gets tired of being
regarded only for the money he represents.

It seemed a sympathetic company which had gathered
to do honor to the woman none of them had known,·
but I shrank from their gaze. The nurse reached out
and drew the curtains between me and them. We must
have waited a long time while the train of carriages
received their occupants, for there were many carriages

though but two mourners. At last I heard the wheels of the hearse grate upon the pavement. I would have given my heart to ease the jar even of the cold clay. I must have writhed in agony. The nurse put her hand upon my arm. The touch soothed me. I did not see her, yet I knew she was not looking at me, but out of the window with a handkerchief pressed to her lips, weeping. Why should she weep?

CHAPTER VI.

A GOOD BIT OF WORK.

It was over in a flash, but it was something to stir one's blood while it lasted. When a span of well-bred trotters really break away, they are the worst of all animals to control. There is not only the fierce desire of the thoroughbred to go—the wild delight of racing with each other and the wind—and the indomitable courage which makes the trotter, after all, the very finest type of the horse ; but there is also the consciousness of wrong-doing to add wings to their speed. When the trotter breaks his stroke, he knows he is doing a forbidden thing and expects to be punished. The fear of this adds to the frenzy which impels him to the unaccustomed gait.

I do not know what startled them. I remembered afterwards that they had been restive all the way to the cemetery, though I thought nothing of it then. The driver was a new one, and lacked confidence, I judge. I did not observe the change of gait at first, being accustomed to rapid driving, and my heart being in the grave we had just seen heaped up. The light had gone out of my life and the darkness had settled down close about me. Black hopelessness had suddenly succeeded a joy so keen that few realized its effulgence. Others, no doubt, love ; but I had known nothing but love and what I had gained for love's sweet sake. The change was from noonday to midnight. I seemed to grope rather than walk from that red mound to the carriage. I saw no one, though I knew many were watching me pity-ingly—curiously. I could only wonder what *she* would be in the life beyond—if there *is* any light or life beyond the grave—and what would be *her* thought of me when she looked back and saw what lay behind the vail which had clouded her knowledge here. Would she ever look beyond it ? Would she ever know the truth ? I hoped not. Selfish as it seems, I think I would rather she should be forever dead—that she should be no more—than know the truth. It is a terrible thought, but I am weak—fearfully weak—and I loved her so !

No, no ! Let me take it back—blot it out ! Let it be unsaid ! It is not true. I would rather endure all wo-fulness forever than that *she* should miss a moment's joy. That is all I can do—all I have ever done. This fact is the key of my life—its one redeeming feature—my sole excuse if any palliation is possible. If I sinned, it was for love, and I will suffer for it, if need be—willingly, gladly, eternally. But harm *her* not, oh, Fate ! Touch not her white soul ! Let her not miss one thrill of rap-ture nor feel one throb of woe ! If penalty there must be, let it fall on me. Even into nothingness—eternal nothingness—I would gladly sink to save her a single pang !

These thoughts and wilder, bitterer, sweeter ones were in my mind strangely intermingled, as we took our way back to the hotel, when suddenly the nurse clasped my arm. I looked at her like one just wakened from a dream. Her face showed very white against the mourn-ing bonnet. We were simply flying; that is the only word to express the sensation. The light carriage in which we were shut up was as nothing to the high-bred beasts striving to outdo each other. I knew at once that the only thing to be done was to choose the least fre-quented streets; steer clear of obstructions and let them go until they had had their fling and were ready to set-tle down to steady work. I pulled open the window and shouted this to the driver. Poor fellow! One will never know whether he heard or not.

I put my left arm about the nurse, knowing that it would be better for her in case we were overturned—especially if I fell underneath, as I would try to do. I was sorry then that she had come with me, and said something of the kind. I do not know what answer she made, but she was very composed for one in such peril. I do not think I ever rode so fast in my life—not since the great race, at least.

Fortunately, few of the Southern city's streets were paved. A glance showed me where we were, and the character of the road before us. A few blocks away a public square lay across our path. On the side we approached, it had been cut down sheer about six or eight feet, to the grade of the streets along the other fronts. At one corner it rose higher, at the other the wall was somewhat lower. The inclosure was thickly shaded with ancient oaks, now clothed in the soft, tender leaf-age of spring-time, through which the sun shone with a mellow, opaline light. Through the openings in the foliage one caught sight of a massive heap of weather-beaten granite. The square was walled with brick, old and crumbling. Upon one corner of it stood an unused office, dating back almost to colonial times; its walls cracked and bulging overhung the parapet below.

I thought of these things—not connectedly, as I have
written them, but in a flash, as one thinks of obstacles
he must pass in a charge over half-familiar ground.
To pass the square we must make two sharp turns in
half a hundred yards. There was little chance of
doing this in safety. Unless the driver had courage
enough to put his horses at the wall, we were pretty
sure to be overturned on one corner or the other, and
then—well, the streets were paved with cobble-stones
about the square, and it was easy to guess what would
be the chances of the occupants of an overturned carriage dragged at the heels of two such horses. The
motion was easy enough until we struck the pavement,
a block or two from the square. The horses were fairly
matched, and their training showed in the evenness of
their stride. I could not see them, but I knew their
necks were outstretched, each black muzzle straining
to get a hair's breadth ahead of the other. Their feet
touched the earth at regular intervals, with the elastic
force of a steel spring. I held the girl tightly, so that I
might be ready to do whatever should seem needful for
her safety when the crash came.

Just before we reached the corner I saw a young man
drop an armful of books and a green bag, and after
a hurried glance up and down the street, turn and
run toward the square. I read his thought in an
instant. The corner was barely twenty steps away,
but we passed him before he reached it. I glanced at
him as we went by and knew that the end of our race
was near, and that this brown-bearded, firm-jawed
young man would be in at the death. I thought very
likely it would be a real death, too. I only wondered
who would die, and hoped it might not be the slender
creature in my arms, nor the brave young fellow who
was about to risk his life to save us.

I saw he knew what he was about, but it was a perilous thing for any one to undertake. He knew the horses must slacken their speed in making the turn ; the momentum would take them well over toward the wall along the side of the square. If they turned to the right, he would have the advantage of position, for they would have to describe the arc of a circle, while he would traverse the chord. Then, if he could get a good hold on the reins, he might force them against the wall and stop them before they reached the other corner.

It was a good plan and would have been entirely successful if we had not had to reckon with the masons of a century ago. The young man did his part splendidly ; that is, he did the right thing—the very best thing that could possibly have been done—at exactly the right time. One had no need to be told that he was a horseman. Every motion showed it. I could not but admire him as he ran, his lips shut, hands well up, chest out, not doing his best, but with every muscle strung like whip-cord and his eyes fastened on the mane of the frantic creature on the off-side as if he were picking out the very handful he was going to clutch. That is just what he was doing, too. It's a good trick and fairly safe, if one has muscle and youth, elastic bones and coolness on his side. But there is always danger in it. A false step, a second's miscalculation—any one of a thousand possibilities—and one who fools with a runaway pays the penalty of his folly, no matter how strong or nimble he may be. As for me, I could only brace myself for the shock.

When we reached the corner, the horses started to go to the left but finally went to the right, swerving over toward the wall about the square. The wheels upon one side left the pavement; those upon the other creaked and trembled. I threw our united weight upon the outside. As I did so, I saw the young man dart by the carriage-window like a flash. I knew he had seized the off-horse by the bridle with his right hand, twisted his left in the mane, and was hanging a dead weight upon his neck, crowding the span nearer and nearer to the wall. Then came a jar, a crash, a curious, unaccountable rumble. We were overturned, of course. I came underneath as I had planned, clasping the girl tightly above me. Just as we fell, I saw my mistake. We had struck the wall near the corner, knocking out the foundation of the old brick office. I tried to turn her over and shield her from this new peril, but could not move. The frame of the carriage somewhat broke the force of the blow, but it was not much beneath the weight of the wall, more than a foot thick, which toppled over and [crushed down upon us.

It was a good while before I knew anything more. They tell me the driver and one of the horses are dead. It is too bad : the man was brave if not skillful. The horse cannot be replaced. Such a span would be hard to duplicate. I may have something the owner would count an equivalent, however. The nurse, poor thing, has a broken leg ; and I—well, I hardly needed the doctor's verdict to understand my situation. The young man was unhurt. He is a gallant fellow. He has looked after my comfort since as faithfully as if I had been his father.

CHAPTER VII.

Since that day I have been an invalid—or rather as one half-dead. The dull limbs defy my will. I live, but life is visibly chained to death. The future holds no hope save that which lives beyond the stars, where love will not be sin, and shame will be unknown. I have written the story of a strangely disjointed life, and the shadows of the past have come trooping to my bedside, mocking my loneliness with the long-forgotten yearnings they inspire. I long once more to be what I was, and dread to die and be remembered only as what I am. It is a strange impulse. I wonder if it is akin to that which makes the criminal fear to die until he has confessed his crime. It is not fear, but only the desire to uncover and reveal the past—to let the world know that Hubert Goodwin did not die in that wild tempest on the Western plains. I wonder if *she* felt something of this when she refused to sleep beneath the shelter of my name? Or did she think that I had shamed and dishonored her purity by bestowing upon her a name that neither of us had any right to bear?

The thought has troubled me greatly. Was her life one long sacrifice to love? I can hardly realize that such may have been the fact ; but why should she ask that this name—our name—should not be placed on her tomb? Did she recall the past? Did she, perchance, remember that she had been another's wife? Did she know or guess that I had been the husband of another? Ah, if she did, how sweet and holy was the sacrifice she made to love! Not one word of regret! No shadow of repining! If she remembered the past, she must have realized something of what I had sacrificed for love, and determined not to make my burden heavier by revealing any knowledge or suspicion of its existence. If she remembered the past, she must have known of that fame I trampled in the mire for her sake. Was this the secret of her life? Was this the interpretation of her deep humility and the tender pride she always manifested in me? Did she think my act which came so near to baseness, was indeed a god-like sacrifice?

I can well see how she may have been thus self-deceived. I never thought to explain everything to her, assuming that she would either but half understand it or that she would be happier if the interval of her affliction remained a blank. I wondered sometimes that she did not ask more—about her mother, about my mother, about my life and hers in those sad, silent years. But I thought she had forgotten. What if she remembered—remembered and was silent? Perhaps it was a mistake. Knowing that no wrong could attach to her conduct, it never once occurred to me that she might imagine that I had reached out my hand to her in that time of half-unconsciousness and leaped with her into a gulf of shame that lay hidden under the name of which I was so proud—John Howgood. How she must have hated it as the mark of infamy—the badge of shame which love had imposed upon her helplessness.

I wonder if it was because of this that at the very last, when she saw my grief at her request that our name should not be carved upon her tombstone, she

expressed a desire that our accumulations—for all I had
was hers, since I counted gold but dust in comparison
with her happiness—might be applied to some good use
which would reflect honor on *my* name. " *Your* name,
Jack ;" that was what she said. If my soul had not
been blinded with the agony of impending woe, I should
have known her thought and made her understand the
truth—that *our* name was my name lawfully and
irrevocably ; that on earth as in the dim future I would
stand only by her side—John Howgood, in time and
eternity ! She should have understood that the old
name died with the old life. But she shall know it yet.
I cannot blazon it above her ashes, but beside them
shall be placed my own, and on the rugged granite
block above them shall be carved the words, John
Howgood. Beside it on the self-same granite—part and
parcel of it, indeed—shall be a slender shaft, with only
those words which in her school-girl days she loved to
repeat :

> " *Illa fuit animæ*
> *Dimiduum meæ.*"

So the world shall know that in life and death she
was half my soul.

The young lawyer has procured several designs for
me, of which I have chosen one which struck my fancy.
I showed it to the nurse the other day, and was surprised
at the feeling she exhibited. It was something more
than anger—almost fury. If it had not been for the
burst of tears that quickly followed I should have had
the worst thoughts of a woman whose conduct seems
altogether inscrutable.

I think this very suggestion has turned my thought
backward with a longing I have never known before.

I cannot help feeling a strange love for the name I disgraced. I am a Goodwin still, despite the gulf that lies between me and the old Goodwin pride. I love the sturdy, boisterous, man-defying stock which served God and the devil with equal fervor. From the fierce Old Harry down to my shrewd, single-hearted uncle, there is not one who ever bore the name of whom I am not proud! How they must detest my memory, who, of all the race, brought it inexcusable infamy! I cannot forget them. Blood is not only thicker than water, it is stronger than the law itself. I wonder if I should leave my estate to this proud stock if any of them would condescend to take it? I do not know what my uncle's children, my brothers and sisters of the half-blood—may be like. I only know that my mother died believing in me. It was natural. I was her first-born, her idol. Somehow, it seems just, now that there is no other love to be considered, that, after some specific bequests, I should leave the bulk of my possessions to those of my own blood. Perhaps that is what she meant.

Why should I not boldly utter the thought that is in my heart? Why not leave my estate to "the heirs of General Hubert Goodwin?" Then there can be no mistake. Whoever chose to claim under that testament would have to acknowledge their unfortunate kinsman. Suppose they refuse to take it? Well, then it shall go to some foundation to do good in his name. The name I in life covered with infamy I will make honorable again in death. If my kindred will not take my bounty, it shall be devoted to some purpose which shall take away the stain I cast upon the old name. What shall it be? I have no wrongs to right, unless it be to one who is beyond the reach of propitiation—whose wrong, indeed, was beyond amendment—the wife

who was so proud of my fame that she would not have
it smirched by my shame, and sought to hide her wrong
that she might in part screen me from blame. For her
sake, it shall be a foundation that will be of benefit to
man. I had thought of choosing the horse as my beneficiary—he has been so linked with my destiny—but
somehow I shrink from associating my father's name
even with that noble beast, which has been the blessing as well as the bane of our family. It is my wish
to re-establish the name in the esteem of men. I am
not a philanthropist ; I do not much care for the poor
and weak, but, after all, I love humanity. Why should
I not leave my estate to benefit those whose commenda-
tion I would secure ? Suppose I should endow an
institution for the " Promotion of Human Progress," or,
better still, " The Study of Methods of Human Better-
ment ?"

"Why not ? I am sure the world *can* be made better,
and that only collective human endeavor can improve
present conditions. I do not know how it can be done.
I have never studied such things, but I do not doubt
that the world would be improved if the mere amassing
of superabundant wealth was not regarded as the highest test of ability and the only worthy aim of ambition.
I think the world would be sweeter, too, if half the
money and more than half the aspiration of the country
were not absorbed in that wild game which we call
speculation—gambling on the rise and fall of values
which are not enhanced or depreciated by such action,
and in which the speculator has no interest beyond the
particular rise or fall on which he has staked his money.

It seems proper that a fortune won on the " Exchange "
should be devoted to the improvement of business
methods and social conditions which that and kindred

institutions growing on the rank stock of our bloated civilization have done so much to debase.

I never thought of it before, but perhaps this is the "call" for which I waited in my young days, and for which I have blushed so often in my later ones. Perhaps my "one talent" may do more good in this way than I could have performed in any other. I can see that only by such isolation from my fellows as I have known could I have been led to make such application of my wealth. I am sure it would please *her*, looking backward from the realms of joy, and that other, whom *she* has no doubt met ere this—she, too, will be glad that the name she cherished with such jealous care is not to be left entirely to dishonor. The thought pleases me and brings a strange content. I seem to see the fragments of a broken life joined into one not altogether discreditable existence—the past and future harmonized, and Fate made not a blind worker of mischance, but a beneficence which blesses when it seemed only to curse.

It may seem a foolish notion, but John Howgood can afford to be foolish. A name that can make a piece of paper worth as much as his is proof even against the charge of eccentricity. When I think of its potency I am proud of this quaint synonym of humiliation and despair, and glad that it has power to wash away a part of the stain from that other name which I love, and leave it revered rather than accursed of man. To-morrow I will give the young lawyer the last instructions.

Through the dull, inert limbs that lie outstretched upon the couch I feel the red mark of Old Harry burning with that fierceness which always presages success. My life has not been as others forecast it, nor as I willed it, but as Fate decreed. I do not feel that I have been worse than most men and believe that I have been better than many. Of conscious evil I have, perhaps, done less and of unconscious wrong more than others. The hopes attaching to my early youth have been sadly blighted. I have been of little service to humanity ; in fact, I do not know that the world is any better, though perhaps, not much worse, for my having lived in it. I wonder if this is not the final outcome of most lives? Perhaps there may be those who would gladly cut off, as I have been compelled to do, the early life of valorous achievements from the latter one of sordid uselessness.

One of the predictions touching the fate of the sons of Old Harry at least, has been literally fulfilled in my life. Ever since my baby-hands caressed a suck-ling's velvet muzzle, my life has been like a post-road with a change of nags at every stage. Some have been good ; some have been bad ; some have borne me exult-ingly on to joy, while others have dragged me down to shame. And now a span of the noblest have brought the end. Why not? Fortune has come to me on horseback more than once ; why not Fate as well ? The son of Old Harry will not forget man's noblest servitor. He shall be the residuary of my grace. If man will not accept my bounty, the horse shall be its beneficiary.

To those who have never tasted renown, I do not doubt that oblivion comes at last as a sweet solace for the woes of life. But to me the fact that I cannot claim the fame that Hubert Goodwin won is now so bitter a thought that no after-success brings consolation. If it were not that to do so would cast discredit upon *her* memory, I would even now throw off the mask of years and proclaim my identity. While *she* lived I did not mind it ; she was all—enough and more than enough. But now—the world is so empty—I am so alone—that the past stirs in my breast a vague but intense yearning which compels me to con over its joys and suffer again, more acutely than ever before, its shame.

Of the friends I have made here, very many are not exactly old comrades, but have an almost equally strong bond of intertwined renown, in that they were our enemies. The soldier's fame is dependent almost as much upon the valor of those he meets in battle as upon his own prowess ; and these men were doughty foemen. They come and visit me, and to cheer the tedium of the lingering hours, tell me stories of the war. Some of them are true, some are fanciful. No matter ; the veteran has a right to multiply his perils and magnify his prowess. As for myself—I keep silence ; I dare not speak.

Perhaps out of my shame some good may come to others. Somehow, good is always strangely linked with evil. Out of disease springs a more secure health ; out of danger comes safety; out of wrong right is born. He that seeth the end from the beginning finds His highest glory in that He "maketh the wrath of man to praise Him." And I, who have so long defied the judgment of mankind, feel at length a strange yearning for approval. It seems as if I were hardly just to that love which pledged itself to me "forever and ever, amen," if I fail to do something to redeem it from obloquy ; and, surely, next to doing good oneself, is that spirit which gives the means of compassing the welfare of others. The past cannot be amended ; perhaps the future may be spared some ill. I do not claim to be a child of Theophilus, but I hope that one son of Old Harry may leave the world no worse for his having lived in it.

CHAPTER VIII.

"AN HOUR OF SUN."

A strange thing has happened. As I have said, the nurse, who was in the carriage with me, has been unremitting in her efforts to relieve the tedium of my situation. Between her and the young lawyer my rooms have been made quite gay. As soon as I was able to be moved, I arranged for the purchase of an old mansion, standing in a splendid grove just on the outskirts of the city. The doctor has somewhat modified his predictions and extended a little my life-limit. I should be almost sorry but for the life they have contrived to bring into its wide halls, lofty rooms and airy porches. It is a charming retreat in which to await the end. Wisterias and honeysuckles clamber about the porches and festoon the clustering oaks. Quaint junipers spread out upon the ground and show dark and columnar between the brown bolls. Evergreens shut out the street and screen the scanty herbage of the lawn, in the red soil of which innumerable bits of mica sparkle when the hot sun shines down through the leaves of the great oaks. Roses and flowering shrubs abound.

The place caught the young lady's eye the first time she rode out after the accident. She was anxious I should go with her, but I have no fancy for being exhibited as a mark for pitying glances and pitiful remarks,

A man who has been a man would rather meet death than pity. She gave me a glowing description of it on her return. She was still using a crutch, and I remember, as she stood by my chair while speaking, that one hand was full of flowers and the crutch was festooned with honeysuckle. The owner had been a wealthy man in the old times, she said. Grievously wounded in battle for the Confederacy, he had dragged out a useless, painful life, dying but a short time before. When she told me his name, it was a familiar one. He was a cavalry officer with whom Hubert Goodwin had crossed swords more than once. The place was to be sold, being more expensive than the family could afford to maintain. Indeed, they had kept it hitherto solely for the father's sake that he might not feel the pain of exile from the home he loved. There were tears of sympathy in the nurse's eyes as she referred to this, but she smiled brightly when I told her that the roses with which she strove to hide the pitying drops were not fairer than those which shone upon her cheeks.

They paled quickly, however, when I added that I would buy the place for her if she would stay and be its mistress and give me a room in it until the end. I had grown terribly afraid that she would leave me. Every day after I recovered consciousness she sent me a note, and as soon as she was able to leave her room had insisted on the servants bringing her in her chair to call upon me, and daily since then her sunny face had lightened the monotony of my hopeless seclusion. She had talked to me, read to me, and, without seeming to do so, had assumed control of my surroundings, even before she was able to walk herself.

As I said, her face grew pale when I proposed to buy for her this place whose charms had captivated her fancy, and she turned away and sat down as if faint. I reached toward the bell-cord that hung beside my reclining-chair, but her eyes caught the motion and she nodded disapproval. She did not look at me, however, but sat with her face turned toward the window, the long dark lashes falling regularly upon her cheeks and the heavy brows drooping over them, while her lips quivered as if under the influence of some profound emotion. I watched her silently. There was something very familiar about her look, yet I could not determine what it was. When I came to think of it, I knew this was what had attracted me toward her from the very first.

"It is the very place—*for you*," she said, finally ; more to herself, it seemed, than to me.

"And for you, too," I answered. "A single visit has made you almost well. I expect to see you lay aside your crutch after one more trip."

She smiled at my banter, but still looked away from mᴇ

"Yes ; I shall soon be well."

She spoke as if it were a contingency not altogether pleasant.

"And then you will leave me, I suppose," I said, pet-tishly.

"I will stay with you—as long—as long as you desire."

"You accept my offer, then ?" I asked, exultantly.

"I cannot."

"It is not enough ?"

She shook her head.

"Well, name your terms. You have become indispensable ; and, after all, it is only anticipating my purpose. I intended to leave you a—well, a considerable legacy."

"I was so informed."

"Indeed ?"

"At least, Mr. Barclay intimated as much when he asked me to give him my full name."

"Ah, yes ; I forgot. Did he tell you how much ?"

" I did not ask him."

"You had no curiosity on the subject, I suppose ?" sarcastically.

" Not the least," decidedly.

" You gave your name, all the same ?" with a shrug.

" I did not."

The deep blue eyes met mine with an angry flash.

" No ? Why not ?"

" Because I did not choose to do so." How proudly the head was raised upon the firm white neck.

" I beg pardon," I said, full of admiration for her independence, but regretting bitterly that she had not been willing to trust my kind intent. I had sent her a check for a considerable amount, a few days after the accident, and she had returned it indorsed " Katherine Parks." My second attempt to compensate her for her kindness had been equally unsuccessful. " You said you would stay with me," I remonstrated ; "if you will not accept my terms, name your own. Don't be afraid of setting too high a price upon your services."

" I am not," she answered, quietly. " I will stay with you as long as you desire—on two conditions."

" What are they ?"

" First, that you will not think of giving me any reward, present or prospective ; and, second, that you will not ask my real name."

" But that would be unjust. You cannot afford—to —to serve for nothing."

" And you have not money enough to hire my services," she said, rising and tucking her crutch under her arm. How charming she was as she turned her flushed face upon me, with a proud toss of the shapely head ! Yet I could not believe that she meant precisely, what she said.

" You will put the terms in writing, I suppose ?" I asked, incredulously.

She turned to the table and wrote out the conditions and handed them to me to read.

" I would not ask a daughter to serve me on those conditions," I said, angrily.

" You would not have her accept any other, would you ?"

" Will you not be my daughter ?" I asked, impetuously, snatching the hand which held the paper, and looking up at her with an earnestness which only the fear of a lonely life could pardon.

Then the strange thing happened. She stood a moment, her bosom heaving with suppressed sobs, then bent and kissed me—not once, but many times—turned and hurried away. I heard her crutch thumping along the uncarpeted hall. When I wiped my face, I found tears where her kisses had been.

I do not know when I have been so badly puzzled. I could have forgiven a mercenary motive, and was prepared to gratify any reasonable or unreasonable wish, for she is very agreeable and seems to understand, not my whims—for I do not think I am whimsical—but my moods. I do not like professional attendants, and would have been glad to persuade this cultivated girl, who has such an attractive individuality, to remain with me and be the chief beneficiary of my wealth. But why should she manifest affection or agitation ?

The incident gave me a bad night, and when Miss Parks came to visit me the next morning, I thought there were traces of tears in her eyes. The hand she placed in the one I held out as a proffer of reconciliation was moist and tremulous. I did not say anything for some little time. In truth, I did not know what to say. The girl's presence embarrassed me greatly, despite the pleasure it gave. While she stood beside me she began to fondle my hair which, though white as snow, is still abundant. At first she touched it very lightly, as if putting portions of it in place. Her hand was unsteady, and it was evident that she was greatly excited. I could feel the crutch on which she leaned tremble. I was sitting in my reclining-chair, but she stood so close to me on the left side, that I could not look up at her without considerable exertion. She did not speak. Presently she stooped and kissed my forehead. I pushed her back by the hand I held, and gazed up into her face. God forgive me, I had for an instant the most infamous suspicions! But when I looked into her eyes they fled away like shadows before the sunshine, and I was ashamed that I had ever felt them. There was indeed a blush upon her cheeks, but it was childlike in its innocence, and the smile with which she looked down upon me was that of purity itself.

"Why did you do that?" I asked.

"Because I wished to," she replied. "Does it annoy you?"

Of course, it did not annoy me—for myself, that is, but it troubled me greatly for her sake. Suppose another should witness her caresses, what would be said of her? The very thought sent a shiver of agony through my veins. But I could not tell her that.

"I wish you were my daughter."

"I am afraid you would find me very troublesome," archly.

She sat down upon the arm of my chair, familiarly holding the crutch upright with her left hand, leaving the right still in mine. It betrayed no agitation now, and her look was one of calm content.

"Why not allow me to regard you as such?" I asked, tenderly.

"I have never objected."

"Then why not accept my name and let me announce you as my daughter?"

"Because I prefer my own name."

"Yet you say the one you bear is not yours?"

"Not the whole of it; when I—came to live with you, I thought it might be better to drop part of it. I did not like to seem to be other than I was, however, and so told *her* the whole truth a few days afterwards."

It is singular that we always allude to the loved dead as "her" or "she," and not by any name. I do not know why it is—I merely note the fact. Upon looking back I find that I have always done so, since I became aware of that other consciousness that once possessed her. I seldom called her Dee, even during her life. Somehow, I do not think she ever became quite the old Dee to me. I called her "dear;" never, unless necessary, addressing her as my wife. There was no reason for this, except that, having become accustomed to think of another as bearing that relation to me, it seemed unnatural to apply the title to *her*. I wonder, now, if she ever noticed it.

"What did *she* say?" I asked, after a moment.

"She wished me to remain with you."

"And she urged *me* to regard you as a daughter," I answered in surprise.

"She was very kind," simply.

"Yet she did not tell me your name."

There was no reply.

"Did she know your—your people?"

"My people?"

" Yes—your father and mother ?—your mother is dead, I believe ?"

Somehow I had gotten the impression that the mourning she wore was for her mother. She bowed her head and I saw, by the trembling lips and the tears that ran over the quivering lids, that the wound was still unhealed.

" There, there !" I said, soothingly. " Don't grieve. Why not let me arrange everything for you ?"

" I thought everything was arranged," she answered, simply.

" How ?"

" That I was to remain as your daughter as long as you desired."

" Suppose you should choose to go away ?"

" There is no danger."

" You might wish to marry ?"

· Then I will ask your permission."

" And if I do not choose to grant it ?"

" Then I will not marry !" with an archness that showed she was at least sincere.

" You are very dutiful."

" I shall try to be."

" I suppose you would do this if I were a poor man, instead of a rich one ?" I said after a moment, lightly patting the hand which still lay in mine.

" I think so—why not ?"

" Yet you are not sorry that I am rich ?"

" I am very glad of it—because you can afford all the comforts you require."

" And you do not object to sharing them with me ?"

" I shall be happy to do so—if it will give you pleasure."

A servant brought me a card just then, and she went to her apartment. It was young Barclay, the lawyer

who had been at work, under my direction, getting my
affairs in shape for final disposition. At least, that is
what he thinks he has been doing. Really he has only
been getting acquainted with my business.

I gave him instructions as to the purchase of the house,
directing him to make no question about price, but to
pay what the owners saw fit to ask, within reason, of
course, and give Miss Parks *carte blanche* in repairing and
furnishing it. He seemed a little surprised at this, but
when I told him that I designed the place for her after
I should be through with it, he offered no objection.

The young lady showed unusual energy in the work
intrusted to her, and displayed an unexpected readiness
and capacity in the application of considerable sums of
money, always, so far as I could learn from Mr. Barclay
—for it was agreed that I should not visit the premises
until all was completed—with the very best results.
After a few weeks the work was so far advanced that
the house was pronounced habitable, and preparations
were made for my removal. The nurse had long since
dispensed with her crutch; I think 1 never saw a woman
who made so light of such a serious injury. She had
been busy and, I judged, very happy—she and the
young lawyer. I had a couple of horses brought from
Tete de Loup for their use, along with a span to replace
those which were lost at the time of the mishap.
The mare I gave to her has the white crest and silken
tail of Gray Eagle, and the white spot above the hoof
which is the mark of old Diomed's favorites among his
progency. A good many have spoken of the resemblance between it and a horse ridden by a young " Yankee " cavalry officer during the war. The young lady
was delighted with the present I had chosen for her ;
kissed me, and called me " dear papa " without any
affectation—quite as a daughter might have done. It

was in the presence of Mr. Barclay, too, who looked
surprised, and I thought a little envious also. Of
course, they met often in preparing the new place.
They rode together a good deal, too, for she is a fine
horsewoman, as I have seen from my window when they
ride away and she tosses me back a kiss from her
gloved fingers.

I suspected a bit of romance between them then, but
had no wish to interfere. Why should there not be?
Love is all there is of life worth knowing, and they are
a fine couple—both splendid types. I wondered, sometimes, it they would not take my old name when they
came to wed if I should put John Howgood's fortune
with it? They would not be Goodwins indeed, but it
would be pleasant to re-establish the old name, if not the
old line. The Goodwins were well enough in their
queer Yankee way, but there would be no fear of the
old marked heel in the new stock, and that at least
would b- an advantage. I used to dream of these
things before I had determined what I would do with
my fortune. It was very pleasant to note the pretty
confidence which grew up between the young people.
They were often with me, and I thought she petted me
the more when he was present, because she dared not
pet him. Perhaps I was mistaken.

The morning after I had solved the problem of my
life—which, after all, does not seem much of a problem
now—I awoke feeling better than I had at any time
since the accident. The terrible burden which had
rested on the base of the brain so long seemed rolled
away, and the prickling thrill, which had accompanied
the loss of sensation and of power, once more pulsed
through my limbs—especially the left—and I felt
the steady, continuous glow of Old Harry's mark
with infinite content. The doctor came before Johnson

had completed his morning duties. He found him rubbing the limb, and incidentally remarked upon the singular character of the mark upon my heel. I told him it was a family inheritance and related the tradition concerning it.

"Yes!" he said, absently. "I think I have seen it before—on another, I mean."

He looked at me keenly as he spoke. I did not ask him where ; the old fear was upon me. So I said, cynically enough :

"You should hunt up the case, and be ready to testify. There are not a great many Howgoods in the world, and such a fact might be very valuable after my death."

"From present appearances there is not much prospect of a chance for one to profit by my discovery," he rejoined, significantly.

I looked at him inquiringly.

"It seems as if you were getting better," he explained, with a smile.

Then he gave me a very careful examination.

"It is always a little humiliating," he said, after his scrutiny was completed, "for a physician to have to revise his verdict. No man likes to see his prophesies fail—especially no scientist. I am afraid, however, that I shall have to extend your time-limit a little. It looks as though you might recover comfort, if not strength. Of course, the odds are still with the former diagnosis ; for any, even the slightest thing, may verify it in an hour ; but it does look as if you might have some months at least of enjoyable life, if you are very careful and your mind is kept quite free from anxiety."

" Well," I said, smiling, " I have nothing more to worry about. My will will be ready to sign at three o'clock, and I am to be moved out to the new place to-night."

"And I am going to take the entire charge of him," said the pretty nurse, catching the last words as she entered.

"Ah, then !" exclaimed the doctor, extending his hand and shaking his head in mock confusion. " Then, there is nothing left for me. I can only send in my bill."

He went off amid the laughter that followed. After a while Mr. Barclay came, and I told him what disposition I had determined to make of my estate. The young lady, who was sitting on the arm of my chair, seemed much affected at this statement, and went and stood by the window until it was completed. I could hear her weeping softly. When I had concluded, she came and kissed me with tremulous lips.

" It was a curious thing," said the lawyer, meditatively, after he had finished his notes and read them over to me.

" What ?" I asked, sharply.

" About this General Goodwin to whose heirs you wish to leave your estate—"

"You have heard of him, then ?" I interrupted, sneeringly.

" Heard of him ! Everybody has heard of him ; but I am almost a relative."

"A relative ?" exclaimed the young lady, her cheek growing pale.

Again I became suspicious of her. Was she a mere mercenary adventuress, after all ? I watched her closely as the lawyer made reply :

" Well, no ; not a relative, of course ; though I feel almost akin to him. I was named after him, you see. My father knew him when a boy, and was afterward under his command—on his staff, indeed—and never got over his love for him."

"And your father was—"

"Captain Christopher Barclay," answered the young man, proudly. "He always insisted that the young General was not so much to blame for the act that cast discredit upon his name as people claimed. He said he was never exactly himself after a wound received at Stone River ; and when I was born, soon after the war, he gave me his name—Hubert Goodwin Barclay. I think the censure he received for this, among his old neighbors, was the chief reason why he removed to this part of the country ; though, I suppose, my mother's death, which occurred at my birth, made the old home distasteful to him. He died a few years ago ; but I naturally inherited his reverence for a man who, it is now generally admitted, must have been acting under some mental distemper. I am glad you are going to do this to redeem his fame."

"Under mental distemper !" I repeated, looking from one to the other in amazement. "Can it be ?   Are we all crazy ?" I asked, in confusion.

"There !   There !" said the nurse, coming quickly to my side. "This will not do. You are having too much excitement. You must go away at once," she said, turning to the lawyer, pleadingly.

"You will have it ready at three," I said.

"Very well," he answered. "And the witnesses ?"

"Bring three or four of the most prominent of my friends."

The will was signed, but the nurse insisted that it would be too much for me to be taken to the new abode that day ; so the flitting was put off until the morrow.

CHAPTER IX.

It was arranged that I should be removed from the hotel in the evening, so as to avoid the curiosity of loiterers, to which I am, perhaps, unnecessarily sensitive. The house and grounds were lighted upon our arrival, and when I had rested for a moment in my reclining-chair upon the wide porch, and looked around, I fully indorsed all that I had heard of the beauty of the place which had been chosen as my last retreat, and was fully prepared for what the daylight might reveal.

There was a strange home-likeness about the premises for which I could not account. Much of the furniture seemed familiar, though I could not recall where I had seen it. As I was wheeled from room to room, this sense of familiarity grew upon me until it almost seemed as if I had lived in the house before. Especially was this true of the room set apart for my especial use. I supposed it to be the result of frequent conversations with the fair purveyor of my comfort, for whose thoughtfulness my admiration increased with every step in this tour of inspection.

In a sense, I was, however, disappointed. The one thing that had not ceased to puzzle me about her was the motive inspiring her devotion. I had long since abandoned the idea of any sinister purpose. In her absence it was impossible to account for her conduct on any other hypothesis; but in her presence it was equally impossible to entertain it for a moment. There was something in her manner—something of freedom, unrestraint and confidence—totally unlike anything I had ever known, which was yet especially soothing and agreeable. I felt sure that this was, in some way, the key to her motive, or perhaps that her motive, when discovered, would prove a sufficient key to her conduct. This secret I had expected somehow to surprise in my examination of the house, and I was disappointed that I did not. Not that I wished to pry into anything she desired to keep from me, but, for the mere pleasure of discovery, I would have liked to surprise this secret.

When we had visited all the other rooms upon the ground floor and I had scrutinized and commended everything while she hovered, flushed and gratified, about my chair, calling attention to this and that which she was afraid would escape my notice, we came finally to the two rooms upon the left of the wide hall which had been prepared for our especial use. I will not attempt to describe them. How had she learned my tastes so well? They were spacious rooms. Mine opened by two broad windows on the porch; hers looked upon a bower of roses in the rear. The one was a man's room—the walls lined with books and prints, strong, manly pictures of sport and battle with touching contrast of nature and affection—a cavalry charge and a wife bidding her husband adieu before mounting the scaffold. Over it all, too, was something of that carelessness and incongruity which is the very essence of the masculine idea of comfort. On the mantel was a silver-mounted hoof of Abdallah; on the desk, already open to my hand, the soiled, grim, writing-case on which these pages have been traced. She had had it brought from the hotel that it might be here to strengthen the sense of accustomedness I already felt.

"And this," she said, passing through a curtained arch, "is my room. There is a door here that shuts with a touch and almost noiselessly, being hung on rubber rollers, but I thought these double curtains would usually be better. I shall be always near, you see, and will hear if you speak even in a whisper. I have taken you at your word, and made my room just as pretty as I thought you would wish a daughter's to be."

She watched me narrowly as my eye went from one to another of its pretty details. It was a girl's room—light in shade, pure in tone, somewhat lacking in adornment—its flushed and expectant mistress its chief ornament. I did not think I could ever again feel grateful for a woman's ministrations, but I think some tears escaped my lids in spite of myself, in recognition of this fair girl's tenderness.

When we turned back into my room, I asked about some pictures which were so heavily draped, that it was impossible to detect their character.

"No," she said, in her pretty, imperious way. "You are not to see anything more to-night. I am afraid you have had too much excitement already. Now you must go to bed, and then I will play to you until you fall asleep. I had a piano put in my room on purpose for that; you can hear it without being annoyed by the performer's presence."

I obeyed without protest. She kissed me, and left me to the ministrations of the deft-handed colored man who had long been my attendant. After he had withdrawn, low, soft strains came from beyond the closed curtains. They were very soothing. Though not a musician, I think every one is, to a greater or less extent susceptible to the influence of harmony. My life had been singularly barren of such experience. *She* had been what was termed an accomplished musician in the old days. I do not think she had any great love for music, but her indomitable perseverance had made her, as I judge, a mechanically expert player. At least, her music never moved me. When she awoke after her long night she had not only forgotten her skill, but had an actual aversion to musical sounds ; they seemed to have a disturbing, unsettling effect upon her. The other—Kitty—had numbered among her attractions an unusual musical gift. As I dropped off into unconsciousness I dreamed of her, and thought I was listening to the airs she was accustomed to play.

The change from the noise and heat of the hotel, which had constantly increased with the advancing season, was very grateful. I was dimly conscious, once or twice, during the night, of another's presence in the room, but made no sign. It was very pleasant to listen to the cicadas in the oaks without, catch the fragrance of the roses, and feel that one so thoughtful and tender was watching over my slumber. After all, it is not so bad to be dead in the midst of life, if the life is only mindful of you.

In the morning I saw the *portiere* that hung across the door leading to her room move a little, and knew that she was listening to learn whether I were awake. It was still almost dark in the shaded room, but I knew from the bird-chorus without that the dawn had come. So I called out cheerily :

" Come in, daughter."

" In a moment, papa," came the ready response in a voice as sweet and contented as the bird-song to which I had been listening.

In a few minutes she glided into the room, wearing a morning-gown of some soft stuff which trailed noiselessly behind her. She buttoned it at the throat, where a bit of white showed, as she passed through the room to open the blinds and let in the soft morning light. The dew was yet dripping from the glistening oak-leaves. She drew aside the curtain that I might look out. The view of the lawn from my window was enchanting. Flowers and verdure, and over all the still morning light. Even the bees had not begun their day's labor. I turned my eyes from this to the beaming face which waited for my verdict. It was a morning face, bright with the light of the coming day. The abundant brown hair was looped hastily back, stray tresses here and there telling of the night's disorder. The soft, warm-tinted gown fell about the lithe figure, revealing its graceful outlines. I extended my hands. She came and put her own in them, her face beaming rapturously.

"My daughter!—my more than daughter!" I exclaimed. "Why are you so kind to me?"

"You will not be angry with me?"

"How could I?"

"You will not send me away?"

"I am only too fearful you will go."

"You will find it hard to get rid of me," she rejoined, with that arch look which always enchanted me. What was the resemblance that haunted me?

"Who are you?" I asked at length in puzzled desperation.

She laughed softly.

"Can you not guess?"

I put her off at arm's length and scanned her features again in the cool white light. She put back her hair above her ear and stood immobile as a statute, only glancing down at me under her dark brows. Again that puzzling resemblance ; but I shook my head despairingly. She seemed disappointed.

Slightly lifting her skirt, she laid a dainty foot on a low hassock by the bedside and pointing to it, exclaimed :

"Do you know that?"

I could hardly believe my eyes. Clearly traced upon the soft white heel was the red, fateful mark of Old Harry's offspring.

"My God !" I exclaimed. "It cannot be !"

"Oh, it is genuine !" she answered, with a glow of modest pride upon her smiling face. "See for yourself."

She placed the foot upon the counterpane beside me, and I took it in my hand. There could be no doubt about it ; the blood-red spur showed bright and hot upon the heel and was securely joined above the instep.

"But you—no woman ever had that mark !" I exclaimed.

"I suppose there were no more boys to wear it," she answered, laughingly, as she returned her foot to the slipper.

"But—but—who are you—anyhow ?"

She turned impatiently and pulled a cord drawing aside the curtain which hung before two pictures at the foot of my bed. They were portraits of Hubert Goodwin and Kitty, his wife. I recognized them at once ; they had been painted by a distinguished artist immediately after my return from the service.

"They were my parents," she said, quietly.

"But you—you—" I stammered.

"You did not know you had a daughter ?"

I shook my head.

"Are you sorry ?" archly.

"I do not know. Your name is—?"

"Katherine Parker Goodwin," proudly.

" After your mother," dreamily.

" Don't you think I look like her ?" glancing at the portrait.

There was no denying the resemblance. Yet she was a Goodwin, too.

" And she—is—?" The words choked me. I could not ask the question.

Her eyes fell. I was answered. When she lifted them there were tears upon the lashes. Yet I could not understand what had happened. The mind will be dull when the body is half dead.

" How did you know that—that I was alive ?"

" My mother found you. She never believed you dead. She traced you by the horse."

" The horse ? What—Damon ?"

" Of course."

" Ah ! I see. She knew then—"

" She knew—everything," solemnly.

" But you ?—How did you come to—to—?"

" To be here ? It was my mother's wish—her dying wish. *I* would never have come—never have spoken, but for that. I hated you ! I hated *her*, too ! But I promised my mother, when she told me the whole story, just before she died, that if you ever needed me—needed care, you know—or if there ever came a chance for me to reveal myself without humiliation—I would do as she wished. When I saw your advertisement for a companion for—for *her*—a few months afterward, I thought that was my chance—and—and you know the rest."

" You say you told *her ?*"

" Everything."

" And she—?"

" She begged me to remain with you—unless you should send me away."

" And you promised her ?"

"I promised to—to do what should seem right."

I could not understand it all. My brain seemed so very dull.

"Why did not your mother let—let me—let me know I had a child?" I asked at length, in desperation.

"She supposed you did know it," was the quiet answer.

"She must have thought me a—a precious scoundrel?"

"She would never hear a word against you—even from your mother. She thought it was the old wound, you know. Besides, she said there was no way for you to undo the wrong after it was once committed."

"Was she very—very unhappy?"

"She was not happy—not as she might have been, that is; but I think she grieved more than anything else for the odium you had brought upon yourself."

"If she had only come to me—and—and," I began, petulantly.

"Do you think the Goodwins are the only people who have any pride?" she interrupted, with an impatient frown.

"Pride? That is true. She must have hated me bitterly."

"Or loved you very foolishly!" was the tart response.

She was patting the floor impatiently with her foot, and I knew the red mark upon her heel was burning hot with anger. All at once she burst into tears.

"If you knew," she exclaimed, "how my mother watched for you and prayed for you—yes, and taught me to pray for you—how she forgave you, and even forgave the woman who enjoyed the love which belonged to her—you would not think so poorly of her."

What a perfect Goodwin she was in her stormy wrath!

"But I—I never thought poorly of her," I said, holding out my hand—"only of myself, dear, that I was so weak—so weak and blind !"

"I don't think she blamed—at least, she excused you, sir," she said, coming shyly to my side, and putting her hand in mine.

What a strange feeling it was to think that the soft, warm hand was that of my child—no, not *my* child—her mother's child ! I had never been a father to her. I had not watched her infancy—directed her childhood—known her life. She had come to me full-grown—fair, enchanting—but not my *child*—only a daughter, having her own life and stooping to me in complaisance—not in duty. We were strangers except for a few months' acquaintance. The thought made me very humble—with the saddest of all humility—that which a parent feels toward the offspring he has wronged.

"I hope you—she, that is—did not suffer any—were not at any time—in want ?"

The question broke the ice of constraint between us.

"Did you think you were the only one who knew how to make money ?" she laughed. "I think poor mamma would have given almost as much to have had you know how well she succeeded with what you left her as to have you acknowledge that you had done her wrong. That was one reason she wanted me to make myself known to you. Oh, no ! We were not poor ! Did you think the Mrs. John Goodwin of whom you bought your house on the avenue was a pauper ?"

It is impossible to describe the regal pride of her manner and the exultant tones of her voice as she uttered these words, or the amazement with which I heard them. The wife whom I had so thoughtlessly abandoned would not lay aside my name, and instead of regarding me with resentfulness, had made excuse for my conduct and jealously guarded my honor.

"Did you think," she continued, "because you were blind that nobody could see? Or that old Sir Harry would desert one who had his mark, just because she was a girl? Mamma told me all about it, and I have seen her laugh a hundred times when she has met you face to face and you did not recognize her. Oh, it was too funny! Because you had your head in a bush, you fancied nobody knew you!"

"Why—how should they?" I asked, in alarm.

"How should they? Do you think any one can see your signature in that peculiar, undershaded backhand, and fail to note its resemblance to the handwriting of General Hubert Goodwin? I have heard more than one speak of it even here."

"I see—but you do not think that—that they suspect —anything!"

"I don't know, I am sure. What if they do?"

"But would you—would it not embarrass you?"

"I think if I am willing to overlook the past no one else will regard it as inexcusable. I am going to let it be known that I am Hubert Goodwin's daughter—and —that you are my father!"

I trembled at what the revelation might involve for me, but could not help being proud of her. How like her mother she was in simple directness and unshrinking courage!

All at once a thought struck me.

"Kitty," I said, hoarsely, giving her instinctively the diminutive by which I had always designated her mother, "did your mother—was she ever at Tete de Loup?"

"I think so; at least, she seemed to know all that happened there."

Then the tide of humiliation swept clean over me. I saw it all then, and knew how utterly weak and selfish I had been in comparison with her.

"Go! Go!" I cried, in an agony of shame. "Leave me—a little while—a little while !"

The sun had long since risen when I called her back. She clasped my outstretched hands and lavished upon me the sweet endearments only a daughter can bestow. The struggle was over, and I was content to submit to her direction. Why should I not? What right had I to object? If the world chose to guess the truth, let them do it, but we could offer no apology. I recognized the correctness of her view, and for the first time in all those long years was quite relieved of fear.

"And you are my daughter ?" I said, banteringly, as I stroked the beautiful hand, pushing her off at arm's length and looking at her with that anxious criticism which only one in my position could ever feel. "What shall I do with such a fair responsibility ?"

"I guess you could—you might dispose of me—if you are anxious to do so," she replied, mischievously.

"Dispose of you—how ?"

"Well, I thought it just possible, you know—that—that Mr. Barclay—"

"Barclay! The rascal! But it is too late ; I see that !"

A deep blush had leaped up into her face before she could hide it on my shoulder. It *was* too late, but I do not mind. And if there is a boy and he has the mark of Old Harry, as I hope he will, he is to take the name of Goodwin, and will, no doubt, be as proud and headstrong as his forbears. I trust he will be as honest and as tender in purpose, too, even if he should be as foolish, also.

But the money will go to the Institute, just the same

—the bulk of it, at least; for the children of Old Sir Harry must always shift for themselves. They are too strong to be pampered with idleness and too weak to be exposed to temptation. I will not curse them with my gains nor unman them with my regrets.

The days are very sweet; but I know they will not be many. Joy is as fell a consumer of life as sorrow. The thrill that indicated hope of reprieve has departed. The limbs arc again leaden. The double-life and the half-life are both drawing to a close. Neither seems so very strange now that I see another life coming on to take its place, and hide in the dawn of hope the shadows of retrospection. So the rising sun screens the ghastly pallor of the waning moon. Death loses its terrors in the rosy glow of coming life.

THE END.

BERYL'S HUSBAND.

BY

MRS. HARRIET LEWIS.

Author of " Lady Kildare," "Sundered Hearts," " Her Double Life," etc.

WITH NUMEROUS FULL-PAGE ILLUSTRATIONS BY G. A. TRAVER.

Paper Cover, 50 cents. Bound in Cloth, $1.00.

A very charming story. It opens on the shores of Lake Leman, in the romantic city of Geneva, under the shadow of Mont Blanc. A young English girl, who has been educated at a boarding-school at Vevay, is suddenly left without natural guardians and means of support. Her beauty and interesting character attract a young English traveller, who induces her to run away with him and marry him. This is the beginning of a romantic novel of extraordinary vicissitudes and adventures. To give an analysis of the plot and situations would mar the interest of the reader. It is sufficient to say that it is equal to the best of Mrs. Lewis's novels, not excepting " Her Double Life " and "Lady Kildare."

For sale by all booksellers and newsdealers, or sent, postpaid, on receipt of price, by the publishers,

ROBERT BONNER'S SONS,

COR. WILLIAM AND SPRUCE STREETS, New York.

BY

ROBERT GRANT,

Author of "Mrs. Harold Stagg," "Confessions of a Frivolous Girl," etc.

ILLUSTRATED BY WILSON DE MEZA.

12mo. 309 Pages. Illustrated. Handsomely Bound in Cloth, Price, $1.00. Paper Cover, 50 Cents.

In "The Carletons" Mr. Grant has given his admirers a fresh and delightful novel. It is a New England story and the characters are truthfully drawn. Boston is the scene of the principal transactions, although the story opens in a neighboring suburban town. The charm of the story is in the humorous delineation of New England family life. The children are interesting, and when they grow up into men and women, as they do in the progress of the story, they are more interesting and charming, and the reader takes a deep and abiding interest in their history to the close. Mr. Grant's amusing and refreshing humor lights up every page of the book.

For sale by all booksellers and newsdealers, or sent, postpaid, on receipt of price, by the publishers,

ROBERT BONNER'S SONS,

Cor. William and Spruce Streets, New York.

EUGENIE GRANDET.

TRANSLATED FROM THE FRENCH OF

HONORE DE BALZAC.

WITH ILLUSTRATIONS BY JAMES FAGAN.

12mo. Bound in Cloth, $1.00. Paper Cover, 50 Cents.

———

"Eugenie Grandet" is one of the greatest of novels. It is the history of a good woman. Every student of French is familiar with it, and an opportunity is now afforded to read it in a good English translation. The lesson of the book is the hideousness of the passion of the miser. Eugenie's father is possessed by it in a degree of intensity probably unknown in America, and to our public it will come as a revelation. What terrible suffering he inflicts upon his family by his ferocious economy and unscrupulousness only Balzac's matchless narrative could show. The beautiful nature of Eugenie shines like a meteor against the black background, and her self-sacrifice, her sufferings and her superb strength of character are wrought out, and the story brought to a climax, with the finest intellectual and literary power and discrimination.

For sale by all booksellers and newsdealers, or sent, postpaid, on receipt of price, by the publishers,

ROBERT BONNER'S SONS,

COR. WILLIAM AND SPRUCE STREETS, New York.

AN INSIGNIFICANT WOMAN.

A Story of Artist Life.

BY

W. HEIMBURG.

TRANSLATED FROM THE GERMAN

By MARY STUART SMITH.

WITH ILLUSTRATIONS BY WARREN B. DAVIS.

12mo. Beautifully Illustrated. Handsomely Bound in Cloth,
Price, $1.00. Paper Cover, 50 Cents.

———

This is a matchless story. It is a vindication of woman. It ends finely, so as to bring out beautifully the glorious character of the heroine, the insignificant woman. The combination of the artistic and practical in this story makes it peculiarly suited to the taste of our times. It is impossible to imagine more beautiful and effective lessons of magnanimity and forbearance, strength and gentleness, than are inculcated in this novel. Every woman who lives for her children, her husband and her home will find her heart mirrored in the pages of this fascinating story. It is told in a manner that must please all readers, and is exquisitely rendered in the translation.

For sale by all booksellers and newsdealers, or sent, postpaid, on receipt of price, by the publishers,

ROBERT BONNER'S SONS,
COR. WILLIAM AND SPRUCE STREETS, New York.

The Breach of Custom.

TRANSLATED FROM THE GERMAN

BY

MRS. D. M. LOWREY

WITH CHOICE ILLUSTRATIONS BY O. W. SIMONS.

Paper Cover, 50 Cents. Bound Volume, $1.00.

———

This is a translation of an interesting and beautiful German novel, introducing an artist and his family, and dealing with the most pathetic circumstances and situations. The heroine is an ideal character. Her self-sacrifice is noble and exalted, and the influence which radiates from her is pure and ennobling. Every one who reads this book will feel that it is one which will be a life influence. Few German stories have more movement or are more interesting. There are great variety and charm in the characters and situations.

For sale by all booksellers, or sent postpaid on receipt of price by

ROBERT BONNER'S SONS, Publishers,

182 WILLIAM STREET, New York.

THE NORTHERN LIGHT.

TRANSLATED FROM THE GERMAN OF

E. WERNER,

BY

MRS. D. M. LOWREY.

12mo. 873 Pages. Handsomely Bound in Cloth, Price, $1.00.
Paper Cover, 50 Cents.

Since the death of the author of "Old Ma'mselle's Secret,"
Werner is the most popular of living German writers. Her
novels are written with great literary ability, and possess the
charm of varied character, incident and scenery. "The Northern
Light" is one of her most characteristic stories. The heroine is
a woman of great beauty and strength of individuality. No less
interesting is the young poet who, from beginning to end, constantly piques the curiosity of the reader.

For sale by all booksellers, or sent, postpaid, on receipt of
price, by

ROBERT BONNER'S SONS, Publishers,

COR. WILLIAM AND SPRUCE STREETS, New York.

WIFE AND WOMAN;

OR,

A TANGLED SKEIN.

TRANSLATED FROM THE GERMAN OF

L. HAIDHEIM.

By MARY J. SAFFORD.

WITH ILLUSTRATIONS BY F. A. CARTER.

12mo. Beautifully Illustrated. Handsomely Bound in Cloth,
Price, $1.00. Paper Cover, 50 Cents.

———

"A thoroughly good society novel." This is the verdict of a
bright woman after reading this story. It belongs to the Marlitt
school of society novels, and the author is a favored contributor
to the best periodicals of Germany. It has a good plot, an
abundance of incident, very well drawn characters and a good
ending. There is no more delightful story for a summer holiday.

For sale by all booksellers and newsdealers, or sent, postpaid,
on receipt of price, by the publishers,

ROBERT BONNER'S SONS,
COR. WILLIAM AND SPRUCE STREETS, New York

www.ingramcontent.com/pod-product-compliance
Lightning Source LLC
Chambersburg PA
CBHW032025120726
47901CB00006BB/1665